CLOSE-UP

Esther Verhoef

Quercus

First published in Great Britain in 2009 by

Quercus
21 Bloomsbury Square
London
WC1A 2NS

Copyright © 2007 by Esther Verhoef

Originally published by Ambo | Anthos Uitgevers, Amsterdam

English Translation © 2009 by Paul Vincent

A CIP catalogue record for this book is available
from the British Library

ISBN (HB) 978 1 84724 797 1
ISBN (TPB) 978 1 84724 330 0

10 9 8 7 6 5 4 3 2 1

Printed and bound in Great Britain by Clays Ltd, St Ives plc

I

It made everything easier, knowing each other so well. It meant that she cooperated without realising, making it intimate, almost safe.

Preparations took three months. First I examined the plan from every angle, trying to visualise it for myself. Once I was sure it was feasible, it was no longer a vague idea, but became part of me. It was a wonderful project, right from the preliminary phase, which consisted of talking to her and the people around us, to acquiring the equipment I needed.

Admittedly, I didn't need much. She herself gave me the idea.

Edith couldn't cope with having her sleep disturbed; next morning her eyes were always puffy and red. And while she was much more than just a pretty face, what mattered most to her was looking good. If you ask me she always did, whether she was all dolled up stealing the show at a reception or fresh out of bed, apologising for her scruffy appearance as she made me a cup of tea, still in her bathrobe. Sleeping pills were the only way she could avoid being woken up repeatedly by things that went bump in the night.

I was looking forward to it. I felt like a kid queuing up for the rollercoaster; one step at a time, closer and closer. The mounting excitement, which reached its climax on the evening when every-thing fell perfectly into place like the pieces of a jigsaw.

We'd finished a bottle of wine together and talked about things that fascinated us. Art, and artists who made the impenetrable and incomprehensible world of imagination and emotion tangible for the general public. Painters, sculptors, writers and musicians. She was very relaxed and leaned against me. More than once she said she felt at ease with me, trusted me completely. She was already drifting away – the drug was working remarkably fast.

I hugged her and said she should take a quick bath. She was tired, it had all got too much for her, and after a refreshing bath and a good night's sleep she'd have a less gloomy outlook. She was bound to feel better in the morning.

I helped her to the bathroom, sat her on the toilet and pushed her body, which was already going limp, to one side, so it could rest against the wall. Then I took the latex gloves out of my trouser pocket and pulled them on. She didn't even notice, her eyes were closed and her breathing was shallow. I turned on the taps. Hot and cold. I put the plug in and waited. The water slowly filled the tub, an enormous bath designed to take two or three people. I opened a cupboard, found some bath oil and poured a little into the water. Then I put the bottle back. To kill time I looked at myself in the mirror behind the washbasins, which took up the whole wall, and smirked at my reflection. In the background Edith slumped against the tiled wall like a collapsed mannequin. She may have mumbled something, I can't remember. I was too full of myself, of the whole plan.

While the bath was filling up, my eye fell on the razor in its case. Not the disposable kind, but a handmade cutthroat razor, the sort you sometimes see in Italian barber shops, extremely sharp. My heart skipped a beat, such was the feeling the sharp razor awakened in me and the ideas – new ideas – that occurred to me. Then

I shook my head. No. Stick to the plan. No improvisations. There's always a next time.

Not for Edith, though.

'For God's sake, Margot, *pink*?'

I look up at Anne and then around me as if I'm seeing my new living room for the first time. Pink, indeed. And that's not all: red, purple, lilac. Each wall a different colour.

I'm amazed she can be so unobservant. Pink shouldn't come as a surprise. Or red, or purple. My hands, clothes and hair have been covered in brightly-coloured blobs for weeks.

'I like it,' I say – quite unnecessarily, since everyone who's here lugging the heavy boxes and packages inside knows that no one can be held responsible for the colour scheme except me.

The flat was grey when I found it – grimy almost. It had put off lots of buyers, but not me. It reminded me vividly of my great-aunt's house, which I visited regularly when I was young. This immediately made it feel personal, and it gave me an indefinable sense of luxury, as well as safety and security.

My great-aunt used to live nearby, in the same kind of old mansion in the centre of town and within walking distance of the cathedral and the historic fish market. Not because it was trendy or close to bars, restaurants and shops, but because she had been born and had grown up there and knew no better,

To a child's eyes her house looked like a museum or a temple. Reluctantly I stepped inside, holding my mother's hand, addressed her as 'Mrs' and fell silent, overawed by the high ceilings with their chandeliers, and the creaking stairs, and paintings so dark it was difficult to make out what was depicted in them. For the duration of the visit, I would stare at all the extraordinary objects, like the shiny organ that I was dying to play but was never allowed to touch. Time seemed to have stopped somewhere in the 1920s or 30s and as a child I was fascinated by what I saw, smelled, heard, discovered and absorbed as I sat, on my best behaviour, on the sofa, knees together and a lukewarm glass of orange squash miles away from me on the elegant walnut coffee table.

An old woman used to live in my new flat, too. I never met her. She had already been moved to an old people's home when her flat was emptied and put up for sale by her children.

I did, though, get to know her a little by cleaning every nook and surface in this two-room flat. I vacuumed up the spider's webs that had been gathering dust behind the radiators, used ammonia to scrub the greasy tops of the kitchen units. And I painted bright colours over the yellowy walls of the living room. The old carpeting was still down when I collected the keys, beige bouclé stretched over boards, worn in various places but like new in others. Underneath was a wonderful untreated wooden floor, which I sanded but otherwise left well alone. I hid the brown marble mantelpiece with its dramatic brown and white patterns behind silver-painted MDF. And every day, regardless of whether it was raining, I opened the windows and polished and scrubbed and painted and glossed till the smell of wax polish, cigarette smoke and wool gave way to the smell of a new, fresh start: paint, turpentine and detergent.

'Well,' mumbles Dick. 'It wouldn't be my choice of colour, either, at least not for a living room. More like a teenager's bedroom.' Out of Anne's field of vision he gives me a great big wink. 'But then our Margot has always been one-of-a-kind.'

I put on an awkward grin and set the box of kitchen utensils on the draining board in the narrow kitchen. Next to the sink are bottles of chlorine and turpentine and thick brushes wrapped in aluminium foil. There are still paint marks on the speckled work top.

As I remove plates and mugs from their wrapping paper and stack them in the kitchen cupboards, I see the blue corrugated roof of Dick's van below. It is parked with two wheels on the pavement. The open sliding door gives a view of the contents: boxes, a rolled-up carpet, wicker chairs, and an old white electric fan. My stuff. On the side of the van it says in white stick-on lettering DICK HEIJNE ROOFING AND PLUMBING WORK. My brother, four years older than me, used to be a total pest, but as the years have gone by he's increasingly proved a beacon of light and warmth in cold, dark times.

Very dark times.

Somewhere deep inside I feel a pang, like something is contracting violently. It's the kind of pain you can't put your finger on, can't have surgically removed or treat with medicine – and there's no end to it.

I take a deep breath and go into the living room. Anne, arms folded, is looking around her. 'You know what: the longer I look at it, the less awful it gets. Maybe it's just a question of getting used to it.'

'It was time for some colour,' I respond without much enthusiasm. I can still feel the knot in my stomach.

Jan deposits a box on the wooden floor with a thud. 'You have a ridiculous number of books!'

Without a word, I follow him into the narrow stairwell and down the stairs. It is dimly lit and there are dirty smudges along the wall. The worn wooden steps creak under our weight. I slide my hand over the smooth walnut banister and realise that thousands of people have touched this old wood before me. People who, long before I was born, lived out their lives in this place, filled with family, work, worries and happiness, but who died ages ago.

Downstairs in the hall there are metal letterboxes hanging from the wall, some with names on, others without. I'm one of the latter: there's been no time to get a name card made yet and maybe I won't ever bother. I've not met the other residents yet – the house is divided into eight flats – though I have listened to them during the hours spent painting and cleaning. Their music, their footsteps in the stairwell and their arguments.

'Can you take this?' Jan thrusts me a red cashmere floor cushion that I bought last week at the market. I grab it with both hands and bend down to catch a candlestick wrapped in newspaper that is about to fall out of the van. Then I tilt my head right back. A uniformly grey sky hangs over the city, colourless and opaque. The weather has never reflected my state of mind as well as now.

In the living room Dick gets down off the beer crate he's using as a ladder. Hands on hips, he inspects the baroque mirror over the mantelpiece as if it were a work of art. The thing is tilting perilously forward. He climbs back onto the crate in annoyance, takes the mirror back off the wall with a great deal of fuss, and starts fiddling with the nylon cord. With the frame balanced on the toes of his trainers, he casts a fleeting glance at his watch. 'I hope we can wrap things up before five. I've got a customer this evening. A repair job.'

'Just as long as everything's upstairs,' I reply. 'I can handle the rest by myself.'

Jan comes in with two boxes piled on top of each other. All I can see are his fingers and legs. 'Where does this go?'

'The kitchen, please.'

Anne shoves a mug of coffee into my hands and flops onto the sofa. I sit down beside her and light up a cigarette. What yesterday looked like a lavish showroom has been reduced by the four people walking around in it and the piles of boxes to the thirty square yards it actually measures. Yet it still doesn't look small, and certainly not poky, thanks to the high ceiling and the large sash windows. The living room looks out onto the rear garden. In the adjacent gardens there are huge trees and their leaves, already fading into autumnal colours, largely hide the other houses from view. When I lie on the sofa and look outside I can easily imagine I'm living in the woods instead of the centre of town.

Dick and Jan join us for coffee, sitting cross-legged against the mantelpiece.

'I've connected the washing machine and dryer, and checked your pipes,' observes Dick. 'It all looks in reasonable condition, although I bet your water pressure isn't very high with that old-fashioned pipework. If it's a problem, be sure to let me know, OK? If that's the case we'll have to set a day aside.'

I nod and take a sip of my coffee. Anne has forgotten to put milk in it, but I feel too unsteady on my feet to get up. My muscles are aching from the heavy carrying and traipsing up and down stairs.

'I'll drop by in the week with another tap,' Dick continues. 'That thing in the bathroom is out of the Stone Age. I think we've got a ceramic tap lying about in the store somewhere that was left over from an order.'

'Thanks,' I say.

I've been alone again for a few hours when I notice that dusk is starting to fall. I stand on the sofa and turn the light on, a chandelier with red, purple and transparent cones. When I bought it

I thought it was incredibly exotic and warm, but now the light from the six bulbs is pretty harsh. I stand on tiptoe and unscrew a couple of them. It makes a difference, but not much. The flat doesn't feel like me at all yet, there's an obtrusive smell of paint and every step I take echoes off the bare walls. Restlessly I walk to the kitchen. There's nothing in the fridge but a tin of evaporated milk. I could go to one of those little restaurants in the area, there are enough of them, but I don't like the prospect of having to sit alone at a table. A Chinese takeaway, then? Call a pizza delivery service?

I stare out of the window, my hands resting on the sill. The lamps along the narrow canal cast a soft orange glow and puddles of rainwater gleam on the cobbles. Across the canal warm light streams from the windows over the paving stones of the street and the parked cars. People are moving about in the windows. Scooters and a few cars with their lights on are crossing the small drawbridge that links the old town with the wide road to the station.

I should be feeling great. Happy even, liberated perhaps. It's over. I've got my own place. Not some stopgap chalet in a messy holiday park, not some dead-end flat on a new estate, but a beautiful, authentic place in the provincial capital of Brabant, bubbling with life twenty-four hours a day.

Except I'm not bubbling.

All morning I dealt with the chores I hadn't yet got round to. Applying for a phone line and an internet connection, for example, and arranging for my post to be forwarded for the next three months. Then I went shopping to fill the empty fridge and store cupboard. As I make a sandwich and listen to the sounds of my new surroundings, it sinks in that two of the four weeks' unpaid leave are already over. Soon I'll be back working flat out again.

In the weeks preceding the leave I was operating on a defective auto-pilot, dazed by lack of sleep and a head full to bursting that just went on buzzing and pounding. That didn't mesh very well with the deluge of complaints I had to deal with. My job is to note customers' preferences, advise them, take the order and coordinate the various departments in the company so that everything is delivered at the same time and on the date agreed. If there's a slip-up in this process it's a complete disaster for the owners of the restaurants, bungalow parks, temporary exhibitions, asylum centres and conference venues. They have to open for business; they can't wait for a follow-up delivery. And when that happens, guess who they call and who gets it in the neck? It required superhuman self-confidence to face the raging customers, self-confidence I was always able to muster by reminding myself that they had nothing against me personally, just against the mouthpiece – or Wailing Wall – of All Inclusive Project Furnishings.

I've always been good at my work, I truly believe that. Sales figures and lots of satisfied customers have confirmed me in that belief. But I know that in the last few months my performance has been well below par. Many incorrect deliveries were a direct result of my mistakes, because my mind wasn't on the job.

Not so long ago the days dawned like tunnels with no light at the end, where I wandered aimlessly, screaming, crying, exploding with frustration. The hole that John had made in my confidence affected everything: my moods, my self-image and my professional performance, and eventually had a devastating effect on my social life. At the end of the period of mourning, when I crawled from the dark earth, dazed, resting rather feebly on my elbows and blinking at the bright sunlight like a bewildered mole, I found my circle of friends had shrunk to almost nothing. Apart from a handful of people, it had ceased to exist. Most people took John's side. He's good company, at least. He has every reason to be cheerful.

My mobile rings. The ring tone, which sounds far too upbeat to me, blares through the flat. It can only be Claudia. She joined the office at All Inclusive two years ago. We were never close; I got the impression she didn't like me because in her eyes I was free to come and go as I pleased, while she was always tied to her desk. A few weeks ago I was forced to abandon that preconception. One evening when I had some paperwork to finish after closing time, I was astonished to find her in a deserted office, crying. At my insistence, she told me her boyfriend had traded her in for a newer model. This forged a bond. Since we weren't going to get any more work done, I suggested we go for a drink. After a well-lubricated evening getting things off our chest, we wound up at her place, sitting at her computer where we booked a weekend in London on impulse. *Shopping, partying, forgetting.*

The last time I had been on holiday with a girlfriend was long before I moved in with John. John didn't like the idea. 'It's not that I don't trust you,' he always said. 'But you shouldn't set a fox to keep the geese. Marriages where the husband or wife has separate holidays or evenings out are headed for the rocks. Without exception.' Looking back, it wasn't me he didn't trust. He'd been talking about himself. But I didn't know that yet.

'Hi Clo,' I say.

'Margot? I'm really sorry, but . . .' As fast as she starts, she stops.

'What is it?'

'God, I'm so pissed off.' Again silence.

'About what?'

'I've got a huge overdraft.'

My heart starts beating faster. I sense immediately where this conversation is heading. 'So?'

'I know how unbelievably shitty this is, and it's just not the sort of thing I do, but I can't come to London with you. I can't afford it.'

'Clo, we've booked. You've already paid for the flight and the hotel.'

'I'll have to write that off. Because if I come, Margot, it won't stop there. Food, drinks, shopping . . . I don't like the idea of not even being able to buy myself something nice, or eat out any-where but McDonald's . . . When I go away for the weekend, I don't want to have to watch the pennies, you know? And I can't do that now.'

There's a lump in my throat that stops me speaking.

'I should have thought about it before,' she continues. 'I feel really shitty about this. I might just have been able to afford it if I hadn't got my electricity bill this morning. I've got an extra 400 euros to pay. I just know that if I take off for a weekend now, there'll be one hell of a mess waiting for me when I get back.'

'I'll lend you some money,' I say without hesitation. I can't imagine a better home for the last of my savings.

'That's very sweet of you, but I really don't want to . . . Haven't you got someone else who'd like to go with you?'

'Not at this short notice . . . Everyone's working. Shit, I'm really pissed off.'

'So am I, believe me.'

So why doesn't she sound as if she is? 'Have you heard anything from Alex?'

'Er . . . yes. We went out for a meal.' She falls silent for a moment. 'Margot? Are you angry?'

'Of course not.'

'Still good friends?'

Without answering, I cut her off. I slam the telephone down on the kitchen table, and then stand staring at the screen for minutes on end.

She doesn't ring back. No text. Nothing.

Was it childish of me to show my feelings like that, selfish to be angry with her, or do I have every right to be pissed off? In the past I could have answered that easily, and would have been sure of how I saw things. Not any longer. I'm no longer sure of anything.

You get to know yourself by seeing yourself through your friends' eyes, the responses to how you look, what you do and say. And while I know in my head that I should focus on the positives, day by day, I can't stop the negative things getting the better of me. Because quite simply they hit you much harder.

Yesterday Anne made a remark about the number of stairs, something like: 'Won't do the figure any harm, though, will it, Margot?' and cast a knowing glance at me. But it wasn't just Anne who upset me unintentionally. Jan – someone I barely even know, who works for Dick – felt the need to call the number of books I own *ridiculous*. Dick once again subtly rubbed my nose in the fact that I'm different from the rest of the family: *one-of-a-kind* – a Brabant euphemism for not quite right in the head.

I clench my teeth and start trembling. A compelling voice whispers in my ear that it's my fault for taking it so personally, not theirs. That must be true. Dick and Anne have helped me through the last few months, each in their own way. Even when I was completely unreasonable and paralysed with grief, powerlessness and rage, when there was no end to the crying fits, they listened patiently. Yesterday they took the day off to collect my things, which were stored at three separate addresses, and transport them to their new location. They wouldn't have done that if they didn't like me.

I'm making heavy weather of everything at the moment. As if that invisible layer that normally surrounds me, filtering things and putting them into perspective, is out of order, so that everything strikes a deep and devastating blow. Every comment, however light-hearted and insignificant, hits me like an incendiary bullet and goes on smouldering deep inside. *Not right in the head.* Ridiculous number of books. Too fat. I can add to that myself: unstable, touchy and emotional. Oh yes, and rejected, of course. On we go.

Something's flowing over my face. Wet and warm. My nose is blocked. I lay my forehead on my upper arm and stare at the table top. My vision blurs while the puddle of salt water continues spreading out beneath me.

I'd pictured the first day of my new life rather differently.

Edith was far gone, very far gone.

I supported her body weight and lowered her carefully to the ground. The red hair fanned out over her face and the natural stone floor. I took my time undressing her. First her blouse and bra, then her skirt. Her large breasts slumped to one side, the nipples big and soft, and her fleshy hips revealed dimples in the harsh light of the bathroom. She had shaved her pubic area, completely, shaved everything off, and the flesh was pink. I slowly slid my gloved hand over her body. I had seen her naked so often before that there was no physical reaction. Finally I pulled her socks off. Pedicured toenails painted light-blue.

She mumbled so faintly I couldn't understand her.

'Come on,' I whispered. 'You've got to get washed. In the bath.'

I put her arm around my neck and pulled her up a little. She weighed more than I expected. She was heavy. Very heavy, a dead weight. Lifeless, drugged flesh.

It took a while, but I managed to lower Edith into the bath without injuring her. She mustn't get any bruises or marks.

I let go of her, her face, turned upwards, seemed to float by itself, as did her breasts. Strange.

My hand pressed down on her face. My fingers spread and pushed her head under water. She twitched in response, but they were only vague, feeble movements. I sat down on the edge of the bath, took hold of her hair and pulled her head back, further under water.

She opened her eyes, stared at me in horror, in panic, as if she knew what was happening, but scarcely put up any resistance. She was in a twilight zone between dream and sleep. Her knees briefly rose to the surface. Just for a moment. Her mouth opened. And again. Bubbles fluttered from her mouth. It took a long time. Longer than I had expected.

And I enjoyed every second.

I bent closer to the surface of the water. I wanted to see how she slipped away, drew the water into her lungs, to see those eyes staring at me, softened by the layer of water separating us. I wanted to absorb every detail. I can't remember ever being so excited.

Until she gently slipped away. The muscular tension disappeared from her body, her eyes stayed wide open. I raised her head above water and closed them, and then let her slip back. Her hair billowed in the water, her arms and legs were spread slightly apart. As if she were floating. Peaceful. Dead. She had never looked so beautiful, so serene.

I pulled off my surgical gloves, put on another pair and laid the strip of pills on the bedside table. I went into the living room, picked up my wine glass, washed it out and put it at the back of the cupboard with the other glasses. Then I rinsed out Edith's glass and half-filled it with the last of the wine from the bottle. I put both the bottle and the glass on the edge of the bath. Then I folded her clothes loosely and put the bundle on the edge of the washbasin.

I looked around. Excellent. No need to do anything else.

It was over.

I didn't dislike Edith, quite the contrary. That's why I did my very best to make the transition as fluid and comfortable as possible for her. And I succeeded.

I always get what I want. I never fail. Never.

My parents' house is on the outskirts of the village, a modest red-brick semi with large windows front and back, built in the 1950s. It's small and unpretentious, but for twenty-five years it was my home.

I park the car in the street and walk up the narrow drive paved with concrete tiles. It is to the left of the house and adjoins the neighbours' with no visible transition. My parents' Passat is not there.

I grab at the top of the green-painted gate, feel my way towards the hook that keeps it shut, and enter the garden.

Whatever the interior of the house lacks in space is more than made up for by the deep, walled back garden. The front section is my mother's domain. A terrace of square brown bricks and a small pond with golden orfes swimming around like timid yellow streaks in the greenish water. Next to it is a small lawn edged with flower borders. Behind that my father has constructed a pergola with a lush covering of ivy and wisteria, which divides the garden in two. In that way my mother, on those rare days when she sits outside enjoying the sun and the peace and quiet, doesn't have to look out on his messy collection of wooden sheds and runs made of chicken-wire which he has linked together with corrugated sheets. These structures are at the bottom of the garden, in the shade of a huge ash tree.

The back door is open. I take a few steps through the half-open kitchen towards the living room, and then towards the hall. I stop at the bottom of the stairs. 'Mum?'

No response. I go back outside, in the direction of the sheds, where I can hear a radio playing. My father is convinced that his animals become less jumpy if they are used to all kinds of noise, so he regales them with upbeat background music and chimes, from early morning to his last inspection before he goes to bed.

The familiar smell of hay, dust and manure wafts towards me as I pull open the outer shed door, push the screen door inwards and go inside.

My father has bred animals for as long as I can remember. His social life is pretty much limited to the weekends, and more specifically to the headquarters of the regional breeders' association and gymnasiums in every corner of the country where small animal shows are held. When I was at nursery school, he was still involved with coloured canaries, later he switched to chickens with very peculiar combs, but when the new neighbours started complaining about the crowing of the cocks, the chicken run was converted into a rabbit house. Quiet animals, you scarcely notice they're there, and though the hutches may be weathered and rickety, my father keeps them clean with military precision. The neighbours stopped complaining.

It's rather dim inside. This is due to the tree, even though it's already lost some leaves, and to the small windows, which are covered with a layer of dirt and cobwebs and let in hardly any light.

My father doesn't notice me. He is completely absorbed in his chore: rinsing out drinking bottles in a bucket. His unkempt hair has started thinning noticeably. And for the last few weeks he has worn glasses, even when he is not reading. The grubby blue overall with which he seems to have fused protects his clothes and on his feet he wears a pair of grey socks and black leather clogs. That's how I've always known him. My father would have liked to be a farmer, but his life turned out differently.

The radio is on a wooden shelf along the wall and is covered in dust. I reach out and turn the volume down a little.

He looks up, with a confused smile on his face. 'What are you doing here?'

I bend forward and kiss him on the cheek. 'Where's Mum?'

'Isn't she in the house?'

I shake my head. 'The car's not there.'

'Then I expect she's gone shopping. I'll be right with you, but I've got to finish this off first.'

'I'm not in a hurry,' I say, distracted by a white rabbit in one of the bottom hutches. I sink to my knees and take the wire-mesh front out of the wooden frame. The animal, clearly still young, is curious and hops towards me, sniffing cautiously at my outstretched hand. Its velvety ears stick up a little from its round head, which, together with its dark eyes, makes him look funny. Almost like an animated figure from the Pixar studio. 'This is a nice one,' I say. 'How old is it?'

'Born in July.'

I stroke the animal, who obviously enjoys being touched and drops its head a little, slowly opening and closing its eyes. Its pink nose bobs up and down.

'Its days are numbered,' my father remarks.

I look up.

My father now has a cigarette in the corner of his mouth. His eyes are focused on the drinking bottles and his hands never stop moving. 'Its ears aren't right. I can't get them to drop. Shame, because the rest is first-rate.'

After a final stroke I close the hutch again and stand up. I look at all the rows of hutches, at all those rabbits in white and black and beige, craning their necks and peering at my father and me, waiting in their dim cages for a clean drinking bottle with fresh water and some greens. An undulating sea of soft, hairy little heads with big brown eyes and floppy ears.

If they're the same colour I can hardly tell one animal from another. It is tiny deviations that mean one is given a pet name and enjoys my father's special, personal attention, while the other ends up anonymous in the freezer. As a child I quite often hated my father for that.

I could be found here regularly when, after about three weeks, the young crawled out of the litter for the first time. I was always delighted when there was one with something funny, unique about it. One who was different from the rest. But I learned not to get too attached to the odd-ones-out. The world is hard on pets that deviate from the norm. In a flash I realised that it's no different for human beings.

Through the window I can see my mother heading in our direction. Her flowery skirt is flapping about her sturdy legs and she has stuffed her hands deep into the pockets of her three-quarter-length coat. I have inherited my figure from her. She has full hips, a large cup size and is generally solidly built. She is also responsible for my hair colour, voice and facial features, to such an extent that more than once my father has wondered aloud whether my mother didn't discover and practise cloning long before the twenty-first century began.

'Hi, darling, I saw your car.' My mother brings a cold wind into the shed with her. She pushes the screen door firmly shut behind her and kisses my cheeks. 'Have you had coffee yet?' She shoots a dark look at my father who continues imperturbably with his chore, and supplies the answer herself: 'No, of course you haven't. Come on inside with me, it's chilly out here.'

'Are you settling in OK in town?'

I tip my packet of cigarettes onto the table top. 'Not really. I've only been there a few days. But I think I'm going to like it. Everything's nice and close.' I don't tell her that I haven't had time to explore the surrounding area yet. In fact for the last few days I've locked myself away and felt really sorry for myself. I didn't want to see anyone. It was only this morning that I felt the urge to get out and drove without thinking to my parents' house. There weren't many other options left.

'It would have been nicer for Dad and me if you'd come back and lived here in the village. There's nowhere to park round there and it's too far on the bike for me. But there you go, you knew that already.'

I just nod and take a sip of my coffee.

'Dick said you've painted everything pink.'

'Not everything,' I say flatly.

My mother is doing her best not to make her disapproval sound too apparent, but the message is clear. Scarcely anything has changed in my parents' house since I moved in with John. It's simply become more lived in. The walls were originally white plaster. Now they've turned beige from the cigarette smoke, as has the ceiling. The same paintings are still on the walls. The brown leather three-piece suite *is* recent, but the same cannot be said of the dark oak cupboards and sideboards.

'Have you considered the fact that your place will be more difficult to sell with bold colours like that?' she goes on.

The Persian rug on the dining table we are sitting at is pricking my bare forearms. With my thumbnail I vacantly trace the angular patterns that stand out grubby white against the dark-red and green. 'It's only paint, Mum. You can easily paint over it again. And I'm not going anywhere for the time being.'

'You never know. When are you going back to work?'

'In a couple weeks or so.'

'Do you think you're up to it?'

I shrug my shoulders. 'I'll have to face up to it sooner or later. Sitting at home is no good.'

'Did you know there's a fête on this weekend? I just know lots of people would love to see you again.'

What rabbits are to my father, the annual village fête is to my mother. All the shops in the centre open their doors all weekend and put out stalls in the streets with special offers. Bands come and play, children have their faces painted. From all over the village and from miles around people flock to it. My mother is on the committee, so I usually put in a brief appearance. It's one of those occasions you try to wriggle out of if you possibly can.

'When is it, did you say?'

'This weekend.'

My stomach contracts. This weekend I should be in London. I haven't even bothered to find a replacement for Claudia. In fact all I've done is put it off, pretended it didn't exist. 'I don't know if I can make it. I was supposed to be going to London, remember?'

'So have you found someone else to go with you?'

'Not yet.'

'Well, see what you decide. It would be lovely if you could come. By the way, I hope we get a chance to drop in and see you next week. We haven't managed it so far, we're so busy at the moment. You know how it is.'

My father comes in, puts his clogs on the mat and turns on

the kitchen tap to wash his hands. He clears his throat noisily a couple of times. 'Any coffee?'

My mother gets up and rummages in the kitchen cupboard for a coffee cup. 'I was just saying to Margot that we must pop in next week and see how she's getting on.'

'I heard from Dick that all those garish colours were driving him up the wall.'

Normally I would giggle at this, but my face is frozen in a wry grin. I can't help reacting. 'I work with interiors every day. I think if you see too much of the same thing, you get jaded. I wanted to try something different.'

'That's nothing new in itself,' says my father, as he pulls his chair up to the table and my mother puts his coffee in front of him with a plastic mat underneath. 'Even as a child you were always different. Do you remember the kind of clothes Margot wanted to wear to school?'

My mother nods in agreement. 'A golden princess's dress and wellies. My dear, you won't believe how often I protected you from yourself. You'd have been a laughing stock if I'd let you make your own choices.'

I was anyway, I think, regardless of what I wore, but I don't say it.

'You were always painting too, do you remember? You haven't done that for years, have you?'

'No, no time these days.'

'You see, you grow out of it eventually,' my mother says, totally missing the point.

'Just act normal, that's crazy enough,' mutters my father in agreement.

I get up and kiss my mother on both cheeks, walk around the table and give my father a hug.

'Are you off already? We've got some cake.'

'Sorry, I really have to go. I've got so much on,' I lie.

'Can I expect you on Saturday?'

'Maybe,' I call out, but I'm already outside.

I'm going alone. The realisation that I'm actually going to do it, that in a few days' time I'm going to board a plane to London, where I know no one and no one knows me, fills me with excitement. I feel positive for the first time in ages. This is good, I tell myself. This is the first step towards regaining my old self, the person I was or wanted to be before I met John. Or towards discovering the new Margot. At any rate this is something I have to do by myself.

Dick told me yesterday he'd love to go with me. He was fitting the new tap in the sink. I looked into his eyes and read something totally different. He didn't feel like going at all. He probably didn't even have time.

The only reason he suggested it was because he had the idea that brothers should be prepared to look after their unstable, damaged sisters. Sweet, of course, but the old rebel stirred deep inside me. I'm not a child anymore, not a spotty adolescent with gangly arms who needs protecting from the wicked outside world. I'm thirty-two, grown up, with a first-class education and job, and OK, I may be a little overweight – but I'm definitely not ugly. What's more: I've never got myself into a mess and I'm not going to start now. I'm just going through a bad patch at the moment, which is pretty normal given recent developments. And I have a strong feeling that the deepest, darkest days are already behind me.

I'm going alone. I can't wait.

III

It wasn't so much the murder itself but the ease of it that surprised me. It's not difficult to kill someone. I suspected as much all along, but now I know. It's child's play. I'd thought through every detail and worked on the assumption that if there were such a thing as a perfect murder, I had committed it on that particular booze-soaked evening. Still, I remained alert.

Murderers who are caught usually have only themselves to blame. Arrests result from carelessness: a tiny oversight, a flaw in the plan or its execution, an impulsive improvisation.

The razor blade on the ledge by the mirror, which drew me irresistibly to it and seduced me with its sharp, gleaming edges, might have given me away. The use of a knife would have said something about me, and nothing about Edith. The short-lived pleasure of indulging a whim would have rebounded on me, since it didn't square with the picture I wanted to leave behind, the image I wanted to sketch. The cuts would have represented an anomalous piece of the puzzle that could eventually have put the police on my trail.

Rule number one for the perfect murder: make sure the forensic puzzle fits, and that all the pieces are to hand and, with a bit of brainwork, fit together seamlessly. Then everything falls into place, clear. But don't make the mistake of making things too easy for the police, since that, too, awakens suspicion.

No, what really surprised me was the aftermath, or rather the complete absence of one. A couple of personal interviews at home, with detectives who looked at me with tired eyes, wore shabby suits and fired off their all too predictable questions. Routine.

I replied meekly, flatly, frequently rubbing my eyes. Yes, Edith had sometimes talked about death. When asked if that had happened often, I answered affirmatively. What I withheld from my interviewers was the plain truth that only a few people around her knew: for Edith such conversations were purely analytical, fooling around – she loved abstraction. But for the outside world her statements could easily be interpreted as a cautious expression of latent suicidal thoughts.

I looked sad. My eyes were red and swollen, my hair uncombed. It didn't take much effort. I did feel sad, I had cared about Edith and now she was dead. Suicide. Awful that I hadn't seen something like that coming, and hadn't been more alert. Then perhaps I could have done something to prevent it, and she would have still been alive.

I played my part well and got away with an ease bordering on the improbable.

Because everything fitted in the picture.

4

I sit at the window staring outside where, in the pouring rain, a succession of fully-laden wagons to and fro across the asphalt delivering suitcases for loading into the hold of the aircraft. Further off, planes are taxiing towards the runway. It's dusk and barely any light is passing through the grey cloud cover. I drove with my lights on the whole way to Rotterdam Airport. October is not being kind to us this year: it's more like January.

I take a magazine from the back of the seat in front and flick through it absent-mindedly, without absorbing the English words. It must be at least six years since I was last on a plane. That was with John, a weekend in Barcelona. Back then life was still fun, we were smitten with each other and there was still no question of the estrangement that cast such a shadow over our last few years.

I look up from the magazine. The seats next to and in front of me are still free. I wouldn't mind at all if the seat next to me stayed empty, but I doubt I'll be that lucky. Passengers are still flocking into the cabin, boarding pass in hand, looking for their seat.

The fête is tomorrow and I won't be there. I knew I wouldn't the moment my mother mentioned it. Even if I hadn't been going to England I would have made up some excuse. The break-up with John is still too fresh. I've no wish to provide nosy village people with juicy background information. It's ten to one that everyone knows exactly what's happened. They just want to hear it straight from the horse's mouth. I can really do without pitying looks and good, or other, intentions. So I rang Dick just before I left to say I was going to London after all. I'd already paid for the ticket, the hotel was booked, and anyway, I'd have to get used to doing that sort of thing on my own from now on. I could tell from his reaction that he was relieved. He would pass the message on to our parents.

That call was a downright cowardly act on my part. I could, should perhaps, have rung them myself, but I couldn't bring myself to. I love them both, but we're too different – always have been. Dick is their dream son. He lives three streets away, and his wife Anne drops in for coffee with the children at least twice a week. In contrast I've neglected my parents over the past few months, because I didn't want to confront them with my anger and at the same time I didn't feel much like being frank with them.

They mean well, I know that of course, but I quite often find their comments hurtful, whereas I would never criticise their decisions or attitude to life. My hands start itching when I see the interior of their house: with a few tins of paint and some off-cuts from the market it could be transformed into a more modern, much more spacious and welcoming home. But I don't even dare offer, scared I'll offend them. Live and let live, it's called. They like it, what we dismiss as 'hackneyed rural-chic' in my line of work. But then why, I wonder, don't they let *me* live? *Just act normal, that's crazy enough* – I've lost count of how many times I've heard that put-down from my father's mouth. My mother expresses herself less forcefully, but she could never appreciate my naïve paintings and she still thinks she 'protected' me from my choice of clothes.

Basically I haven't changed at all inside. I still express an inner urge to convert emotions into something tangible – it's just that over the years I've changed the way I express them into something that pays the bills: a nice respectable job.

Nevertheless, whenever I enter an empty room where a restaurant or exhibition is planned, in my mind's eye I colour everything in. It takes no effort, the ideas come by themselves. An empty space has so much potential. Sometimes I manage to talk a client round, rouse their enthusiasm for my tentative suggestion to go for chairs with a tiger print in combination with bright red walls. Far more often I don't. Your average client doesn't want to get his fingers burnt and plays it safe. Just like my parents and almost everyone I know, John most of all. I can still see his face when he got home from work and I took him to our new apple-green bedroom. I'd spent my whole day off on it and wanted to surprise him. His shocked, almost angry reaction made it clear I couldn't have been quite right in the head to undertake something so idiotic without his permission. How could I slap that cheap green over patterned wallpaper? But that anger paled beside the shock wave that greeted my cautious hints that I was considering having dreadlocks and maybe even a tattoo at the base of my spine. 'You'd better find a new man while you're at it,' was his cold reply. 'I'm not going to bed with a woman with a spoiler and fake hair.' And he didn't stop at that by a long way.

In retrospect I should have left that same day. But I stayed, and in the years that followed I closed off, hid away, put the lid on those undesirable aspects of myself as well as I could. Until he eliminated *me* from the game.

Was that really the end of the world, I wonder now? For months I went around tormenting myself, screaming at the walls, cried myself to sleep and felt rejected, ugly, fat, ridiculous even. But now I'm on my way to London. Alone.

Perhaps the break-up with John is the perfect moment to steer my life in a direction that suits me better. I could even retrain as a stylist, a window-dresser or an interior designer – or something like that. Why not?

Something is fluttering around in my stomach, tumbling and giggling and my face breaks into a smile, the first of the day. You see, Margot, you've not even taken off yet and the future no longer looks pitch-black, but bright red, fuchsia and screaming yellow.

The plane has filled up without my noticing. Two men have sat down next to me. I give them a fleeting glance and then pretend to be engrossed in the magazine. Establishing contact, certainly with men, is still a problem. I worry that if I strike up a conversation myself I'll come across as a naive chatterbox, and the way I feel right now the slightest rejection would be enough to plunge me back into the well I've been thrashing around in for months. But if I go on staring stiffly into space, it's bound to turn into a couple of very lonely days. That's not what I want at all. This weekend has to be special. I'd like to meet some nice, new people. Recharge my batteries.

The man right next to me has ginger hair. He's wearing a dark-blue suit and a white shirt and I'd put him at about fifty. He's reading a Dutch paper and has shut himself off from everyone and everything. His stocky build is taking up so much space I have to keep my left arm jammed against my body to avoid touching him. My hands are in my lap on the magazine and I am leaning slightly to the right.

When the stewardess comes past to check with a professional

smile that everyone has fastened their seatbelts, closing the overhead lockers here and there, I look sideways again.

The other man, in the aisle seat, is clearly taller, slimmer and considerably younger than my immediate neighbour. He is wearing jeans and a black roll-neck sweater. Part of his face is masked by a lock of dark hair. He's preoccupied with his mobile phone.

The stewardess puts her hand on the back of his seat, bends over to him and asks him to turn off his mobile. He pretends not to hear, doesn't even look up, but a few seconds later I see him slide the cover shut and put the phone away. I notice he has slender hands, strong, rather bony, with small black hairs on his fingers.

The aircraft starts moving and taxis to the runway. I stare out at the lights on the runway, and the bustle of the airport as it moves slowly but surely away from us.

Less than five minutes later the wheels finally leave the ground of Rotterdam and the plane heads westward.

5

He's staring at me, the dark-haired man in the aisle seat. In the last twenty minutes I've looked in his direction a few times because I was curious about the face that went with those beautiful hands, and each time our eyes met. I feel uncomfortable, because he's not saying anything, just looking at me. It's not intimidating, in fact he's rather reserved, deep in thought, as though he's constantly on the point of saying something to me and thinking better of it. No, more than that, for a moment that look strikes me as familiar, as though we've known each other for years and found someone seated between us due to a mistake at check-in. A buffer in the form of the ginger business suit, who is now asleep with his chin on his chest. The broadsheet he was furiously leafing through a moment ago lies carelessly folded in his lap and threatens to slip off at any moment.

Disconcerted by his gaze I turn away and look out of the window. Grey skies.

'There's something about you . . .' I hear someone say beside me. A pleasant voice in which I think I recognise a faint Brabant accent.

I turn my face to the left to make sure it was him who spoke those words, and not my sleepy neighbour. But there can be no doubt about it. I produce a fleeting smile, waiting for what follows.

He shakes his head. Laughter lines appear around his eyes, and then he looks straight ahead again.

Despite my initial confusion I think I know what he's getting at and it immediately has a negative effect on my mood. I get reactions like this from strangers all the time.

I have different-coloured eyes. One is blue and the other is brown. There's an official name for it: *heterochromia iridium.* Some people who have this are deaf in one ear or are left with it as the result of an accident, the best known example being David Bowie. That's not true in my case. I was born like this and there's nothing wrong with my hearing. If I'd been a rabbit, my father would have used me as the progenitress of a new breed of which he would be the proud inventor, or else if I didn't come up to scratch I'd have wound up in the pot. That thought crossed my mind more than once when I saw my father selecting rabbits in the shed. But I wasn't a rabbit, I was a human being, a child, their child, and so they thought I was wonderful just as I was – what else could they do? That opinion wasn't always shared at school and in the neighbourhood. Some children, and even some grown-ups, kept staring at me, like this man, to the point of rudeness. Some thought my blue eye was made of glass. They couldn't believe that someone could naturally have two differ- ent-coloured eyes. More than once I was accused of being a witch, or a supernatural being. Later, in my teens, coloured con- tact lenses were all the rage on the club scene and they put it down to that. Then my brown eye was the fake one. In reality I regularly used brown contact lenses to blur the difference. After a while you get tired of constantly having to explain, having to tell the same story to total strangers over and over. If you diverge from the norm, there are only two possibilities: people find it attractive, or it turns them off. Show or stew.

I can't figure out which category this man belongs to or which group he's classified me in. He's looking straight ahead. It's just plain rude, staring at someone for ages, finally speaking to them and then completely ignoring them. It hurts, perhaps because of all the people sitting around me he's the one I would have most liked to talk to. He looks unusual, like someone with a story. Not devastatingly handsome, more interesting, with his dark, almost shoulder-length hair, cut in messy layers, partly hiding his sharp features.

He turns his head towards me again. I decide to stare back and lift my chin slightly defensively.

'It's still bothering me,' he finally says, so softly his voice scarcely rises above the noise of the engines and the piercing squalling of a baby at the back of the plane.

'What is?' Perhaps I put just a bit too much defensiveness into my voice, and it sounds just a bit too harsh, but right now I don't care. If he dares make just one snide remark, I'll give him a piece of my mind. He'll get a real bollocking. I've had thirty-two years' practice.

He says nothing and looks the other way. Didn't he hear me? Uncomfortable with the situation, I put my hands in my lap and start fiddling with my cuticles.

'Women always immediately assume there's something behind it if I say.'

I turn my head to the left. 'Say what?'

He makes a brusque gesture with his hand. 'Nothing. Leave it. Forget it.'

Not on your life. 'What were you going to say?'

'As long as you don't bite my head off.' The corner of his mouth curls. My reaction simply amuses him and it infuriates me. 'You've got an open face. Beautiful eyes, big and clear. But at the same time you're withdrawn. You know? It's as if something so devastating and painful has happened it's made you close yourself off from the world around you. You pretend you're not interested because you're scared of getting hurt again. And you do it so well that few people see how beautiful you really are.'

I stare at him breathlessly. Nothing about my eyes, at least nothing about their colour. He looked right through them. Just like that.

'That's what I do,' he says in response to my unspoken question.

'Are you a psychiatrist or something?' I manage to blurt out.

He grins, unfastens his seat belt and without another word walks down the aisle towards the back of the plane.

I wriggle out of the belt, turn ninety degrees and watch him go. He's really tall, at least six foot. At first sight his hair looks nonchalant, but you see that kind of nonchalance in glossy magazines. The same applies to his clothes. Yet he doesn't strike me as an arrogant, old-money type. There's something raw about him; the way he looks around him and the way he moves remind me more of a street fighter than a psychologist, lawyer or doctor.

Alarmed at my own reaction I grab the magazine out of its compartment in the seat back again and start leafing through it. The pictures and the words fail to hold my attention. Involuntarily my eyes stray outside to where everything is uniformly dull and grey. For the same price I could have been on a plane to Barcelona or Malaga right now. At least the sun would have been waiting for me there, and blue skies. It was Claudia's idea to go to London. She's crazy about that city, and I was happy to go along, never having been there. I feel a momentary pang of regret.

Am I mistaken, or is the aircraft starting to descend already? The clouds glide past the small window like shreds of mist and now and then I see a grey sea with white horses. I press my temple against the plastic and lower my head. Yes, land, a little way ahead. We're almost there.

'Are you visiting someone?'

I look up. The man I was talking to is back in his seat. At the same time the lights come on and everyone starts fastening their seatbelts. Through the speakers comes a crackly, inaudible announcement from the captain.

I fasten my seatbelt and shake my head. 'No, I'm on holiday. A weekend away, in fact . . . out on the town,' I add.

'Alone?'

'Yes. Alone.'

'Have you been to London before?'

'No, never.'

He raises his eyebrows. Beautiful, thin, slightly angular eyebrows above two dark eyes. 'So you're going to London alone, going out drinking, but you've never been there before and you don't know anyone there?' He sounds alarmed, as if I've just admitted I'm off to Afghanistan in a bikini.

'That's right.' I'm irritated by his attitude. A complete stranger the same age as me doing his best impression of my father. Why doesn't he mind his own business?

'What hotel are you staying in? In what area?'

I shrug my shoulders. Claudia and I booked the hotel on the internet. It was one of the few affordable ones we could find, two stars or less I think. We were only going to sleep there anyway. The website says it's situated in the beating heart of the city, with all the shops, pubs, clubs and restaurants within walking distance, so who needs a luxury hotel with internet and room service? The name of the hotel has slipped my mind and I'm not sure exactly where it is, either. I intend to work that out in a minute, when I get there. It looks like the London underground connects you with everywhere in the centre. It can't be all that difficult.

'I can't think of the name right now,' I finally say. 'It's in the centre anyway.'

'Did you book through a travel agency?'

'No. Why?' Again that defensive tone in my voice. Why am I defending my choices to a complete stranger?

He looks away and seems to be lost in thought.

Between us my neighbour wakes with a start, clutches at the newspaper, puts his hairy ginger hand on it possessively and shuts his eyes again.

The man bends over and rummages in the black rucksack wedged between his knees throughout the flight. He pulls out a file, tears a piece off and starts writing, and then thrusts it at me. 'Here, my mobile number. I'll be in London for the next four or five days. If there's a problem, or you feel like some company, or whatever, you can call me. In fact, you must call me.' He gives a wide grin. 'I'm a very good guide. And I don't bite.'

I stare at him in astonishment, but my hand grabs automatically at the scrap of paper he is holding out to me and stuffs it in my trouser pocket.

6

I forgot to ask his name. That's the first thing that occurs to me as I see him walking off on those long legs of his, his rucksack slung casually over one shoulder. All my fellow-passengers know where they're going or at least give that impression. They're being met by people holding up signs with their names on, or walk straight out through the sliding doors.

On a column in the middle of the bright concourse a news ticker is spewing out information on public transport, details that are probably very useful for those who know their way around, but none of those names means a thing to me. Sticking out of the column are tourist maps of the centre of London and fold-outs showing the tube lines. I grab them from their plastic holders and sit down on a bench with my rucksack beside me. I take the booking confirmation that has been sent to me by e-mail out of the flap. It contains a very cursory set of directions. Not very clear, all in all. In any case the hotel must be some-where in or around Soho, a name that does ring a bell. It could be Chinatown, but I'm not sure.

The green, blue, red, pink, brown and grey lines that indicate the London tube routes dance before my eyes. Oxford Circus, City Line, Camden Town, Marylebone . . . None of the tube lines goes all the way out to the airport. If I'm not mistaken, I should be taking the Docklands Light Railway to the nearest tube sta-tion, which is called Canning Town, where I can change to a tube train that will get me close to my hotel. The grey line – the Jubilee – goes north and south from Canning Town, but I can also opt to stay on the DLR train as far as Tower Hill, which sounds very much like Central London.

I hold the simplified map next to it to figure out exactly where I need to go. It's hard to say. I can find my way thereabouts and of course I can ask for directions, but I'll have to change trains a few times. There are stations where at least six lines seem to converge. My head is spinning. Suddenly I have a sneaking feeling that the London Underground may not be all that safe for a woman travelling alone who quite plainly gives the impression that she doesn't know the way. Aren't I an easy target for pickpockets, clutching tourist brochures, peering at signs and looking for entrances and exits?

Through the glass sliding doors I can see old-fashioned black taxis pulling up and leaving. Perhaps I shouldn't make things too difficult for myself on the first day. This afternoon I can explore the underground at my leisure, after I've had a shower and something to eat and drink. City Airport is near the centre, so the fare can't be that exorbitant.

I gather my things together, get up and go out through the glass sliding doors. A little way away, to the left in front of the building, are the taxi ranks. The vehicles are strikingly old-fashioned, with high roofs, looking like they date from the 1920s or 30s. The driver of the first taxi, an older man with grey hair and a knitted V-neck sweater over a checked shirt, looks friendly.

I bend over towards his opened window and read out the name and address of the hotel, before asking what the fare will be. The man frowns and casts a sideways glance at my piece of paper. It'll cost me about twenty pounds, he reckons.

Back home I took £250 out of the bank – my budget for the next few days. The taxi fare has already put a considerable dent in it, but the alternative is even less appealing now it's started raining. I sit on the leather seat in the back. With three feet of space in front of me, the flat black luggage compartment and host of brochures and announcements stuck to the partition, the taxi reminds me of a small local bus more than anything. It makes exactly the same kind of sound as it does a U-turn onto the road.

The rain lashes against the windscreen and the roof, making diagonal streaks across the glass, reducing visibility. With my arms clutching my rucksack I look at the buildings in brown, beige and grey that we pass at high speed. It's terribly busy. All around there are pedestrians, scooters, cars and motorbikes. Here and there the traffic is held up by vans and small trucks delivering orders to shops and restaurants. One in every three or four vehicles in the centre is an exact replica of my pre-war-style taxi. They're not all black, but yellow or bright pink and covered in advertising stickers. It's a very different world from the one I left behind this morning.

In the distance I catch a glimpse of a medieval fortress or castle. I'm inclined to ask the driver what sort of building it is, as it's bound to be a tourist attraction, but there is a thick sheet of glass between us and the man is at least five feet away from me. I try to make eye contact with him via the rear-view mirror. He doesn't look at me. This man is not the talkative kind who enjoys showing disorientated tourists around his city. I fiddle with the zip on my jacket and look at the black floor of the vehicle. I won't admit it to myself but I feel naked without someone beside me. There's no one to talk to, laugh, exchange a knowing look or discuss things with – not even anyone to get annoyed at. Travelling alone isn't nearly as much fun as I'd hoped.

IV

Edith turned out to be vulnerable, though that was the last thing she projected. Most people, even friends who knew her well or thought they did, described her as 'strong'. That was also the word that cropped up a lot in the speeches at her cremation.

A strong woman.

Yet she was just as mortal as everyone else. Fragile.

Everyone has a weak spot. In fact most people have more than one. If you take the time to search for them, have a good eye for social relationships, use your eyes and ears and are receptive, you'll find them.

With Edith it was vanity. Because she wanted to be beautiful she couldn't afford a bad night's sleep, so she took sleeping pills. There was also her bluntness, an abstract, hypothetical, detached viewpoint she affected and let loose on all kinds of topics, regardless of their importance. Edith could easily distance herself from what she personally felt or believed: what she really enjoyed was the debate. If everyone in a discussion was against the death penalty, you could be sure that she on the contrary would come up with cast-iron arguments for reintroducing it. Those kinds of things were her forte. She stoked the fire, held up a mirror to whoever she was talking to that seldom flattered them and often made them feel uncomfortable. I appreciated that quality in her. It was her strength, definitely her talent, and at the same time her second weakness.

It has struck me that people seldom listen to the meaning underlying words. There are only a few who recognise the silence behind the scream, the gentle weeping that hides behind tough statements. They hear only the words, the sentences, when there is so much more to take in. People are too self-absorbed to notice, really see or fathom others.

Often they don't even know themselves.

7

My cosy Victorian hotel in the pulsating heart of London is down a narrow, dark alley, and actually looks like a run-down boarding house. That may be due to the bad weather: dark clouds have gathered over the city, making everything look gloomy.

I throw away my lit cigarette end and push against the thick wooden door with the flat of my hand. It doesn't budge. Only when I put my shoulder against it does it grudgingly open.

Once inside, my eyes have to adjust to the lack of light. Hardly any daylight enters through the door pane. I'm standing in a small hall with a worn dark-red carpet on the floor. It's quiet and there's a strong smell of dust and mould. The hall leads to a narrow staircase carpeted in the same fabric. A counter has been knocked together in the left-hand corner of the entrance, finished in marbled plastic that curls up at the joints. There's no sign of anyone behind it.

I look round in disbelief. The reality I find here doesn't tally with what I saw on the website at all. Or does it? On my right is an armchair next to a marble bistro table beneath a painted portrait. I recognise the combination – only just – from one of the tiny low-resolution photos next to the inviting description on the internet. The painting turns out to be a reproduction and someone has scratched a moustache on the pale nineteenth-century female face. On the table there is a can of Coke and a plastic cup that once contained coffee. The armchair itself is almost totally obscured by an old fax machine and a mound of files piled up on the seat. When I look up I see a ghostly carnival reflection of myself in a low ceiling covered with plastic mirror tiles so warped they give the impression they could crash down from their grimy brass frames at any moment.

Against my better judgement I take the A4 sheet out of my pocket, and look again at the address and name of the hotel, but they haven't miraculously changed. I take a deep breath and close my eyes for a second. Perhaps the room will be fine after all, I tell myself, trying to keep my spirits up, but without really believing it.

Feeling worried, I approach the counter. On it is a notepad covered in all kinds of jottings in a language I don't recognise. The writing looks like either Polish or Czech, or at any rate Eastern European, with lots of c's and z's. I clear my throat loudly. Did no one hear me come in? Is there anyone here at all?

In the dimly-lit area near the stairs a door I hadn't noticed before – being papered in the same brown-and-green as the wall – swings open. Someone has cut round the outline of the door with a Stanley knife, so it can be opened and closed without taking the rest of the wallpaper with it.

A huge man appears with a blond crew cut and small, close-set eyes in a broad face. His skin is marked with spots and scars and there are stains on his polo shirt. His hand – with three tattoo dots between thumb and index finger – grips a cigarette. The open door reveals a living room with a grubby three-piece suite and a TV tuned to a sports channel. Timidly I place the booking confirmation on the counter, tell him my name in stuttering English and explain that I've booked online for two nights.

Giving me an odd look, he casually snatches my paper off the counter and grabs the notepad. Only then does he focus on the booking, scribbling something on the paper, turning round and yanking open a wooden cupboard. His huge body leans heavily over the counter as he hands me the key and stares at me, brazenly, as if I'm an animal in the zoo – a curiosity. I've already stepped back and take the key at arm's length, in order to keep as much distance between us as possible. The metal feels heavy in my hand. Keys like this are used for garden gates and are widely available in hardware shops. There's a plastic tag hanging from it bearing the number 18 in blue ink.

The man, who still hasn't uttered a single word, points to the stairs with his chin and raises two fingers.

I turn away from him and climb the stairs, conscious of his fixed gaze. My heart is pounding against my ribs and I can't stop shivering. The hotel is downright creepy and the porter or whatever he is has the look of a deaf-mute criminal. Not someone you'd approach to complain at length about the absence of clean towels.

I find room eighteen on the second floor at the end of a long, unlit corridor with a fussy patterned carpet. The smell of mould is even stronger here than downstairs and the floor under the carpet sags with each step. The key looks simple enough, but only after minutes of fiddling do I manage to open the door.

The heat hits my face immediately, a tingling dryness that reminds me of an old-fashioned drying hood at the hairdresser's. The central heating must have gone haywire. I put my bag down and take off my coat. It's boiling hot in here. The source of the heat turns out to be an old radiator hanging below the window, with no regulator valve on it. I slide the curtains aside and put my hands under the wooden sash window, which finally budges after creaks of protest.

I wipe my fingers on my trousers and survey my accommodation. There's not much to discover. The room is scarcely bigger than the bed. In the corner next to the window, barely twelve inches from the end of the bed, there's a narrow plastic shower cubicle. The plastic folding door is open and reveals a shower hose without a head. The unfortunate hotel guest before me had black curly hair. The proof of this is still clinging to the shower tray and hanging around the waste outlet. A washbasin next to the shower is not in much better shape. Two taps: one for cold, one for hot. No plug.

I edge past the bed and go to the other side, where there are two wardrobe doors. One wardrobe is empty, the other turns out to contain a chamber pot next to a small pink towel. 'Terrific,' I say aloud. 'Absolutely bloody terrific.'

Everything has gone wrong since the airport. The taxi driver, who seemed friendly at first, turned out to be a rip-off merchant. By the time we reached our destination there was thirty-three pounds on the meter, thirteen more than he'd said he would charge me at the airport. He didn't even apologise for his miscalculation, but just blamed it gruffly on circumstances: red lights, streets closed off, forced detours.

And now this.

I flop onto the bed and lie motionless, staring at the damp patches above the shower cubicle blotting the plywood ceiling like beige and pale-green Rorschach test patterns.

What on earth was I thinking, coming to London on my own? That the no-star hotel would be a cosy, comfortable hidden gem? That the sun would shine here every day and that it would be teeming with nice people who'd welcome me with open arms the moment they saw me? Maybe, just maybe, there are such people walking around, but to find out I'll have to go outside, past the porter. How can I be sure he won't rob me – or worse? I don't trust the lock on the door one little bit. And apart from that the guy is sure to have a skeleton key. Hotel rooms have to be cleaned after all, although that's probably not a top priority in this place. I'm still shivering when I think of the look he gave me.

I won't get a wink of sleep tonight, that's for sure.

The rain patters against the window pane and onto the windowsill. The heat gradually subsides and gives way to a damp chill that brings with it the smell of wet concrete.

As I poke at a burn hole in the bedspread with my nail, I fight the impulse to start crying and never stop.

I've already paid   180 for two nights at Hotel California. If I try to find a better place to sleep I'll have to shell out twice as much again.

This dreadful boarding-house is my base for the next couple of days. I'm stuck here like a prisoner. It feels like a nightmare.

This was supposed to be *my* weekend, and I was so looking forward to it. Exploring the city, forgetting everything for a little while: going out, eating well, shopping . . .

I've stopped believing that's going to happen. The way I feel right now, what I'd most like to do is go back to the airport and take the first flight home I can afford.

8

John and I met seven years ago at a trade fair in Utrecht. The company I was working for on a temporary basis had a stand there and for just under a week my job was to support the sales team – which amounted in practice to serving coffee, handing out files and being regularly dispatched to buy rolls, Mars Bars and cigarettes. We sold complicated hot-air heating systems for large buildings – not very exciting – and it gave me absolutely no outlet to use my diploma in advertising. But that didn't matter back then. At least I was gainfully employed, while in the evenings and at weekends I would scour the papers for job adverts and send off applications till I was exhausted.

What I learned in that week and what my subsequent experiences only confirmed, is that stand holders work under enormous stress. It may all look relaxed and informal, but that's just on the surface. Everyone's under inhuman pressure. Not infrequently, profits depend on orders taken at a trade fair like that and the new contacts established there. So everyone's on their toes, dressed to kill and armed with a forced smile, alert to every potential customer – *prospect* in the jargon – who may make all the difference.

Our stand was no exception. Everything and everyone was poised for action. On the stand itself there was a lot of showboating, bragging and joking, while out of sight of the visitors, in the pantry or the kitchen for staff, people let off steam. That was where you had the outbursts, the bitching about the competition or awkward customers, the painfully contorted faces and the fiddling with blister plasters and very occasionally – when everything had gone pear-shaped – the tears.

I was twenty-five, it was all new to me and I didn't mind that my job involved so little. The high hopes, the passionate emotions and the people, all those tens of thousands of visitors from all over the country with their different accents, who shuffled past the stands trying to look uninterested and who were regarded by those manning the stands as walking scratch cards . . . it was a world in itself, an invigorating cosmos buzzing with energy. That week I came to understand that for some people working at fairs can be addictive, just as others get their kicks from nightlife or extreme sports. I also was carried away to some extent. Later I did many more fairs and I still do them now, but I never got the same adrenaline rush as back then, at that first fair in Utrecht.

And that was all down to John.

He was working for a rival company on the stand directly opposite us and he soon caught my eye because he exuded such great calm amid the hustle and bustle of the hall. Everyone was racing around, making contacts, running to and fro with forms and calculators, while John gave the impression that none of it had anything to do with him and he was above it all. It was only later that I noticed his appearance, which was also to my liking. John was older than me, not quite thirty-five. He wore his suits with flair and moved around his sixty square yards of territory with the confidence and ease of an alpha male. Even on the first and second day we made lots of eye contact. On the third day he spoke to me at the buffet in the refreshments hall and on the fourth day he invited me out to eat with him in town after the fair. That evening I couldn't eat a thing and kept pushing my food around my plate. I didn't need to say much: John did the talking, he was full of stories. He stayed at a hotel near the fair complex and I went home, but not without butterflies. On the fifth day I realised I'd fallen in love with the newly-divorced technical manager of the competitors across the hall, the enemy camp.

Not long after the fair I joined another company where I had more responsibility, but John and I continued seeing each other. Our relationship grew deeper in a very natural way. It turned out he'd got divorced because he flatly refused to have children. He was very adamant. His ex-wife Linda couldn't accept that and after a fruitless attempt at marriage guidance they had decided to go their separate ways. John didn't only not want children, he never wanted to get married again, and I didn't have a problem with that. I wasn't feeling broody, and thought marriage was old hat. It was something your parents did. Living together was fine. I was happy, John was happy, and that's how it always would be.

It's stopped raining. The damp persists in the hotel and has crept into the sheets and the duvet. The bed feels clammy, but oddly enough I can no longer smell the mould. I look at my watch. More than two hours have slipped by, with me just lying on my bed and staring into space. Not the best of starts to a whirlwind weekend.

I fiddle restlessly with my nails and run my hands through my hair. I need to get out and *do* something, otherwise I'll go mad. I unzip the rucksack and start folding my clothes and putting them in the wardrobe. Two sweaters, two pairs of trousers, some skirts and blouses and a plastic bag full of underwear, including a new red lingerie set I bought specially for this weekend – just in case. God, where on earth did I get that idea?

When I've finished, I lean against the wardrobe door and throw my head back. The John I met seven years ago would have laughed at all this, at this dreadful hotel, the creepy porter, the rain. He would have tested this wobbly bed and my body for shock-resistance and simply relished me and the freedom: no work, no phone calls, no deadlines. But the John who could take on the whole world with his laconic attitude no longer exists. I lost him long ago. I lost him bit by bit, and beneath the peeling veneer appeared a man who was a stranger to me. He mumbled in greeting when I came home and when I got into bed beside him he didn't even look up from his book. No more attentive gestures, no cuddles, no feeling I was special. The butterflies fluttered off one by one through the window of our semi and escaped into the darkness, until all I had left was a hollow emptiness.

I stuff the red set of lingerie back into the bag and put it behind my modest pile of clothes. It gradually dawns on me that what I am doing is pointless. John is history. But still, I can't help feeling I may have contributed to the way he rejected me. Perhaps things would have turned out OK if I'd taken a different attitude and done my best to live up to his expectations. I should have listened to him, been stricter about dieting and exercise to regain my old shape.

Perhaps that's the worst thought of all: that it wasn't John who wrecked our relationship, but me, because I was inadequate on so many fronts and more or less forced him away from me.

Cold wind from outside mingles with the dry heat given off by the radiator and makes me shiver. 'Stop this,' I whisper to myself. 'Right now.'

I could stay here for hours, driving myself crazy with questions I can't even answer. It won't really make things any better. I must go out, take the plunge, do something, to stop myself going round the bend. My jeans are still damp from the rain, and the same applies to my socks. Mindlessly I empty my trouser pockets. Keys, chewing gum, my mobile and a scrap of paper. I unfold it and stare at the hastily scribbled telephone number that's already started to run with the damp. It feels like two days since I took it from the man in the plane, but it was actually only this morning. Above the number it says in powerful letters 'Leon'. Nice name.

I store the number in my phone.

V

Last week I went out with a girlfriend to a new restaurant. Small and trendy, no more than twelve tables, with room for about forty diners. Every seat was occupied. The mint-green paint on the walls was scarcely dry. There were no menus, the food on offer was written in black capitals on the ceiling. The result was that customers sat there with their heads tipped back and their mouths wide open like fools, staring at the ceiling. Apologetic, embarrassed giggling. The people around us found it funny, I think. Innovative, fresh.

She was sitting there looking up in the same way. A young woman, obliquely opposite us, together with a guy of the same age and two older people. She had mid-length red hair, which looked soft, with a lock across her forehead and an almost round, flushed face. Her full, pink mouth formed a perfect O as she studied the menu.

'Anything wrong?' asked my girlfriend.

I gazed at her intently and smiled. 'What could be wrong?'

'You look like you've seen a burning bush.'

'We live in stressful times,' I said, treating her to my friendliest smile. She went back to her carpaccio.

The rest of the evening passed as if in a trance. I pretended to have an upset stomach and went to the toilet a couple of times to be alone with my thoughts.

It was eleven months ago, my last night with Edith, but I

remember every little apparently irrelevant detail with astonishing clarity, as if it had happened only yesterday. I think back to it regularly, and at first this helped to keep the compulsion under control, but its effectiveness is wearing off. The feeling I got from killing her just as I had planned and on precisely that evening, as if I were God, was the best experience I've ever had. A cliché, forgive me, but there's nothing else like it. The high of alcohol or drugs pales beside it, shrivels to a trifling, insignificant experience. The power I had over her that evening had a euphoric, almost erotic effect.

I understand myself better than anyone. I know what it is I'm feeling, and also know that it's getting stronger and stronger.

Hunger.

In the toilet I stood against the tiled wall and rubbed my face with my hands. I visualised the redhead in the restaurant, imagined how she would soon be leaving and waving goodbye to her boyfriend and parents-in-law – I observed them closely enough to make sure. How she would walk home through the park and I would follow her and finally speak to her to gain her confidence. It wouldn't be that difficult. I always make a good first impression.

I entertained the thought for a moment, just for a moment, and then suppressed it. Thoughts become words, words become acts, acts become your fate.

Edith's death was meaningful. I cared about her, I really did, but finally she got in my way.

With this woman everything would be different. I didn't know her personally, knew nothing about her habits or weaknesses. And perhaps even more importantly: her death would be completely meaningless – would be carried out purely and simply to satisfy base, animal instincts. I recognise and accept them in myself, but I'm no animal. I know very well what there is inside me and how it got there. But I also know that the moment I give in to it, everything can go wrong. Will go wrong, I'm sure of it. If I were to embrace those thoughts, those wonderful tingling thoughts, actively allow myself to toy with the idea, it would be the first step towards wandering round at night like any other disturbed freak, dragging people off their bikes and having my way with them.

Not my style. That's for lower life forms.

9

Soho must be Chinatown. Street after street is full of Chinese restaurants and gambling arcades, their fronts covered with signs in Chinese characters. The city is damp and foggy, and all the cars have their lights on.

I don't feel like Chinese food, and definitely don't want to go back to the hotel. I feel strangely frantic, so I keep on walking, with one hand on the lapel of my coat without consciously taking in anything of my surroundings.

Pedestrians stream past me, I hear the traffic driving by, the hissing of the buses and the pounding music coming out of the shops, but the overwhelming noise is that of my own footsteps on the wet paving stones and the beating of my heart.

The busier it gets, the more I realise how alone I am. I have no part in this teeming anthill of Londoners, tourists, pavement artists, and homeless people, that cacophony of sound and colour, flashing neon signs and exhaust fumes. None of it has anything to do with me. I'm just walking here, random and aimless, and I've no idea where I might end up. Here and there open doors to bars and restaurants beckon, but when I look inside as I pass and see people together, drinking and talking. I walk on even faster.

Lost in thought, I reach another district, where the streets are wider and still more pedestrians pass me, though I see only their legs and feet because my head is bowed, as if that will help me shut myself off so that nothing can reach me.

The sound of a horn wakes me from my dazed state. I start as a white van hurtles towards me without slowing down, and only just manage to step back onto the pavement in time. Water splashes all over my jeans and coat. The driver beeps again angrily.

Next to me an old woman in a grey raincoat tries to make eye contact. She is smiling and her bright blue eyes look friendly. She says something that gets lost in the din of the traffic. Her trembling hand points to the ground: it says LOOK RIGHT in thick letters on the asphalt, underlined with two arrows. Look right. Of course. 'Thank you,' I say, but the woman has already disappeared into the crowd.

Across the road in a side street, there's a pub, The Black Horse. It sounds cosy and very English. I cross the road looking left and right till I reach the other side.

In the pub it's nice and warm and rather dimly lit. Gleaming oak floors, dark-green panelling almost to the ceiling, dark-red striped wallpaper above it and lots of oil paintings and copper utensils. The customers are mainly balding men in shirtsleeves clutching large glasses of beer. I choose a seat by the panelling, take off my coat and reach for the well-thumbed menu.

My mobile bleeps. A text from Claudia. My mood sinks to an all-time low.

How's London? Met any nice men yet? Thinking of you.
Love, C

My first impulse is to send back a trite message. My thumb is already poised over the keys and I'm formulating the craziest replies in my head, but I think better of it and tuck the mobile back in my trouser pocket. Claudia's feeling guilty, otherwise she wouldn't be texting me. Fine. The guiltier the better: let her wonder why I don't text back.

No one comes to take my order. A little way away a young barman serves wine and beer to a young couple, turns on his heel and goes straight back to the bar without so much as looking round, as if I'm invisible. I want to believe the man's a lout, the umpteenth one I've met today, but he's chatty with the other patrons. I run my hand through my curls, which have become bouncy with the hazy atmosphere in town. It's impossible to make eye contact with the barman. It takes another ten minutes before I realise no one has their order taken at their table.

I get up, holding the menu in my hand. The moment I reach the bar, sure enough I have their full attention. The ginger-haired barman leans over and takes my order. He keeps his head turned aside, as if he's hard of hearing.

'Small or large?' he asks, making a gesture with his thumb and forefinger.

'Sorry?'

'The wine. A small or a large glass?' A broad, mischievous smile. 'It's nice wine, love.'

'Make it a large then,' I say. 'Large is fine.'

All that's left on my plate are some hard bits of chip and a leaf or two of lettuce. The Scotch hamburger with pepper sauce was one of the tastiest meals I've ever eaten. That sauce was really divine, and this pub is also the nicest place I've ever been in. I can't help casting a professional eye over the interior and admiring the person responsible for the consistent, warm style that envelops you like a comfortable blanket. All that copper and wood must have cost a fortune. They're playing music I haven't heard for ages. A minute ago there was a Sade tune from the 80s, and now Frank Sinatra's 'Fly Me to the Moon'. I hum along soft-ly, as I fold my beer mat so it breaks into pieces. I'll just finish this glass of wine, I tell myself, and then I really must go out-side, onto the street. I can't bear the thought. I feel rosy and happy and want to hang on to this feeling for longer, but I know that I can't sit here for ever. Finding my way back to the hotel will be tricky enough, because I can't remember how I got here. If I let myself get drunk – and that will happen if I have another now – it could easily end in tears. A dark voice inside me protests against this train of thought. Bring on the disaster, it whispers. Wander through London drunk? Why not? Maybe I'll blend in with my surroundings better then and no longer feel like I'm alone and different from everything and everyone.

To spin out my stay in the pub I play with my phone, read old texts and delete some of them. It's a sorry sight, my inbox. As well as Claudia's last text I find old messages from my cus-tomers and Dick. The paltry content of my mobile phone accurately reflects my impoverished post-John social life.

I have another sip of wine and go through all the numbers of my family, friends and acquaintances. For Anne I have three numbers, only one of which is correct. To my shame my late granddad's number is still there. Why didn't I delete it before?

The next name on the list brings a cautious smile to my lips. Leon. The man from the plane, with his beautiful hands, dark eyes and long legs, whom I was supposed to call if I needed a guide, had any problems or just needed company. He said some-thing like that, with an air that suggested he assumed I'd call.

I stare mesmerised at the screen. Would it be terribly naive and impulsive to accept an invitation like that, to just call a guy you barely know? Isn't that foolish at the very least? I have no idea what he expects from me. Is he just a nice guy who enjoys showing tourists round a city he knows well? A psychologist who's discovered a particular character trait in me that he'd like to study in more detail? He could be a drug dealer for all I know, and this is his way of drumming up trade. I won't absolutely rule out the one obvious answer, but he really doesn't strike me as that type. With his looks it can't be too hard to find women who'll cater to him. So why should he give his number to me of all people? I'm nothing special. I'm not blonde, or dark and mysterious, not slim – and at the moment I'm not very good company at all. I was special once, at least I thought so for a while, before John trampled that idea ruthlessly underfoot.

What am I thinking? Why on earth should I call him? If I do he'll know that my London weekend has turned into a fiasco on the very first evening.

So what? I hear that wicked voice inside my head say. What difference does it make? I don't know the man, he doesn't know me, it's a strange city – if he has other ideas, if I make a fool of myself or if we just don't click, it won't have any repercussions. I wanted a special weekend, didn't I? Well, it's started, but it's not been particularly special so far. Just sad.

I reach for the wine glass and take another sip. The remainder of the wine slides down my throat and warms my gullet.

Before I can change my mind, I head out into the street, light a cigarette and put the mobile to my ear.

10

'It's Margot.' I nervously flick my cigarette ash. 'Margot Heijne. We were on the same plane this morning. You gave me your number.'

Hubbub in the background. Leon is in a bar or a restaurant. 'Margot . . . nice name.'

'Thank you.'

'What can I do for you?'

Some people have an arsenal of carefully polished remarks and jokes up their sleeve that they can serve up effortlessly. I'm not so lucky. Only afterwards, when I'm lying in bed at night and replay all the conversations I've had that day at leisure, do the witticisms come to mind.

Nervously I run my hands through my hair for the umpteenth time. When I open my mouth, no sound comes out.

'How do you like London?' he asks, breaking the silence.

'It's OK.'

'And your hotel?'

'The pits.'

'Define the pits.'

'An escaped convict for a porter and a filthy broom cupboard for a room.' I'm quite proud of that.

He chuckles. 'Sounds like fun. I'd invite you over to mine, but that might give you the wrong impression.'

'Is your hotel better then?'

'Oh, probably just as bad. It's swarming with businesspeople sounding off so everyone can hear how wonderful and widely travelled they are. And besides, they've run out of Entre deux mers.'

I have to laugh. I can't help it.

'So I was just planning to escape and go AWOL for a while. Have you eaten yet?'

'No.'

'What do you say we eat together? That's more fun than alone, isn't it?'

'But how –'

'The Oxo Tower. O-X-O. The taxi drivers will know it . . . Shall I see you there around eight-thirty?'

Disconcerted, I agree. He rings off with a short 'ciao'.

Trembling, I stub out my cigarette and look at my watch. Seven o'clock. I have no idea where that restaurant is or how far it is from here, but I assume I won't be terribly welcome in the old jeans, comfortable boots and knitted cardigan I'm wearing at the moment. If every taxi driver knows it it won't be a run-of-the-mill place.

As I start walking back to the hotel, I realise that the wine has already gone to my head. Those were three big glasses after all. And all three of them were irresistible. The pavement is bouncing like rubber under my feet and that's not a good sign. I'm not going to drink any more tonight, I resolve. Not a drop.

I plunge purposefully through the lamplit night, it's cold and windy. When I get to Oxford Street I remember exactly where I crossed the road. The traffic is quieter now than this afternoon.

I smile when I pass a group of giggling girls in high heels and miniskirts. It occurs to me that I'm one of them now. I have a goal, a prospect, somewhere in the city I have to get to on time.

More by luck than judgement I find the hotel. In my room everything is as I left it. The central heating is still on full blast, as if it's serving a factory rather than a glorified chicken run. As the heat leaks out of the window I opened earlier the curtains waft gently up and down in the airstream.

I undress and turn on the shower tap. Water sputters out of the hose, which immediately snakes in all directions. I grab my shampoo, wet my hair and lay the hose back on the floor, with my foot on the plastic end to keep it in place. Then I rinse the shampoo out and repeat the procedure with conditioner. Dripping wet, I walk across the dirty carpet to the cupboard concealing the toilet, squeeze the water out of my hair over the toilet bowl and dry myself with the pink towel. It's too small to wind round my head, as I always do at home. I hang it over the radiator. I have no illusions about the towel service in Hotel California. I spray deodorant under my arms, dab some perfume in the nape of my neck under my hair, and open the wardrobe. The red set of lingerie? The alternatives are a washed out sports bra and a skin-coloured underwired model that I wear under white clothes. The lingerie hasn't been worn and the labels are still hanging from it. I bite them off impatiently and look at my watch. Ten past eight. My hair is still dripping. It's thick and curly and always takes ages to dry. No problem, since I always wash it before I go to bed: it's dry by the morning. How about a quick, straight ponytail? With an elastic band between my teeth I drag a brush through my hair and hold the ponytail with one hand. The light's coming from the wrong side, so I can barely see myself. No, that ponytail looks hideous. Not today. I work mousse through my hair to stop it frizzing up all over the place once it's dry and take up the sides to fasten them back. I take another look in the mirror. With a bit of luck it will dry attractively, with curls falling over my face. I quickly wriggle into my black skirt and the only smart blouse I have with me. It is black with red roses, long, wide sleeves in a thin fabric and quite daring. The blouse diverts attention from my sturdy upper arms and hips to my cleavage. I paid a fortune for it last year and afterwards there was simply no opportunity to wear it. Too flashy. Now it's perfect. I rummage feverishly through the pile of clothes in the wardrobe. No tights, I forgot to bring any. Bare legs then: the skirt's long and you can hardly see my ankles.

Quarter past eight. Make-up, I'd almost forgotten. All I can do is pray that Oxo Tower isn't too far from here, since I'm not going to make eight-thirty. Shit. I really have to get a move on. Foundation, brown mascara, blusher that I rub on my cheeks and eyelids, since there's no time to do a proper job. A peach-coloured lipstick to finish it off. A last look in the mirror. To be sure I rub my jaw and neck with wet hands. If there was a tide mark there before, it's gone now. Ready. Eight twenty-three. I grab my bag off the bed and put my coat on as I hurry down the stairs and out of the hotel. There's no one in the hall. From behind the hidden door comes the sound of a television. A match.

11

It's a quarter to nine. My heart rate has doubled by the time the taxi driver drops me off. He says the restaurant's on the top floor and the entrance is at the back, and you can get to it in one of the lifts. He also told me that the building used to be a factory where they made Oxo stock cubes.

You can recognise the restaurant from afar, with its gigantic advertising letters, each almost as wide as the tower itself, a glowing red unfinished game of noughts-and-crosses against the dark sky. There's a pedestrian promenade in front with the Thames flowing past – a wonderful spot for a restaurant.

I tip my head back and hold my lapel tight against the bare skin of my cleavage. At the top of the building I can see people sitting at tables and waiters dressed in white and black moving to and fro. I walk down a corridor to the rear of the building and find the lifts, where a group of people in evening dress are waiting. Next to the metal lift doors there's a colourful sign listing what there is to do on the various floors. The building is partly residential and partly used as an exhibition space and showroom for both interior and fashion designers. I must remember to drop by here again this weekend. You never know, I might pick up a few good ideas. Then all I need is to find a customer willing to try them out, I think wryly. Fat chance.

My companions in the lift are mainly women with bleach blonde, perfectly styled hair wearing higher heels than I can walk in, and a few men in smart suits. When the lift doors slide open there's a narrow corridor, and at the end of it you can either turn left, to the restaurant, or right, to the brasserie. I stand there rather uncertainly. Restaurant or brasserie? Hesitantly I walk in the direction of the restaurant. It's busy near the cloakroom but I can't see Leon anywhere. It was a good idea to get changed at any rate. This is not your average restaurant. In fact it's anything but average, with its floor-to-ceiling glass walls giving a breathtaking view over the Thames, the bridges and historic buildings across the river, each bathed in warm light.

As I walk back towards the brasserie another lift door opens and out gets Leon. Now I can examine him closely at last. I'd say he's five or six years older than me and in good shape. He's wearing the same jacket as this morning, and the same cowboy boots, but now with jeans and a black shirt open at the collar. Not much chest hair, and smooth, slightly tanned skin. But it's his face that catches my eye. He's not good-looking in the classical sense, his face is just too narrow and angular for that. But he has nice dark eyes, a straight nose, and something very important to me: a sharp jaw-line.

Before I can say anything he puts an arm round me and kisses me on the cheek. 'Sorry I'm late. I got tied up.'

'I was late too, I've just arrived.'

'Brabant time?'

'You're from Brabant too, aren't you?'

A grin. 'Yes. It takes one to know one . . . Unfortunately the restaurant was full, this place does a roaring trade, but the brasserie's fine. Perhaps even better.'

He puts his hand on my lower back and leads me to the brasserie like we've been married thirty years, where he takes my coat and leaves it at the cloakroom together with his own. He gives his name and telephone number to a woman behind a small counter. His name is Wagner. Leon Wagner. That sounds like a step up from John van Oss. I can't help smiling inside.

A young hostess leads the way. The ceiling is very high, a metal construction that slopes down to the glass wall. Almost all the tables are occupied. They are small and white, with chairs on either side in chrome and light-blue leather. The tables are arranged in rows and are close together. There's one free right by the window and the hostess leaves us there. A black man of about fifty with short grey frizzy hair hands us the menus.

'Will you join me in a bottle of Entre deux mers?'

I didn't really want to drink. 'OK. But I don't drink very much.'

'Don't you like white wine?'

'I like all kinds of wine. That's the problem.'

'Good! The first thing we have in common.'

I feel like a cigarette. I quickly look around. There are no signs for a smoking area anywhere. Slightly alarmed I ask: 'Don't they have a smoking room up here or something?'

He looks at me in amusement. 'Over there at the back there's a door onto the terrace, so you can smoke outside if you want.'

'Not very enjoyable, smoking outside without a coat.'

'I'll come with you in a bit. Or do you need one right now?'

Need . . . 'Not at all. I was just wondering.'

He's clearly not entirely convinced.

'The first thing we don't have in common?'

Leon opens the menu. 'I gave up, two years ago. But I have no problem with it, if that's what you mean. I'd go for the salad. It's really superb here.'

'Do you come here a lot?'

'When I have to be in London, I eat here often.'

'And do you have to be in London a lot?'

'Six or seven times a year.'

'For your work?'

'Sometimes,' he replies without taking his eyes off the menu. Then he snaps it shut. 'I've decided. How about you?'

I've scarcely had chance to take in the dishes. 'Not yet.'

'Do you like pasta?'

I nod.

'Just leave it to me then.'

As he looks up the waiter is already on his way to our table.

It strikes me that Leon speaks English almost without an accent. With most Dutch-speakers it's painfully obvious they come from abroad. Not with Leon.

'You speak good English,' I observe.

'I come to England a lot. You soon learn.'

I want to ask him what he does for a living, but he beats me to it and I explain what I do, why, and what parts of my job I find fulfilling and what parts I can't stand.

'If you want to be in business, you have to make concessions,' is his brief comment.

'I'm beginning to hate them more and more. The job's starting to take over my life, it seems. I don't want to complain, really I don't, but increasingly I feel like all I do is take orders. My input doesn't matter very much. The customer usually already knows what he wants and all I have to do is see if we can deliver everything on time.'

'Your customer is at the point where you started years ago. You deal with interiors and furnishing on a daily basis and if you're any good, you'll know your stuff. You visit trade fairs, you get ideas from international magazines and want to put them into practice together with your own ideas. You want to create, leave your mark. If I'm not mistaken, you've now hit the ceiling of what you can achieve, because that kind of customer doesn't want to leave the beaten track, true or not? It's good if you're aware of that. A sign that you're good at your job, that you're evolving and you're a creative person and not some two-dimensional sales robot. And that it's time to move on.'

I stare at him breathlessly. Everything I've been trying to get across to Claudia, Dick, Anne, and yes, even John, till I'm blue in the face, he understands immediately, without having to come up with examples and without having to explain what furnishing an empty space means to me, how much satisfaction I can get from creating a special, unique atmosphere just by combining colours, shapes and materials. For a moment I'm speechless. Then I say: 'You clearly know what you're talking about. Is that from personal experience?'

He shrugs his shoulders. The waiter appears and pours a few drops of white wine into Leon's glass. Leon takes a sip and nods. 'It's fine.' The waiter fills my glass too and puts the bottle into a cooler full of ice cubes, before disappearing again without a sound.

'If you really can't stand it,' says Leon, raising his glass to me, 'then you'll have to find a totally new direction. Follow your heart, otherwise you'll lose yourself.' There's no hint of the lecturer in his voice or attitude. This man sitting opposite me, brushing a lock of dark hair from his forehead in an incredibly masculine way, knows what he's talking about. He gives advice so casually it's like we've been friends for years and he knows exactly what I think and want. More than that: he puts his finger on something I hadn't yet worked out for myself.

I take a sip of my wine and notice that my hand is trembling slightly as I put the glass back on the shiny table top. 'I've already thought about perhaps doing an interior design course. Or something to do with window dressing. Windows can often be more adventurous because they're temporary, and cheaper.'

'Even then you're tied to the customer's requirements. In practice window dressing often comes down to putting certain products in certain places, exactly where the customer wants them. The chains you rely on for most of your work, because they have the budget for a professional window dresser, want the same window displays all over the country. It boils down to a production-line all the same.'

I take a bite of the bread that the waiter has just put on the table unnoticed. It's warm and fragrant and tastes of walnuts. 'Well, I'll have to see about that,' I say, once I've swallowed the bread. 'Window dressing's new for me, and I've got a lot to learn in that area too. Besides, I've got a mortgage.'

'What a pain,' he says dismissively, as if financial obligations are outside his experience. That may be the case: for the price of a simple starter in this restaurant you could get a three-course meal elsewhere, including drinks and coffee.

My eyes wander for a moment as I ponder what he just said. To our right, six or so square tables further on, is a high-tech open kitchen. Behind a high, brushed-steel counter cooks in immaculate uniforms are preparing the dishes. It reminds me of English cookery programmes on TV, where flamboyant chefs race the clock, turning out one haute cuisine dish after another. These are young people cooking and they are going about their work in a serious, accomplished way. Do they still enjoy it, I wonder. To what extent can these people express their own creativity in the dishes they make, day in, day out, for a whole season?

As if Leon is reading my thoughts, he says: 'True freedom only exists in art. The problem is you have to be incredibly good. No, I'm putting it all wrong: you don't so much need to be outstanding, what you really need are connections, if you don't want to be dependent on all kinds of government foundations who will impose their ideas and restrictions on you in turn. It can be touch and go in the beginning: it takes guts to let go of everything. But if you make it, you're free. It's worth a try, it seems to me. You've got commercial talent, judging by what you say. If you combine that with your creativity, you could go a long way.'

'I can't afford that freedom,' I say softly.

'Can't or won't? Are you afraid?'

I look up. 'Afraid? Me? No. It's got nothing to do with fear. I'm just being realistic.'

'Your house and your holidays are more important to you, that's what you're saying. It's a question of priorities and in your case they obviously don't lie in the creative field. Shame . . . For you, mainly.'

I feel the urge to tell him I'm not ready yet, that it's not a question of priorities, but that he's jumping to conclusions. That I've been through a bad patch that was overshadowed by the past and have barely had time to think about the future, so he's jumping the gun with his snap judgements, but the waiter appears at our table with the starter.

The salads are piled up in the shape of a pyramid, with dried strips of bacon, pine kernels, spinach leaves and cheese to bind it together. I feel good when I eat salads. I should make them more often at home, but I simply never get round to it. Every so often I spend a fortune on fresh vegetables and fruit, but by the time I'm free to transform it all into a healthy snack, I find it's all gone mouldy, wilted and rotten.

We've scarcely finished the salad when Leon pushes his chair back and nods to me. 'Cigarette break?'

I take my bag and follow him, past the tables and the open kitchen, behind a glass display case in which art is exhibited and outside via a sliding door. I love the way Leon walks. Many men walk with their feet turned out, shoulders hunched or with wooden movements, but not him. He exudes a self-confidence with every step that everyone notices. Men stand aside for him and one by one I see the countless bleach blondes check him out and then feel their appraising glances slide over me, as if they're weighing me up, assessing me, and wondering if we're a couple and if so what kind of relationship we have. Could someone like Leon ever be with me? At any rate he's not at all like the men I let into my life until recently. Maybe that's precisely a point in his favour.

The terrace is an extension of the brasserie, has no roof and looks out onto the illuminated bridge and buildings on the other side of the Thames. It's cold. I grab for my lapel without thinking, but only then realise I haven't got a coat on. The wind blows right through the thin fabric of my blouse and I'm getting goose pimples all over.

I rummage in my bag, find my cigarettes and light one up. As I'm about to put the packet back in my bag, Leon puts his hand on mine. 'Give me one too.'

I look up in disbelief. 'You gave up.'

'I can handle it.'

'Are you sure?'

He just looks at me in amusement, almost condescending. 'Trust me.'

We stand next to each other smoking in silence. The wind tugs at my blouse and carries the smoke up towards the roof.

Then he he gives me a sidelong glance. 'Cold?'

'A bit. Not really.'

His grin draws up on one side. 'Be strong, Margot. Just stay strong.'

'What do you mean by that?'

'It's just comical. You're freezing to death, but you won't admit it. What are you trying to prove?'

In my confusion I try to run my fingers through my hair but they catch on the pins I put in a few hours ago. Christ, I haven't been to the ladies' yet to check the end result now it's dry. The loose locks are being pulled in all directions by the wind. I must look like a scruffy ghost.

Leon just finds it amusing. His dark eyes are twinkling.

'Do you do this often?' I ask.

'What?'

'Ask out women you don't know, for your personal entertainment?'

He turns to me and shields me from the worst of the cold with his tall body. Then looks down at me. 'You're first-class entertainment, Margot, but my evening won't be a success if you don't have some fun too.'

I don't know what to say.

'Have I succeeded up to now?' he asks.

I can't help laughing. I shake my head and look at the floor: wooden planks of the ridiculously expensive, sanded kind. When I look up again, he's standing closer to me, almost touching me, and then he leans over me. 'Well?' he says in a whisper.

'You're a fast worker, Leon.'

Before I can react he grabs my jaw and presses a little kiss on my mouth. It all happens too fast for me to return it or pull my head away. Anyway the latter didn't even occur to me.

'Come on, princess, we're going inside before you catch your death out here.'

He goes towards the sliding doors without looking round and to my annoyance I throw away the half-smoked cigarette and hurry after him. In the warm interior, the annoyance fades as quickly as it arrived and I realize that I've been feeling great all evening. Relaxed, ecstatic, light – frisky almost. I don't want it to end, this evening with a man who reads me like a book – an interesting book.

12

The evening is going too fast. Over the main course I told Leon all about my parents, how they met, and my childhood as the younger sister of an infuriating brother I only learned to appreciate when I grew up. Over dessert we talked about the advertising course I did at college, and I dished up anecdotes I thought I'd long since forgotten. I skirted around the subject of John as best I could and when Leon asked me questions too close for comfort I managed to steer the conversation in another direction. John wrecked lots of things but I'm not going to let him spoil this evening. He's history, in the past, he has no part in my present and none at all in my future.

Leon talks easily, but listens far better. I have the feeling that we could go on talking for days, weeks, even months without the conversation flagging for a moment or either of us getting bored.

I've no idea what I've done to deserve a date that's turning out better than I imagined in every way. But I do know that such self-disparaging thoughts have been pushed into the background and I'm enjoying the here and now. Lapping it up.

We wait outside for a cab. We've finished every last drop of the wine and after the meal we had cognac with coffee. I can handle my drink better these days, probably because I've put on weight. That's my salvation now, because if I'd drunk this amount of alcohol a few years ago, I'd have had to be carried out, slurring my words. There's no question of that now. I am firmly on my feet, but the alcohol is making me light-headed and I barely feel the biting cold. Leon raises his hand and a taxi pulls over.

'I'll take you to your hotel,' he says, helping me into the cab. 'We can have another drink there.'

I had forgotten what a dump my hotel was. 'There's no bar,' I reply. 'Just a creepy guy.'

'I'd like to take a look at him. What's the hotel called and where is it?'

I tell him the address and he passes it on to the driver, who makes a U-turn and heads back towards the centre. Some eight pounds fifty later he stops with his engine idling at the entrance to the alley.

'Wait here,' Leon tells the man, thrusting him some money.

The door from the hall of the hotel to the living room door is wide open. My porter is in the company of two ladies in red high heels and a man who could be his brother. They have the same build and the same expression. The men are watching us with prying eyes and raised eyebrows. The women are sitting on the floor in front of the sofa braiding each other's hair.

'Very professional,' comments Leon. 'Are you sure it's a hotel and not an undercover brothel? What kind of sleazy site did you find this on for God's sake?'

'Ha ha.'

'It wasn't a joke.'

My room is too small for two people. It's full the moment we cross the threshold and shut the creaky door behind us. During my absence the walls seem to have moved even closer together. There's a damp, penetrating mouldy smell that almost takes my breath away. Did I really lie here dozing this afternoon, untroubled by that stench?

With his hands in his coat pockets Leon takes a look around, at the shower, the ceiling, the bed, the open window. 'OK,' he says without looking at me. 'You're not sleeping here tonight. I wouldn't even leave my dog in here.'

'Have you got a dog?'

'I used to. His name was Dalí.'

'What a funny name.'

'It suited him. He was just as crazy and had a black moustache.'

I can't help laughing again.

'Well, what are you waiting for? Pack your things. I'll go downstairs while you're doing that and check you out.'

I look at him in astonishment. Pack my things? Check out? I'd like nothing better. Away from this den of thieves, nowhere could be worse than here. But something protests inside me – could it be common sense? 'Listen, Leon . . .' I begin. 'If I go with you and it . . .' My voice falters.

He looks at me so intensely I expect him to start kissing me at any moment, not fleeting and friendly like on the terrace of the restaurant, but slow and intimate. But he just stands there. 'What are you trying to say?' he asks.

'If . . . I go with you and it turns out I'm lacking in entertainment value, tomorrow – or even tonight . . . then I need somewhere to . . . Christ. Well, what it comes down to is: I'm not going to check out just like that, if you know what I mean. However grotty this hotel may be, I've paid for it.' I look him straight in the eyes and go on, more gently now: 'In your world €180 may not mean very much, but for me it's a lot of money.'

He closes his eyes for a moment and rubs his nose with his thumb and forefinger. 'You don't have to check out. You should do what *you* want.' He throws up his hands. 'But . . . with all due respect, I wasn't planning on taking you to my room. That's a bit of a cliché, don't you think? Taking a woman out for a meal then asking for payment in kind . . . I was planning to offer you a decent room in my hotel for the rest of your stay. A separate room.'

So there it is. My first gaffe. I've been waiting for it all evening, and now it's made its entrance, centre stage. The evening has gone so well, I didn't put a foot wrong, and now this. He sees me as a protégée, not a mistress. He doesn't even *want* to go to bed with me, he simply wants to protect me from this hotel, because he's grown fond of me and clearly won't lose any sleep over one more hotel bill. For him it must be like giving loose change to a beggar.

I wish the ground would swallow me up. Mechanically I start taking my clothes out of the wardrobe and stuffing them awkwardly into my rucksack.

My good mood is almost gone.

'But that's not to say it won't go any further,' I suddenly hear a voice say behind me.

I turn round, rucksack in hand.

He's leaning against the peeling wallpaper with a broad grin, but his eyes aren't smiling. 'But only when you're ready, princess, and preferably later. Much later.'

'*Later?*'

He grins. 'I like seeing a woman suffer. I really love that.'

13

My last remnant of intuition hasn't deserted me. The taxi just stopped outside a distinguished-looking building bearing the name Waldorf Hilton, every brick in the façade exuding luxury and history. The style inside is different from what you might expect: clean lines, spacious and modern, with soft colours. As I look round the lobby, absorbing the numerous details, Leon is talking to two members of staff. The hotel is fully booked, that much is clear, and even the helpful receptionists who would bend over backwards to help him can't magic up an extra room for him.

A hotel in the same chain still has two rooms available, but it's almost midnight and it's a bit out of the way. Leon doesn't see any point in what he calls a complete 'migration of peoples', so we decide not to be difficult and share his room. Two rooms, in fact. His suite turns out to consist of a bedroom with a gigantic white bed and a full sitting room, with comfortable furniture and a plasma TV.

'Do you always stay here when you're in London?' I ask as we go in, trying desperately not to sound too keen or provincial.

'Not always. I often stay with friends. Or at the St James or Great Eastern. But this is OK.'

OK. The understatement of the year. The bathroom alone is almost as big as my living room at home, with thick glass doors, recessed lighting and extremely expensive fittings. It crosses my mind that one night in this suite – I can't call it a hotel room – must cost about the same as camping out for well over a week in Hotel California. I take my shoes off straight away, hang my coat up and leave my rucksack by the door.

Leon moves through the room as though he owns the whole hotel, kicks off his shoes and pours whisky for us. He takes the remote and switches to a music channel. The volume is low, and the music scarcely audible. He flops into an armchair and watches me in amusement.

His whole behaviour confirms what I already suspected : he's used to this kind of hotel, just as he's used to eating in top restaurants. For him this is not some special treat that you can afford every now and again, if you're lucky, but an acquired right.

I still don't know what he does for a living – for some reason the way this evening's conversation went we only talked about me – but I'm beginning to have serious doubts whether it's all above board. Over the years I've met thousands, tens of thousands of people from all walks of life and have learned to recognise old money a mile off. One thing is clear: Leon is no scion of a wealthy family. His movements are too rough, too animal for that, his skin is too weathered and his accent too broad. The latter is a plus for me: he has a magnificent voice that puts me at ease. Whatever the case, the man sitting opposite me in the armchair is not the kind to ask Daddy for a handout. He's earned this for himself. He can't be a psychiatrist, as you obviously don't strike it rich like that. The other options I've already considered are drug dealer, or nightclub owner. I'm still not ruling that out. It crosses my mind that maybe, just maybe he's one of those lucky few who've made their fortune with a dotcom business. He's the right age at any rate but his appearance and behaviour fall midway between the two preceding options.

'You haven't told me what you do yet,' I say, sitting down opposite him and taking a glass of whisky.

'I'd rather tell you tomorrow. I don't want to frighten you off.'

'Drug dealer then,' I blurt out. I slide to the far edge of the armchair and watch closely for his reaction. If this man makes his living from crime of any sort, I'll thank him for the lovely evening and that will be the end of it. The reason I rang him and went out with him is because I'm fully prepared to take the plunge, but there's no way I'm going to do that knowing in advance that the current is treacherous and that sharp rocks lurk beneath the surface.

'Interesting notion,' he replies, and bursts out laughing. Then his face clouds over and he falls silent. He turns the glass in his hand and gives me a piercing look. 'I'm not a drug dealer.'

I sink back into the armchair in relief. He's not a drug dealer. Great: 'But what then?'

'I'll let you see for yourself tomorrow. Or do you have other plans?'

I shake my head and realise at the same time how stupid this must sound. I have no plans, no goal, and no appointments. I don't know anyone in London and he's all too aware that he saved my evening, perhaps my whole weekend.

I take a sip of the whisky. The liquid burns my throat. A moment ago I still thought I wasn't feeling the alcohol, but it seems to be catching up with me now. Resolutely, I push the glass away. 'I shouldn't drink any more.'

He casts a quick glance at his watch. 'Go to bed then.'

I look around. The only bed is in the adjoining room.

Leon follows my gaze. 'You take the bed. I'll sleep in here.'

'No, you have the bed.'

'I'd never forgive myself if I let that happen.' He gets up and puts an arm round my waist to support me. 'I'll put you to bed. You may be on holiday, but I've got to be up again in five hours . . . The trials of the middle classes.'

Instinctively, I put my arm on his shoulder. It feels nice and hard and strong. Leon smells wonderful. I hope it will 'go further', as he put it.

Half-stumbling, I get into bed. It's soft and clean and very comfortable. My muscles relax at once and the tiredness falls on me like a blanket. I turn automatically onto my side and stuff the pillow into the space between my shoulder and head.

Leon strokes my hair and mutters something, but I no longer hear it.

14

It wasn't John's idea to break up. I made the decision after a lot of thought, two months after the discovery, and I stand by it now. It was him or me, and I chose me. If I hadn't, I would have been damaged even more. Consciously, but mainly unconsciously, I'd already adapted to his demands and expectations more than was good for me. Partly out of insecurity and partly because I was anxious not to disappoint him and wanted to be his perfect girlfriend. I wasn't the only one who tried to please him. My parents were crazy about him. He fitted in well with the family and even better with our circle of friends. As a couple we couldn't have been more compatible with those around us. Perhaps that was a background factor, or maybe our busy social life served as a kind of glue that basically held our broken relationship together. For a while there had been rumblings of discontent beneath the surface. They only came to light when we were alone, usually when we had nothing to do. That was the unspoken reason why we never went on holiday on our own together, but always with friends, my parents, his parents – any company was OK, as long as we weren't alone. For a long time I blamed myself. Gradually I'd lost more and more of myself, and what was left of the foundations began to show sizeable cracks beneath his harsh words, critical looks and occasional sulky silences. That increasingly made me feel like I was inferior to him and secretly I began to hate him for it. In spite of everything, our relationship could have plodded on for years before either of us truly realised what we were doing to each other.

The inevitable break-up was precipitated when Mieke, whom I trusted completely and regarded as my best friend, fell in love with John and he with her. At some dark moment in space and time they must have decided to tell each other, but not their partners. A period of lies and evasions followed, with trysts in his car and even in our bed when I was away at a fair, until last summer when the time bomb they had constructed exploded. Mieke had come clean about the affair to her husband Tom, the father of her two young children. After days of talking and arguing a furious Tom came round to have it out with John. He'd managed to get everything out of her, every sordid detail, and I heard them one by one from Tom's mouth, while John sat silent and deathly pale in his deckchair, incapable of defending himself since everything Tom was confronting him with was completely true.

Leaving seemed the only way of dignifying the situation and hanging on to my last shred of self-respect.

But it was far from easy. I hadn't noticed that John had become a larger part of my life than I was prepared to admit. John was everywhere. He prowled around at my work, crept into every e-mail I sent, and joined in every conversation I had. I felt his presence in my every waking hour. John's words, looks, silences, actions, his whole legacy had invaded me, like a stubborn parasite gnawing away at my insides all day long and delighting in whispering to me that I'm not good enough, that I've failed, telling me how unattractive I am, how naive, impulsive, abnormal and stupid.

I blink at the sunlight streaming in through the big windows. The whole room is light, spacious and modern without a hint of sterility and smells intoxicatingly of laundered sheets and lavender. It takes me a moment to realise where I am. I push the blanket off and sit up. Waldorf Hilton. It wasn't a dream, I slept here last night.

I put my feet on the floor next to the bed and give myself a moment to come round. My skirt is crumpled and has ridden up above my knees and my blouse is twisted, revealing the red lace bra.

I stand up, still slightly unsteady, and straighten the blouse. The marble feels cool to my bare feet. No sign of Leon anywhere.

In the bathroom there is a wet towel in a washbasin and there are puddles on the floor, silent witnesses to the fact that he showered here a short while ago. This is where the smell of lavender is coming from.

Only when I return do I see the note on the coffee table, with the hotel logo on it.

Princess, you were out cold yesterday. This morning as
well, for that matter. Grab some breakfast downstairs or
call room service and then come to The Photographers'
Gallery, Great Newport Street. See you there.
L.

'You're pretty sure of yourself,' I whisper at the powerful handwriting, but my fingers holding the card are trembling just like they were yesterday.

I rummage in my bag for my mobile to check the time. Quarter past eleven. I'm not hungry, not yet. I hardly ever have breakfast in the morning, but a shower would be welcome.

I get my wash bag out of my rucksack and go into the bathroom. I wash the red G-string out in the washbasin and hang it over the heated towel rail to dry, with a towel underneath in the hope that it will speed up the drying process.

My hair has made it through the night OK. I don't see a wild ginger mop in the mirror, but acceptable curls that actually still look shiny. I take a thin shower cap from its disposable packaging and have a quick shower.

There's no question of not going to the Photographers' Gallery, whatever that may be. The name evokes associations with museums, exhibitions, and suchlike. Is Leon a gallery owner, or an artist? I rack my brains for anything he said that could give me something to go on. In any case he knew a remarkable amount about creative processes.

Gradually snatches of the short conversation in the plane come back to me. I remember him saying something like: 'When I ask a question like that, women think there's more to it.'

My mouth breaks into an involuntary – albeit trembling and nervous – smile.

VI

Wonderful art can spring from misery, I'm the last person to deny that. I'd go even further: the best works of art of all time have probably stemmed from deep human sorrow or hellish frustration, built on the bloody ruins of a rejection, the death of a loved one or a divorce – and yes: jealousy. Heartache and impotence as the mainspring for making the unverifiable verifiable and for giving it a face. How romantic, beautiful and especially useful pain and misery can be.

Yet recently I've caught myself thinking that, although art is my world and most probably always will be, there is something that has begun to fascinate me even more over the past year: myself, and more specifically the interesting process I clearly find myself in.

Last week I bought a book that really grabbed my attention. I finished it in odd free moments in a few days, with increasing irritation. A bunch of American scientists had put their heads together and analysed the 'phenomenon of the serial killer'. The bite-sized morsels were collected in countless interviews conducted by the writers with people serving life sentences or on death row. This produced a few juicy facts, graphs and definitions, plus a load of waffle about IQs. In one chapter it says that serial killers – contrary to what had always been thought – actually have an average to low IQ. And they had the cheek to call that scientific. The IQ tests were taken by prisoners, that is, people who allowed themselves to make mistakes, succumbed to the temptation of improvising in the stupidest ways. It stands to reason that brings down the average.

Admittedly that part of the book irritated me a bit. But I didn't take it personally, because according to the guidelines used in it, I don't even qualify as a serial killer. You earn that honorary title automatically after three separate murders committed within a reasonably short space of time.

Edith was already a year ago.

The way I've been feeling recently, I know she won't be the last.

15

My nervousness reaches a climax when I finally catch sight of the black-tiled façade of the Photographers' Gallery looming ahead. I took a taxi again rather than the tube and am getting used to the idea that travelling around a big city is pricey if you don't take the time to get the hang of the public transport system. I feel strangely reckless. My job, flat, Holland, everything seems so far away, like it's no longer part of my life.

The gallery is located in a narrow building squashed unassumingly between others. There is a busy junction almost on the doorstep. In the hall on the right is a desk where a young woman in a white blouse is talking to two visitors, but the enlarged photos on the walls immediately catch my eye. They are parts of faces. I stand there, mesmerised by all those staring eyes on photographic paper that are not only looking straight at me, but also seem to speak to me. Blue male eyes ringed with deep wrinkles, and grey bags. Big, brown children's eyes. Green, heavily made-up eyes of a young woman. Dark, almost angry-looking eyes in a face that's otherwise veiled. They talk to me, they communicate. They send shivers down my spine. Deeply impressed, I go from one photo to another, and am so engrossed that at first I don't notice the white cards below the photos. Finally my eyes wander.

LEON WAGNER (1968), THE NETHERLANDS
ALL PRINTS FROM THIS SERIES ARE AVAILABLE

Leon is a photographer. An art photographer. And the prices he's charging for his prints and the eager faces of the visitors around me, hastily making notes in their brochures and PDAs, explain his penchant for expensive hotels and restaurants.

It's marvellous, what he's done. More than marvellous. Impressive.

'Well?'

I turn round.

Leon. With the same amused look in his eyes familiar from yesterday. That, and something else: tenderness.

The butterflies that long ago fluttered one by one out of my bedroom window are back. I can feel their soft wings brushing the inside of my belly. They are tumbling over each other and there are more and more of them. 'Yes, marvellous,' I say. 'They talk. They all tell a different story. That one especially,' I say, pointing to the photo of the old man with his blue eyes, 'that's really brilliant.'

'But ultimately it's my story,' he says, surveying his photos. 'There's too much pain in the world, in all shapes and forms. That's what these people represent. Pain from losing their home, the death of a loved one, failing an exam, having a leg amputated, not getting a residence permit after years of hoping for a better life . . . That's what binds them, that's what they portray. Pain.'

'You know these people – all of them?'

'I've met them, saw something in them, a certain look, an attitude, I spoke to them if I got the chance, and listened to their stories.'

'The same as with me?'

He chuckles. 'I don't take everyone back to my hotel room, if that's what you're wondering.'

'Do you sometimes get people who don't want to be photographed?'

'Not many. But there are some.' Leon is talking to me but isn't looking at me. His eyes are focused on an invisible horizon, miles away. 'Photography is like stealing. You rob someone of a moment that exposes something essential about their character, their soul if you like. You capture it and take it home with you, and from then on the subject has no further say in the matter. There are people who are very conscious of that, who find that terrifying. The thought that everyone, friend and foe, can get so close to you, look you straight in the eye and judge you without you having any control over it or being able to respond. A part of them has become the property of the photographer. And in my case . . .' he looks around, 'you're laying yourself open to half the world and your soul becomes a commodity. Did you know that in some non-Western countries people don't want to be photographed because they're frightened it will take away their soul?'

'It rings a bell,' I mumble.

He snorts. 'In this society most people are only too keen to sell their soul. For fifty euros, sometimes a hundred. Or just for a cup of coffee and a nice chat. For some of these people I was the first person in years who listened to what they had to say. And I like listening. Every human being is unique, everyone has their own story.'

'And where do I fit into this?' I ask, thinking aloud.

He looks at me pensively. 'I can't deny I saw the same thing in you on the plane that I saw in these people. I haven't got this series completely out of my system yet, even though I've started on a new one. You have heterochromia – I doubt that's news to you. I would have liked to include you in this series. Your eyes are a little further apart than in most women. Combined with the colour deviation it gives an unusual picture.'

'You know the term?'

'Heterochromia?' For a moment a shadow seems to pass over his face, just for a second, and then he recovers his composure. 'I knew someone who had it.'

'Couldn't she sit for this series?' I ask.

'What makes you think it's a she?'

I shrug my shoulders. 'I was guessing. The way you—'

'You were right. It was a she. But she's dead.'

'Oh,' I say. 'I'm sorry.'

'So am I.' He sniffs and looks around restlessly. 'Well, Margot, you now know I'm not a criminal, but have made an honest living from stealing and trading in other people's souls in exchange for a cup of coffee. Anyway, I've promised the owners here to hang around till six o'clock to explain things, shake hands and socialise. Even in art freedom has its limits, it would seem, so . . .'

Leon puts a hand on my shoulder. It feels so nice I wish the gallery would dissolve around us, so that I can feel free to lean against him, let my hand wander over his chest and kiss him. My desperation, and a sense of reality clouded by alcohol, explain why I wanted this even last night, and much more besides. But I'm standing here now, slightly hungover, and I still want it. I actually want it even more than yesterday.

He squeezes my shoulder gently and lets go. 'Feel free to wander round if you want to see more. Make sure you're at the hotel at seven. We'll go for a bite to eat again. I look forward to it.'

I just nod. Just as I'm about to leave, he grabs my chin and plants a kiss on my lips. Fleeting and soft, but his kiss, however innocent, burns its way through my skin, triggering all sorts of reactions.

'Ciao.' He winks and without looking round goes into a room behind the entrance.

The woman at the desk gives me a sheepish smile. I imagine I'll smile back at her like that on my way out.

16

That last evening we visited an Italian restaurant where the pasta was homemade and waitresses spoke Italian. The food was divine. But even if we'd been wolfing down fish and chips under an awning in a street filled with rowdy youths, I wouldn't have relished each second any the less.

I've become attached at dizzying speed to Leon's reassuring presence, to the ease with which he moves among people and the inner calm and self-confidence he radiates. He seems to fathom people at a glance and then win them over, from taxi driver to waitress. It takes no effort at all. I've never met a man who is so well-balanced, who gives off such strong signals that he knows his place in the great scheme of things. Everything seems to revolve around him and everything comes naturally to him.

My flight home is tomorrow afternoon. I'm very conscious of this and it drives me on, the tingling, hectic energy races through my veins. I don't want to go back, I want to stay with Leon, hide away in his world. I want to cling with every ounce of strength to the feeling he gives me and never, ever let it go, because I know that the abyss I'm falling into is deep and bottomless. It won't be a soft landing.

When I left the Photographers' Gallery this afternoon, I immediately went in search of lingerie shops and spent a lot of money on a new set. Daring purple, shiny and strong; the only one I could find with an effect that didn't disappoint. No elastic seams to cut into my flesh and no squashed breasts or breasts bulging out on either side. The bra contains them where necessary and also makes them a little rounder than they actually are. Then I bought a new skirt. It's black, with a slight sheen and quite short, slightly elasticated, giving my hips a smooth rounded look, evening out any lumps and bumps. The purchases do mean that I have only twelve pounds left to get to the airport tomorrow, but I'll worry about that later.

I was careful not to drink too much. Two glasses of Chianti then an amaretto, followed each time by a glass of water to dilute the alcohol. I'm feeling a little light-headed, pleasantly so.

We are back in the hotel, where Leon has again poured out some whisky. I haven't yet touched the glass. There is a huge ladder in my new tights, right on my knee and thigh. I get up and behind the frosted glass of the bathroom door I peel them off and throw them away. I wash my hands and check if my hair and make-up still look OK.

When I return to the room Leon is sitting there playing pensively with his glass. He swirls the liquid round and looks at me over the rim of the glass.

'Did I miss a striptease?'

'I had a ladder.'

'It was there all evening.'

'I only just noticed.' I sit down in the chair and put the glass to my mouth. I just wet my lips, just for show, and put the glass back on the table. 'Leon,' I say, trying to meet his gaze. 'I want to thank you, for everything. For this weekend, for the food, for your company. I've got to be at the airport at eleven tomorrow morning and I'm not exactly itching to go home. If I hadn't met you I'd probably have stayed in my hotel room for two days . . .

I'd like to do something nice for you in return, but I've no idea what.'

'You could pose for me.'

'But your series is finished, isn't it?'

He nods, slowly. 'That series is, yes. I'm working on the next one. You'll fit into that just as well.'

'What kind of series is it?'

He tips his glass to one side and looks at it. 'Nude portraits.'

I clench my jaw and shake my head. 'No way.'

'Why not?'

'I just can't. I really can't. I . . . I'm too fat.'

'Says who?'

I shrug my shoulders and at the same time am annoyed at the childishness of my reaction. I say nothing.

He takes a sip of his whisky. 'I mean it. *What's your bench-mark?*'

I roll my eyes and wave my hand in his direction as if I can dispel his words like this so that their meaning is lost in the twilight. 'I . . .' I begin. 'God, it must be obvious, surely.' For good measure I point to my waist, like a bird with deformed wings.

He goes on looking at me imperturbably, deadly serious. There is not even a smile playing about his lips. His eyes are like black holes in his angular face. He is giving nothing away.

He makes me nervous. I put my hands in my lap and stare past him at the lights of the city.

The silence hangs between us. A compelling silence that forces me into an inner dialogue.

What's your benchmark? Good question. The parasite that John implanted in me flicks its tail. It sniggers and gnaws away at my insides.

When I met John I was a perfectly acceptable size 14. Now I'm an 18. In the shops where I like to buy my clothes that's the absolute limit.

I scrabble for my glass and take a big gulp of whisky. 'I'm a size 18.'

'So what?'

'If I put on any more weight, I'll have to buy clothes in plus-size shops.'

He raises an eyebrow. 'So your self-image depends on clothes shops?'

I can feel myself getting rebellious. 'Basically, yes.'

He lights a cigarette and watches me. Biding his time.

'I have the feeling I don't belong anymore, you know?' I continue. My voice sounds harsher than I intended. 'The fact that I can no longer go into ordinary shops with this body of mine, but have to go to specialist outlets. That's the writing on the wall, isn't it? A benchmark, as you call it?'

'Off-the-peg clothes are made for the masses, sweetheart.'

He flicks the ash from his cigarette, deep in thought. 'All it means is that the masses, that large group of women who buy lots of clothes, are generally size 18 or smaller. It says no more than that. It says nothing about what is beautiful, or how you should look. It says everything about what is bought and by whom. The masses are not a benchmark.'

'And . . . and the people who set the trends. then? They really don't use slim models because that's what the masses look like. They do it because it's more beautiful.'

'Guys aren't driven wild by six-foot stick-thin models with an arrogant look on their emaciated chops. They don't even see models as women. It's got nothing to do with reality, it's illusion, art. The majority of men love a bit of flesh. Take it from me: hips, breasts, buttocks. Something to hold on to. Real women, not bony caricatures.' Leon is no longer sitting back but has moved forward in his chair, emphasising his words with his hands. 'For Christ's sake, since time immemorial plump has stood for fertility, that's how it's always been. You only have to look at the paintings by the old masters to see how attractive they all found ample women. In countries where commerce has not yet taken hold, that still applies. That should be evidence enough.'

His argument confuses me. The way he puts it, it all sounds so simple, so obvious. But it doesn't feel like that. 'It's common knowledge that you should lose weight if you're too fat, that it's unhealthy, that it puts too much strain on your body. Surely that's a benchmark, too?'

'Do you feel unhealthy then?'

'Not because of my weight.' I've talked myself into a corner where I really don't want to be. It's my own fault. Now it looks as if I have a serious problem, as if I weigh 30 stone and can no longer drag myself out of bed. Or as if I can't stand it all, find my own weight a dreadful burden, when all I want is to be a size 12. A 14 would do, just so I can wear nice clothes. Brand-name clothes that look good on me. . . . Why on earth did I start talking about this?

'Because of what then?'

I'm staring at my packet of cigarettes on the table. 'I'd like to stop smoking. I feel it's bad for me. Sometimes I wake up in the morning just as tired as when I went to bed the night before, and I know it's because of the smoking, because I gave up before and I felt great. Or in any case better. Physically, that is.'

'And yet you started again.'

'I put on over a stone in two months. Everyone says it's because I ate more, to compensate for not smoking. But it wasn't that. My metabolism slowed down. I'm sure that's what it was.'

'So you smoke not out of conviction, from choice, but because the alternative frightens you more: the fear of putting on weight, and hence becoming ugly, or uglier, in your perception.'

I throw my hands up. 'Yes.'

'You arrange your life based on what "everyone" thinks of you, or what you think they think of you, whoever everyone is . . . Your neighbour? The assistants in clothes shops? Come on, Margot!'

I grab for my packet of cigarettes, tap one out and light it with a disposable lighter. The flame illuminates my trembling hand.

'Because going to church is out of fashion,' he continues, 'the Western world now obeys the precepts of commerce. A bloody demanding religion, if you ask me. The dos and don'ts change every season and your "everyone" doesn't want to be left out, so they rush headlong to comply. That continuous change has a function, a single aim, princess: maximum consumption. They want to go on milking you, from cradle to grave. Face it: you're a brainwashed, walking purse, a robot, the fuel the multinationals run on.'

I look down. I don't want to be having this discussion. Not with Leon, who looks spectacular sitting opposite me in the dusk. His black shirt half-open, and that penetrating look. The energy surges from him because of the passion he puts into his argument. As if he is on a prime-time talk show rather than in the privacy of a hotel room.

I don't want this, not this evening. It was supposed to turn into, to be, a nice evening. *My evening.* But now we've got into a discussion of my size, my inability to stop smoking and the multinationals that run my life – and the fact that I value what people think of me.

I feel like shit. I could crawl away into a hole.

But I stay sitting there.

Leon gets up, moves the table dividing us aside and sinks to his knees in front of me. His hands grasp my knees, kneading, massaging, pushing up the material of my skirt and ending up on my hips.

My body reacts violently, but passion is tempered mercilessly by an all-powerful sense of inadequacy.

Leon looks up at me. 'A woman *should* be plump. Plump women are sexy. Bloody sexy.'

'I don't feel sexy.' My voice sounds faint, almost broken.

He kisses the inside of my legs. 'You're out of your mind,' he mumbles. 'Completely nuts. I've seldom met anyone with such a screwed-up self-image.'

His kisses are burning my skin. Without realising it I have slid down, little by little, I want him to carry on. Carry on with that kneading, those caresses with his fingers and mouth, higher, closer. I start moaning softly.

Suddenly he stops.

I open my eyes in confusion. Leon is standing up, has taken another cigarette and is standing at the window, looking out over the city – or towards a horizon only he can see.

I pull my skirt down and pick awkwardly at my blouse. 'What . . .' I begin, but he doesn't let me finish.

'I want you to beg for it.'

I look up. Did I hear that right?

He has turned round, the cigarette between thumb and forefinger. His eyes are coal-black, hypnotising me, sucking me towards him and I can only look at him, as if we are on either side of a shaft and nothing else exists. He and I.

'Beg?' My voice sounds faint and trembling. 'Did you say that?'

He looks me up and down, his eyes sweep very slowly across my face, my neck, my cleavage, further down. His eyes are almost physically tangible, more erotic than words or a touch can be. It is impossible not to react. My heart starts beating faster, almost audibly in the silence. I take shallow breaths. My whole body is tingling.

'I want to know how much you want this.' He sits back opposite me in the armchair, takes a puff and cautiously exhales the smoke. His movements remind me of a cat approaching a rival, or prey; weighing me up, feeling his way. He doesn't take his eyes off me for a moment. 'Show me how much you want it, Margot.'

I'm now breathing audibly through my mouth, which is slightly open. For a second I feel the urge to burst out laughing or to make a light-hearted remark to break the charged atmosphere, but I realise it's a hopeless attempt to disguise my nervousness. Too transparent – he knows that as well as I do.

Suddenly we find ourselves in a different dimension, I am in his territory, in a new phase that is unfolding on his terrain. I play a part in it, a crucial role, but only he knows the limits.

'You're magnificent,' he whispers. 'The most beautiful thing I've seen for a long time. Let me see you. Completely.'

I now know what he means, where he is directing me. Instead of frightening me it turns me on even more. Yet I do not react to his direction. Not yet. My toes claw nervously at the patterned carpet, while I think feverishly. The general framework is clear, but the details are still unknown territory. *Terra incognita.*

'Just you and me, princess,' he says softly. 'The walls have no eyes, no ears. It's OK. You want to – I know you want to. Go with your feelings. Do it. Make this beautiful.'

I swallow but my throat is dry as I roll my skirt up a little and, trembling, separate my legs slightly, giving him a glimpse of the purple thong, and lots more. All that flesh, my superfluous flesh.

'More explicit. That excites me.'

I'm shivering all over. I sink down further and put my hand between my legs. Beneath his dark gaze, the silence, the unbearable tension, I almost explode under my own hand.

My uncertain movements are closely choreographed by Leon, whose eyes linger alternately on my face and my crotch. One hand rests on the arm of the chair, the other holds the cigarette, still between thumb and forefinger. His face is not giving much away, but physically he is visibly aroused. He absorbs me, registers every detail, each breath, the tiniest movement of my eyes, nothing escapes him.

It gives me a strange feeling of power, of satisfaction. I matter. He is the director, but without me there is nothing to direct.

'Take it off.'

I think I'm panting, but I'm not sure. I pull my skirt up further and hook my thumbs behind the lace to take the thong off. Although I try to do it alluringly, it is clumsy.

'Carry on,' he says, slowly blowing smoke out.

My fingers are now on my bare skin, which is velvety and warm and smooth and feels so different from usual, as if my hand does not belong to me but has a life of its own, stroking, feeling, moist, rhythmical.

My God, what's happening here? What am I doing? I pant, moan, squirm, while Leon watches me almost motionless from his armchair, sucks me up into him and I keep on looking at him, finding in his dark eyes the confirmation I seek, the approval and encouragement I need to go on, to feel no more shame, but to give in to the pressure building up inside me, swelling, becoming almost unbearable. My left hand is searching for a breast as if of its own accord, my fingertips finding a nipple through the soft material of my blouse and the satin bra, hard and sensitive.

Leon closes his eyes briefly and nods, almost invisibly in encouragement. His hand now lies loosely at his crotch. He looks madly attractive. It is the whole picture that he forms in the armchair and the way he makes me do things simply through subtle body language and limits his words to the bare essentials.

I throw my head back. This is madness, I think for a second, this is pure madness, but now I give a moan that continues, grows louder, groaning, while every muscle in my body contracts, my pelvis and breasts thrust forward, proud, liberated, in a last, wonderful, overwhelming spasm, after which I sink back shivering into the soft upholstery of the chair.

Leon is with me in a few steps and puts his arms round me. He pulls me up and presses me against his chest. I lean heavily against him, my legs won't carry me. I lay my cheek against his chest and feel the pounding of his heart.

He kisses my crown. 'That was very beautiful, my girl. Impressive.'

'Did you think so?' my voice still sounds as if I'm panting.

One hand pushes my chin up. 'Yes, I thought so.' His lips gently caress mine, his tongue, slow and loving.

Still shivering I return his kiss and put my arms round his neck. It's the first time that he has been this close, that I taste his tongue, smell his smell, that I can stroke his body. Light stubble scrapes my nose and cheek as I stroke my face against his and inhale his smell.

'You've never done this before, have you?' he asks.

I shake my head. 'No, never.'

'Wonderful.'

17

During my absence the requests for sales visits in my area have been placed in a tray on my desk. Urgent matters have been taken care of by colleagues. I leaf through their reports and then the pile of requests – both print-outs of e-mails and handwritten notes from office staff – which don't include many complaints, thank God. While reading them I draft a rough schedule for the week. Next to the print-outs is a file where I keep my reports of customer calls. I write them out in the car, after each visit. They contain notes on how meetings went, but also customers' personal details like birthdays, births and hospital admissions. People appreciate it when I show interest in things they told me about on a previous occasion. They're often surprised when I manage to remember them. Tomorrow I intend to go to a semi-municipal institution in the region, a regular customer that buys chairs for asylum-seeker accommodation. Jos van Dam, my contact there, told me last time that his wife was eight months pregnant. That was two months ago, so all being well he must have become a father by now. I make a note so that I can ask him about it.

My mobile is vibrating in my trouser pocket. I hold my breath for a second. I fish the little white thing out of my pocket and slide it open. A message from Dick: there's a new series on TV tonight. I can't miss it: it's terrific. In Dick's opinion, that is – the sweetie. Disappointed, I send him a brief thank you and slide my phone shut. Then I take a sip of the now cold coffee and grimace.

It's extremely quiet this morning. I'm sitting alone at my desk in a space where four other salespeople are working. Their presence here is just as unusual as mine. No one is here longer than a few hours, twice a week at most. It isn't exactly the most attractive space in the building, either. Our red furnishings come from a catalogue published six years ago and in the flower boxes on wheels groups of sub-tropical plants are wilting under the unforgiving striplights. We look out onto the car park and the wide access road into the industrial estate.

After each compulsory office visit, my colleagues and I can't wait to rejoin the tail-backs, which offer no more freedom, but where we can at least smoke and sing along with the radio at the top of our voices. Basically our cars are our offices.

Restlessly I take another sip of the cold, machine-made coffee. I've been sitting here for over two hours and was half expecting at least one colleague to come over and ask how my month off was, Claudia at any rate, or the receptionist, but clearly they have other priorities this morning.

I have brought it on myself to some extent. I could just as easily have popped into their departments to show my face. That might have been friendlier, more sociable. But instead I rushed to my office as quickly as possible this morning, in the hope that no one would notice me. I didn't feel like bumping into Claudia. While I'm now grateful she stood me up, it's typical of her. I didn't respond to her message and she didn't try texting again. So it was a courtesy text, she wasn't genuinely interested. I was a temporary shoulder to cry on, and you can underline 'temporary'.

A small UPS van pulls up in the car park. I see a dark young man leap out of the cab. He disappears into the back of the brown van and a moment later walks into reception with a number of packages in his arms.

I turn back to the reports and the requests, and grab the telephone to ring customers and set up appointments. It all goes smoothly and my diary fills up. This isn't such a bad job in itself, it strikes me. Without doubt the best job I've had up to now, and it's a piece of cake. And there's the rub. It's not enough. Not anymore.

I can't stop my mind wandering. It's over a week ago since I left London. Nothing more happened that evening. Leon tucked me in, lay down behind me with his arm around me and stroked my tummy. He didn't go any further and he didn't have to. I enjoyed his warm body against my back, squeezed his hand and felt happy. We talked for a while, whispering into the silence, but that was all. The next morning he ordered me a taxi, paid the driver thirty pounds in advance and waited, hands in pockets, till the cab disappeared from sight.

I looked round and that was it.

I've no idea if I'll see him again. We didn't make any arrangements or promises or exchange addresses, but Leon definitely told me on that last evening that he wanted to photograph me for his new series. It was a statement not a question. So then why doesn't he call me? He must be back from London by now. If I'm not mistaken, he was due back last Wednesday or Thursday.

For a week I haven't gone anywhere without my mobile, anxiously checking it was charged and even taking it to bed with me. I've lost count of the times I've looked at the screen in the hope of seeing an illuminated envelope.

As I gather my things and head for the exit, I resolve to make serious enquiries about a window-dressing or interior design course when I get home. Perhaps I can even surf the internet for vacancies. Who knows, there may be opportunities I haven't thought of, jobs that suit me better and give me more input, real challenges. Do they even exist?

'Margot?'

I look round. Marlies the receptionist is standing behind me in the corridor.

'I was beginning to think you were still off work,' she says. 'I didn't even see you come in.'

'Today's my first day back,' I say, quite unnecessarily.

'We've just had a package for you.'

'For me?'

'Yes, wait a moment.' She goes into the office.

I wait in the corridor. Through the open door I can hear the hubbub of the office staff and the purchasing department. I catch snatches of telephone calls in broken English and German, order numbers, apologies.

Marlies reappears and hands me an enormous brown cardboard tube.

I take it from her and look at the address label. The package is addressed to the company and underneath in capital letters it says: PERSONAL, MARGOT HEIJNE.

'Bit early for a Christmas box from a customer, don't you think?' says Marlies. Boundless curiosity is written all over her face.

I shrug my shoulders.

'Aren't you going to open it?

'I'll open it at home tonight,' I say. 'It's probably a calendar or something like that. Or a poster for an event.'

VII

I've parked my hire car at the entrance to the Keervliet industrial estate. It's a desolate jumble of ghastly low-rise buildings, banished to the edge of town. Not very inspiring surroundings.

Just now I got out at the information board and stood looking rather inanely at the map, with an advertising brochure in my hand. Just for show, because I know exactly where I have to go. I don't need the information board for that. I'm just someone trying to find his way round an industrial estate and making the odd phone call. I could be anything: a rep, an IT specialist, perhaps someone with his own business. Passers-by don't notice anything strange about me.

Preparation is everything.

Perhaps I'm going on a bit, that's possible, but I'd rather be prepared. Better think ten steps ahead than find out at the last moment that you didn't brief yourself properly. Then the moment passes, and you've lost control.

The only nuisance is that I can't hang about here for hours. Half an hour is OK, an hour's too long.

Annoying.

I make sure I create the impression that I'm working. For that purpose there's an open laptop next to me on the passenger seat. The funny thing about the whole situation is that I actually am at work. The telephone hasn't stopped ringing. My mouth tells them what they want to know, but my eyes are fixed firmly on the office building.

It's a low, white block, with a brown frieze running round it and windows only at the front. The car park is separated from the main road by low municipal shrubs.

There is little movement around the premises. She was supposed to be going back to work today, but I don't know if that means she'll be in the office. She may be working from home, and in that case I have a problem. A temporary problem, mind you, as I'll find out more about her soon enough. But I've become curious and don't just want to let things take their own course. Preparation is everything, haven't I said that already? You can't start early enough.

For example, I now know it's not easy getting hold of a fake passport. My second identity – just in case. It wasn't cheap either. I just hope the moment never comes when I need it, but should something go wrong despite all the thorough preparations, then I know I can always fall back on it.

A reassuring thought.

18

It's a photo. It's lying unrolled on the floor of my flat, shiny and slightly curled at the edges, and I stand and look at it with my arms crossed. Blue eyes in a lined face: the photo I loved so much. Maybe I told Leon in the Photographers' Gallery, I can't remember. He remembered, or guessed. The photo is numbered and bears his signature. At some point during that whirlwind weekend I must have told him the name of the company I work for. He remembered that too.

Over the past week I've often been on the point of calling him, but didn't. I can't handle a rejection, not after literally exposing myself to him. It may have been just a one-off in his eyes; a weekend fling, a pleasant way of passing the time. The fact that it meant so much more to me, infinitely more, is my problem. If Leon never got in touch again, I'd be really sorry, though it wouldn't make the weekend any less wonderful or special in my memory. But an awkward silence, a transparent excuse or a blunt rejection would taint it forever. I daren't risk it. And I still don't know what to do.

'What next?' I say out loud to the blue eyes on the wooden floor. They stare back at me in torment, unable to answer. A snapshot of an unknown man, a piece of his soul, stolen by Leon.

I run my fingers through my hair. How am I supposed to interpret this gift? Is it thank you and goodbye, the way you send someone a bunch of flowers to thank them for help with a move or illness, or a dramatic invitation to get back in touch?

Very carefully I roll the photo up and slide it back into the tube. Whatever happens I will buy a frame for it this weekend and hang it in my bedroom. Not in the living room. It's too private.

The kitchen timer goes off. I go into the kitchen to take my pizza out of the oven. I sit down on the sofa with the plate on my lap. The TV is on low, but my mind is elsewhere.

Shall I call him? *Should* I call him? I can send him a text – that would be safest. But suppose he doesn't reply? Then I'm back to square one. Texts often don't get through for some reason or other. And yes, I want to hear his voice.

I put off the decision and take a few bites of the pizza. I'm not enjoying it. I put the plate back on the coffee table. Restlessly channel hopping, my eyes are drawn to the mirror, which only just shows my feet and calves. Shall I call? Why on earth not? Surely I can just ring to *thank* him? Keep it light-hearted, non-committal, as brief as possible?

Light-hearted is not going to work; I'm frozen with tension and my voice is bound to give that away. I get up and return to the kitchen, this time to pour myself a glass of wine. A little alcohol can do no harm. Without even tasting it I down the glass in a couple of gulps. I walk restlessly back into the living room, grab a packet of cigarettes off the table and light one up. I slide my mobile open and find his name in the address book.

Suppose he's with another woman?

Suppose he's in the middle of . . . with someone

Suppose . . .

Call, Margot, now.

The phone rings three times. Four times.

'Leon?'

I sit up and clasp the mobile with both hands. The alcohol is not helping one bit. Perhaps I should have waited for it to kick in. 'Hi, it's Margot,' I say finally. 'I hope this isn't a bad time? I was just calling to say thank you.'

'It was the right one, wasn't it?'

'Yes, absolutely. I'm over the moon with it. Nice of you to remember.' There's something strange about my breathing. It falters for a second.

'I've got an exhibition in Amsterdam on Saturday with a couple of artist friends of mine. Should be fun. I'd like to introduce you to a few people. How does that sound?'

I fall silent for a moment. I was expecting something different: in my world I could think of only two options and they didn't include this one. 'Yes,' I mumble, 'Sounds fun.'

'Great. If you give me your e-mail address, I'll get someone to send you directions.'

19

I didn't pick up on the strange atmosphere in the house at first. I was too wrapped up in my own thoughts to sense the subtle changes in my parents' behaviour. As I was driving over to see them it struck me that I really wanted to tell them I'd met a man in London. But if I let anything slip, they'd start asking questions I'd rather not answer. It's difficult anyway to put my feelings, or desires, or even thoughts into words. It's all still too fresh, my head was all over the place.

I was still weighing things up when I came in so I didn't notice how my mother greeted me rather nervously, rubbing her hands a lot and avoiding my gaze. Only when my father poured tea for me with great ceremony did alarm bells start ringing.

My mother does the tea and coffee. She looks after the guests, her children, my father, everyone. That's the role she's taken on and clings to. The only time there was a departure from that pattern was when she was in hospital for an operation on her womb.

On my guard, I look around, as if the interior must contain clues to their abnormal behaviour, but nothing catches my eye. Everything's the same as ever and in its proper place. The only novelty is a big bunch of flowers on the coffee table.

My mother still isn't looking at me. I take the cup from my father, drop a sugar cube into the boiling hot liquid and look in alarm at my mother, who's still standing by the window with a distant look in her eyes. For a second I imagine she's been to the doctor or the hospital and been given bad news. Typical of her to hide a chronic ailment only to own up when she's at death's door.

'Is something wrong, Mum?'

She looks up, smoothes her skirt and starts moving. then sits down diagonally opposite me at the table, next to my father, her hands folded on the tablecloth.

'Mum, is there something wrong?'

She shakes her head almost imperceptibly. 'Nothing at all. I'm fine. Did you have a good time in London?'

I frown. Did they have an argument just before I arrived? Did I interrupt them them in the middle of a flaming row? And if so, what was it about? I look from one to the other, but can't see any bloodshot or red-rimmed eyes indicating a crying fit or a sleepless night. No trace of telltale body language as if they're avoiding one another. None of that, they're still a team. A silent team.

It's got something to do with me. I can just feel it.

'London was fun,' I reply, without much enthusiasm. 'Sorry I couldn't drop by earlier. The last couple of weeks have been busy.'

'Doesn't matter,' is all she says. She takes a sip of tea and looks outside again.

I follow her gaze, but there's nothing important going on in the back garden.

There's a long silence. Only the old pendulum clock and the pilot on the water heater make any sound.

'The fête,' I say, trying to break the silence, 'did it go well?'

My mother nods. 'Yes. We had a good time. Shame you couldn't make it.'

Again silence.

This is too silly for words. 'Are you going to tell me what's wrong?'

My parents look at each other. They pause for a moment, a fraction of a second, and then, as if pre-arranged, my father says: 'John was here yesterday.'

John. My hand jerks involuntarily and I spill my tea. The boiling hot liquid burns my hand and I jump up, run to the kitchen in a couple of bounds and turn on the cold tap. With my hand under the tap I look at the flowers on the coffee table then at my parents and back again. My mother lowers her eyes.

I hadn't made the connection. Not yet: I assumed my mother had been given them by the committee as a thank you for her hard work on the fête, or something like that. 'Those flowers are from him,' I say loudly, so they can hear me over the splashing water. 'From John.'

My mother nods in resignation.

'And you put them in a *vase*?' I turn the tap off. The pain in my hand is gone already.

'They're beautiful flowers,' she replies weakly. 'A shame to throw them away.'

'You let him in.' Against my better judgement I hope for a negative reply. But the silence only continues, which confirms my suspicion. Yes, they let him in. Not only that, my mother accepted his flowers, cut them carefully, put them in her nicest vase and gave them pride of place on the coffee table. And I just know they gave the bearer of gifts something to drink, perhaps even a slice of cake to tuck into. In my parents' house. *My* parents' house.

John has fouled my nest.

I cross my arms and make a show of standing in the kitchen, right by the door.

My mother shrugs her shoulders in a gesture of helplessness. 'What was I supposed to do?'

'He's no business coming here,' I retort. My voice breaks with anger and frustration. 'How *dare* he show his face here? He's got some bloody nerve!'

Again that shrugging of the shoulders, as if there's nothing she can do about it. 'John visited us here for years,' she says, so softly I strain to hear her. 'I can't approve of what he did. You know that. Nor can your father, But you can't just wipe away all those years. It didn't feel right to leave him at the door.'

'He rang the doorbell,' adds my father, as if that makes it all better and excuses their treachery. 'He didn't come straight through.'

'No, that's all we needed,' I say. My hands shoot up. 'John walks in like he's never been away, like nothing's happened. He has no right. Not now!'

'Will you sit down for a bit?'

I shove myself away from the draining board and sit down reluctantly at the dining table.

'He's in a bit of a mess, at the moment,' says my mother.

'The lad's at the end of his tether,' adds my father. 'He's . . .'

'He's got Mieke, hasn't he?' My voice is dripping with sarcasm. 'That's what he wanted so badly, wasn't it?'

My father shakes his head. 'It's not like that. He said he really missed us, not just you, but us. He's never had the chance to give his side of the story, and he wanted to tell us how he sees the whole situation. He feels awful about it, Margot. John didn't want to lose you.'

'He should have thought about that before.'

My mother rubs her face with her hands. 'Darling . . . John made a mistake, he knows that now. We all make mistakes in life. Moments when you do things you later regret, because they ruined everything, but which help you in the end to grow as a person. Sometimes you need that to get a better understanding of who you are and what you want.' Something in her voice makes me even more alert than I already am. It's the way she's choosing her words. My father's awkwardness.

I look from one to the other and realise what they're trying to say. My father looks away.

'It's hasn't all been plain sailing for us either,' says my mother. 'You father and I, we—'

'I'm really not in the mood for this at all,' I interrupt her snappily. 'Really. John is history. Why can't you two understand that? I never want to see that man again. Never!' My voice breaks. Perhaps I'm shouting, but I no longer care. 'Have you any idea what he did to me? I hope he dies, a long and painful death. The day that happens, I'll put the flags out.'

I look from the flowers to my parents, who are looking at me almost accusingly, and back again. I feel more helpless by the second. Now it's suddenly my fault. Not John, poor soul, who has the right to make mistakes, but Margot, who won't see reason.

'And . . . you know what . . .' I jump up. 'You two can go to hell as well!'

I run outside and slam the door behind me. The glass rattles in its frame.

I'm surrounded by truck drivers having lunch in their cabs. A man casts a curious glance through his open window, but I look right through him. I've stopped the car in a car park next to a petrol station because I couldn't concentrate on the road any longer.

I sit trembling at the steering wheel and put my head in my

hands. In a quarter of an hour I have an appointment with a hotel owner who's looking for new chairs. The hotel is ten minutes' drive from this car park along the A2, but I can't seem to control myself and calm down. I'm trembling all over with anger and frustration. I'm fighting the impulse to drive over to John's place and sling a brick through his window. Too good for him. Negative attention is attention all the same. But it would be a relief. He's got to get out of my life, completely, totally: emigrate to Siberia, dissolve into thin air, go, disappear, die – so I can be sure I'll never bump into him and I can draw a line under it once and for all. The way he's widened the battlefield to include my parents, and sat smarmily in their house convincing them of his good intentions, is unforgivable.

I only dropped in to see my parents for a cup of coffee, catch up a bit and then get back to work. I was passing through the area where they live and it was lunch time. It occurred to me that I hadn't been in touch since I got back from London ten days ago. At the same time I reminded myself that they hadn't taken any initiative either. My parents haven't been round to see my new house even once and haven't even sent a card, flowers or anything. They haven't accepted the fact that I've moved into town. There's a reason for that. When it became clear that things were going wrong with John, my father, without consulting me, sorted out a house for me in the village, a terraced house on a new estate, whose owner had to go abroad for a year.

'Then you won't have to make a hasty decision,' he said. 'You'll patch things up with John before you know it and then you'll have a house on your hands that you've got to sell. It's a waste of money and effort. And if things turn out differently, it gives you the chance to take your time and find a nice place round here.'

He'd taken a lot of trouble, and by his own account he had to go and talk to the chap a couple of times to explain that his daughter wasn't a drug addict who would strip his house bare or neglect it, and wouldn't take in enough dogs or cats to start an animal shelter either. The man, his name has slipped my mind, finally agreed. Six hundred euros a month, more than I'm paying for my mortgage now, and I could move in right away. It wasn't even such a bad option in itself. But the owner had a catalogue of restrictions. The most important were that the furniture had to stay where it was and nothing in the house could be changed. The walls were not to be whitewashed, the curtains had to stay up: everything had to remain exactly as it was. After all, the owner would be coming back and wanted to recognise his own house, which meant I would be allowed to pay a fortune to house-sit for a year – with no chance of it ever feeling like home. It was a non-starter in my eyes. In all his enthusiasm and mania for organising things my father completely overlooked the fact that I might have other plans. Dick understood me, or at least he did his very best to respect my decision. He and Anne even helped me move, which I'd have done for them too in a heartbeat. My parents on the other hand kept out of it, as a silent protest. Childish almost. And now they've welcomed John back like the prodigal son.

I'm never visiting them again. They've gone too far.

20

It's a short walk from Amsterdam Central Station to the gallery. I'm glad about that, as I haven't worn my boots in yet. They have high heels, much higher than I'm used to, and they're tight round my calves. They're fantastic, but walking elegantly on slippery cobbles is not an unqualified success.

I've left the car at home. I know from the time I had to fill in for a colleague that parking in this city is a disaster and costs a bomb. Quite often I've had to drive around for three-quarters of an hour to find a parking space.

I'm nervous. Nervous and excited. It's almost two weeks since I saw Leon. I would have strongly preferred to meet him alone, or go for a drink with him first before being thrown to the lions – because that's kind of how it feels. But at the same time I'm curious about his friends and acquaintances and how they interact.

I pass canal-side mansions, avoiding the puddles and holding the lapel of my coat firmly against me. I memorised the directions at home. So far I'm still on track: the gallery can't possibly be much further.

Dick has been almost stalking me for the past few days. He's called and texted me twice a day and even dropped by last night to try and put things right. He's terribly upset about the situation. Dick is a family man and thinks there's nothing you can't talk over. Maybe so, but not yet.

I told him it would be best if they could leave me alone for a bit. That I love them, but that what they've done has caused me pain and I don't want to see them for a while. Their betrayal hurts too much for that. He understood, or pretended to. It's sometimes hard to tell with Dick.

The gallery is located in an old, distinguished-looking building. Everything is white inside: the high walls, the ceilings, the huge movable partitions, some of them displaying only a single framed photograph. Extra light is coming from above, where parts of the roof have been replaced by pointed glass constructions, like in a conservatory.

I wander through the various rooms, looking for Leon. Groups of people are clustered together. They are holding glasses of wine or champagne and talking in muted tones.

As soon as I see Leon, all those people seem to disappear for a moment. The surroundings, the photos, become hazy and transparent and I see only that tall, dark figure. His eyes devour me. 'I'm glad you came.' He kisses me gently on the forehead. His fingers burrow in my neck for a moment, under my hair, tickling my skull. It expresses an intimacy that seems out of place in these surroundings.

Bystanders are watching us, watching me. They look me up and down and whisper among themselves.

It makes me feel uncomfortable. Why, I wonder, does he not call for almost a week and a half and then, when he does, want to meet me here of all places, among all these people in this clinical space?

'I want to introduce you to a couple of good friends of mine.' He puts his hand on my back and steers me into another room, where the ceiling is lower and the photos small and more numerous. They are shots of rubbish tips, not in Holland by the look of them. In some photos dark-skinned children are grub-bing around.

There is a small round table with glasses of champagne on it and he hands me one. When I take the glass my hands tremble slightly.

'You look terrific,' he says.

I smile. 'Thanks.'

He shifts his gaze from me to something behind me and his smile broadens.

I turn round.

The woman he's smiling at is gorgeous. Blonde, straight hair with red strands twisted into a kind of bun, a narrow waist and long legs. She walks towards us through the white space with natural feline grace. She's holding a glass between her slender fingers. Her nails are painted the same champagne colour as her dress and shoes, and her whole image has been carefully thought out. As she approaches, the corners of her mouth curl up. The movement causes barely a wrinkle in the smooth sur-face of her skin.

'Margot, this is Debby, she's a close friend of mine and does my PR.'

She looks at me curiously, but slightly hesitantly at the same time, sizing me up.

'PR?' I ask, shaking her hand. Her handshake feels firmer than I'd imagined. 'I thought photographers always promoted their own work?'

'Not all photographers.' She gives Leon the friendliest of knowing smiles. 'It's the secret of our success, isn't it, Leon?'

Leon smiles. 'I'd have thought more your success, actually.'

She pinches his arm playfully and turns back to me. 'Leon told me you met in London, but he didn't tell me what you looked like. It's startling. You strongly remind me of someone. But I suppose he's told you all about it already.'

I shake my head. 'No, why?'

Next to me Leon moves into action and I see the blonde retreat a little. The charged silence lasts only a second, perhaps two, in which all kinds of things are said without a word being spoken. It's confusing.

'And he didn't tell me what you do either,' she says, once she's fully recovered from Leon's silent reproach. 'Are you in the art world too?'

I shake my head. 'No, I . . .'

'She will be soon,' Leon says next to me. 'I'm working on it.'

I turn and look at him in surprise, but don't have chance to respond.

'What are you doing at the moment then?' asks Debby.

'I work for a company that sells business furniture. As an adviser.' It's not actually a lie. I advise clients on a daily basis to buy furniture from our collection.

'Have you been doing that long?'

I have to think. John and I had been together for a year when I started working there. 'About six years.'

'Does your work take you abroad?'

'No, I'm based in Holland.' I want to leave it at that. This doesn't strike me as the kind of place to explain I have a sales territory. That sounds so . . . limited.

A man in his sixties with a shiny bald pate and a garish bow tie comes towards us. He nods at me aloofly and shakes Leon's hand, calling him 'my boy', even though Leon towers over his bald pate and I've not been able to discover anything boyish about him. Then he grabs Debby by the arm and leads her away from us.

'What do you know that I don't?' I ask Leon, in hushed tones. 'Why?'

'Well . . . I'll be working in the art world "soon"?'

'It's a surprise. Be patient, princess. First I want to introduce you to my manager, Richard. I know you'll like him. He has the likeability factor.'

Before I can ask him what Debby meant with her comment about how I strongly resemble someone – startlingly even – Leon puts his arm firmly round me and pulls me with him towards a group standing near a large and quite depressing black-and-white photo of a burnt forest and drinking wine. I take a quick peek at the card. It's not one of Leon's.

'There he is, that blond guy,' says Leon, raising his voice: 'Maestro.'

The blond man turns away from the group. Richard looks about the same age as Leon, but physically they're poles apart. If the words dark, angular and sharp define Leon, you could describe Richard as light, round and soft. A human teddy bear, but without the paunch. His face is friendly and open, and his skin is a little ruddy, as if he's just returned from a winter walk in the woods. He's not unattractive, and his warm handshake feels pleasant. 'I've heard so much about you, Margot. Welcome.'

'Thank you,' I say.

Richard runs his eye over me without the slightest embarrassment. There's nothing erotic in his gaze, I notice. He's appraising me, like a painting. Or a statue. 'Leon tells me you're going to be part of his new series. I can only agree with his decision. Have you ever modelled?'

I shake my head.

'All the better. You're in good hands with him, I can assure you. But that's not news to you, I imagine.'

'I don't know much about photography. I've just seen the series in London, but that was really impressive.'

'The eyes series?'

I nod.

'That was beautiful, very beautiful, but not commercial enough. There aren't that many clients who want a challenging photo like that on their wall. Leon will have to concentrate on commercial work again for the time being. Anyway, I've set up a number of wonderful assignments for him. Here in Holland, but also in Berlin, Barcelona, Copenhagen . . . They're queuing up for him.'

I glance at Leon. He's lost interest. His eyes are fixed on the photo of the burnt forest, but I get the feeling he's not really taking it in. He's lost in thought.

'Leon is really good,' says Richard. 'The best photographer I know – in his field, that is. People are his strong point, though I dare say he could do a portrait of a light bulb that would take your breath away. He has a talent that you can't learn in any class, you've either got it or you haven't. Leon uses the light to his advantage. There are no duds in his work, ever. Not even a mediocre photo.'

Richard says lots of flattering things about Leon, but I have trouble registering his monologue.

Leon's hand is round my waist and his fingers are absently stroking the material of my blouse. The skin underneath is tingling and the tingling is spreading through the deeper layers of my body. I press myself closer to him, very subtly, but it's not enough. I want to curl up with him and hide. Away from here. I want to be alone with him.

'There he goes again,' mutters Leon beside me. 'She's not a buyer. Have you seen Rolf and Joost?'

'I just saw them loitering near the champagne.'

Leon's arm slips away from me. 'Wait here a second.'

I watch as Leon walks away. The way he moves catches my eye once again: fluid and natural, with straight shoulders. Then he disappears into another room. Richard is still standing next to me, watching me curiously.

'Have you been Leon's manager for long?' I ask, for want of a better subject.

'For three years now . . . You know, you must mean a lot to him, Margot, for him to invite you here. The exhibition is only open to the public from tomorrow. Today is exclusively for the in-crowd, special guests, the elite. By inviting you here he wants you to be accepted. Or he's putting you to the test. One of the two.'

I frown slightly. 'Why do I need putting to the test?'

Richard looks away from me. When I follow his gaze I see Leon in a passageway talking to two flamboyantly dressed men in their late twenties. One of them is wearing a kilt and a yellow T-shirt, the other is dressed in black, his hair dyed bright red. They are gesticulating and nodding.

'Because not everyone can hold their own in this environment,' says Richard. 'There aren't many interfaces with reality. There are no frameworks, no limits. That attracts misfits. There are people in this world who do disgusting things under the common denominator of art. It's part and parcel of letting go of the familiar, transcending yourself, creating new realities and trying to see new paths. You mustn't disturb a creative process, you must give yourself the freedom to follow your instincts. If you have to think about everything you want to create and wonder if you're working in a morally responsible way, you might just as well start making passport photos. So, on the one hand it's good, that continual renewal. But if you ask me, some of them go too far. In their creations, but also also in their private lives, which sometimes mirror the art and so go just as badly off the rails.' He looks at me seriously. 'The bottom line is that in this world you have to learn to set your own limits, because if you leave it to others, you'll only discover your own personal limit long after you've exceeded it.'

'Drugs?' I ask, slightly alarmed.

'Drugs, sex, self-mutilation . . . everything you can think of, and lots more you could never have imagined or wanted to imagine.'

Richard's monologue confuses me. I look around at all the people talking and drinking. They don't strike me as particularly perverted. Of course, it would turn quite a few heads in my parents' village if a man in a kilt or a drag queen walked down the street – even I was considered quite a spectacle – but that says more about the villagers than about these people, who see themselves as a work of art or want to make a statement with their appearance. Still, the finger-pointing stopped me reinventing myself. For years I wore a coloured contact lens to hide my blue eye, never got dreadlocks, or a tattoo for that matter. I simply didn't dare, scared of being ridiculed, of making a total fool of myself. Around me are people who have gone much further than that and who seem to be fully accepted. They're in their place here, in their natural habitat. It feels right. So what's cooking that I know nothing about? You find people overindulging in drugs and sex everywhere, they're not restricted to the art world. But Richard's seriousness as he says his piece must have some basis. I turn to him. 'What can go wrong with taking photos? How badly can you go off the rails if you photograph a burnt forest or a naked woman?'

'Do you know Günther von Hagens, the German who dissects and plasticises dead people? He's been in the news a lot, and still is. It's clever what that man does, but he's tinkering with corpses. Ever heard of Marc Quinn, who made a cast of his head with eight pints of his own blood and froze it? Saatchi bought it for over two million euros. That's still quite tame. What about Marina Abramovic, who had herself cut open for an audience in the name of art and let people drink her blood – and set herself alight at one point. Spectators have saved her life more than once. That's pretty weird, isn't it? But there's more. Letting goldfish drenched in paint thrash over a canvas till they die, or letting museum visitors grind them up in a food mixer . . . Is that still art? Call it art, call it whatever you like, but in my view these are twisted minds acting out their obsessions. Some of them lose their way entirely.' He suddenly looks at me as if he's really noticing me for the first time. Then he puts his hand on my shoulder. 'Sorry, I shouldn't frighten you. You're right, there's nothing wrong with photographing burnt forests or naked women. Though personally I prefer looking at the results of the latter category. The point is that this world's different. And that you've got to be strong to hold your own.'

I'm still wondering what his argument has to do with putting me to the test. Behind us a woman starts laughing, and her laughter is bordering on the hysterical – or am I just imagining it?

'And Leon?' I ask. 'How does he fit in to this?'

Richard leans over intimately and I catch a whiff of his after-shave, or shampoo – a light, slightly sweet smell. 'Leon is a natural talent, Margot. He's fond of comparing photography with stealing, I'm sure he's already told you that, but I see it more as hunting. I've seen him at work, the concentration, the flair, he stalks, he focuses. And I can tell you that when he has something in his sights, he hits the mark. Always. He's a born sniper. The same applies to his taste in women. He's pretty consistent in that too.'

He doesn't answer my question. His response only raises new questions. 'I know nothing about his previous girlfriends or wives,' I say. 'He hasn't told me anything about them yet.'

'That doesn't surprise me. He's crazy about you. That's obvious. He's only known you a short time, hardly any time at all actually. What's a weekend? How much can you find out about one another, how much time do you have to talk? Assuming you get round to talking, that is,' he chuckles. 'You've awakened something in him. I think I know what it is, but I suspect he hasn't told you yet.'

I repeat his words in my head but even then I don't understand what Richard is really trying to tell me. What he's hinting is that Leon has a secret. Something he hasn't told me yet that I ought to know. Is it connected with the rest of Richard's monologue about screwed-up people in art and having to be strong to hold your own?

I see Leon coming towards us out the corner of my eye, with the two flamboyant-looking men in his wake.

Richard leans closer, lowering his voice. 'Give him space, don't put any pressure on him. He doesn't come with a user's manual, but he's OK, that's all I wanted to say to you.'

'You're whispering, Richard.'

Richard puts his hands up with his palms facing Leon. 'I've just been telling Margot, there are a lot of oddballs on the loose in this world.'

'I bet you didn't tell her you're the oddest one of all?'

They laugh, roar, Leon, Richard, and even the two men who

have come over to us with Leon, but I don't join in. Richard's grisly stories have given me the creeps.

'Let me introduce you to Rolf and Joost,' says Leon.

They shake hands with me, and look at me full of expectation and genuine interest.

'They have a restaurant here in Amsterdam,' says Leon, continuing the introduction. 'A long narrow place that's been crying out for a revamp for ages. It needs a completely new look. You can really go wild with it, and I've told them you're very good at that.'

My hands are clasped in front of me. I look from one to the other and I'm sure the look on my face must be betraying my excitement. This is what I want, I realise, at last, after all these years: a client who's happy to 'go wild' – how often have I hoped that someone would say something like that? But my excitement soon turns to nervousness when I meet their hopeful gaze. They're looking at me eagerly, as if I'm the answer to all their questions. What on earth has Leon told these two people about me? What do they expect from me? Yes, this is what I want, but at the end of the day my practical experience doesn't go far beyond a well-trodden path of order numbers in my portfolio.

Leon stands diagonally behind them, hands in his pockets, grinning broadly. It's clear from his whole attitude: he's taken care of the introduction; the rest is up to me.

'We have some ideas,' says the man with the bright red hair, 'but we don't really want to be involved in the work. You know? Nothing personal, mind: to each his own.' He looks very young. But his eyes are bright and convince you that he's more capable than you'd first think.

'Because you're more interested in cooking?'

'That's my job mainly,' replies the man with the kilt who was introduced to me as Joost. 'Rolf's a photographer. He specialises in food. He's involved in the restaurant, but doesn't cook himself.'

'We've got a budget for the refurbishment and labour,' adds Rolf.

'Can you drop by sometime soon,' says Joost, 'to see if you can do something with it? Or if you . . .' – he wiggles his fingers like he's playing air piano – 'get good vibes from the space?'

'Leon said that was your condition and we totally understand that. You're completely free, of course, to accept the commission or not.'

'How about today?' I ask.

Joost and Rolf look at each other for a moment. 'Today? Well, why not? It's round the corner.'

I want to ask them about the type of restaurant it is. The sort of food they serve, the kind of clientèle, and whether they want to keep it that way or use the makeover to attract new business. I want to visualise things, consider the possibilities right now, before I go there and they expect me to conjure up all kinds of ideas on the spot. But before I can open my mouth, Leon interrupts.

'We'll drop in for a bite later,' he says. 'What time does your place open?'

'I'm leaving in an hour to get things ready,' replies Joost. 'Officially we open at seven, but you're welcome anytime, Leon. Whenever suits you.'

'Fine. See you later then.' Leon puts an arm round me and leads me away from them. The he turns his face towards me slightly. 'Good?'

'Yes, fantastic. But . . .'

'No buts. You wanted a break, and now you've got one. They're nice lads, those two, they're pretty easy-going, and it'll be hard to botch it up. And they've got plenty of money, so don't feel sorry for them. If you accept this job it'll take you a few weeks. You can stay with me if you want, then you won't have to commute back and forth the whole time.'

It sounds very tempting: spending two weeks with Leon and refurbishing a restaurant. But the unpleasant thought of my job sticks in the back of my mind. The management will go ballistic if I ask for more time off after my leave. They'll never agree to it.

I can't bear thinking about it. 'So you live in Amsterdam?'

'I've got a flat here in Amsterdam and a little bungalow in Brabant, on the edge of a wood. I mix it up a bit.'

'You live in two different places.'

He shrugs his shoulders. 'Why not? I enjoy the change.'

As we've been talking I haven't noticed that we've ended up in a different part of the gallery. The gentle hubbub has died down and our footsteps are echoing on the laminate in a narrow corridor. The walls are unpainted and there are no pictures. This part is not meant for visitors.

Leon opens a door and leads me inside. It is dim and chilly, a room as big as the average living room with a low dark ceiling. There are frames packed up on racks.

'Are you allowed in here?' I whisper.

He grabs my wrists and pushes me against the wall. 'I could have taken you to the toilets, but that seemed too vulgar.' The next moment I feel his body against mine, his tongue, that tastes of champagne, slides over my lips. He tightens his grip on my wrists. 'I've been walking round with a hard on for an hour.' He pushes his lower body against me to add force to his words.

His sudden action takes me by surprise. Everything in me feels instantly weightless. I let out a soft moan and want to bury my face in the space between his shoulder and neck.

The next moment he lifts me slightly off the ground and sits me on a metal sideboard. 'Pull your skirt up.'

I don't think to protest. I shift my weight jerkily from one buttock to the other, while my hands tug the material of my skirt up impatiently to reveal the thong I bought last week. Red, this time. Dark red.

Leon has let go of me. All at once the distance he created in London is back, that sudden appraisal, assessment. One hand is gripping his upper arm and the other is at his waist.

I look at him in the half-light, a frozen silhouette and only now do I think I know what he's doing and why. He's taking photos in his head. He's framing the shot, directing and recording at the same time.

I don't need much encouragement. Before he's even asked, I take off my thong and throw it on the floor. I challenge Leon and try to make eye contact, but his eyes are fixed on my crotch.

'Come closer,' I whisper. 'I don't want any distance, Leon. I want you here with me.' In me, I think. In me, in me, in me. Now.

He shakes his head slightly, as if I'm interrupting his train of thought, and stands there motionless. 'Your blouse.'

'No, I—'

'Do it.'

I fiddle with the fastenings on my blouse. They're small hooks, like on a bra, and are easy to undo. I shake the blouse off my shoulders, but keep my bra on for now.

I can hear people talking in the distance. Are they coming here? I look at the door in alarm. Someone could come in at any moment and expose us to the intense, unforgiving fluorescent light. Leon is fully clothed, but I'm sitting here with my skirt pulled up and only my bra and boots on. Instinctively I put my arms protectively over my breasts and press my knees together.

'Focus, Margot. Focus,' he whispers.

'But what if someone . . .'

His mouth curls into a smile. 'They'll leave again at once. People aren't easily shocked here.'

While I listen to the footsteps and conversations in the corridor, I become even more aware of my nakedness and my body and feel how fast my heart is beating against my ribs. It's raging and whirling inside me. My mouth is dry with tension and slightly open so that I can take in enough air. Somehow the idea that we could be caught excites me enormously.

I adopt a more relaxed position and drop my arms. My back touches the wall behind me; it feels cold and rough against my hot skin.

'Keep going,' he whispers.

I lean forward a little and my hands reach behind my back searching for the fastener on my bra. I'm trembling all over now. The bra goes the same way as the thong and lands somewhere on the floor.

Leon clicks his tongue, very softly, and takes a step in my direction.

I reach out to him, trying to hold him, seeking the intimacy we had that night in London in the hotel bed, skin against skin, stroking each other, listening to each other's breathing and heartbeat, but again he shakes his head and grabs my wrists, pushing them with one hand against the wall above my head.

'I don't want to hurt you,' he whispers, while his hand strokes my thigh and my body shivers beneath his touch. 'I'd never forgive myself.'

'You're not hurting me. You can—'

'Ssh.'

His free hand slides along my knees and I spread my legs for him. I thrust my pelvis forward. I feel feverish, like I'm ill, the room is spinning round me.

When his fingers find the soft flesh and push through, into me, I let out a muffled scream. I'm shocked by my own reaction. Then my lower body starts moving against his hand as if automatically, faster and faster, harder and harder. The palm of his hand is lying on my pubic bone as a counterweight. I can hear him panting, smell him, feel the heat radiating from his body, right through his clothing. I want to touch him, embrace him, but his hand keeps my wrists pressed to the wall and doesn't move.

The moment his mouth seeks out my breast and I feel the pressure of his teeth and lips, I explode into a thousand pieces, no, a million, a billion, innumerable astronomical fragments, and I know I'll never be able to find all the pieces and become whole again. Parts of me that were always so essential, or just seemed so, have disappeared for ever, floated away, tumbling and swirling into the stratosphere.

21

'Mum and Dad are really upset,' says Dick.

I'm kneeling by the coffee table playing with a packet of cigarettes that I tip over onto the table top.

Dick is sitting diagonally across from me on my sofa. His arms are resting on his thighs and he hangs his head slightly as if there were deaths to be mourned. Anne is sitting next to him, feeling awkward. She keeps running her tongue across her front teeth and wiggles her foot nervously.

'If they're so upset, they can come here. If they can find the place, that is . . . I don't think it's right of them to send you, it's got nothing to do with you.'

He looks up: 'What makes you think I've been sent here?'

I shrug my shoulders, pull a cigarette out of the packet, light it and inhale deeply.

In the bedroom Bas, aged three, and his older brother Thomas are jumping on my bed. I can hear the mattress springs squeaking and the patter of their feet on the wooden floor as they chase each other.

'I don't like this any more than they do,' Dick goes on. 'I'm trying to understand exactly why you stormed out.'

I look away in annoyance. 'Dick, surely it's not that hard to understand? They let John in. *John!* That . . . that shit came to the door with flowers and they just let him in. And that's not all—'

Dick throws his hands up. 'I don't think you should have

stormed out. You should have talked it through with them. Now it just makes everything more complicated.'

Anne sits next to Dick fiddling furiously with some loose threads hanging from the seams of her jeans. It's obvious she's been instructed to stay out of the conversation. Why she's come is a mystery to me. Maybe she's curious and wants to hear everything with her own ears, be up on the latest news.

'I couldn't face it,' I say. 'There was nothing to say to them. I was seething. Try to understand.'

Dick makes eye contact with me. His voice is soft. 'Margot, I can really understand how shitty this must be for you. John messed you around and he hasn't heard the last of it from me, you know that. If I get the chance, I'll spell it out to him. But what you're forgetting is that you're not the only one in the family who got close to that idiot. Personally I couldn't give a damn about John, but it's different with Mum and Dad. They were very fond of him. It all happened so suddenly that John never had a chance to say goodbye to them. So why can't you allow them to talk it over together? It's got nothing to do with you, basically.'

Dick has barely finished before I start shaking my head wildly. 'No! He wasn't there to say goodbye, he really wasn't. He was there to strengthen the ties, to justify his bad behaviour, to clean up his image. And it worked as well, because I found myself sitting opposite two people who were making excuses for his cheating. And now suddenly it's all my fault. You should be talking to Mum and Dad and John, not me.'

'No, that's—'

'Dick!' I interrupt him. 'I'll tell you exactly what's happening: they're making me look like the villain of the piece, it's as simple as that. John made a mistake that he regrets, all perfectly human, the poor soul admits all his mistakes and I'm supposed to just accept that. Can you see why I'm so pissed off? Have sympathy for John, have sympathy for Mum and Dad. Why am I always the one who has to make allowances and see the other person's point of view?'

Dick fidgets with his coarse red hair. 'You're taking it all too personally.'

I roll my eyes. 'That's exactly what I'm talking about. You think I'm the one with the problem as well.'

'I don't mean it like that.'

'I'm the one who's taking it too personally. That's what you're saying, isn't it?'

'I don't want to get bogged down in a tit for tat slanging match, Margot. I'd rather find a solution to this whole shitty situation. We're not kids anymore.'

I tip my head back and exhale noisily.

There are screams from the bedroom. Thomas and Bas must have turned my bedroom upside down. I can hear snatches of their game. Thomas is pretending to be a ghost and is chasing his younger brother. I can't see through the wall, but I'm pretty sure that they've taken my duvet off the bed. Or worse: they've opened the wardrobe and taken sheets out to play with. Who knows what else they're getting up to? And Anne's just sitting there.

'Anne? Would you go and sort them out for a moment? Please? I'm busy enough as it is without spending an hour clearing up after them later.'

She gets up without a word and disappears into the bedroom. I can hear her grumbling in a faint voice.

'Dick,' I say. 'Once again, I hugely appreciate the way you're taking the trouble to patch things up, but there's really no point. They should have stood firm, taken my side. That's what family's for. I've said it ten times already and I'll say it again now: if they want to talk, then just let them come here, to my house. But there's no rush as far as I'm concerned.'

Dick looks down and just shakes his head. He doesn't want to hear what I'm saying.

'Home should be a sanctuary,' I continue. 'Not hostile territory. I don't want to have to check if John's car's there every time I drop in on Mum and Dad. Or have to watch my words because Dad's going to discuss my antics with him every week.'

Dick frowns in annoyance. 'Oh, come on, that's nonsense.'

'Believe me, Mum was trying to make excuses for John's affair. She was arguing in his favour. He's pulled the wool over their eyes, and knitted a sweater with it.'

Anne enters the room. 'I've cleared it up,' she says timidly. She gives Dick a rather startled look and seems unable to decide whether to sit down again or stay standing up.

'Call the two of them. We're off anyway,' says Dick, getting up.

Without a word Anne darts into my bedroom and comes back holding Thomas by the hand with Bas on her arm. 'Say thank you to Auntie Margot, for letting you play and giving you something to drink.'

'Thanks for letting us play!' shouts Tomas cheekily, in an odd voice.

Bas turns away and leans against his mother to avoid having to look at me.

Dick turns round in the doorway. 'Mum's birthday's coming up.'

'I know,' I say flatly.

Anne and the children are already half way down the stairs. Thomas shouts that he wants to slide down the banister, but Anne won't let him. Their voices boom through the stairwell.

'Do you think you'll be coming?' he asks.

I stare at him in silence and then say: 'I'll see. OK?'

He bites his lower lip. His body language and facial expression radiate gloom. 'Fuck it, I'm sick of this.' Then he kisses me on the cheek and goes downstairs.

22

Frits Leenders is in his fifties with thin grey hair and small beady eyes in a round, unhealthily red face. He's the manager of a hotel in a nearby town. Leenders has summoned me because the chairs in the conference suite are well past their sell-by date style-wise. The same goes for the carpeting in my professional opinion. It's an ancient-looking shade of grey-blue with a hint of yellow, but I didn't mention it. Thank God.

'The chairs must match the carpeting,' is his requirement. 'And of course the tables as well – a muted kind of colour.'

I nod and do my best to feign interest as I walk round the room with its modular ceiling and low sideboards along the walls. In the corner there's a coffee machine with plastic cups. 'We have various fabrics that would be a good match,' I say, with little enthusiasm. 'Grey, blue, maybe soft red.'

'Can you show me some examples?'

I take the fabric samples out of my case and lay them on the table next to the open catalogue. He goes quickly through it and stops at a greyish shade. He holds it against the carpeting and then puts the sample on the table top. He takes a step back, puts his hand to his chin and says: 'This is right, I think. Can you tell me roughly what it would cost?'

'The price depends on the model. All models come with and without arm rests, and *with* is obviously more expensive. The advantage of this . . .' I rattle off my spiel without really thinking about it.

For the last few days I've been racking my brains for a way to get two weeks off from work. But I just can't come up with a convincing excuse. Maybe I should call in sick. I really want to get going with Joost and Rolf's place in two weeks' time. There are sketches spread out on the coffee table at home, last night I was working on it till three and this morning it was the first thing I reached for over coffee. The more involved I get in planning Ce Truc ('That Thing' in French), the less I can be bothered to concentrate on my regular work.

My finger floats automatically to the bestselling model. 'I'd recommend these. They're comfortable and really strong. We hardly ever get any complaints about these. And they're stackable, which is ideal if ever you want to use the suite for something else.'

'Stackable? That's certainly handy. So what are we talking, roughly?'

I take out the list and pretend to look up the price. In truth I know them off by heart. We can decide for ourselves how much of a discount we give up to a certain percentage. If I suspect the customer won't be scared off by a higher price, then I give the recommended price. People who've also asked our competitors for quotes or obviously don't have much to spend are given a lower price. I'd put Leenders in the latter group. Nevertheless I'm going to start a little higher. Leenders strikes me as the type who likes to haggle. He needs to feel good about it too. 'Let's say a hundred euros per chair, and you need twenty-eight.'

'Pooh,' is his reaction.

I study his face. He isn't genuinely shocked.

My mobile rings. I grab it out of my pocket. Leon. It's the first time he's called and I can't answer. Not now. I slip the mobile back into my pocket but it keeps on ringing. The sound goes right through me.

I look Leenders straight in the eye. 'Do you want to decide today?'

'Maybe. Depends.'

The ringing has stopped.

'Then I think I'd better just call my boss now. Very occasionally we can offer a discount on larger orders. I'll be right back with you.' Without waiting for his response I hurry outside to the car park, and get into my car. I light up a cigarette and ring Leon's number.

He answers immediately.

'Hi,' I say. My heart is in my mouth. 'I was with a customer.'

'And now?'

'Outside, in the car.'

'Are you up for it?'

'For what?'

'For the shoot? If you're still feeling brave enough, that is.'

Instantly my whole body is aglow, like I'm on fire. The photo shoot. I fall silent for a moment. I've been fantasising about it a lot over the past week, about posing nude for Leon. About seeing blown-up photos of my naked body hanging in galleries and in the homes of art collectors, who find them, no, who find *me* beautiful or interesting enough to spend a small fortune on them. The very idea is enough to keep me awake, to keep every fibre of my being tingling with tension and excitement. I'm ready for a new experience, even though I'm nervous about the outcome. What if it hits too close to home, gets too confrontational? Undressing for Leon is one thing. That's still private, still between him and me. Showing myself naked to the whole world is something else. I'm acutely aware of that. I have the feeling I'm on the edge of the abyss, blindfolded, arms outstretched, ready to jump. The thing is that Leon is down below waiting to catch me. If someone else had asked me, I'd have refused pointblank. 'Yes, completely,' I reply. My voice isn't quite right: it's trembling.

'Fine, Can you come to the studio on Thursday evening?'

'Where is it?'

'I'll get Debby to e-mail you directions. And Margot, don't bother with underwear. Not even a thong, nothing.'

My tummy contracts. I take a nervous drag on my cigarette.

Out the corner of my eye I can see Leenders looking at me behind the sliding glass doors, with the samples in his hand. He's clearly waiting for me. Can he see my face or is the reflection on the windscreen shielding me from view?

I turn my head away from him.

'Before you get the wrong idea,' he says with a chuckle, 'underwear and socks leave a mark on the skin. Jeans, tight sweaters with seams, things with elastic: avoid them all. Great nudes have skin without red weals. If you have a bathrobe, bring it with you. And don't do anything you wouldn't normally do with your body . . . Nervous?'

'A bit.'

Chuckling. 'No need, princess. We're going to make a beautiful job of it together. Trust me.'

'I trust you.'

'Great. See you Thursday. Ciao.'

I sit there, with the mobile against my cheek listening to the beep. Thursday evening seems so much further away than just a few days. It dawns on me that I'd have turned the ignition key and driven to Moscow if he'd asked. I'd have just dropped everything and gone to him, without a second thought.

I cast a cautious glance at the building. Leenders is still standing there. I stub out my cigarette in the ashtray, let out a very deep sigh in an attempt to rid my body of the tension, and go back inside.

23

I remember his last series was on the theme of 'pain' and wonder what the new one is supposed to portray, what atmosphere or feeling he wants to evoke. Because that's also what he sees in me, or thinks he discovered when he asked me to pose for him.

'What sort of series is it going to be?' I ask.

Leon fiddles with his camera and unrolls a flex. 'If you don't mind, I'd rather not say. If I do, you'll act accordingly and it'll be a fake.' He goes over to a computer on an old desk in a corner. 'I often work with music, do you have a preference?' He looks up inquiringly.

I'm sitting on the floor, wrapped in my dressing gown. It's chilly in the studio, perhaps a little too chilly to be naked. My feet slide nervously across the floor, coated with black cement paint. 'I can't think of anything right now. Silence is OK, I think.'

He drops his chin slightly and looks at me from under his eyelashes. 'Don't be afraid. Listen to yourself and it'll always work. We're not going to force anything. Just sit down, lie down, stand up, whatever you want.'

I slowly take off my bathrobe. It feels strange to be completely naked in this tall, dark space. Leon's studio is a small hangar, tucked away on an industrial estate in a village beneath the fumes of Schiphol Airport. Aircraft are passing overhead the whole time, and I can hear the roar of the turbines.

Leon keeps his distance. When I came in he gave me a peck on the forehead and then became withdrawn. I'm no longer a sexual being in his eyes, but a subject that must represent what he feels or wants to convey to his public. I felt that detachment growing as soon as I started to undress, when he seemed to have eyes only for his equipment. I get the feeling he's deliberately creating a distance.

'Forget about me,' he says suddenly. He's still not looking at me. 'I'm not here. You're here by yourself. Look at yourself.'

My eyes shift towards the huge mirror dominating the opposite wall and I see myself standing there, caught in a cocoon of studio lights. At first I turn away in embarrassment, but with my curiosity aroused I finally lift my chin, with my arms awkwardly by my sides, fully conscious of my nakedness. For a long time I've found my body unattractive, even ugly, repulsive, so I've avoided looking at it whenever I could. Yet my nakedness is bothering me less now. I stare at myself in the mirror, following the white contours that contrast with my dark red, curly hair. I'm not ugly, the mirror says. Stripped of my clothes I look different. So much better. Curvy and soft, feminine. Why am I only seeing this now? Perhaps, it strikes me, the problem only arises in clothes shops, because my body just won't fit into clothes that look so promising on the hanger. Everything seems to be squeezed in in the wrong places. The material leaves a mark on my back, the sweaters are too short, making my tummy bulge out underneath, trousers pull at the hips or divide my bum horizontally in two – and when it comes to jackets I can never do up the top button because my breasts are in the way. Now nothing is in the way, everything is in proportion.

A glaring flashlight startles me out of my thoughts. I turn my head towards the camera, look for Leon who must be in the shadows behind it, behind the glass eye that records everything, but the studio lights blind me and I screw up my eyes.

'Don't pay attention to me,' he says. Another flash. His voice is softer now, more accessible: 'Go back to how you just were.'

I lower my eyes for a moment, stare at the floor, which consists of a dark kind of plastic cloth over several square yards. My feet stick to it when I move them. 'I want a cigarette,' I say.

Leon comes out from behind his camera. I hear him rummaging in the dark, see a flame flare up and then he steps into the light and thrusts me a lit cigarette. I take a grateful drag, and another. The flashlight is coming from two sides, maybe also from behind, I can't really pinpoint it. I turn round and see two flashes on the floor pointing diagonally upwards.

Only now does it sink in that every movement I make can be captured and later exhibited in galleries all over the world. Perhaps I'll be made into a post card or a cheap reproduction, as happened to Goya's Maja, or the countless naked men with their babies you can buy at kiosks. Do I want to be recognisable? Do I want people to see my face, walk past me in the street and turn round, wondering if I'm that woman they have hanging on the wall of their student house or office?

I step forward out of the light, stub the cigarette out on the floor and walk back. Then I sink to my knees and lie down with my back to the camera. I cross my arms in front of my body and raise my knees. Flash. I screw my eyes shut and put my hands over my face. The floor is cold and hard and the cold is seeping into my skin, through my flesh and layers of fat into my bones. Flash. I start shivering. It crosses my mind that this has absolutely nothing to do with sex. I've unleashed all kinds of fantasies about this that kept me awake at night. But this whole setting, everything around me, is hard and cold and business-like. I curl up even more. Flash.

'Relax,' I hear him say, closer than a moment ago.

I look up. He's standing diagonally across from me, his legs slightly apart, looking down on me intently, with the camera attached to cables in his beautiful hands. Flash. I close my eyes and turn away from him. No, this has absolutely nothing to do with sex or sensuality. I put my hand under my cheek to protect my face from the rising cold.

'We've finished, princess, get dressed before you freeze.'

In slight disbelief I look up, but in the place where he was standing just now there is only emptiness. I push myself up stiffly off the floor and see that he is rolling up the cables. 'Already?'

'I've got what I need.'

I stand up and look for my clothes. Loose tracksuit bottoms and a sweatshirt. They were the only items of clothing I could find that fitted the bill.

'Come on, let's go, we're going to have some coffee.'

We go over to a small room built within the hangar. Here there's a heater on full blast and a black leatherette three-piece suite. I flop down on it. On the prefabricated walls there are cards and photos, simple computer printouts and calendars. 'Are these all your own photos?'

Leon pours out some coffee from a thermos flask and hands me a mug. It's cracked. 'Most of them. I share the studio with a couple of colleagues.' He looks up. 'By the way, have you started on the design for Joost and Rolf yet?'

I nod. 'That same evening. I'm really fired up about it. But I'm also uncertain. I've nothing to fall back on.'

He raises his eyebrow as he takes a sip. 'Qualifications, you mean?'

I nod again. 'I've never done a course, anything.'

'All the better,' he growls.

'Because?'

'On a course or a degree programme you're steered in a particular direction, everything's pigeonholed and taught as established fact, though essentially many things can't be classified. You become more and more aware of those rules and restrictions, you start putting your own work into perspective with comparable work by other people, and by doing that you limit yourself. That's not right, in my opinion.'

'Didn't you do a photography course then?'

'I quit after a few weeks. They didn't teach me anything I didn't already know myself or couldn't learn from experience. Courses take years, wasted years if you ask me. It's a waste of time, cramming yourself full of theoretical knowledge that's not a damn bit of use to you in the end. It just inhibits you.'

'Isn't it easy for you to talk? You're good. You're a star.'

'I had to start somewhere.'

'As what?'

He smiles shyly. 'Have you got a cigarette?'

I hand him one and am about to give him a light, but he takes the lighter out of my hand and lights his own. 'I began as a press photographer on a local newspaper. In practice that involves driving round the area all day long photographing the same people again and again. Owners of a new shop, aldermen, police spokesmen, supervisors of children's day centres. At least I tried to do the best I could.' His smile broadens. 'Eventually the management sent the journalists out themselves with digital cameras, which was cheaper than employing someone separately. In their view anyone could take photos. Exit Wagner. What leaves a nasty taste in the mouth is that the public often can't even tell the difference between a photo that's taken with love and one that isn't . . . Or they can see it, but they're not interested. It wasn't till I ended up back at home that I realised I'd got into a rut.' He sniffs and looks away from me.

'I take it from Richard that he discovered you. He said something like that.'

'That's right. I joined a camera shop part time and started doing a few jobs on the side to forget about it all. It was a time when I was looking for something, and didn't really know how to move forward, but I did know I wanted to carry on with photography. I did a series on factory workers and daily life in a crisis centre for drug addicts. I got so involved in it I sometimes forgot that I could barely pay the rent. All my money went into photography and travel. I didn't care, I didn't give it a second thought. Looking back, that may have been the best time of my life. Searching, feeling my way, unfettered by knowledge. No assignments, expectations, deals, agreements . . . no necessities.' He runs his hand through his hair. It immediately falls forward again. 'After a while I came into contact with a couple of art photographers and they really liked my work. They put me in touch with Richard and Debby, and we clicked straight away. Within a month I had my first group show and my photos were sold for amounts of money that would have previously taken me a week or two to earn. Without them I'd still have been wandering through the polders and city centres, in search of God knows what.'

The heater is making the small room very warm. I feel rosy and languid and pull my knees up next to me on the sofa. I try to imagine Leon, in his younger years, still an undiscovered photographer for a regional paper. Did he already have this aura about him? That intangible, dark quality that still seems to surround him? Did he always have it?

Leon looks at his watch. 'I hate to have to shoo you away, but the next lady will be on the doorstep any minute.'

A jolt goes through me. Up to now I haven't thought about the practical side of a photo series. How naïve of me. It's only natural that Leon won't just be photographing me, but a whole bunch of women he must have spoken to in the street. Women he's convinced that they are beautiful time after time, or special enough to be the subject of his photography. Women who have his telephone number, women he's had coffee with, or more. It hurts that I have to go, have to make way for the next woman who will shortly be wriggling naked across the floor for him. I look at him over the rim of my mug.

He just grins. 'Jealous, princess?'

I shrug my shoulders. It seems too childish to answer in the affirmative, but that's essentially what I'm doing by not saying anything. 'It's your work,' I say quickly.

Leon gets up and takes the mug out of my hands. He puts it on the table and sits down next to me. He takes hold of my jaw and brings his face close. 'Jealousy is a human quality,' he whispers. 'It suits you.'

'I just have to get used to the idea.'

'Can you come to Amsterdam after work tomorrow? On Saturday I'm flying to Berlin for an assignment. I'd like to see you before then.'

I frown. 'I can't do tomorrow. I've got a meeting at five-thirty.'

'I bet *that's* important.'

Suddenly I feel myself getting angry. 'Perhaps not important to you, but I recently took a month off. There's no way I can miss it.'

'You could if you quit your job.' He lets go of my chin. 'Then no one would be surprised if you no longer showed up at meetings.'

'Quit my job?'

Leon doesn't move a muscle. 'What the hell do you want? In London you were moaning about your job for a whole hour, and now it's suddenly become important? Or am I wrong and do you secretly like it after all? Or do you just like moaning?'

I look away from him to the photos on the wall. One of them is hanging askew. 'Don't you know the expression about burning bridges? I can't just quit my job on the basis of a single odd commission I've barely begun and that might not work out. It could be a disaster . . . You make it all seem so simple. But it's not as easy as that.'

He looks at me so intensely that I stop talking for a moment. 'It is as easy as that, Margot. It's a question of taking action. Free your mind. You'll have enough money left from that job to see you through the month, maybe even six weeks or so, and believe me, new clients will follow soon enough. Joost and Rolf have loads of connections, and don't forget about me . . . And Richard and Debby. Even if you achieve only half of what I expect from you, you'll be fighting them off.'

'You sound pretty sure about it.'

He takes the coffee mugs off the table and starts rinsing them out under the tap. 'If you're serious about something, you've got to give one hundred per cent. You hate that job of yours, so it leeches your energy. Energy and time you could spend on developing yourself.' He turns round, pulls a grubby towel from the draining board and dries his hands. 'How long have you been thinking about a career change?'

'About two years. Maybe three.'

'I rest my case,' he says, coming and sitting next to me again. 'And what have you done in all those years to change things?'

I say nothing. He knows as well as I do that I've done nothing, nothing at all.

'I'll tell you what I think you should do,' he says. 'You quit that job of yours, as soon as possible, preferably Monday, then put your flat on the market. I'll look for a studio for you in Amsterdam, that's where you'll be working mostly for the time being and that way you won't have to drive back and forth. Or you can come and live with me for a while. But do me a favour and don't worry about money. Your work starts now.'

'But I have no guarantees at all.'

'That longing for certainty of yours just gets in your way. It's a shame you won't see that.'

I can feel myself getting angrier and angrier. Angry and rebellious. I get ready to leave. 'It's easy for you to talk, Leon. You've got enough money, half the world at your feet and you can do whatever you like.'

Leon looks at me darkly. 'I didn't achieve this by clinging to certainties. I took the plunge as well. There's no getting round it. You can't grow without any kind of risk. In order to move on you have to dare to let go.'

'I'll have to think about this,' I say softly. 'It's all taken me a bit by surprise.'

Leon doesn't respond.

I see something moving behind him. A woman's face appears at the window. She is young, no more than twenty-two, and has big dark eyes. She watches us hesitantly. When our eyes meet, she waves at me rather timidly, and smiles.

'Your next patient,' I say flatly.

Leon quickly looks round, casually raises his hand to her and scribbles an address and a rough map on a piece of paper, which he thrusts into my hand. 'This is my address in Brabant. Come over on Monday night. We've got a lot to discuss.' He kisses me hastily on the forehead and opens the door. He gives me no chance to respond.

'Hello,' says the woman to me as I pass her. She can't hide her unease, and looks at me then at Leon and back again. Like me she's not exactly underfed, but otherwise I see no similarities. What on earth went through her mind, I wonder, when Leon asked her to pose nude?

'See you Monday,' Leon says.

I nod and walk past him out the door.

VIII

There is so much to discover here. So many objects jostling for priority, each of them telling me its own story and providing me with new clues. An overwhelming stream of information, caught in the beam of my torch.

The flat smells vaguely of paint. Typical of newly-decorated houses, everything is still clean and tidy. But it's far from clinical. In a year's time it will look very different, messier. The first signs are already showing.

In the sink are dirty dishes and a there's a dying plant on the windowsill. I pull off a latex glove and feel the soil. Bone dry. Did someone give her this specimen, but she doesn't care about it and is neglecting it deliberately? Or did she choose it carefully and then forget to give it water? That would mean she's careless, or has been preoccupied with other matters for so long that she no longer notices mundane things.

I crouch down and open the refrigerator. In the door there are cartons of milk and orange juice and a bottle of white wine. On the shelves are a pizza, a half-eaten wedge of semi-mature cheese, diet margarine, small cartons of fat-free yoghurt, and some withered vegetables. Margot watches her figure. Not that you'd notice. In the freezer there's nothing but a plastic bag full of ice cubes.

I stand up again and look through the kitchen cupboards. Bags of crisps and bars of chocolate, tins of peeled tomatoes, beans, spinach, plates, mugs – the usual stuff.

On the kitchen table there's a magazine lying open. I shine the torch across the pages. It's an English interior design magazine – did she buy it in London? –which she's scribbled notes on in blue biro. I sit down on the kitchen chair and imagine her sitting here – this morning, yesterday? – leafing through the magazine. She must have started having doubts. That's literally what she's written, followed by a question mark: warm or cold? She has nice round handwriting. Below the question mark there's a small circle instead of a dot.

Next to the magazine there is some opened post. I put the end of the torch between my teeth and go through the letters. Utility bills, bank statements: All Inclusive has paid her salary.

I tuck the letters back into their envelopes and go into the living room. On the coffee table there are sketches that had caught my eye when I first came in. The interior of Ce Truc to scale, carefully drawn out on large sheets of graph paper. Beside them is a file, new felt tips, swatches of fabric, newspaper cuttings, set squares and rulers. She's hard at work on her first job.

I run my hand over the sofa and sit down. Looking into the mirror, I shine the torch at myself and grin at my reflection.

I know who I am and I know what I'm capable of.

But who is Margot? Who is Margot really?

The beam flashes through the room and comes to rest on a bookcase. Most of the space is taken up with interior design books – I'm not surprised. On the bottom shelf there are a couple of bound leather photo albums. I lay them out on the floor in front of me and start leafing through them. This is interesting. Her whole life is summarised in a couple of albums. Margot in a garden, with a red-brick house in the background. It looks like an average working-class house – her parental home? – and there is a hedge of conifers. She's wearing a white dress and is standing behind a garden table with a couple of white rabbits on it. She is keeping the creatures together neatly with her hands, so that they stay in line with their heads facing the camera. She looks serious. She's the spitting image of her mother who is depicted a few pages further on. 'Dad and Mum married 12.5 years' it says underneath. Yes, she has the same figure. She gets her curly hair from her father. Further on in the album she is already years older and is wearing a brace in a class photo. That explains her nice straight teeth. And she wasn't always such a big girl, not even as an adult. That must have started not so long ago. In the last album there are recent photos, but a number are missing. They've been torn out, the paper is ripped. 'John and me on Texel'; 'BBQ at Tom and Mieke's'; 'Mieke on the boat'; 'John asleep'. Why has she removed them? I flick through quickly: there are lots more missing. All photos John or Mieke should be in. At the back there is a file from a camera shop, filled with photos stuck together. I carefully separate them and study them intently. A sleeping man with tousled blond hair, his mouth slightly open. John asleep. Interesting. The woman with the shiny, auburn hair must be Mieke. In various photos she is sitting arm in arm with an Indonesian-looking chap – Tom. A couple, like Margot and John. 'Something went very wrong on the way to heaven, didn't it, Margot?' I whisper. She hasn't thrown the photos away. She could have done: torn them up, burnt them. But no, she's taken them out of the album and banished them to a file at the back, so that she can still look at them whenever she feels the need.

She has trouble letting go.

I find further indication of this on the shelf over the photo albums. Next to a huge collection of interior design books there are well-thumbed children's books with her name in them.

Crusade in Jeans, Daddy is a Dog, Hunger Winter, Snub Nose and Pim. Childhood memories. I'm sure of it now: she gets attached to things. Let's have a look. Perhaps she still has a cuddly toy from when she was a little girl, or a doll. If so, I'll find it in her bedroom. I still need go through that too, as well as her bathroom. And if there's any time left, I can see if I can get into her computer. Computers are like the blueprints to someone's personality.

The way I feel now, I know I've got to be careful. I've had that idea for quite a while, that I get carried away too easily. The feeling of power it gives me just to snoop around in her house is addictive in itself. And I know that this wonderful feeling will grow a thousand times stronger if I don't leave it at that.

I can kid myself that I simply want to find out more about her, but deep inside I know that I've crossed a line. I know myself. I don't need much more encouragement.

24

I park the car diagonally across from my house and get out. The church clock strikes ten within earshot, but the sound is almost completely drowned out by the rain. It's dark, cold and bleak, perfectly reflecting my mood.

The meeting was a marathon. A four-hour ordeal in which I watched each minute pass on the clock above the door, waiting for the moment it would be OK to leave. Sales meetings at All Inclusive are all about figures, sales figures to be precise. Has everyone hit their target, and if not, why not? Who is salesperson of the month and who is lagging behind the rest? I've only been at work for two weeks so my figures couldn't be compared. Silently I cursed myself, the company, my colleagues, everyone, for having to spend the best part of the evening within the stuffy confines of the office, when I could have been with Leon.

Stooped forward I walk towards the front door, put the key in the lock and close the door behind me. It's pitch black, even though it's a house rule that the light in the hall has to stay on all the time. I feel my way to the switch, but whichever way I press, the light won't come on. Could there be a power cut?

Gradually the outline of the stairs begins to emerge. A faint, ghostly light is coming from above, through the skylight which has been positioned immediately above the stairwell three storeys up. Only when I hear noises from the other flats, talking and the faint sound of televisions, do I go upstairs. Each step creaks under my weight.

When I was a child, my mother always had to wait at the foot of the stairs until I was safely in bed. Until I was at least fifteen she faithfully kept watch every night and her presence frightened away all the monsters, spirits and ghosts. I thought I'd grown out of that, but I can't shake off the completely irrational feeling that I'm being watched.

My outstretched hands touch the front door and finally find the lock, into which I insert the key with trembling fingers. Inside I flick the switch and am relieved when everything turns out to be working. I close the door behind me and quickly lock and bolt it.

I turn the TV on straight away and flick through the channels till I find a light-hearted talkshow. Then I go to the kitchen. There's a bottle of Entre deux mers still in the fridge. I get a glass and fill it to the brim. I go back into the living room with the glass and the bottle and flop down on the sofa, kick my shoes off and tuck my legs under me.

Even though the whole flat is bathed in light and the television is giving out the reassuring sound of laughter and applause, I keep looking around me rather anxiously. I wriggle closer to the back of the sofa with the glass in both hands and drink the wine like a mug of hot chocolate. I look around once more: at the mirror, which reflects my legs and lower body and the red of the sofa, and at the closed door with the hall behind it – that big, dark, echoey hall with its ghostly light. I can't shake off the feeling that a sinister atmosphere has pervaded the whole building. In the beginning everything here felt so personal, so familiar, now suddenly everything seems hostile. For a second, in a strange, inexplicable moment, I imagine I'm rising, higher and higher, straight through all the floors of the building, the wooden loft and the slate roof, ever higher, all the while looking down on myself and on my red sofa, becoming an ever shrinking doll in an ever expanding city. I see myself sitting there, enclosed by four walls, and many more walls besides, houses, streets, cars, people, water, trees, fields, and finally just by the darkness around me.

This is my home, the first home of my own, but it doesn't feel good at all.

I turn the television up, and finally down again. I pour another glass of wine and drain it in a few gulps. The last one makes me shiver.

I shouldn't have gone to the meeting. I could have refused pointblank or made up an excuse, I could have done so many things, but instead I showed up promptly at five-thirty at Industriestraat 19.

It must have been habit. I can't think of anything else. Leon was right when he said that I clung to certainties. It must have been the reason why I held on to John. I may well have moved into town because of that, but I'm still in the same province and just fifteen minutes' drive from my old village.

Yet recently I've been doing things I would never have imagined myself doing years ago. New, exciting things. I went to London by myself, where I put myself in a vulnerable position with a man I hardly knew. It led to me falling in love, posing nude – my God! – and I came away with a design commission. These events can't possibly be disconnected. They're like a chain reaction, a line of collapsing dominos. They're connected, part of the same whole. And it all feels good. Exciting, inspiring, thrilling.

I pour another glass and look at the purple, pink and red

walls, and at the sketches for Ce Truc on the coffee table. Isn't it true that you sometimes get only one chance in life and have to grab it before it passes you by?

I take my mobile out of my trouser pocket and call Leon. The telephone rings for ages before he answers.

'It's me,' I say. 'Sorry to ring you so late.'

His voice sounds sleepy, mumbling. 'It's OK.'

'Were you in bed?'

'No, I've just got back. How was the meeting?'

'Shit . . . I . . . Actually I wanted to tell you that I've thought about what you said to me yesterday. I shouldn't have got so worked up. You're right, I think. Maybe I am stuck in a rut with my job, the routine. But . . . well, I'm thinking about giving it up.'

'Well done, my girl. Terrific.' He still sounds tired.

Suddenly I feel troubled. 'Leon, I . . . I miss you.'

'Try and get through the weekend. We'll see each other on Monday. By the way, I've got a nice surprise for you. I was going to call you about it tomorrow, but I'm talking to you now anyway. A friend of mine has a nightclub. He's thinking of giving it a makeover and would like to see you. Wait a moment.'

I can hear rustling and rummaging on the other end of the line.

'Write this down.' Leon reads out a name and telephone number.

I grab a felt tip off the table and write everything down in the margin of the sketches. The name and the number don't ring a bell. It's ages since I've been clubbing. 'When can I call him?'

'Not now. He works at night. But you can reach him in the

afternoon after twelve. I told him you might be able to drop by on Monday at the end of the day. It's not far from the bungalow, so you can drive straight on afterwards. Then we'll celebrate your second commission together.'

25

A pale sun is shining in the cloudless sky. The patches of fog that held the traffic up this morning have lifted and the atmosphere is tingling. Everything feels fresh, young, like a new spring. But even if there were rain or ice, I don't think it would make any difference to the way I feel right now; I'm unstoppable. I burst out laughing at stupid jokes on the radio and move as though I'm five stone lighter. I even feel the urge to skip and dance. But I control myself. Instead, only my foot is tapping and I hum along to the rhythm of the music playing in the café – 'Sing it Back' by Moloko.

The feeble winter sunshine is casting a yellowish light over the brown interior of the café. I spoon chocolate over the frothy head on the cappuccino and savour every mouthful.

My excitement from this morning hasn't died down. In my head I'm fully aware that I've taken a risk, that I may well have done something very foolish, but it feels so wonderful I don't want to give in to that persistent, nagging schoolmaster haunting my mind. Things are going to be different, radically different. I've taken the first steps towards that. I've had the whole weekend to think about it, made lists of pros and cons, screwed them up, torn them into pieces and started all over again until last night, when I took the plunge.

I have no children to look after, not even a pet. There's only one person I have to care for, and that's me. And up to now I haven't made a very good job of that simple, manageable task. When I think about it, I've neglected myself in recent years, on all fronts. It's time for a breath of fresh air.

Before I drove to All Inclusive this morning, I stopped at a car dealership on the same industrial estate. My shiny new set of wheels is parked in a garage a few streets away. It's a small, six-year-old Japanese car which looks and smells like it's just rolled off the factory floor. According to the salesman it's reliable and economical. The price was a nice surprise, but I mustn't make too many more leaps in the dark for now and I need to get hold of some money quickly. Leon's idea of selling my flat briefly crossed my mind. It's probably worth more now than when I bought it. It looks so much more modern. But I've decided to wait a bit. I can always sell if everything doesn't go to plan.

I've never seen my boss look so surprised as he did this morning. I took the car keys off my keyring and laid them on his desk together with the sample books, my files containing customer details and everything else I kept in the car. After he'd recovered a little from the astonishment, his blue eyes twinkled suspiciously behind his thick glasses and he pointed subtly to the competition clause in my contract. He simply couldn't believe I was quitting just like that and hadn't been head-hunted by a competitor.

I went outside, tilted my head right back and took a deep breath of fresh winter air. It was like a load off my shoulders. The dead weight was gone. A new, exciting life lay at my feet and all I had to do was pick it up. I walked to the car dealership and we drove to the post office together to transfer ownership of the Japanese car. That was that. I was free. Completely free.

I nibble the biscuit that came with my coffee. It's one o'clock and Leon's friend isn't expecting me till three. There's not enough time to drive to Amsterdam even though that's what I'd really like to do, to reassure myself about the commission from Joost and Rolf. Hopefully I'll get a chance to drop in on them this week and they can decide between the three proposals I've come up with. The Ce Truc restaurant specialises in organic food and there are a relatively large number of vegetarian dishes on the menu. That's why I've designed an interior based around recycled natural materials, giving them a new lease of life. The second design is more daring. Everything, from the walls to the furniture and materials, is a different shade of green, which I want to combine with half tree trunks with the bark still on. They can serve as pillars, immediately breaking up the length of the room. As a third option I've come up with something totally different: a sleek interior of steel and glass, based by no coincidence on the concept of the Oxo Tower in London. I'm curious to find out what they'll make of it.

My mobile starts beeping and vibrating. I slide it open, half expecting Dick to have sent me another message. But it's not Dick.

Sorry I've made such a mess of things. Wasn't my intention. I hope you'll believe me. Once again: sorry. Regards, John

I raise my eyebrows. John sorry about something and apologising? Twice in fact? I slide the mobile shut again, lay it on the table and keep looking at it, as if the device might sprout legs and walk off at any moment. Then I slide it open again and re-read the message. I wasn't mistaken, there it is in black and white: sorry twice.

I take a sip of the cappuccino, reach for my packet of cigarettes and light up. If John had got in touch a few weeks ago, then ten to one I'd have rung him straight back and given him an earful. I'd have probably got hysterical, and then immediately regretted letting my true feelings show. But now his message arouses no more emotion in me than a text from Orange telling me my monthly credit has been activated.

I haven't thought about John for quite a while, either in a negative or positive sense. He hasn't even disturbed my dreams. I've been too busy with my own life. The photo shoot, quitting my job, the designs, the doubts about moving and Leon. Mainly Leon. John suddenly seems so unimportant.

Obviously he *has* been thinking about me. I can just picture him waiting for my furious telephone call after his visit to my parents. When I made no contact, the doubts must have set in and that led to this message. My smile broadens. 'One–nil to me,' I whisper to myself.

I gently bite my lower lip and realise it's not just John who's dropped off my radar, but also two people who didn't deserve that at all. I slide the mobile open, select a number and press the call button. The telephone is answered almost instantly.

'Hi, Mum,' I say.

'Oh. Margot, I'm . . .' she's panting as though out of breath. 'I'm glad you've called.'

'I'm calling to say I'm not angry anymore, Mum. And I want to say sorry for giving you such a hard time.'

'Oh, that—'

'I meant to drop by,' I say, interrupting her. 'But I've got loads of things going on at once right now and I can't possibly get away. Is it OK if I come to your birthday party?'

'Of course it's OK! For goodness sake . . . You don't have to ask.' Another deep sigh. 'You've no idea how glad I am that we've talked this over.' That's typical of my mother. We haven't talked anything over.

'Has John dropped by again?'

She's silent for a moment. 'No,' she says finally. 'Though he did ring us to say sorry for causing so much trouble.'

'How does he know that?'

'When you stormed out your father called to tell him we'd had an argument and he's no longer welcome here.'

I chuckle under my breath. 'You're both sweethearts. You really are. Mum, I'll see you on your birthday.'

'Wait a moment. What if we dropped by this week? We should have done that long ago, Dad and I were talking about it. We left you in the lurch a bit.'

'That'd be lovely. But I'll probably be in Amsterdam for the rest of the week or even longer.'

'Have you got another fair?'

'No. It's something else, a long story, but I'll fill you in later.'

'Nothing serious, I hope?'

'No, Mum, quite the opposite actually. I'll tell you later, OK? Later. I've got to dash.' On impulse I add: 'I love you, Mum.'

It's getting on for three when I pull into the empty car park of Taco's night club. I've no idea if that's his first name or his surname, or maybe just a nickname. I get out and take a look at the premises. It's a whitewashed 1970s villa, with a park-like garden full of mature conifers and a relatively large car park covered in white gravel. Weeds are poking through here and there. Nevertheless the whole place looks well maintained. On the front of the building, close to the eaves, is an orange floodlight. The large windows are hidden behind wooden boarding painted plain white, same as the bricks.

I walk towards the front door, which is covered in a coat of glossy red paint, and ring the bell. I can't hear any ringing inside. To be on the safe side I ring again, but hear nothing except the continuous roar of cars on the main road and the lowing of cows further away. I wonder whether a night club so far from the town centre can attract enough punters. The villa is scarcely visible from the road, and the whole plot is surrounded by a thick screen of poplars and beeches. Even though the trees have shed most of their leaves by now, it's still difficult to see the meadows and the road through the tangle of overgrown branches and trunks.

As I raise my hand to ring again, the door opens. A well-preserved man in his fifties with dark wavy shoulder-length hair, strikingly light eyes and a tanned face, is watching me curiously. He's wearing a white tracksuit with blue and black stripes over his shoulders. 'You must be Margot.'

'That's right. Taco?'

'Taco Sanders, come in.' His accent is not local. He rolls his r's and could be from Rotterdam, but in that case he must have moved away some time ago.

'Do you live here?' I ask, as I follow him down a jet-black hall to a large well-lit room that smells strongly of cigarette smoke and alcohol. I notice that Taco has difficulty walking. He drags one foot. Then I see that one of his feet is in a leather slipper and the other in plaster.

'Next door,' he replies, without looking at me. 'When I bought this place, I split it into two.' He goes over to the bar. 'Coffee or tea?'

'Tea, please. Is this the room we're talking about?'

'Yes. Feel free to take a look around. There's no one here yet.'

With my arms crossed rather awkwardly I walk past the sofas

arranged against the walls in a U-shape, with low tables in the middle. Attached to the wall in each alcove is a large photograph measuring at least 30 inches square. They depict women in black-and-white, with only their lips and their lingerie coloured red. Did Leon take them, I wonder? I don't know his work well enough to know for sure. I tear my eyes away from the photos and try to concentrate on the rest of the interior.

The light is bright and shows up imperfections and wear and tear that no one would probably notice in subdued lighting. Black-painted wood with damaged, worn red velvet on the sofas, covered in stains and burn holes. In the middle of the room, which is about the same size as three large living rooms, is a droplet-shaped stage, also black. At the rounded end is a metal pole. The bar is on the left, directly opposite the stage and the wings, which are hidden from view by heavy velvet curtains.

It dawns on me that I'm in a strip joint. I've seen them on TV, and I've heard people talking about them, but it's the first time I've actually been in a club like this. I feel slightly intimidated.

'Well,' says Taco, setting a cup of steaming tea down on the bar, 'do you think you can do something with this?' He looks at me, friendly enough. Yet there's something about the man that puts me on my guard. It could be the tracksuit, combined with the surroundings and the knowledge that he's the owner – but it's not only that.

'That depends on what you want,' I say cautiously, sliding onto a bar stool. I know from All Inclusive that people often get very attached to certain aspects of their decor. They seldom see what's wrong with it. I learned early on to keep my opinion to myself and find out what the customer thinks first.

'I've been staring at this for fifteen years now,' he says. 'It's paid for itself. As far as I'm concerned it can have a complete makeover.'

I put sugar in my tea and start stirring. My hand is trembling slightly. 'How complete?'

'As long as I've still got a stage. And the customers like the alcoves. Of course it needs to be quite dark, that goes without saying.'

I turn round on the bar stool and run my eyes over the room. I get a brainwave: purple. Purple and pink, why not? Strip clubs are kitsch: glitter, lamps, neon lights, flamingos, palm trees . . . anything goes. I suddenly feel enthusiastic. 'I assume you've got a budget in mind?'

He purses his lips. 'I could easily blow a hundred grand on it. But then it'll have to be really swanky.'

A hundred thousand euros. Three times my annual salary. I do my best not to seem too eager, though I seriously doubt if I'm succeeding. 'That should be enough,' I hear myself say.

I brush my hair out of my face, sit on the stage and look around again. I think I've seen enough. The layout of Night View, with every fixed sofa, table, platform, step and power socket, has been mapped out. I need to come back again and take some photos, at least before I make a proper start on the design. There are so many possibilities my head is spinning. Ideas keep popping into my head, from water and fountains to neon tubes. I have doubts about the floor. At present it's covered in red carpet with black designs. I'm strongly inclined to go for plain purple, deep purple even, but I'm afraid the effect might be too sombre over such a large area. That's why I need to go and talk to specialist carpet suppliers who have experience with this. And that's not all: I also need to talk to

companies who can make sofas to measure, lighting special-
ists, and so on.

There's something else. If this commission goes ahead, a lot
of things will have to be ordered. Expensive stuff. With Joost and
Rolf I've arranged for the invoices to be sent straight to them
and they will just pay me an hourly rate. Taco, however, is
assuming I'll handle everything for him. He wants 'as little fuss
as possible'. But he must surely understand that I can't just
advance such huge sums of money?

I take a sip from my glass of water and put it back on the bar.
It's starting to get serious. I'll probably need to register as a company and open another bank account. Am I liable for VAT? I'm
sure I am. And that means I need a accountant, and insurance
too perhaps. God, I haven't a clue where to begin. So many ideas
are flashing through my mind. I've barely begun and already I
don't know what I'm doing anymore. I'd better not say anything
to Taco. I'll talk to Leon about it first this evening. I'm finished
here for today.

Still no sign of Taco. He went into the house an hour ago.

I gather up my things, put them in my briefcase and go outside. Behind the club there is a paved area with a tall white
fence in front of it. A large dark-haired dog starts barking loudly when he sees me. He jumps up and down in his kennel
covered with corrugated sheeting and gets angrier and more
aggressive the closer I get.

'Calm down, boy,' I say, 'I'm welcome here.' The dog continues
regardless.

I walk round a large BMW towards an extension. There are
pink vertical blinds at the windows and to the left of them is a
door. I tap on the windowpane. 'Hello?' I have to shout to be
heard above the barking dog.

Taco opens the door. 'Come in.'

I go in hesitantly, as he orders his dog to be quiet with a short yell. I find myself in a kitchen with a low ceiling that leads straight into the living room. There is a deep-pile wall-to-wall carpet. The furniture is made of glass and tight black leather. In pride of place on the wall there's a plasma screen and below it an impressive music system on a low cabinet. A little white dog makes a beeline for me. Its long hair hangs down in front of its eyes in tousled strands and its whole body shakes as it greets me by wagging its tail. I bend down and stroke the creature. It rolls over and displays its pale, almost hairless belly. Its long hairy tail whisks two and fro over the antique pink carpeting.

'Take a seat. Anything to drink?'

'No, thanks. I just came to say I've finished. Could I drop by tomorrow or the day after to take some photos?'

He shrugs his shoulders. 'As long as it's before six and you ring in advance. Then I'll make sure the gate is open.'

I go a bit further into the living room. The little dog follows at my heels, still demanding my attention.

'Loulou,' explains Taco, slightly embarrassed. 'Belongs to my girlfriend. A spoiled brat.'

'Your girlfriend, you mean?'

His grin reveals perfect white teeth. 'Her too, yes. Just the same.'

In the living room a door stands open. Through the chink I see a glass desk with a huge colour photo of a woman above it, a close-up of her face. She is heavily made up, dramatically, like in old films. Her eyes are ablaze. She's holding a cigarette and is blowing smoke towards the camera. For a moment I think I'm mistaken, but when I take few steps in the direction of the office, I can clearly see that the woman has two different-coloured eyes. I stand there.

'Beautiful, isn't it?'

I turn round in alarm. 'She has heterochromia. And red hair. Like me.'

'Don't you know her then?' He leads the way to his office and holds the door wide open.

I walk a few steps behind him. Then I cross my arms and gaze at the eyes of the unknown woman. They sparkle. 'No. Should I know her?'

'That's Edith.' There is a lot of love in Taco's voice, as he studies the photo intensely from a distance as though he's seeing it for the first time. 'Leon's previous girlfriend. I bought that photo a few years ago – that's how we got to know each other. After her death Leon wanted to buy it back. There are only five of them in circulation and he's destroyed the negatives. Shitty for him but I wouldn't sell. I've become too attached to it. It's not about money.' He glances at me. 'You look a bit like her. Same physique, your eyes.'

I clench my jaw. *Leon's previous girlfriend . . . After her death . . .*

'How did she die?' I ask.

He exhales slowly, as if I'm asking an impossible question. For a moment he says nothing and then his voice adopts a confidential tone. 'I don't know if I'm the one who should be telling you this. But if you're Leon's new girlfriend, you'll find out sooner or later anyway. She committed suicide. He found her in his own bath. She'd been lying dead in it for a couple of days. Fucking awful, if you ask me.'

26

The journey to Leon's house passes me by like a film reel unwinding at speed. I peer through the windscreen into the dark night, registering virtually nothing of my surroundings. I automatically press the brake pedal when a light changes to red, pull away with the rest of the traffic and continue on my way like a zombie.

I can't get over the fact that Leon has kept something so vital from me. It's not hard to imagine that the suicide of your previous girlfriend is not something you can talk about easily. Certainly when you've only known someone for a short time. Inevitably it casts a dark shadow over something that's beautiful and hopeful, but also vulnerable – it's no accident that I haven't breathed a word about John.

But Edith is not the same thing as John. John and Leon are not alike, physically or mentally. But it's impossible to avoid my own resemblance to that woman who stared out at me with her misty eyes from Taco's wall.

Heterochromia is an extremely rare affliction and definitely not an unobtrusive quality. Whenever Leon looks into my eyes, he must see something he lost in a dreadful way. I'm pretty sure it's not me he sees then, but a second chance, an opportunity to regain what he lost. That's what I'm afraid of, afraid that it's true, that I'm a substitute for his dead girlfriend, maybe even a project, someone he wants to transform quite deliberately into her image.

I grip the steering wheel and fight back the tears.

When I turn into his street, I can't help thinking back to the odd remarks made by Debby, the pretty blonde in the gallery in Amsterdam. Leon's manager spoke in riddles too. Their remarks now appear in a very different light. She used the word *startling* when alluding to my resemblance to someone, but didn't say any more because Leon intervened. I can't remember what Richard said exactly, but the gist of it still sticks in my mind, which was that Leon had a secret.

Number twenty-six is the last house in a long avenue just before the asphalt turns into a woodland path. It's one of the lesser known access points to the biggest nature reserve in Brabant. Dunes surrounded by hilly coniferous and deciduous woods and peat bogs. I came here often enough with my parents as a child, it's no more than half an hour as the crow flies from where I used to live. At the weekends you're constantly tripping over families getting a breath of fresh woodland air. Now there's no one. Bare, gnarled branches loom up in my headlights and there's nothing but darkness beyond. Closer by there are horses' hoof prints in the damp woodland soil.

At a walking pace I turn right, between rhododendron bushes into the narrow drive, and park my car behind Leon's new-looking blue Audi. Before I get out I take a good look at the house: a small white bungalow with narrow, vertical windows. Light falls through the curtains onto the moss-covered paving. I stub out my cigarette and push the door open.

Leon has heard me coming. Before I've had a chance to take two steps he appears in the doorway. He's wearing black tracksuit bottoms and a grey long-sleeved T-shirt, and his hair is wet, as if he's just showered or come back from a jog.

I run my hand awkwardly through my hair, brace myself and keep walking. On the threshold I glance at him. In that one second I realise without doubt that this is the man I'm in love with, the man I've quit my job for, exposed myself to and posed nude for. This is the man who's turned my life and my self-image completely upside down.

And he's someone I barely know.

What demons haunt him? What kind of warped mind lurks behind that attractive, overpowering mask of testosterone and self-confidence? The next second, in which we stand looking at each other in silence, motionless, in the soft light of the hall, I curse Taco Sanders. I wish he'd not told me anything, wish I'd never gone there, never seen that photo. I wish I'd remained oblivious, so I could now just enjoy this man, who's looking at me so intensely I want to reach out to him, straight through all the anger and doubts, and hold him.

But I can't.

'What's wrong?' He closes the door behind me.

In the small square room everything is white, black and apple-green. It's clean and sparsely furnished. On the wall are various prints of black-and-white photos and on the wooden floor there is a black woven rug in front of a modern open fire. When I sit down the leather of the two-person sofa creaks under my weight. I rub the apple-green leather restlessly and keep my coat on. 'I went to see Taco.' I clear my throat and force myself to look him in the eye. 'Edith. I saw her photo.'

He raises his eyebrows. 'Were you in his house?'

I ignore his question. 'She looks like me. She looks too much like me.' I shake my head. The anger vanishes and I feel an intense sadness growing in me. 'No coincidence,' I whisper.

He stands in front of me, his hands in his pockets, and

observes me silently from under his eyelashes. Only the taut sinews in his neck betray his alarm.

'Leon . . .' My voice sounds high-pitched and unnatural. 'I've come out of a relationship that was pretty painful for me and I don't feel like getting hurt again. I had the fright of my life.'

'Right,' he says, so faintly I can scarcely hear him. 'It was naive of me to think that . . . I'd have preferred if you'd heard it from me.' He closes his eyes for a moment and then turns to me again. 'Did Taco tell you everything? About how . . . How I . . .' He gives me a searching look. 'I bet he did, didn't he?'

I nod and try to say 'yes', but all I can produce is a sort of squeak.

Leon curses under his breath and runs his hand angrily through his hair.

'It must have been terrible,' I whisper.

He lifts his head and focuses on a spot on the wall behind me. 'She'd been lying there for two days when I found her. Do you know what happens to a body that's been in the water that long?'

He doesn't want an answer, he's not really asking a question, so I say nothing.

'It swells up,' he continues. 'It goes purple for Christ's sake, the skin hangs off as if it's been stripped off. Flayed. The jaw hangs open, the tongue bulges out, swollen. You don't want to know what it smells like. That smell, that vile stench of decay, it hangs around your house for weeks, months. I still smell it sometimes.' He looks straight at me, forcing me to look at him. Then he says, more softly: 'Just like that, when I think I've forgotten about it. Or if I'm brave enough to think I have the right to go on living, to be happy, even though she chose to put an end to it all. And occasionally, Margot, very occasionally, when I wonder if I could have done anything to stop it, listened to her better perhaps, read the signs – then I smell it again. As if I'm in the bathroom again and see that my girl, my everything, is dead. Dead and purple and swollen.' He clenches his fists. 'And there's nothing I can do . . . Nothing at all.'

The tears are running down my face. I don't know why I'm crying. For Leon, for Edith, or for myself. I brush them away angrily. 'Why didn't you tell me?' I whisper. 'You could have told me.'

'When? In London, over the meal? Or in the hotel perhaps, when we were in bed together?' He walks over to me and kneels down, holding my hands and rubbing his thumbs over my fingers. 'Or in Amsterdam, when you were so delighted at getting your first job from Joost and Rolf? Should I have told you then, just before we said goodbye and you threw your arms around my neck to thank me?'

'You could—'

'There was never a good moment. Not so far.'

'But there must be—'

He doesn't even hear me. 'Or should I have told you during the photo shoot? Hey, Margot, before you hear it from anybody else: my previous girlfriend happened to have eyes just like yours. Oh yes. Don't be afraid, she's dead. Suicide . . .' He laughs cheerlessly. 'What would you have done? Be honest.' His eyes are so melancholy it hurts to look at him.

'I don't know,' I say.

'I'll tell you: you'd have packed your things and run off like a bat out of hell.' He shakes his head and tips it back. His fingers make massaging movements in the nape of his neck. 'There was never a good moment.' He gets up and sits down diagonally opposite me in the only other seat in the room, a black arm-

chair, and rubs his eyes. 'It's not something you just tell someone you hardly know. After Edith, everything died. Not only her,
I died too. I didn't want to talk about it with anyone. It's only
recently that I've felt some of that fire in my belly again, and
have been able to think about the future. Partly because of you,
or rather, *precisely* because of you.'

In the car I'd rehearsed this conversation and knew exactly
what I wanted to ask him. But now I really have to concentrate,
keep my wits about me, because my whole being is reaching out
to him and all I want to do is hug him, console him. Kiss him. It
hasn't even occurred to me that Leon might be unsure of my
feelings. Not for a second. The way he seems to take everything
in his stride and the people around him do anything he wishes,
leaves no room for that. But there's nothing dominant about
the man sitting opposite me now, looking at me expectantly. It's
his other face, I realise, that only a few people must know. His
vulnerable, human face.

'She looks like me,' I squeak. 'Your Edith looks like me. And
that frightens me, it frightens me to death. Do you understand
that? Quitting my job this morning, and giving back my company car, and leaving all my insecurities behind, only to
discover . . .' I shake my head wildly '. . . that you're not really
interested in me at all, but in *her*. And that I've never felt so
utterly stupid as . . .'

Leon jumps up out of the armchair and sinks to his knees in
front of me again. He grabs my face with both hands and forces
me to look at him. His eyes are searching my face. 'Listen to me
carefully, because I'm only going to say it once. You don't look
like Edith one little bit.'

'Except that she was overweight like me, had red hair and different-coloured eyes?'

He frowns in irritation. 'I go for well-built women with naturally red hair. So it's not that odd that you caught my eye on the plane. I wondered if the guy next to you was your husband and looked at your hands in the hope that you weren't wearing a wedding ring. When I saw that you had different-coloured eyes, I jumped out of my skin. It just made things complicated. But I didn't want to let you go. You were too beautiful for that.' He snorts. 'I could have gone with you to your hotel, and believe me, that would have happened if I'd wanted it to. But I left it to you to take the initiative. That's the reason I gave you my number. If you rang me, showed an interest in me, then I'd go for it. Then it was meant to be . . . And you rang. Do you know what was nice? You were Margot Heijne right from the start. Not Edith Benschop. You're a completely different person.'

He lets go of my face and gets up. 'Have you got any cigarettes on you?'

I rummage in my pocket for my pack and thrust it at him.

He pulls a cigarette out and lights it up, inhales deeply and slowly exhales the smoke. 'There's one thing I want to know: do you trust me?'

The pain in his eyes touches me deeply. I've grown to care about this man, and the overwhelming emotion right now is shame.

'Because it's simple,' he says, in response to my silence. 'If you think I'm lying, it would be better if we broke it off right now. Now, right here. Because that will be the end of it. Then— '

'Yes,' I say quickly, before he says anything else that makes me wince. 'I trust you.'

He raises an eyebrow. 'Don't just say that for the sake of it. If you want me, you get my past into the bargain . . . I've explained the situation, what happened, and as far as I'm concerned this is the last time we ever talk about Edith. It's over. I want to move on. Take it or leave it.'

'I'm not just saying it, Leon.'

He snorts, staring at a point on the wall above my head.

I think I know now what he's seeing on his own personal horizon, and they're not nice things.

He rubs his upper arm absently. 'I could do with a coffee now. How about you?'

Without waiting for an answer he goes to the kitchen and busies himself with his espresso machine.

I watch him adjusting the handles, pouring water into the machine and getting cups out of the cupboard. It looks so normal, so everyday. But even if he does ordinary things, Leon is far from ordinary. What went wrong between him and Edith, so terribly wrong that she bottled up her rage and frustration so forcefully until it had that devastating, irreversible effect? I can't ask him now.

Leon comes back with two metal cups and puts one down in front of me.

Only now do I notice that my shoulders have been hunched the whole time. They're totally rigid. I breathe deeply and relax them. Then I take my coat off.

For minutes on end we say nothing. I look at the cigarette smoke spiralling up to the ceiling.

Leon breaks the silence. 'And I had such lovely plans for this evening . . .' He softly clicks his tongue.

I burst out laughing, but don't know why. It must be to release the tension, the rush of emotions. I put my hand to my mouth and can't stop.

The corners of Leon's mouth curl up. Very gradually. Little

wrinkles appear around his eyes. 'Cow,' he says. 'You're laughing at me.'

I put my hands up. 'Sorry. It's got nothing to do with you. I suddenly thought of Taco. He looks just like one of those perma-tanned crooners. How on earth did you meet him? Or is that something I'd rather not know?'

He slides his hand under his T-shirt and rubs his midriff. His grin broadens. 'Taco likes women and photography. So if, as in his exceptional case, you've got too much dirty money burning a hole in your pocket, it's only natural you're going to find your way to my door sooner or later.'

'Did you take the photos in his, er . . .'

'Brothel, you mean?'

'Is that what it is then?'

'No. It's a respectable strip club that a lot of businessmen go to. Innocent. I wouldn't have sent you there otherwise.'

'Did you take those photos of those women?

'Yes. I was commissioned. They're girls who work or have worked for him. The idea was to give the photos as end-of-year presents and that did happen, but eventually they found their way into the bar as well.'

'I liked them.'

He purses his lips briefly. 'They're not bad, but I wouldn't say they're fit to hang in a gallery. Tell me, have you eaten?'

I shake my head.

Leon grabs his mobile off the table. 'Pizza?'

'That's fine . . . Quattro stagioni, if they've got it.'

'They've got that everywhere.' He slides his hand under his shirt again, revealing a patch of his skin. That body under the T-shirt that I've barely had the chance to discover yet. He looks at me while he orders the food. His mouth is smiling, but not his eyes. They're deadly serious and pin me to the sofa. No more jokes, they're telling me. No confessions, no Edith, no pain. His mind is on completely different things. He's focusing.

To mask my unease I take a sip of coffee, but the cup is empty.

What's he brooding about? The uncertain prospect of him knowing exactly what's about to happen and me groping in the dark – the very thought immediately sets off a chain reaction of tingling and contractions in my body. A glance, a few words, a slight inflection in his voice – no more than that, and I know I can't win.

Leon puts the phone back on the table, and just as I think he's going to sink into his armchair and keep me at arm's length with his words, he says: 'Come here.'

To my annoyance his simple remark only raises questions in my mind. How? I wonder feverishly. Walking upright, or crawling across the floor? Seductively, or normally? The question 'how?' is on the tip of my tongue, ready to be spoken, with only fear holding me back – the fear that it might not be what he wants, and the fear of my own readiness to act on his instructions. Yes, I'll crawl to him if that's his wish; it turns me on more than I thought possible. What in heaven's name is happening to me? Who is this person who's taken control of my body, this person, until recently a complete stranger, who's penetrated every fibre of my body and my brain, making me do all this – and *willingly*?

The confusion must be written across my face.

'I want to cuddle you,' he says.

I get up, aware of every movement I make, walk over to him and stand in front of him, expectantly.

His hands glide over my waist and come to rest on my hips.

They gently massage my flesh and increase the pressure, pull me downwards so that I find myself sitting astride him.

He moves over a little and places his outspread hands on my buttocks. He pushes his pelvis against me. 'You should have put a skirt on,' he mutters, burying his face in my neck and leaving a trail of kisses. 'That black thing you had on in London. That gave me a few angles at least.'

'I thought you just wanted a cuddle.'

His face is now level with my breasts. I push them forwards instinctively.

Leon pulls down the narrow zip of my sleeveless top. Slowly, without rushing, he unhooks the fastener on my bra and peels my top and bra from my arms. His breath brushes my naked skin and I shiver. Between my legs his excitement is tangible. So close. I have to control myself to stay still, I want to mount him. There's too much material between us.

'I want to take things easy with you,' he whispers.

'There's no need.' Cautiously I start moving, rocking slowly forward and back again. 'I don't want to take it easy.'

'Take those trousers off.'

I stand up, shaky and giddy, unbutton my jeans and put my thumbs behind the waistband, taking my thong with them in a single movement. Then I bend down to take off my socks. While I'm doing this he strokes the inside of my legs and then moves his hands further up. When I look up, and try to crawl back onto his lap, he stops me.

'We'll do this my way.'

He holds my hand and takes me to an adjacent room. There's a double bed, neatly made up with a dark plain cover. The floor feels cool beneath my bare feet.

Leon lets go of me and pulls the door shut behind us.

Suddenly it's dark, the room is submerged in shades of grey. The only light enters through the door frame, a luminous right angle.

'Lie down on the bed.'

A shiver creeps up my spine. Breathlessly I ask: 'How?'

27

They went for 'green', design number two. Joost and Rolf were wildly enthusiastic about the tree trunks and just couldn't get over my idea for jazzing up the design with a 3D representation of Ce Truc – that thing, or better, the little monster – subtly repeated throughout the restaurant. It already existed, Rolf the photographer had designed it, but it was only featured on menus and napkins. Now it's going to play a bigger role. Every bar or restaurant calling itself The Angel is full of pictures and statues of angels, so why can't a restaurant called That Thing simply have its own little things? The idea is good but the execution will take time. I can't even begin to find all the companies I need off the top of my head – how do you source half tree trunks, for example, or find someone to make little monsters for a reasonable price? Still, I have every confidence that a year or so down the line I'll have a reliable network of regular suppliers.

Overseeing Ce Truc and designing a brand spanking new interior for Night View is extremely intensive work, but it pumps me full of new energy – and ideas, crazy, exciting ideas I hope to put into practice someday. It's not just the new challenge and the completely different schedule that are making me feel better than ever. At the same time it seems as if I'm predominantly meeting people with unconventional ideas. The conservative Frits Leenders types from my All Inclusive days appear to be extinct. Yet all these new people I've met were around long before I became aware of them. Strange really, that worlds can exist alongside each other, and can even be intertwined, without really coming into contact with one another.

'Are you staying for dinner?' calls Joost from the kitchen. He's been working in there for a bit while I make calls to suppliers. I want to try to set everything up so that the actual work can be finished in five or, at the most, six working days. Then the restaurant will only have to close for a week.

'I'd be happy to cook something for you,' he continues. 'Do you like fish?'

'That's sweet of you, but I've arranged to meet someone and I'm a bit late.'

Joost comes out of the kitchen carrying a checked tea towel he's using to dry his fingers. His long blond hair is in a ponytail half way down his back and he's wearing a white apron covered in splashes. 'Will you be in again tomorrow?'

'No, tomorrow I have to go to Brabant, to the workshop where they're making the Truc monsters, for a start.' I run through my diary in my mind. 'Then to a carpet manufacturer, and back to Amsterdam after that for the upholsterer.'

Joost drops his head onto one shoulder and then the other, back and forth, as if it were on a spring. 'Girlfriend, you're busy. Far too busy.'

'Don't be silly.' I say. 'I'm loving it. I'll call you, OK?'

'Are you going to manage?'

'Course I am,' I say, with the door handle already in my hand. 'We'll be starting work in three or four weeks.'

I go outside and wrap my coat round me. A biting wind is whistling past the canal-side buildings and blows my hair in all directions.

Last week, after spending the night with Leon in his bungalow, I went with him to Amsterdam. We're now living together
more or less. He has a loft on the top floor of an old warehouse,
right on the River IJ and with high windows which I, unlike
Leon, can only look out of if I stand on tiptoe. Access is by lift
and the ceiling must be twenty feet with the original metal roof
construction still visible. The walls are built of large brown
bricks, and whole sections of damaged wall have been covered
over with a rough layer of cement. Nevertheless it's become a
real living space. There are rugs on the stone floor, modern
paintings on the walls and three huge sofas in an oriental fabric, with thick loose cushions you sink right into. You see
everything the moment you enter: the living area, the big metal
bed and the kitchen decorated in chrome, wood and stone. Only
the bathroom is partitioned off from the rest by a plastered
wall. The half-sunken bath is big enough for three people. When
Leon showed me the bathroom he didn't behave any differently
than usual. For my part I tried not to show that it gave me the
creeps. I don't dare ask him if he moved after Edith's death. I
expect so. But to be on the safe side I avoid the bathroom as
much as possible for now.

I push the café door open. It's warm and filled with smoke.
Richard is not here yet, so I take a table by the window and open
my new attaché case to check my papers again. Yesterday Leon's
manager offered to go through my business plan with me and give
me a helping hand. It was music to my ears. I'm now a freelance
entrepreneur, but I've got no experience of the business side of it.
To be honest, I couldn't care less about it, but I understand as well
as the next person that I have to keep things in order.

When a waiter appears next to me, I look up from my papers
with a start. 'Cappuccino, please.'

'Shall I bring the menu?'

'No, no need. Thanks.'

The man disappears again.

My mobile vibrates. I slide it open without looking at it, half assuming it's Richard saying he'll be coming later.

'Margot?'

'Hello. It's me.'

I frown. 'Sorry, who's this?'

'Er, John.'

The waiter puts down the cappuccino and leaves the bill under a vase of artificial flowers.

'John,' I repeat curtly.

He clears his throat. 'I was tidying up over the weekend and found a whole lot of stuff that belongs to you. I was going to drop it off yesterday evening, but no one opened the door. You weren't home.'

'Maybe so.'

'Will you be home this evening?'

'No.'

'Later this week then? Or next weekend?'

'Probably not.'

'Not home as in not home, or not home for me?'

Don't flatter yourself. 'I'm in Amsterdam at the moment.'

'Have you got a fair or something?'

'No, I live here now. More or less.' Although Leon thinks I should sell my flat – which is just a ball and chain in his opinion – I'm not going to. Things are all moving very fast and I want to keep an escape route – a place of my own I can retreat to. Leon is away a lot. Richard drags him halfway round Europe for lucrative assignments. The idea of having to hang around in Leon's loft for days on end when he's not there doesn't appeal to me much.

'Wow,' John sounds surprised.

'I've got a new boyfriend.' I could kick myself, but there, I've said it.

'Wow,' he repeats, clearing his throat again. 'Well . . . what shall I do with that stuff? That red Samsonite case, a pile of CDs, I found more books of yours in the loft, and your belt, the wide one, you know? A file full of old school stuff, reports and things.'

'I thought they were still at Mum and Dad's.'

'No, we took them with us when they cleared out your room. Have you forgotten?'

It starts coming back to me. That was the time when our relationship was already going downhill pretty fast. The box stood in the hall for a week, until John put it in the loft. 'Yes. Now I remember.'

'So?' he asks.

This is a pain. I can hardly expect him to drop my stuff off at my parents' house. That's out of the question. Meeting John is definitely not high on my list of priorities, but I would like to have my school reports back. And if I'm honest: part of me is curious. It's months since I've seen John and now he's on the telephone, it doesn't upset me. His voice just sounds pleasantly familiar. How will I react when I see him?

Someone is standing by my table. I look up. It's Richard. He puts his hand up and squeezes his eyes shut as a signal that it's no problem as far as he's concerned if I continue my phonecall.

'Margot? Are you still there?'

'Yes, I'm still here. I had to think for a moment. Tomorrow I have to see a client and I could pick up my things from your place after that.'

'What time?'

'Wait a sec.' I search my case and find my diary. It's filling up nicely. 'About twelve?'

'I've got to work, but I can come home for a bit during the day.'

'You don't have to come home from work specially. We can arrange something in the next week or so if that suits you better.'

'No, tomorrow's fine. I'll sort something out.'

'Great. See you tomorrow then. Bye John.' I end the call before he can say anything else.

'Wonderful things, mobiles, aren't they?' Richard comments. 'You don't get a moment's peace.'

We get up at the same time to greet each other. He kisses me on the cheek and gives my back a friendly rub.

'It was my ex,' I confide. 'He's still got some of my stuff. I'm going to fetch it tomorrow.'

'I see,' he says absently, putting a file on the table and pushing it towards me. 'I've worked out a plan for you. You're going to be a lot busier in the near future.'

I leaf through the file of bound laser-printed A4 sheets. It contains an action plan and addresses, the kinds of things I should be doing. The information is specifically tailored to my situation. 'I can't thank you enough, Richard. That's really very sweet of you, doing that for me just like that.'

He waves his hand as if brushing off a fly. 'I'm just glad I can help you. Everyone's happy that Leon's got some fun back in his life. It was about bloody time.'

It's on the tip of my tongue to ask Richard about Edith. Was she mentally ill and was her suicide unavoidable, or could Leon have prevented it? What sort of relationship did they have, what kind of woman was Edith? What was she interested in? Richard knows all that. He knew her and should be able to tell me everything. But I don't ask. Richard and Leon have known each other for a long time and are very close. If I interrogate him about Edith, there's a good chance he'll tell Leon.

A whole hour passes, in which Richard explains the main points of action. I have to find a slot in tomorrow's overfull diary to go to the Chamber of Commerce. I have to register my new business and fill in a form for the tax authorities. I need to think up a company name and design headed notepaper for invoices. From now on all receipts must be kept: for food and drink, paper, printer cartridges etcetera. The list seems to go on and on.

'But having said all that,' says Richard, gathering up his things and stuffing them into his briefcase, 'creative spirits shouldn't be burdened with this wretched stuff. You should focus as far as possible on things you're good at and enjoy doing. You'll earn most in the long run that way. All the hours you put into administration are essentially wasted time, which just saps your energy and stops you generating turnover. So my advice is: save all receipts, mileage records and invoices in an old-fashioned shoebox and take it to your accountant every three months. Let him sort it out: that's his job.'

I like the sound of the shoebox concept. 'That really *would* be great.'

'Have you got an accountant yet?'

'No. I don't know any.'

'Do you mind having someone you know sort out your business matters?'

'I don't think it makes much difference.'

'My partner Marianne was an accountant for years, but since

having Lola she's been working from home. She's doesn't charge that much, she likes the work and she's good.' He digs a card out of the inside pocket of his jacket and pushes it towards me. 'Call her this week to arrange a chat.'

28

It's almost twelve-thirty by the time I park the car on the drive of the semi-detached house which is only two districts away from where my parents live.

I should be feeling tense at least, slightly uneasy perhaps, or curious at any rate, but funnily enough I don't feel anything of the sort. Maybe it's because I haven't been able to think about it today. I simply haven't had time. The only thing that crosses my mind as I get out is that I can't stay much more than a quarter of an hour if I don't want to jeopardise my schedule for the whole day.

Daily life is beginning to look more and more like a roaring express train driven by a deranged driver sending it hurtling from station to station. Compared with my new schedule, working for All Inclusive was like a leisurely cruise down the Rhine.

This morning there was an accident near Utrecht and I crawled along for almost an hour, an hour I spent as productively as possible by ringing all sorts of people, including Marianne. I can go and see her this afternoon. Her voice sounded decisive, a bit posh even, but she seemed really nice all the same.

The long drive to Brabant gave me the chance to think about yesterday's conversation with Richard. He made me promise in future to charge a fixed hourly rate considerably higher than what I quoted Joost and Rolf. According to him I should have invoices sent direct to the client, keeping things manageable and minimising the risk. The hourly rate he suggested is much higher than I'm used to, but he urged me to stick to it. I'm no longer making pension contributions and I can't rely on a reasonable income on benefits. In addition I'm going to have to turn a considerable part of my income over to the taxman. But above all, the fact is good creative people simply cost money – that's what Richard impressed on me: in the circles he moves in people are used to high hourly rates. Indeed it serves as a recommendation, because someone who's good is in demand and will therefore automatically charge more. According to him I need to start giving out that impression, and believe in it. If I can, the clients I'm aiming for will follow as a matter of course. He was so certain about that that I thought it better not to tell him I found it rather difficult to look successful and sought-after while driving up in a six-year-old dodgem.

John has lost weight. That's the first thing I notice. In recent years he was well on his way to developing a middle-aged paunch, but there's no trace of that now. His light pink shirt lies flat above the belt of his blue trousers. We bought those in town together with a sports jacket and two shirts, and got a silk tie thrown in for free. He was already having an affair with Mieke then, though I didn't know it at the time.

'Come in,' he says, holding the door wide open. 'You're looking good.'

I can't say the same for him. His cheeks are sunken and there are dark shadows under his eyes. He's clean-shaven at least and his tousled dark blond hair has been gelled into place.

I've wondered often enough how I would feel if I were back in our old house. Now I'm there it just seems familiar, no longer hostile. There's still a hole in the panelling next to the TV. John promised me at least ten times that he would mend it, but something 'important' kept getting in the way.

He goes straight into the kitchen and comes back with two dark-red mugs I don't recognise: they must be new. John puts them on the table by the window and stands there rather ill at ease. 'I'd like to apologise,' he mumbles, without looking at me. 'I've been an unbelievable bastard.'

'It's OK,' I say flatly, to discourage him.

'Are you happy with that new boyfriend of yours? Is it serious?'

I nod. 'Yes and yes. Where's my stuff?'

'Aren't you going to drink your coffee first?'

'I haven't got much time,' I say, but sit down anyway and stir the coffee. It's already got milk and sugar in it.

'That tin can outside, is that a courtesy car from the garage?'

'No, I've quit my job. And it's a great car.'

He raises his eyebrows in disbelief. 'I didn't know that. What are you doing now then?'

'I've gone freelance.'

'Freelance what?'

'Stylist. I design restaurants and things like that.'

The distance between John's eyes and eyebrows is growing all the time. 'And is it going OK?'

'So far, yes. At the moment I'm working on a restaurant in the centre of Amsterdam. If everything works out, I'll be moving on to a nightclub.'

John chews on his cheek and looks at me analytically. 'That new boyfriend of yours, do I know him by any chance?'

'No. I don't think so, but his name might mean something to you: Leon Wagner. He's an art photographer. And quite successful too.'

'Art photographer . . . where did you dig him up from?'

'In London.'

'Oh yes, of course. Your mother told me you'd been to London.' His face clouds over. 'Sorry for calling on your parents. I didn't realise for a moment that—'

'I didn't come here to talk, John.' I force myself to take big gulps to finish the coffee quicker.

He chuckles joylessly. 'Recently I've become persona non grata at your parents' house. It really upset you, your father said. Do you know how odd that is, not being able to go there anymore. I went there more often than to my own mother's flat.'

I give him a piercing look. 'I told you I wasn't here to talk.'

The enlarged holiday snap that used to hang above the TV has gone. It was taken in Crete, three years ago. We were both in it, John tanned and me sunburned, laughing at the camera. In the background you could see a little harbour, white houses and a clear blue sky above.

John follows my gaze. 'It's in the loft.'

I shrug my shoulders. 'It's your house now.'

'Yes,' he says softly, and plays with the spoon in his coffee. 'I know.'

I down the last of the coffee and make a show of looking at my watch. 'OK, I must be off. Where's the stuff?'

'In my car.'

We go outside and John transfers the two small boxes – it's not much – to my boot. They only just fit.

Before I have the chance to get in, he suddenly grabs my arm. I look in astonishment at his hand and then at his face. 'Margot . . . I want to say that if you ever need someone, or . . . well, just want a chat one evening, my door's always open.' He lets go of my arm. 'I miss you.'

I don't respond. He should have said this months ago, and then I'd have been like putty in his hands. Now it's too late. I get behind the wheel, start the car and wind down the window.

John is still standing next to my car with his hand on the roof. 'Give my regards to Mieke,' I say, and drive off.

IX

After Edith, because I make a clear division between the degree of awareness I had before and afterwards, I started to see not only myself, but other people with different eyes.

I've begun to pay even more attention to the people I come into contact with during the day. Take a gallery owner, a cashier, a postman, yes, even my snooty neighbour: however different their lives may appear at first glance, for me there's absolutely no distinction any longer, because basically there is no distinction. Everyone is vulnerable, and everything can be destroyed.

But not everyone is worthy of my undivided attention.

I can't help admitting that my premature fantasy regarding Margot Heijne is taking ever more concrete form. You could picture that remarkable process as separate images, snatches of movements, facial expressions, sounds, which steadily grow into coherent scenes that slowly, very gradually, merge into one beautiful, glorious, orgiastic final shot.

For a long time that was enough, but Edith's murder has changed everything. However overpowering and impressive that mental film may be, it cuts a sorry figure – I know that now – compared with the real-life version.

Fantasising is not sufficient. Not anymore.

Yet for now I'm going to have to content myself with that. I owe that to myself and my values.

She hasn't done anything wrong yet. Her death would serve no greater purpose.

But that can always change.

29

Marianne is four or five years older than me and has thin, naturally curly blond hair that she wears up. Her face is wreathed
with rebellious hairs that refuse to be caught. She reminds me
of a china doll: her skin is the same colour and she has delicate
features. 'Shoe box?' she asks.

'That's what Richard said, and it seemed quite handy. I'm not
such a whiz at administration.'

'It's up to you, but if I sort everything out for you it'll cost
more.'

I've been sitting for a quarter of an hour in Marianne's office,
a sort of conservatory off the living room. Her glass desk stands
in the middle of the room, and she works at a white laptop. Her
eighteen-month-old daughter Lola is within earshot, playing
with blocks in the living room.

'Richard said I could better spend my time designing.
Contracting out the administration would pay for itself.'

'There are carthorses and racehorses.'

'Sorry,' I say, 'I didn't mean to . . .'

She shakes her head. 'Don't worry. It's something between
Richard and me. I don't want to burden you with that.' She gets
up abruptly. 'I haven't offered you anything to drink yet. I get so
few visitors I've forgotten how to be a good hostess. What can I
get you?'

'I don't really mind. Whatever you have.'

'There's a bottle of wine open. Red.'

'Then I'll join you.'

Marianne disappears from view. It gives me the chance to have a good look round. Leon's manager and his partner live in a modern house north of Amsterdam. It's completely detached and is accessed via a narrow private bridge. The office-cum-conservatory looks out over green meadows, pollard willows and a windmill. The sky stretches as far as you can see. A wonderful spot.

The interior of the house is as austere and impersonal as the surroundings are idyllic. One of the two, or maybe both of them, must have a great liking for minimalism. The only furniture there is has an immediate function and everything is extremely tidy. The walls and the ceiling are white and there is beige carpeting. It looks like a showroom. Lola crows and crawls in pursuit of a sinewy Siamese cat, which accelerates when it realises the child is after its tail, and jumps out of reach onto a white sideboard.

Marianne comes back with two huge glasses a quarter full of red wine. She puts one down in front of me and remains standing as she takes a sip. Only now do I notice that Marianne's clothes are a perfect match for her interior. She is wearing beige trousers, and a white starched blouse with a turned-up collar.

'Richard told me you're an accountant.'

'I worked at Deloitte. When I got pregnant with Lola we had to make a choice.' She looks straight at me. Her narrow nose is a little crooked, the only discrepancy in her otherwise perfect face. 'So I stayed home. I only recently started working again.' Then she looks outside, at the meadows. 'We used to live in Amsterdam, and there was always something to do. Here you could fire a cannon and no one would hear.'

'It is very beautiful, though,' I say. 'Rural. There aren't many places like this left.'

She sits down on her office chair and has another sip of wine. 'Grass and cows – I couldn't care less about either.'

'Why don't you move then?'

She shrugs her shoulders. 'Richard loves coming home to peaceful surroundings. His work is very hectic. He chills out here.'

'But he's away a lot, and you're here . . . the whole time.'

She leans towards me confidentially. 'He doesn't sense that at all. That's just how he is. So many men are like that.' She's silent for a moment. 'Except Leon.'

I'm suddenly on the alert. 'Why's that?'

'Leon's a different kind of man,' she says, and her eyes soften. 'Different from the others.'

'I don't quite follow you.'

She puts the glass down on the desk. 'I'm chattering too much. That's what happens when you're alone all day. Well, not completely alone.' She means Lola, who has now pulled herself up by holding onto to the sideboard and crows all the while as she grabs at the Siamese cat's tail.

'You can't have an adult conversation with Lola,' I say. 'Can't you do something, voluntary work, for example?'

'Not while Lola's still at home. Richard doesn't want me to put her in a nursery.'

'Why not?'

'He grew up mainly in care and it's given him an aversion to institutions. At any rate he doesn't want his daughter to be "put away" as he calls it.'

I look at Lola and at her mother. I don't have any children, but I was a child once, and unless I'm very much mistaken Lola would be far better off with playmates of the same age, even if only for a few hours a week, with a happier mother as a bonus. 'Haven't you got any friends here?'

'Not yet.'

I start feeling rather sorry for this beautiful woman with her perfect doll's face and her gruesomely perfect house. I down the rest of the wine in one and put the glass back on the desk. 'I've got to dash,' I say. 'It's getting dark.'

'Leon's waiting for you,' she adds, almost breathlessly. 'What have you got planned for this evening?'

I put on a rather forced smile. 'Nothing special, a bite to eat. Then sleep, I'm shattered.'

'Sleep? With Leon around? I find that difficult to believe.'

I smile again, but it's getting harder to make it look genuine. 'Well, I'll be going then.'

Marianne follows me, picking Lola off the ground. She waves me off as I drive over the wooden bridge and is still standing in the doorway as I turn onto the road.

A feeling of oppression lingers with me as I park the car along the canal side and rummage in my jacket pocket for Leon's spare keys. The river flows past the concrete banks and laps softly against the wooden supports. It's grown dark. Exhaustion is pulsing through me and I'm ready for a cup of coffee and something to eat. In the lift to the top floor I wonder if Leon has cooked something. Silly idea. If Leon is hungry, he reaches for his mobile without thinking. He has speed-dial numbers for every takeaway restaurant.

I close the door behind me, put my briefcase on the floor and hang my coat on the hook by the door. Inside it's warm and the room is sparsely lit.

Leon is stretched out on the sofa. He doesn't react. From here I can see only the crown of his head and his bare feet, which are resting on the other arm. The TV is switched to a news channel and there's an ashtray on the coffee table. Next to it is a packet of Gauloises. I'm a bad influence on him.

I approach him from behind and kiss him on the head. Thick, smooth hair that smells wonderful.

He extends his arm lazily. Without taking his eyes off the TV he rubs my tights. 'Take those off.'

'What thing?'

He pulls at the elasticated material of the tights. 'These.'

I unzip my boots, take them off and wriggle out of the tights, wondering whether to take my thong off as well.

'Just those tights and your thong,' he mumbles. 'Keep the rest on.'

'My boots too?'

'Why not. There's nothing wrong with them.'

I take my thong off, roll them up in my top and put the bundle in a heap behind the sofa. Then I step back into my boots and zip them up.

'Come here.'

Again his hand slides along my legs, higher. His fingers find the way as if by themselves, probing and compelling. 'What were you doing at your ex's place?'

I look up, but his eyes are still focused steadily on the TV.

'Collecting my . . . things. He still had stuff of mine, from school.'

'Why didn't you tell me?' His fingers slip inside, two, three.

I give a moan and my legs start trembling frantically. I can't possibly stay standing; if I tried I'd sink to my knees. Jerkily I try to support myself on the arm of the sofa.

'Well?' he insists.

'Because . . . because I didn't think it was important.'

In. Out. In. Out. 'We could have gone together.'

'I can . . .' I moan '. . . think of nicer things we could do together.'

'Oh yes?' He gets off the sofa and stands behind me, moving my hair aside and licking upwards along my neck, in the direction of my ear. 'You know what they say about exes,' he whispers.

I roll my head to the side so that he can reach it better. 'Is Richard your personal spy or what?'

'Perhaps.' He yanks my skirt up till it gets caught round my hips and won't go any further.

'John's harmless,' I moan.

'Oh really?' He puts his hands possessively on my breasts and pulls my bra up with one quick tug. 'He rings up with a transparent excuse and you rush to meet him the very next day . . . How harmless does that sound?'

'Leon . . .' I can't think anymore, it's just impossible. Leon's hands are everywhere, his mouth on my neck, the belt of his jeans scratching my bare skin. 'There's nothing going on,' I manage to say.

Suddenly he stops his caresses and grabs my hair. Not so hard that it hurts, but I have to tilt my head back to ease the pressure. He steers me ahead of him round to the back of the sofa and pushes me forward, so that my upper body lands on the wide back and the cushions. I close my eyes and bury my face in the thick cushion, claw at the fabric and enjoy his teasing caresses along my spine. His fingers follow the curve of my neck down to the crevice between my buttocks and I shiver.

He moves my legs further apart with his knee. 'You're not

going to see that prick anymore,' he says, with his mouth close to my ear, still holding my hair tight. 'Promise me.'

'I promise,' I whisper.

For a second, in a moment of confusion when I lose all sense of space and time, I assume he's putting his fingers inside me again, simply because I've never been any closer to him, and he has never let our physical contact go beyond that. But then it dawns on me that one hand is still gripping my hair and the other is round my hip, under my skirt, while the pressure between my legs is building slowly but surely.

'How much do you want this?'

I can scarcely speak. 'Very much,' I gasp. 'So much.'

'Beg for it.'

'Do it, Leon. Now . . . Please. Fuck me.'

30

'Apple pie or cheesecake?'

'Er, apple pie would be fine,' I say.

My mother is wearing a new glittery dress with a kind of stole. I suspect she bought it to wear at Christmas but just couldn't leave it hanging in the wardrobe. And she's been to the hairdresser's. Her red hair has been cut a little shorter and blow-dried into shape. Anyway, today's also a special occasion: her sixty-second birthday.

The living room is packed with family and friends. A grey veil of cigarette smoke is gathering up on the ceiling. I'm doing my best to maintain it by lighting up one cigarette after another. As per usual all the men have gathered round the dining table on the garden side and the women are sitting on the other side of the room.

I'm sitting on a kitchen chair against the wall beneath the grandfather clock, and looking at the women who have installed themselves on the three-piece suite, bags at their feet, packets of cigarettes, cups of coffee and glasses of soft drinks and wine on the oak coffee table. Auntie Agatha is there, my mother's sister, and their neighbour Anneke with her daughter Charlotte. She's slightly younger than me and calls my mother 'auntie', since the families have grown so close over the years they've lived next door to each other. The one with most to say for herself as usual is Els, a childhood friend of my mother's.

Next to her is her complete opposite in every way, my mother's mother, my last surviving granny. She's sitting quietly in a corner of the sofa listening to the conversations, rolling a cigarette between her parchment fingers. It's painful to see how this is getting harder and harder for her. My father collected her from the old people's home earlier today.

Anne sits next to me, in a denim jacket and with her hair up. Bas has climbed onto her lap. He leans against her with his thumb in his mouth, waggling his legs. His big brother Thomas is playing upstairs in my old room. After I moved in with John it was turned into a playroom for the grandchildren, full of Dick's and my old toys. All that's left is my bed. Thomas thinks it's just like a museum, and I suppose he's right.

Laughter rises from the men's table. Their conversations have scarcely changed over the years and still relate to the magic quartet of cars, work, politics and football. There are empty beer bottles on the table beneath the yellow lamplight, and bowls of peanuts and cubed cheese that hands are constantly dipping in to.

'Hey, haven't you just been to London?' Anneke asks.

'That's right.'

'Did you see Buckingham Palace and Tower Bridge?'

I shake my head. 'No, actually I spent most of my time shopping.'

'Pick up anything nice?'

'Yes, a new skirt. And some lingerie.'

She giggles.

'And I visited an art gallery,' I blurt out. 'There was a photo exhibition on . . . pain. All kinds of pain, pictured through the eyes of the . . .'

She raises her eyebrows. 'Pain?'

I nod.

'Gosh.' She turns away and grabs for a piece of cheese, after which she strikes up a conversation with Charlotte, who's sitting next to her.

'Margot, I was wondering if you'd heard from John at all.' The question comes from Auntie Agatha, her voice sounds shrill and harsh and suddenly all eyes are on me.

'No,' I say abruptly, hoping she'll leave it at that.

My mother puts a piece of apple cake down on the coffee table in front of me with a freshly washed-up fork. It's still wet.

'Is he still with that . . . what's her name again, that friend of yours, that Mieke?' Auntie Agatha persists.

'I've no idea,' I say truthfully, and continue more sharply: 'And I couldn't care less. If you don't mind.'

'I saw him on Saturday at the Smithy, but he didn't have a woman with him,' Anneke remarks to Agatha. 'He didn't look good. Scruffy.' She nods and frowns, as if to say: he had it coming.

'Oh, don't worry, dear,' cackles Els at me, completely oblivious to the possibility that John may be a closed chapter. 'Better for something like that to happen now rather than when you've got kids. Then you've really got problems. A mountain, not a molehill, shall we say.'

Everyone thinks the same, judging by the nods of agreement in the women's group. A discussion ensues about unfaithful husbands, which segues into news of Uncle Anton. My father's brother is in hospital and yesterday had his third operation in the space of a few weeks.

'Margot?' My mother is standing by the bar in the kitchen and beckons me.

I put my plate back on the coffee table and go over to her. Out of sight of everyone she asks me conspiratorially: 'You haven't told me what you were doing in Amsterdam.'

I don't want to tell her that I've quit my job. 'I've got a new boyfriend. He lives there.'

She squeezes my arm hard enough to break it 'How marvellous. Why didn't you bring him with you?'

I look past her into the room. I can't imagine Leon here, in the midst of my family, sitting drinking beer from a bottle at the men's table and joining in the talk about the pros and cons of a station wagon. 'He couldn't make it tonight.'

'What does he do?'

'He's a photographer. An art photographer.'

She frowns. 'Does it pay?'

'Very well actually, Mum.'

'Art photographer,' she repeats. Then she looks up again. 'What's his name?'

'Leon. Leon Wagner.'

'Beautiful name.'

'He's a beautiful man.'

'Erica? Is there any more beer in the shed?' I hear my father shout.

My mother is already on her way to the back door and changes into her casual shoes.

I stop her. 'I'll go and get some, if you'd like to put your feet up for a bit. You've been running around all evening.'

'But I like it,' she says sincerely. 'It's lovely to have everyone here. And I'm even happier you're here too. I'm really curious about your new boyfriend. Will you bring him over sometime?'

'Of course,' I say, without much enthusiasm.

'Can I tell your father?'

'Dad, yes, but wait a bit with the others. It's all very early days.'

I go outside, switch on the shed light and take out as many

bottles of beer as I can carry from the crates under the workbench. On my way back I see everyone sitting there through the large slightly steamed-up window. Out here their voices are muffled. I've known most of them all my life. They're family, even though not all of them are strictly related. I know their backgrounds and who does or doesn't get on with whom. I've talked to them about their hobbies and their frustrations. I was present at the important events in their lives and they were present at mine.

These are my roots, I suddenly realise. My origins. My nest. These people have, to a large extent, shaped my cultural views, my standards and values and how I see the world – or how I saw it until recently. Why do they now seem like complete strangers to me?

31

I'm sitting at Leon's desk. My eyes have almost gone square from staring at the computer screen and I feel stiff from sitting still for hours on end. Next to me is a notepad that is slowly but surely filling up with phone numbers, prices and contacts. I've been working all day on the design for Night View. This afternoon I contacted the owner of a lighting company that can supply starry skies for ceilings and walls. He has worked with a small company in the past that makes custom ceilings, partitions and stages, and so he'd prefer to do this job with them. Through them in turn I made contact with a one-man business that can make anything to order in the way of neon lighting. There's going to be neon along all platforms and staircases so that no one need break their neck when the main lighting is turned off during the shows and customers can easily find their way to the toilets and bar. In addition I want to move the erotic photographs from the alcoves to the hall, which at present is rather dull. Arranged in rows and columns they will take up almost a complete wall. The idea is to print the photos on shallow light boxes, with the sections that are currently red coloured bright pink – an updated wink at the old days.

This morning I went through the design for Taco with Leon, because I was a bit worried about his photos. My reticence was unnecessary: Leon had no problem with them appearing in a different form. He called his commissioned work uninspired production-line pieces and the customers could light a fire with them for all he cared – he wouldn't lose a moment's sleep over it. I was a bit shocked at the harshness in his voice, mainly because he takes photographs on commission almost every day.

I look at my watch. Quarter to eight. Leon thought he'd be home around eight and said he'd bring something to eat. Only when I get up from the leather office chair do I realise how stiff my muscles are. I arch my back, stretch and then turn on a few lights. In the bathroom I brush my teeth and glance at the bath. The enormous bath and I still have a difficult relationship. It looks luxurious and inviting enough; there's a big chrome knob on the side to make the water bubble, and special recesses where you can rest your arms and head. But I wouldn't dream of having a bath when I'm alone, an irrational fear since I found out last week that Leon has only lived here for eight months. So Edith can't have lain in this tub.

I undress and turn on the shower tap. When I catch sight of my naked reflection in the mirror, I realise I no longer lower my eyes as I used to. The shame has gone. I can look at myself for minutes on end, at the body that under Leon's eyes, words and hands has been transformed into a sensual female form. I'm fully aware that this is the same body that disgusted John, that it's not my body, but my self-image that's changed so quickly. Something essential has changed in the space between my ears, and that is manifested on all kinds of levels: my choice of clothes, the way I approach people, and a greater confidence in my own decisions at work. I probably radiate my new self-assurance and others haven't failed to pick up on it. Recently I've discovered from the looks and comments of clients and suppliers that Leon is not the only one who finds me attractive. That subtle recognition gives me extra energy and inspiration, and permeates everything I do. The only thing that still grates is that I needed a man to make me learn to see myself differently.

As I'm drying off I hear stumbling and laughter in the hall. Leon's brought guests home. I quickly put my clothes on and go into the room. Leon comes towards me with two carrier bags of takeaway food and Debby and Richard in his wake. I swallow my disappointment. I'd been looking forward to an evening in together.

'Hello, princess.' Leon bends over and kisses me on my neck. 'Debby and Richard are staying for dinner.'

'Cool.' I give Richard and Debby a quick kiss on the cheek and make my way to the kitchen to get plates. Leon takes the knives and forks out of the drawer and I see Debby getting glasses, while Richard opens a bottle. The two of them act like they live here. They both have a front door key and come and go at will, regardless of whether Leon's at home. While I've grown to like Richard more and more, and have also started to appreciate Debby since it became clear she doesn't constitute a threat to me, I'm less happy with the fact that I can never have this place entirely to myself. The front door can swing open at any time. Leon's fine with it: as far as he's concerned, Debby and Richard are part of the entourage.

I watch as Richard fills the wine glasses and Leon opens the packaging and dishes out the kebabs. As we are sitting down to eat, Richard's mobile goes off. He looks at the screen and answers in irritation. 'Why are you calling?' Silence.

Debby and Leon have already started eating and pay no attention to Richard, which confirms my suspicion that this must happen quite often. I think I know who's calling him and who he's shouting at while his friends are within earshot: Marianne, in her isolated house, alone with Lola, surrounded by meadows, ditches and pollard willows.

'I'm still in a meeting,' he says. 'I'll see you at about ten, OK?'

My jaw drops. As Richard is putting his mobile away, I can't help saying something. '*Meeting?*'

'There's lots to discuss.'

'Don't you think it's a bit—'

'How's it going with Taco?' asks Leon, interrupting me. The message is clear: Marianne and Richard are none of my business.

'Better than I expected. I've been surfing the internet and making calls all day and I think I've already found most of the suppliers. I'm just looking for someone who can do frescoes, but there are enough of them on the internet so that should be fine.'

'I'd love to do that,' says Debby beside me.

'Do you do murals?'

Debby nods. 'As a hobby.'

'Debby used to be a painter,' explains Leon. 'But she didn't get on too well, so she went into PR.'

'How come it didn't work out?'

Debby smiles shyly. 'The world isn't ready for my vision.'

Leon burst out laughing. 'Come off it, Debby, you give everyone the creeps with your paintings.'

'You like them!' she cries.

'Go on, rub it in.'

'But your murals are terrific,' says Richard soothingly. 'You have good technique.'

'Drop by tomorrow if you have time,' says Debby softly. She puts her hand on my arm. 'I've got a portfolio of photos, maybe you could use a painting of mine in your design as well. I'd really like that.'

Richard looks at her in amusement over the rim of his glass. 'Debby, darling, the only place those paintings of yours are in vogue is in TB clinics. I wouldn't go hawking them around if I were you.'

Debby lifts her chin and her face hardens. She opens her mouth to say something, but changes her mind and carries on eating.

'What's wrong with them?' I ask Debby.

Richard raises his hand 'Don't tell her, Deb. Let her see for herself tomorrow.'

32

Black, expressionless eyes. Knives. Primitive, hooked brush-
strokes in black and red in which at a distance I discern
screaming faces and bloody tears. In one painting there are at
least a hundred such figures, their crudely attached heads bent.
In others they are lying on the ground staring at a dark red sky
in an ink-black landscape. Because a lot of paint has been used,
long red drips have formed, suggesting blood, as if blood is trick-
ling from the sky. Leaning against the wall there are dozens of
watercolours that are totally different in terms of colour
scheme and technique. There are people lying dead in their
coffins. Men, women, children, with folded hands and closed
eyes. So realistic they look like photos.

It sends a shiver down my spine.

Debby is standing beside me, beautiful and serene as ever in
an immaculate white suit, her arms loosely folded. 'Well?'

I bite my lip. 'I can see what Richard means, I think. It's all
rather . . .' I search anxiously for words that will offend her as
little as possible: ' . . . gloomy.'

'Munch's "Scream" is just as gloomy. Do you know it?'

'Of course I know it,' I reply, thinking of the painting of a
screaming figure holding its hands to its face. 'It's world-
famous.'

'It was originally called "Despair". Well, he's not the only
one.' She closes the door of her studio without warning – the

viewing is suddenly over – and walks over to her house. She lives simply, in an old little house squashed between other little houses in Amsterdam South.

I walk beside her, still searching fruitlessly for something nice to say about her personal work. Nothing comes to mind. She's right, there are lots of *gloomy* paintings and quite a few of them are famous. But Debby's work goes beyond gloomy. It's really unpleasant to look at. When we went to the studio – a wooden shed with a pointed roof – from the house, she told me that her paintings are all concerned with death, which terrifies and fascinates her at the same time. Her personal work is a creative form of control freakery. Now I've seen them, I start seeing Debby with different eyes. There's much more going on inside her than you might think at first, and maybe even second glance. And what is smouldering under her skin is not very nice.

'So you don't think your client can use these?'

'I really don't think that men who are out for an evening with the boys and want to stare at naked women are on the look-out for a challenging painting.' The words leave my mouth before I realise what I'm saying, and I could bite my tongue off.

'I can do other things as well,' she says resolutely, opening the back door. 'That no one would be offended by,' she adds cynically. 'Neatly coloured in, inside the lines.'

'Sorry, I didn't mean to . . .'

She puts her manicured hand on my forearm and gives me a penetrating look. 'Don't be sorry, Margot. I'm used to this sort of reaction. I just hoped you were different. One of the few people who could appreciate my personal work, besides Leon, was . . .' She suddenly stops talking and takes her hand off my arm. 'But you're not her.'

Edith. She's talking about Edith.

Debby kneels down at a sideboard and takes out a couple of heavy, leather-bound albums which she puts on the table. 'It's a bitter pill that I represent artists,' she continues, leafing through the books, 'and evidently do a good job so that everyone around me becomes acclaimed and well-known, when I can't sell my own work. Not to museums, not to galleries . . .' She looks at me meaningfully '. . . and not even to some strip joint.'

Not another word about Edith.

I look at the albums over her shoulder. They contain photos of all kinds of works, mainly paintings of Mediterranean-looking scenes. 'You could try a different approach, dream up new themes. There's a world of difference between what you showed me in your studio and this. Are all these paintings your own work?'

'Yes, all of them.'

They're nicely done, as far as I can tell: realistic, very detailed. 'So what's wrong with them?'

'They're not art. In Asia there are factories churning out paintings like this all day long. You're not going to get any critics singing their praises. Oh well. I don't mind doing them and I can supplement my income.'

'Don't you earn enough from your work?'

'You mean PR for a handful of artists? No, sadly not. I do it for sixteen hours a week.'

'And Richard?'

'Richard gets half of all the photographers' income. That's a completely different story.'

I raise my eyebrows. '*Half?*'

'That's normal.'

'But aren't you and Richard doing more or less the same job?'

'No, don't be silly, there's no comparison. Richard arranges all the assignments for the photographers.'

'Photographers?' I ask, with the stress on the final letter.

She looks up. 'Leon's not the only one Richard represents. Anyway: Richard has the international contacts and he's good at selling the work. I write the press releases, keep the media informed about exhibitions, possible awards, that sort of thing.'

My mobile rings. I look at the screen and slide it open.

'Hi,' it's Dick. 'Have you got a moment?'

I turn ninety degrees. 'A moment, yes.'

'It just dawned on me that we've got that family do on Saturday. I was wondering if you knew.'

'No, how was I supposed to know?'

'Agatha sent you and invitation. You've probably not been home?'

'No, not for a while.' I make a mental note to drop by my flat this week. The letterbox will no doubt be bulging, even if only with junk mail. I forgot to put a no-thanks sticker on it. There might not even be room for any more post now. 'Who's the party in honour of?'

'It's Paul and Agatha's fortieth wedding anniversary. The whole family is coming. At least seventy or eighty people: all the nephews and nieces and even Anita and Cor are coming over from Switzerland for it.'

'Where is it?'

'They've hired out a function room at Van der Valk, the same one we had for Mum and Dad's fiftieth anniversary. Er, Margot . . . ' There is silence for a moment. 'Seeing as you've got a new boyfriend now . . . Have you had a change of heart about John?'

'What do you mean?'

'Listen, if you want to make an issue of it then I can ring him and take care of it, but it turns out Agatha has sent him an invitation. It was a pretty clumsy thing to do in my opinion and I don't expect him to turn up, but . . .'

'Doesn't matter.'

'Are you sure? I don't want all that—'

'Don't worry. I really don't care anymore. If John wants to come to the party, that's up to him.'

'You're an angel. If you do change your mind, let me know, OK?

I wish him good day, send my regards to Anne and the children and slide my phone shut.

Debby looks at me inquiringly. 'Party coming up?'

'Family do.'

'Fun?'

'Usually.'

'Of course it's nothing to do with me, but who's John?'

'John van Oss, my ex. He's probably going too. My family are quite fond of him. So I suppose I'll just have to get used to bumping into him all the time.'

'I don't know how you put up with it.'

I shrug my shoulders. 'I'm not mad at him anymore.'

'Does Leon know him?'

'No, John has nothing to do with the art world. He's technical director at a heating company in Eindhoven, Lentico.'

Debby's already lost interest. She bends over the photos and taps a Roman female figure with her fingernail. 'Look, could this be what you're looking for?'

'Something like that, certainly. Taco has alcoves and I want the paintings on those walls. Not all the same of course, but they have to go together.'

'That goes without saying. I'll scrape a few more examples together. That won't be a problem, but it'll easily take me a couple of weeks.'

'I don't think I can persuade Taco to close his club for two full weeks. Basically everything has to be finished in a week.'

'I'm really not going to be able to do ten murals in a week.' She purses her lips. 'You can also have panels made, then I can paint them here in the studio and you can stick them in the alcoves later. If you do it properly you won't see the difference. How does that sound?'

'I think that's the only option. When could you start?

'As soon as I get the panels.'

'Fine,' I say, and make a move to leave.

'Can you stay for a bit?' she asks.

I look at my watch. 'I'd like to, but I'm due at Joost and Rolf's at six.

'You could always ring and say you'll be over later. They won't mind. I don't see you that often, without Leon.'

She won't take no for an answer. I flop down in a plastic bucket chair – there are four, all bright orange. 'Do you mind if I smoke?'

'Go ahead,' she calls out.

I light up a cigarette, watch Debby fill two blue glasses and marvel once again at her almost eerily perfect appearance. There are never any hairs or fluff on her clothes, and even close up her skin is flawless. Debby is frighteningly perfect. Leon said he thought she was very sweet, but too artificial and definitely too thin for his taste. I don't think she's thin, at least not bony or knobbly, but she has such a narrow waist that I'm amazed all her organs can fit in it. Perhaps she has tiny little organs – dwarf intestines, mini-kidneys and a

Lilliputian liver. When she hands me the wine I lower my eyes. She does her very best to be pleasant and hospitable and all I do is look for her weak points, so that I can breathe a sigh of relief.

'Edith liked my work very much,' she says. 'Especially the abstract stuff. We had the same kind of . . .' She giggles. 'I suppose you could call it perversion.'

I don't respond and look at my glass. I want to ask her if she was very upset by Edith's death. She must have known her well, so it would be a perfectly acceptable, logical question. But I don't ask anything. This conversation could easily find its way back to Leon and then he might think I've been fishing for information from Debby. I divide my attention between my wine glass and the toes of my boots and feel myself growing more nervous by the second.

'He's banned you from talking about her,' Debby concludes.

I shrug my shoulders and say nothing.

'I understand, believe me. It knocked him for six, still does. Leon and Edith had all sorts of plans. Everything looked rosy, and then . . . wham. I wasn't expecting it, no one was really. But still, when you think about it later, you can only conclude that she may have been giving signals the whole time. On the one hand she was cheerful and positive, but she also had regular spells when she talked about suicide. It wasn't always easy to fathom her.'

'I don't think we should be having this conversation,' I say softly.

'Well, I happen to think this is a perfectly normal conversation. I could tell you a lot more, but I'm not the right person. Ask him, tonight, because this is really all wrong.'

'It's really not my place to bring it up.'

'Just say I mentioned it,' she insists. 'That guy of yours and I go back quite a long way, believe me, and he can be very persuasive, but you mustn't let your whole life be ruled by him. That's what it's beginning to look like, and if you do you'll end up like Edith.'

33

Although I can't get Debby's words out of my head for one second, there hasn't been a moment all evening when I could ask him anything. As soon as I got home I had a quarter of an hour to put my make-up on and change, after which we drove to Nijmegen in the Audi to attend an opening. The invitation came as a complete surprise. Leon leaves for Copenhagen tomorrow, which made me think we'd spend the evening together. We didn't get round to talking in the car. Driving along, we had other things on our minds; his hand never left my thigh and I didn't want to spoil the intimacy. The closer we got to Nijmegen, the more convinced I became that this evening wasn't the right moment to confront him with my questions about Edith. We could always do that later when he was back from Denmark, or better still even later, after the family do.

The evening is a succession of animated conversations with all kinds of people from the art world who I didn't know, but who greeted Leon like a long-lost friend. In a packed gallery people were talking to him virtually the whole time. My job was restricted to smiling pleasantly, and now and then, when asked, I said something about my current projects. Fortunately I no longer have the handicap of my old job, so I don't have to keep up appearances, although I'm still not feeling completely secure in my new role.

It's almost eleven-thirty when Leon turns onto the motorway and we head for Amsterdam. My unspoken questions are weighing me down like heavy stones in my stomach. Although I try to put it out of my mind, it seems to be getting worse and worse, so bad that I can think of virtually nothing else.

'Dick called this evening to say they're expecting me at a family do,' I say, to break the silence. 'Next Saturday. It's my uncle and aunt's fortieth wedding anniversary.'

No reply.

'Will you come?'

'To a fortieth wedding anniversary in Brabant?' He rummages in a packet of cigarettes on the dashboard, pulls one out and lights it. 'Is that a joke or something?'

'My parents would like to meet you, and my ex is coming too. So I'd really like it if you came along.'

His eyes narrow. 'Just explain to me what that guy is doing at your family celebration?'

I pull a helpless face. 'I lived with him for seven years. He had more contact with my relatives than I did. I'm afraid he's become one of the family.'

'That's rubbish. You split up on bad terms.'

'I'm not angry with him anymore.'

Leon looks at me impassively for a second and then turns back to the road.

'Anyway, I'd love it if you could come,' I continue. 'I don't really fancy going on my own. Apart from that I'd like to introduce you to my parents. I'm more or less living with you now. In fact it's odd that we've never met each other's families . . . don't you think? You've never told me anything about yours. I don't even know what sort of family you come from, whether you have any brothers and sisters and—'

'Maybe because you've never asked. There's nothing very shocking.'

'So I'm asking you now.'

He takes a drag on his cigarette, looks in his wing mirror and overtakes a lorry. 'I'm an only child and my parents split up when I was twelve. I stayed with my mother in Eindhoven. About six years ago she remarried and left for Sicily with her new husband. Last time I saw her was last year. We phone and e-mail each other every now and then.'

'And your father?'

'I never see him,' he says flatly.

'Why not?'

'Because we just don't get on.' He takes another deep drag on his cigarette. The end glows brightly and colours his face orange. 'Personality clash.'

'In what way?'

'My father is a grade-A prick. When he was still living at home he believed that people bringing up kids were completely responsible for shaping their children's characters. That was the prevailing norm at the time and he also preached it in his practice – he was a psychologist. He had no notion of genetic predisposition, that there's such a thing as an innate temperament, so that there were limits to that shaping of his. If I wanted or did something he disapproved of, he saw it as a shortcoming in the way he'd brought me up, a fault he had to put right. If talking didn't help, he'd chase me all over the house, beating and kicking me.'

'Did that happen often?'

He snorts. 'What's often? I didn't keep count. Our characters were so far apart that it was impossible to meet his standards.'

'What did your mother do when that happened?'

'Nothing. Usually she walked away so she didn't have to watch. She couldn't handle confrontation.'

'It must have been difficult.'

'At the time yes, but it's a long time ago.'

'And it doesn't bother you anymore?'

'There are so many people who've been through things like that. I've yet to meet anyone with a perfect childhood. You told me your parents never accepted certain aspects of you. That's not a problem for you anymore either, is it?'

It certainly was till a month or so ago. 'My father didn't hit me,' I say. 'There's no comparison. You were abused. I can't imagine how you wouldn't have problems with that.'

He frowns in annoyance. 'Come on, Margot, that's bullshit. It's absurd to blame everything on your childhood twenty-five years after the event. That's fine when you're eighteen. Things happened the way they happened and it's gone, over.'

'Like Edith?' It slips out before I realise. I'm so shocked by my own words that I clap my hand over my mouth.

His eyes narrow. 'What about Edith?' The sudden tension that sparks from him is almost tangible, like static electricity. Angrily he changes gear.

I run my fingers awkwardly through my hair and hardly dare look at him. At the same time something snaps in me. I've bottled it up for too long. 'Have you ever stopped to think,' I say, louder than I intended, 'that I wonder every day what sort person she was and what kind of relationship you had?' I continue more softly: 'You don't talk much about yourself, Leon. I don't need to know all the details, but I need more than what you give me to feel a connection with you that goes beyond just physical attraction.'

When I look up, I see an emotionless mask in the faint dashboard light. He has cut himself off completely. It probably runs in the family.

It would probably be better if I backed down down a bit, but the words keep on coming, there's no stopping them. 'I'm not allowed to talk about Edith, even though she was an important part of your life. I understand that it's difficult, but having a relationship is also about sharing, not just the nice things.'

'I don't want to talk about this. Not with you, not with anyone, not now, not ever. Do you understand?'

'No, I don't understand a thing. This afternoon I was at Debby's place. She made a remark about Edith and I didn't know where to look, I was so stressed out. Is that normal? I don't want that to be normal. Debby, Richard, Taco, even Joost and Rolf, all those people I meet are completely in the picture, and I know absolutely nothing about her. And perhaps there isn't anything to know, perhaps it's all very unimportant, but because you say nothing about it and I'm not allowed to mention it, it's growing bigger and bigger inside my head. It makes me start thinking about our relationship, what we have . . .' I catch my breath. 'Actually I don't even know if you can even call this a relationship.'

He presses down on the accelerator even harder. The wheels race over the surface of the road. 'For Christ's sake, you live with me.'

'We don't talk.'

'I told you Edith is a no-go area. And perhaps it was naïve of me, but I really believed you respected that. I appreciated that in you.' He stubs his half-finished cigarette out in the ashtray and shuts the lid hard. 'I was wrong.'

I have no idea what to do. I rub my hands restlessly and search anxiously for words, but nothing comes to mind. The minutes creep past. I listen to the droning of the engine and watch the windscreen wipers sweeping to and fro.

After a long silence the contours of the old warehouse loom up and Leon drives into the car park under the complex.

He yanks the steering wheel to position the car between the white lines and jams on the brakes, so that I'm thrown forward. Only then does he look at me. 'Why? Why are you so fixated on Edith? You think it says something about you and me, but it's got nothing to do with it. Not a damn thing.'

My silence is taken as agreement.

'Edith and I had a different kind of relationship than you and I have.' He focuses on the concrete wall in front of us. 'And Edith was a completely different person from you. She came from a family of market gardeners, with strict near-religious maniacs for parents and two screwed-up elder brothers with wandering hands who tormented her day in day out. I met her five years ago when she was visiting a gallery – she was twenty-four. She moved in with me the same week. We explored our limits together. Actively. All in the name of art, with a solid cultural base . . . Of course.' He pulls a tortured face, as if he could burst into tears at any moment, but his eyes stay dry. 'But her limits, because of what she'd been through, were a whole lot closer to home than mine, and I should have seen that. I should have understood, put the emergency brake on, and I thought I already had, but obviously it was too late.'

I remember the conversation with Richard in the gallery. He was also talking about limits, about acclaimed artists who were basically crazy, and how you had to be strong to hold your own. He must have been talking about Edith. Was it a veiled warning? 'So what the hell did the two of you do?' I ask, on my guard.

He pulls the key out of the ignition and gets out. I release my seatbelt and follow him to the lifts. Our footsteps echo through the basement and I have to struggle to keep up with him. In the lift he still doesn't look at me, he has stuffed his hands in his pockets and just stares at the doors.

'Leon, how am I supposed to interpret *exploring your limits*? I'm trying to picture it, but I've no idea what . . .' Richard's words are tumbling around in my head. 'Cutting,' I blurt out. 'Hurting each other. That sort of thing?'

The lift doors slide open. He steps into the hall, opens his front door and turns on the light.

Just as I'm about to repeat my question, he turns round to face me and grabs my chin. 'You're dying to know all about it but can you put it in the right context? Do you actually know exactly what a relationship involves? Because I'm beginning to have serious doubts. Were you the same woman with John as you are with me?'

The question confuses me. I don't get the chance to formulate an answer.

'I know the answer,' he says, with a harshness in his voice that makes me recoil, but he keeps hold of my jaw, so that I have no choice but to stand close to him and look at him. 'The answer is: no, you weren't. You weren't surprised that he went off with someone else, because you were ugly anyway, unattractive and fat. I was able get rid of that idiotic self-image in one evening, though you'd been telling yourself that for years. It affected the way you functioned, approached people – especially in bed.' He lets my chin go. 'And it works just the same the other way round.'

I feel the sore marks his fingers left on my jaw and rub them.

'To put it briefly, people will adapt their behaviour according to the circumstances. They will opt to function within the limits of what is socially acceptable to the group they belong to at the time. For us, in a broader perspective, that's Western culture, and it narrows progressively via school or work to neighbourhood, friends, family and partner. It means that a new social circle, a new job or a new partner automatically elicits new behaviour. It doesn't mean that your character changes, but it does mean that certain behaviours or traits can be exaggerated or suppressed, or that you can discover potential within yourself that you were unaware of before. It was already there, but you only discover it when the social circle to which you belong requires it of you, or stimulates you. Pure conditioning. People sometimes say that they discovered themselves by going through a certain event, when basically they have only discovered a new facet of themselves. How was your sex life with John?'

I give him a withering look. There was scarcely a sex life to speak of, and he knows that. For the last few years sex was an obligation in the dark, under the covers, me underneath, him on top, me hoping that it would be over quickly and suspecting from John's uninspired grinding that he felt the same way. 'Shit,' I say. My voice is hoarse.

He brings his face very close to mine. 'And what's it like now?'

'You know what it's like,' I whisper, and lower my eyes beneath his feverish gaze. 'Why are you making me say this, I—'

'Complaints?'

'No. Quite the contrary.'

'Do I force you to do anything? Do you do things against your will?'

I shake my head.

'And what if that John of yours had asked for this? Say last year John had said to you, as I did this evening: I don't want you to wear any underwear to that première?'

'John would never have asked that.'

'I said: if.'

I look at the floor and pause. He's right. I wouldn't have dreamt of it.

'Do you follow me, Margot? You're not the same woman for me as you were for John. Not sexually, and not in countless other ways. Can you understand that I'm not the same man for you as I was for Edith? If you recognise and accept that, then you'll see that your questions about Edith are beside the point. They say nothing about you, about me or about us. They only say something about the interaction between Edith and me. And you have no part in that at all.'

'I understand that and I accept it,' I find myself repeating his words. 'But it's not only about that. It's also about basic information, things that everyone seems to know except me. I live here, you introduce me to everyone as your girlfriend, but at the same time I'm an outsider. Debby, for example. I would really have liked to stay at her place a bit longer, I don't know all that many people here yet, but I couldn't get out of there fast enough.' I shake my head. 'If I don't talk about Edith, it has to be out of respect for you, and in the certainty that I know what went on and choose to let it rest. But without that knowledge I'm not even fit to talk to your friends.'

'Touché,' he says joylessly and goes over to the kitchen.

I cross my arms awkwardly and realise that I'm almost shaking with tension.

Leon opens a kitchen unit and pours some water. Two glasses. So he's not planning to throw me out tonight. He comes towards me and shoves one of the glasses into my hand.

Gratefully I take a couple of big gulps.

Leon stands in front of me, still as a statue, his face clouded over. 'We played mind games,' he says softly.

'We experimented with drugs. Too much of everything, too often, too hard.' He snorts.

No pain, no cutting. Thank God. 'She was suicidal,' I say gently.

'She was so young, addicted to sleeping pills, she was full of memories she hadn't dealt with and she'd completely lost her way. That was the problem.' He looks up with a tormented expression. 'I should have protected her against herself, but I did the opposite. Sometimes she wanted pain. She asked me for it. I should have said no. But I didn't.'

I look up 'Pain?'

'Yes, pain,' he says darkly. 'I don't want to say any more than that. Now you know more than my friends.' His expression hardens. 'If this isn't enough for you, then as far as I'm concerned we can call it a day here and now.'

'It's enough.' I have the urge to put my hand on his arm, but I don't dare. It seems inappropriate, since I caused his mood. 'I'm glad you've told me. Now I can put it in perspective.'

He turns away from towards the bathroom. *'You* can.'

The alarm clock reads two minutes past four when I start awake. I had a terrible dream. A lioness had escaped from a zoo, she was as big as a house and was running roaring through the town. I wasn't familiar with the town and had no idea how I came to be there. I ran to my car for safety, but it wouldn't start. Anyway the steering wheel had gone. In the back of the car was Debby, with one of her paintings on her lap. She had her immaculate white suit on and seemed quite untroubled by the imminent danger. Her eyes were sparkling and she was bursting with laughter: 'Are you afraid? Are you afraid? You're not afraid, are you?' I told her to get out of there, but she just laughed at me. I managed to get out of the car and was about to flee into a building, but the deserted streets were made of a sticky substance, like thick treacle, my shoes stuck to it and I was making hardly any headway while the lioness got closer, roaring, with enormous claws. Gasping for breath, I managed to reach a shop – I can't remember what sort of shop – and it was full of people I knew. Dick and Anne, my parents, friends I hadn't seen for ages. They had fled just like me. They stared at me wide-eyed with fear and as the ground beneath us thundered I dived in among them, waiting anxiously and peering outside through the shop windows.

The dream is very real, so terribly lifelike, and my heart is pounding like crazy when I open my eyes wide and realise that I'm in bed. No lioness, no shop, no treacle on the road and no danger. I'm lying in the foetal position with the pillow wedged under me. It's damp with sweat. I brush my hair out of my face and crawl closer to Leon's side of the bed. My eyelids are heavy and I feel myself drifting off again, back into the twilight world between waking and dreaming. I want to take hold of Leon's hand and pull his arm round me like a protective shield, but his side of the bed is empty.

X

If you're condemned to the drudgery of a nine-to-five job, your body adjusts. You get to bed by ten at night and wake up of your own accord before the alarm goes off – you function more or less as a robot.

My internal clock went chronically haywire long ago because I'm not tied to fixed working hours. Over time I've come to enjoy being wide awake and lucid when the public at large is tucked up in bed. The night is beautiful, with its ear-splitting silence. There are no phone calls, no people at the door, no obligations. Alone with my thoughts, wonderful thoughts.

Last night I couldn't sleep. I got up, poured myself a glass of wine and then booted up the PC. I read the news headlines, surfed to the cultural pages and joined in a forum discussion on sex and art as a twenty-two-year-old female student – one of my aliases. What was being discussed at that time of night wasn't very edifying. From the idiotic, oafish reactions full of typos and language errors I deduced that only drunks and sex maniacs were still online. I logged out and began surfing aimlessly.

I found myself – as often before – on a site giving information on South Africa. I'm not ruling out the possibility of my going out there to live one day. It's far enough from Europe and yet a bit like home. Great weather, interesting history. No one in my life knows how much that country attracts me, and always has, and I want to keep it that way. I like to think that when I go there, it will be in style and not from necessity. But if it should be from necessity, then it would be to my advantage if I've never breathed a word about it.

My feet were prickling and starting to go to sleep, but in my head the roaring continued, a tingling surge of electricity that kept me sharp and awake. I finally ended up on a site trying seriously to measure people's IQ. Multiple-choice questions, sums, logic problems, spatial awareness. I keyed in the answers impatiently and after about twelve minutes the result appeared on screen. You could print it out: a kind of diploma, lousily designed. Are there really people who frame a scrap of paper like that and hang it over their desk? I'm sure there are – I have no illusions on that score.

This score puts you ahead of over 97 per cent of the population, it said, adding quite superfluously: You are highly gifted.

Terrific, as I feared.

I shut down the computer and crawled back to bed. By the time I slowly fell asleep, the first birds were starting to sing.

34

'How fantastic of you!' Debby hugs me and kisses me on the cheek, pressing her whole body against me. 'Do you see now that you were getting upset over nothing?'

I smile shyly and pat her uncomfortably on the back. I don't share her enthusiasm. After last night's conversation Leon packed his case, after which he went to bed almost immediately. This morning the farewell was pretty chilly. He gave me a kiss and got into the lift without looking round as if he had already forgotten me and his mind was on the next assignment. It didn't feel good to see him leave like that.

Out of necessity I shake off that feeling. I've got three packed days ahead of me. I've set up a gruelling schedule in order to have as little opportunity as possible to feel lonely.

'But from now on I'm going to let it rest,' I say, extricating myself from Debby's hug.

'I quite understand. Take a seat. I've made some tea.'

I sit down in one of the orange designer bucket chairs and look for my cigarettes in my handbag. 'I really can't stay long. I've got to be off again in a minute.'

'Yes, yes, I'm getting to know you,' she calls from the kitchen. 'Always in a hurry. No good for you.'

Debby comes back with two glasses of tea and sits opposite me. She crosses her legs. When I came in I noticed she was looking sloppy by her standards. She's wearing dark-blue tracksuit bottoms with flared legs and a tight-fitting training top in the same colour, which makes a rather dishevelled impression. Her blonde hair, with the garish red streaks, looks less shiny. Perhaps she hasn't had time to run a comb through it or blow-dry it. She has no make-up on, so her eyes look a little lacklustre and the skin beneath them grey. It makes her more approachable, more human.

'I've crammed these few days as full as possible,' I say, 'because I don't want the opportunity to think too much.'

'It's only three days, you'll survive. A few months ago Leon was in Italy for two weeks. He was exhausted when he got back and had to go straight on to Berlin. That's how it is when you're popular.'

I take a cautious sip of the tea. 'I expect I'll get used to it eventually, but right now I don't like it one bit. Leon's place is great, with those Persian rugs and the lovely sofa and kitchen, but the exposed walls and the metal joists up by the ceiling make it so much like a factory, and not enough like a home. And I'm not used to there being no dividing walls or doors. It's so open, your back is never covered. There are no curtains at the windows. I'm not really anxious by nature, but it's no fun staring into those black holes in the evenings. When I'm alone, I hear every little noise.' I look up. 'Sorry, I shouldn't moan like this.'

'Don't be silly, I understand perfectly well. Will you be staying in Amsterdam for the next few days?'

'I think so. In a moment I have to go to that workshop you recommended, for the panels, and then on to Taco. I want to try and pop in for coffee with my parents at lunchtime and afterwards I'll be working for Joost and Rolf till about six. There was a problem with the fabric.'

'What was that?'

'The fabric they'd chosen couldn't be delivered for three weeks at the earliest. I have to collect some new samples from the upholsterer so they can make a selection. Then I have to go to a company that makes LEDs in wall panels . . .' I stare vacantly ahead of me. 'I'm completely flat out tomorrow and the day after too, mainly with appointments in the area. I've got to—'

'Margot,' she interrupts. 'Do you realise how hectic you sound? You remind me of that white rabbit from *Alice in Wonderland*.'

'I'm just starting out. I want to get it right, so I can't bear the thought of messing up my first two commissions.'

'I mean it. This isn't good.' She gets up from her chair and stands behind me. Suddenly I feel her hands in the back of my neck. Her thumbs are turning in slow circles along my spine and neck vertebrae. 'Leave it to me. Everything's tight,' she whispers.

I let her continue. How she does it is a mystery to me, but her fingers press down in exactly the right places and I can feel myself warming up, relaxing.

'Better?'

'Yes, lovely.'

'You really are far too tense,' she says softly, while her fingers and hands maintain pressure on my neck and shoulders. 'Let your shoulders drop for a moment. You keep hunching them up. You should really watch that, otherwise you'll have problems.'

'I know I'm doing it and I should pay more attention, but it's automatic.'

'You've been through a lot recently.'

'Lots of nice things,' I say, 'they shouldn't stress me out.'

'Positive stress is stress just the same. You've quit your job, gone freelance, got a new boyfriend and more or less moved to a new city. That's quite a lot all in all, wouldn't you say? You should take better care of yourself, Margot. Take more time out for yourself, try to find a balance.' Her thumbs glide from the top of my spine and up my neck to the groove in my skull. 'Nice?'

I close my eyes. 'Yes, wonderful. How do you do that?'

She chuckles. 'I'm a qualified masseuse, but I make far too little use of my skills. Deliberately, mind: I find myself chasing my own tail often enough, that's why I recognise it in you . . . Listen, I'm going out this evening, but I haven't got anything on tomorrow night. Shall I sleep over at yours?'

'Oh no, don't be silly. I don't need a babysitter.'

'Relax those shoulders,' she says sternly. 'I'm not your babysitter. We'll make a fun evening of it. A girls' night in – I haven't done that for ages either. We'll have a bite to eat, then on to a pub, a nice hot bath and then bed. How does that sound?'

'Great.' Apart from the hot bath, I think to myself.

'Fine. I'll pick you up at seven, OK?'

A few hours later the rosy feeling I got from Debby's massage has been wiped out by the busy traffic and the countless calls I've had to answer. Perhaps Debby was right and I'm too frantic and nervous. It's all still so new and I'm so keen to get it right. Still, despite the lack of anything to compare it with, I have the feeling things are going according to plan. The labourers will be coming on Monday to demolish the interior of Ce Truc. A skip will be placed outside on the pavement for the occasion and will be collected the same evening. The following morning is set aside for plastering and the afternoon for laying the floors and positioning the tree trunks, so that it should be possible to start fitting and painting from Wednesday onwards. The first furniture will be delivered the same day. To be on the safe side, Ce Truc will stay closed until Friday; on Saturday afternoon there will be a reception for special guests and only on Saturday evening will the restaurant officially open again. The schedule isn't too tight, so it should all go smoothly.

The only thing I'm slightly concerned about is that there are no new clients on the horizon as yet. I can easily get by for three months on the proceeds of these first two commissions, as Richard worked out for me. But what happens after that? Supposing no one else turns up?

As I turn into my parents' drive, I deliberately drop my shoulders. Unconsciously I'd returned them to their familiar position next to my ears.

35

When I got back from Brabant yesterday I didn't find Joost at Ce Truc. Instead a young man I didn't know of about twenty with thin flaxen hair was in the kitchen smoking a cigarette. A dark-skinned girl with striking freckles was stirring two saucepans. They both looked up in surprise when I asked where Joost was. Joost and Rolf had taken a day off and gone parachute jumping on Texel.

Today Joost is back. He's understanding about the problem with the fabric and will leave the choice to me – I could have done that from the start, he says. The design is my department. He prefers to concentrate on cooking.

'You really must try this.' Joost pushes a plate towards me, turns it ninety degrees and quickly wipes a few drops of sauce off the edge. 'I'm thinking about putting this on the Christmas menu.'

I shove my diary and mobile aside to make some space. On the plate are two pale chicken nuggets with all kinds of protuberances. I take a bite. 'Divine,' I say, with my mouth full. 'This is wonderful. What is it?'

'Tempura noix St Jacques – deep-fried scallops, Japanese-style.'

'Normally I'm not a great fan of shellfish, but this really is very good.'

'I knew that,' says Joost with a satisfied smile and clears my plate away.

At the same time my phone starts vibrating. 'Margot? Hi. It's

John. Guess where I am?' It sounds as if he's walking outside somewhere. He seems a little out of breath and I can hear noise of the city in the background.

'How should I know?'

'In Amsterdam. We're doing a fair in the RAI Centre this week, but I've got the afternoon off, so I'm painting the town red right now.'

'They don't need you for that here, John. You'd do better to look after yourself.'

'I couldn't help thinking of you. I want to thank you for not making an issue of me coming to the party. Dick rang yesterday to say the coast is clear.'

'Great to know my own brother and you are in cahoots.'

'Is it not true then?'

'It's true. I told Dick I don't care.'

'I'm really glad. I was rather surprised too . . . Listen, you told me the other day you're refurbishing a restaurant. I was wondering if I could see it?'

'Not yet, I'm still getting everything ready. We don't start till Monday.'

'Where's the restaurant? It suddenly occurred to me I could walk right by it without knowing you were working there.'

'I'm there now, but there's not much point in coming over. There's nothing to see yet.'

'Er . . . to tell the truth I've had something on my mind for a while. I'm afraid I need to talk to you about it. Would now be OK by any chance?'

I look at my watch. I have to leave in three quarters of an hour and need to make a few calls before then. 'I could see you very briefly.' I give John the address and slip the mobile into my pocket.

Joost is watching me with interest. 'A new client?'

'No, my ex. He's in town and wants to talk to me.'

'You should give exes a wide berth,' he says abruptly.

'This one's harmless.'

'That's exactly when it gets dangerous, when you're no longer aware of it.'

I ignore his remark and sit down at one of the tables to ring a couple of suppliers.

Almost half an hour has passed by the time John's face appears in the front window. He taps on the glass and waves when he sees me look up.

'I'll leave my stuff here,' I say to Joost, quickly putting on my coat. 'You'll be here for a bit, won't you?'

'Take your time,' is the cynical reply from the kitchen.

I go outside and first button up my coat before saying hello to John. He stands rather awkwardly at a distance, as if I might bite him if he kissed me on the cheek.

'Well, what's it about?' I ask irritably.

'Shall we go and have a drink?' His breath is clouding up in the air.

'Sorry, I haven't got time. I have to go in fifteen minutes.'

'Can we go in here for a minute then?' He raises his eyebrows and nods in the direction of Ce Truc. 'It's too cold to stand out here. Or would you rather walk?'

John's looking remarkably good, much better than the last time we saw each other. He's put on weight, so his face has filled out again. His ruffled dark blond hair, which is going rather grey at the temples, is cut shorter and he's wearing a new suit with an exceptionally nice dark woollen overcoat – a technical director in his professional attire. John has always been a trade fair animal. He'll be in his element this week, and will doubtless be a big hit with the countless women attending. Suddenly I see the man he once was for me long ago. It's a strange sensation.

'Margot?'

I look up. 'Yes, let's go in here. But no coffee, I really have to go in a minute.'

As expected, Joost immediately scampers out of the kitchen, shakes hands with John and looks him up and down. Then he disappears into the kitchen, but positions himself so that his white apron is constantly visible out of the corner of my eye. On the one hand it annoys me, on the other hand I find it reassuring. My conversation with John is none of Joost's business, but he's so suspicious he could have got all kinds of ideas into his head if he'd seen John and me walking off together. This way it's obvious I have nothing to hide.

'Right then, come on,' I say when we're sitting opposite each other.

John leans forward intimately. 'I've got a problem with your Dad.'

'What's wrong with him?'

'The last time I was at your parents' house, I promised I'd help him build the new rabbit hutches. He said Dick promised to lend a hand months ago, but hasn't got round to it. The guy's worked off his feet at the moment, in the run up to Christmas. But well, then he phoned me—'

'You want to help my Dad build new rabbit hutches?'

'I really do.' John looks away from me for a moment in Joost's direction and then tries to make eye contact. 'Your Dad isn't getting any younger and can't do as much as he used to. I'd like to help him.'

'Well, go ahead and help him.'

He raises his eyebrows. 'Are you sure? You realise in that case I'll be at your parents' house every Sunday for a while?'

'I realise that.' I realise a whole lot more, such as that this means I'm now lifting my own banning order on John and that from now on I'm going to run into him at every party, barbecue and birthday. 'It doesn't bother me.'

'The last time you got very angry.'

'I thought it was disrespectful. And it *was* disrespectful. But I've changed my mind since then.'

'Why?'

I sigh deeply and follow a wayward grain in the wooden table top with my nail. 'I don't hate you anymore. I've often wished you'd get run over by a train, and Mieke as well. . . . But everything that's happened . . . my new job, and my new boyfriend, has made me see I didn't behave all that well myself.'

'I acted like a prick.'

'That's true.' I scratch my eyebrow. 'But let's not go into that. It's over. I'm happy now, and I hope you are too. If you want to help Dad with his hutches, feel free.'

'Are you coming to the party?'

'Yes, of course.'

'And your boyfriend?'

'He's coming too,' I lie. Leon hasn't said yes yet.

'Great. I'd like to meet him.'

I look at my watch. 'I really must be going.'

John leaps up and plants a cautious kiss on my cheek. 'Thanks. You really are a wonderful woman, Margot.' He looks around. 'Best of luck next week.'

As he steps outside, I see Joost scoot back to the kitchen.

*

The Italian restaurant Debby whisks me off to consists of two floors packed with noisy diners of all ages. The walls are beige, covered with hanging copper pans and paintings and the ceilings are made up of dark beams in the same colour as the wooden furniture, creating a pleasant, warm atmosphere. The waiters' Dutch is poor without exception.

Debby pours us another glass of Chianti. Her hair is shiny again and she's wearing a white blouse with a plunging neckline. I'm reluctant to admit it to myself, but I still feel slightly intimidated by her.

I stick my fork in the homemade pasta. 'I was wondering, do you have a boyfriend?'

'Not anymore. I've put my profile on a couple of sites. Not for a serious relationship, you understand, I'm past that stage. More for fun.'

'Why are you past that stage?'

She shrugs her shoulders. 'If you want a serious relationship, you find the dating pool shrinks dramatically over thirty. You can't be that choosy. The men who appear to be nice are usually married. Not that they tell you . . . You know, those guys who pick you up with a rose in their teeth but have forgotten to take the child seat out of the back of the car. They lie about everything, and so transparently it's almost sweet.'

I burst out laughing. 'You can't be serious.'

'I'm afraid I am. I thought there'd be less of that if I took myself off the books of all the dating agencies and put my profile on some of those casual sites, you know. I hoped to find kindred spirits, men who like me are no longer looking for a longterm relationship, but a friend to go to the cinema with occasionally, or have a drink with – and the rest, of course, I'm only human. Well, I was wrong.' Her lips pout slightly, and arch into a smile. 'Those places are absolutely teeming with horny husbands. They just want a quick shag to boost their vulnerable egos, or are secretly on the look out for something better than what's at home on the sofa. Pathetic little sods.'

Even close up Debby's perfection is almost unearthly. Not a wrinkle on her face, not a single blemish, as if she's been created rather than born, and rolled off the factory floor just this morning, fresh and pristine. I can imagine that someone with her looks must get lots of interest, but I find it harder to imagine that she can't get lucky the normal way. Unless the answer is that men are made to feel as insecure by her appearance as I am. 'Don't you meet any nice men through your work then?'

'Oh, sure, I'm not complaining. The only thing that gets to me are those overconfident husbands. Usually I can spot them easily, but occasionally one slips through the net. And then my whole evening goes down the drain.'

'But surely that's not the reason why you're no longer looking for a serious relationship?'

'Not really. I've lived with four guys, never for very long. Permanence is obviously not my thing.' She gives me a piercing look with those big blue eyes and long lashes. 'I like hunting. It can't be too easy, or I lose interest. I like a challenge. Strange, isn't it, for a woman?'

'Oh,' I say, scraping the last bit of sauce from my plate. 'You're probably not the only one.'

Her hand reaches for mine across the table. 'I'm glad we're here together. It's ages since I've been out with a girlfriend. After Edith I didn't think I'd ever find anyone I could get on with so well.'

'Were you close?'

She nods. 'We understood each other without words. Leon fell into a black hole after her death, but so did I and I couldn't talk to any one about it. Richard shut himself off from it completely and acted as if nothing had happened. I don't have much contact with Marianne anyway and Leon . . . well, you know all about that.'

'Did Edith have other friends besides you?'

She shakes her head. 'In the final months before her death she'd definitely turned a lot of people against her with her stubborn behaviour. In reality she was only teasing, she liked doing that, but not everyone appreciated it or understood what she was getting at. It's a shame you never knew her.'

The waiter appears, clears the table and comes back with the dessert menu.

Debby lets go of my hand. 'I hated not being allowed to see her after her death. Even if it hadn't been a pretty sight, I still might have been able to paint her. The funeral was completely controlled by her family, people she despised, and they excluded us from everything. Her parents and brothers sat in the front row – they were just ashamed. What she had done was a sin and they shunned us as if we'd driven her to it. They didn't even shake Leon's hand. A dreadful service and an awful day.'

'I'd like to let it rest,' I say, when she pauses for a moment. 'I can imagine that you want to get things off your chest, but it feels a bit like . . .'

'I'm betraying Leon – you don't have to explain that to me. Sorry. I'd forgotten that. Have you still got room for ice cream? It's fabulous here, especially the lemon.'

I've completely lost my appetite after Debby's account of Edith's funeral. I feel rather gloomy. 'I think I'll have a cappuccino,' I say, flatly.

'That's good here too. But I'm going to have the lemon ice

cream. With a liqueur. How about you? They've got a fantastic walnut.'

Two glasses of wine, a walnut liqueur and two hours later we stumble out of the lift giggling like schoolgirls. I open the door and Debby turns on the lights.

'I'm going to have a quick bath.' She goes straight over to the wall that divides the bathroom from the rest of the flat.

'If you don't mind, I'm going to bed.'

She stops. '*Bed?*'

'It's almost twelve-thirty and I'm out again at seven. I had a great time, I'd really like to thank you for an amazing evening, but I've got a killer schedule and if I stay up any later now, it'll all go pear-shaped tomorrow.'

For a moment Debbie says nothing, as if she doesn't know how to handle the situation. Then she says: 'Oh, of course, I never thought about that. You're used to all the foam and bubbles. I've only got a shower at home, so I have a bath here whenever I get chance. Do you mind?'

'Not at all.' I yawn and rub my face. 'Go ahead.'

Only when I hear the taps running do I take my clothes off and pull one of Leon's T-shirts over my head that comes half way down my thighs. I slip between the sheets and listen to the sounds from the bathroom in silence. I hear her open a cupboard and close it again. Then, after about ten minutes, I hear splashing. I'd be lying if I said I'm not curious about what Debby looks like under her clothes – probably equally perfect. But to find out I'd have to have a bath with her and that strikes me as a bit odd. Maybe I'm hopelessly old-fashioned, even prudish, and it's perfectly normal. and I'm just uptight while Debby's a lot freer and more spontaneous. After all, women have visited the sauna together since time immemorial and men shower communally after sport. Nevertheless the idea of sharing a bath with Debby is slightly repellent. We'd sit opposite each other and . . . then? I wouldn't know where to look, it strikes me as too intimate.

I hug the pillow, bury my face in it and breathe in Leon's smell. Suddenly I'm overcome by a nagging, hollow feeling, as if I could burst into tears at any moment. Now that I can smell his scent and am alone in bed, I realise how much I miss him. Perhaps Debby's presence makes it all the harder to bear. Against my better judgement I grab my mobile out of my trousers on the floor next to the bed. No messages. I'm not surprised: Leon never sends texts. Still, I'd hoped he'd make an exception today after this morning's cool farewell. I don't want to text him. If he didn't respond, it would upset me for the next few days. I know I'm being needy again, and that's not what I was aiming for, it's not healthy. But I don't know how to stop it.

I lie looking at the alarm clock for over half an hour, watching every minute pass.

When Debby comes over to the bed with a towel wrapped round her head like a turban, I squeeze my eyes shut and lie motionless. She dives into bed next to me. Anxiously I wait to see if she might cuddle up to me, but she only pulls the covers over to her side a little. Soon enough I hear her peaceful breathing.

I find it inconceivable that Leon isn't attracted to Debby. She has a frighteningly beautiful body.

36

'How was Denmark?'

'Very Danish mainly.' Leon squeezes me tight and rubs his face against mine. 'And cold and depressing, with no plump red-haired ladies.'

A weight is lifted from my shoulders. For three days my emotions have yo-yo'd from one extreme to the other, but I forgot all about it the moment I saw him come through the door in his long black coat with that devastating smile on his face.

'Did you miss me?' His fingers caress the hair of my neck and he kisses me softly on the mouth.

I mumble something inaudible and hope that he can't distil a 'yes' from it. I'm not going to concede that yet.

Leon lets go of me. 'I'm ready for some coffee. Richard too, I think.'

Richard has been standing watching in amusement. He steps forward and kisses me on both cheeks. 'Hello, dear, did you manage to make it through the days without your boyfriend?' His eyes are twinkling.

'Very funny.' I go over to the espresso machine in the kitchen. 'Fortunately I've been too busy. The demolition work is starting at Rolf and Joost's place on Monday.'

Leon takes his coat off, tosses it over the sofa and grabs a pile of post off the coffee table, focusing all his attention on it. I've lost him again, this time to bills and invitations.

'Great,' says Richard. 'That's what I like to hear.' He comes over to me and helps with the milk and sugar. 'Oh, in Denmark I talked to the owner of a restaurant chain who's going to open a couple of Japanese restaurants.'

'In Denmark?'

'No, in Holland. But that makes no difference in principle. They already had certain ideas about the style and the ambience and they want to be involved in the design, but they were looking for someone who can develop their rough plans in detail. Seems like a good in-between job, you can work from home and they pay well. I said you'd give them a ring. And there was someone else. Wait a second.' He fishes a couple of business cards from his coat pocket and shuffles them in his fingers as if they are playing cards and reads them with a frown. 'A holiday park in Zeeland wants to give some of its chalets a makeover. The owner's brother is an art dealer I've known for years, reliable guy. To tell you the truth I doubted whether it would be interesting enough, but you should see what you can do with it.'

'I can't afford to be too fussy at this stage.'

He raises an eyebrow. 'Actually my advice would be to cherry-pick. In that way you'll build a good name for yourself. Compare it with an actor: he can't allow himself to take on everything that comes his way either. Image-building. But then . . .' He puts the business cards on the draining board. 'This happened to come up. At any rate they know who you are, I sang your praises. It's up to you whether you ring them or not.'

'Thanks,' I say, resting my hand on his arm for a moment. 'I truly appreciate what you're doing for me.'

He shrugs his shoulders. 'It's no trouble. If you're happy, Leon's happy. And it's best if you set those pretty little hands of yours to work, otherwise you'll only get bored.'

I look past him. Leon is now sitting on the sofa, completely absorbed in his correspondence. He's kicked off his cowboy boots and is resting his feet on the table.

I want Richard to leave. I want to be alone with Leon and cuddle up next to him on the sofa. But that's not the only reason why Richard has outstayed his welcome. Richard puts me in touch with new clients and has really helped me find my feet, and I'm more than grateful to him for that, but I can't escape the image of Marianne climbing the walls in that house in the polder. Richard has come straight from Schiphol with Leon and is not giving the impression he's about to go home, wants to go home, or has even rung his wife. 'Speaking of boredom . . .' I say, cautiously. 'Have you been home yet?'

He raises his light blond eyebrows. 'Home?'

'Yes, home. To Marianne and Lola.'

He gives me a stern look. 'No, why?' he says curtly. 'Is there something wrong then?'

'No, nothing. I was just wondering. I could imagine that—'

'Marianne isn't expecting me before eight,' he interrupts me gruffly.

I refuse to let him fob me off. As I hand him a cup and walk in Leon's direction holding two others, I say, 'So do you always go with Leon? I mean on all his foreign trips?'

'Not always, but if I possibly can, I do. You get to hear things, more than if you sit at home on your backside. Say, Margot, I heard an old friend came to see you at Rolf's restaurant.'

'Yes, that's right. That was John, my ex. He's in Amsterdam this week for a trade fair.'

Next to me Leon slams the post down on the table. He rummages in his pocket, pulls a cigarette out of a packet and lights it.

Only then does it really sink in what Richard said to me. 'Who told you that then?'

'Joost. He was quite impressed. Very handsome guy, he said.'

I cringe. I wanted to tell Leon about this myself, this evening or tomorrow. The way Richard's brought it up, it sounds like I've had a secret rendez-vous. 'I can't understand why Joost would mention something like that to you. It's really not important.'

Richard looks from me to Leon and back again. 'Did Joost overstep the mark then?'

'Of course not. I've got nothing to hide.' I lift my head but can feel myself growing more nervous by the second. Richard forces me onto the defensive, where I don't belong. It's none of his business whether I've been talking to John. I don't even need to respond. But next to me Leon has been still for the past few seconds. I can feel the tension sparking off him.

'I split up with John quite a while ago,' I say to Richard. 'For a long time I couldn't stand the sight of him, but now I . . . see him more as a friend, or a close acquaintance.'

'Always nice to have a close old acquaintance to hand,' says Richard knowingly. He takes a sip of coffee and says nothing else.

Leon looks straight at me. His eyes are flashing fire. 'Perhaps I didn't make myself sufficiently clear when I said I didn't want you to see him. That implied automatically that he should not come to see you either.'

I jerk upright. 'Come on, Leon! This really is a load of fuss about nothing.' In my confusion I try to make eye contact with Richard, but he is suddenly interested in his fingernails.

'He called me yesterday to say he was in Amsterdam for a trade fair,' I continue. 'He had an afternoon off unexpectedly, was wandering the streets and remembered I was designing a restaurant in the centre of town. He was bored, and he was curious.'

'Of course he was.'

'He was just interested, no more and no less. And he wants to help my father with his rabbit hutches and was asking my permission. He was only being sweet, don't you think?'

'The way I see it, no sooner have I turned my back than, what-do-you-know, John turns up in Amsterdam. What a coincidence.'

I roll my eyes. 'Oh, think about it. If I were going to make a secret date with my ex, would I pick Ce Truc of all places?' Anxiously I look at Richard again. 'Can't this wait till Richard's gone?'

'I've got to go anyway,' says Richard, getting up.

'You don't need to go on my account,' says Leon beside me.

'It's OK. I'll see you tomorrow. Hang in there.' He looks at me for a moment. 'Sorry, I didn't know it was an issue.'

As soon as I hear the door close I say: 'This is completely absurd.'

'I've told you before that I want you to stay away from that guy.'

'You can't expect that, he's family. And you don't even *know* him, so how can you judge him?'

'I had the privilege of picking up the pieces and trying to stick them back together,' he says, his face oozing sarcasm. 'That tells me enough about how sweet he is.'

I close my eyes and count to ten and put my hand over my mouth. I don't want an argument. Not now. I'm delighted that Leon is back, I had all kinds of plans and now this. 'I don't want an argument,' I say softly.

Leon gets up from the sofa and heads for the kitchen.

'You're blowing it out of all proportion,' I say. 'John is . . . just someone from my past. What are you afraid of?'

He rounds on me. '*Afraid*? Have you got a screw loose or something? Your ex visits you here in Amsterdam. He cosies up not only to your family but to you as well, and I'm supposed to find that perfectly normal? I want nothing to do with the guy, Margot. He's pissing in my backyard.' Leon grabs his coat and makes for the door.

'Where are you going?'

'To get some air. It'll give you a chance to think about where your priorities lie.'

He slams the door shut after him.

For at least ten minutes I stare into space, incapable of doing anything or even thinking straight. Then I pull my legs up, put my arms round them and rest my chin on my knees. Is John cosying up to my family? And if so is that normal or is Leon just pathologically jealous? I just don't know. Richard's reaction was disapproving, Joost's just as negative – are they right? I don't want John to become an issue, as Richard put it, he's not worth that. But it's already happened. And now I'm sitting here alone, fighting back the tears, after longing for Leon's homecoming for three days and nights.

Two painfully slow hours later I hear fumbling at the door. I jump up and head straight for him. 'Sorry.'

He wraps his arms around me. 'Bitch,' he whispers in my ear. 'I don't want to fight. I want to fuck.'

'So do I.'

'So why do you do those stupid things?'

'Because they didn't seem stupid yesterday. They do now.'

'Listen. You're going to that damn party tomorrow. After that

I don't want to hear anything more about him. Exit John.' He grabs my jaw and gives me a piercing look. 'Can I count on that, princess?'

'You can count on that,' I say, letting my fingers wander over his cheekbones and cheeks.

He grins. 'So now let's see how much you want me.'

37

I stand in front of the wardrobe looking at my clothes and don't know what to do. Despite the busyness of the last few days I found time to buy a new outfit. Pretty hot stuff. Officially it was for the party this evening, but unofficially I bought it for Leon. I would never have dared buy it if I hadn't looked at myself through his eyes in the changing room, hadn't imagined that slight nod, the corners of the mouth curling in approval. But now if I wear it, I could fan the flames of Leon's jealousy. He could interpret it as something I'm doing for John. So the rose blouse then? I was wearing that on our first date so that rules that one out as well.

This is ridiculous. I really wanted Leon to come to the party with me, but it's simply not going to happen. After yesterday I don't even dare broach the subject.

'What are you standing there for?' Leon is lying on the sofa in an oversized T-shirt reading a magazine, looking at me out of the corner of his eye.

'I don't know what to wear.'

'You said you'd bought some new clothes.'

'I have.'

'So why don't you wear them?'

'They were for if you came with me. If you stay home, I'll have to think of something else.'

'Are they so spectacular then? Put them on.'

I take my new clothes out of the wardrobe, bite the price tags and labels off and wriggle into them. Then I turn round and take a few steps towards him, hands on hips.

He takes a drag on his cigarette and slowly exhales. 'You're quite right. You're not going to the party alone in that.'

'Thanks. Great. Now I'm completely clueless.'

He gets off the sofa with a sigh and slings the magazine under the table. 'Keep it on.'

I look up in surprise. 'What do you mean?'

'I'm coming too.'

'Are you sure?'

'No. And I'm even less keen. I can't bear thinking about being sociable for a whole evening at a Brabant family do at Van der Valk. But if I must, I must.'

'You're from Brabant yourself.'

He takes a puff on his cigarette and squeezes his eyes tight shut for a moment. 'So I know what I'm talking about.'

'It's not that bad.'

He stubs his cigarette out in the ashtray and goes over to the wardrobe. 'That remains to be seen.'

'Leon?'

He slides the door open and pulls a plastic dry cleaning cover off one of his suits. 'What now?'

'John'll be there too.' I add softly: 'You're going to act normally, aren't you?'

'I'm not promising anything.'

It's raining when we park the car outside the restaurant and function room complex. As we make our way to the building stooped over – Leon has put his arm around me – we pass a gleaming Mercedes with a Swiss number plate. It must be Anita and Cor's. They emigrated to Switzerland about five years ago for Cor's work and I haven't seen them since, though every year they faithfully send a Christmas card of a snowy mountain landscape.

'That car belongs to my Uncle Cor and Aunt Anita,' I say. 'They live in Switzerland.'

Leon doesn't respond.

I'm looking forward to talking to everyone again. There are many people I only see at this sort of occasion. And I'm curious to know what my parents will make of Leon, a little nervous even. He doesn't have the jovial, sociable manner of John or my previous boyfriends and I can't really see him giving my father a hand building rabbit hutches . . . Will they have anything to talk about, I wonder?

In the large hall with travertine tiles, clean masonry and dark stained panelling there is a sign listing various family names. The sign says we need to go to a room in the basement. We descend the wide wooden staircase and leave our coats with a blonde girl in a black-and-white uniform. The doors to the room stand wide open: a large square space with narrow mirrored columns and a low ceiling. Here too the walls are exposed brick. The floor is tiled in a mixture of shades of beige. Opposite the entrance a band in glittery waistcoats – a dark female singer and a blond male singer and someone at a keyboard – is playing a Tom Jones number.

Some people are standing talking, others are on the dance floor or sitting eating at one of the tables arranged along the walls. There is buffet laid out to the right of the band. In the soft light shining from spots in the modular ceiling I can see many familiar faces. Els's hysterical laughter, which I locate somewhere on the right, is audible above the music.

I bend over to Leon. 'The woman you can hear shrieking is Els. A good friend of my mother's. She's a bit peculiar.' I point to the dance floor. 'And that bloke over there, with the braces, dancing with that woman in the green dress is my Uncle Anton. He's just out of hospital.'

'There's no need to introduce me to everyone,' Leon says. 'Or it could take all night.'

'I can't see my parents.' I stand on tiptoe and scan the crowd with a frown. 'Or Anne and Dick either. Dick's my brother.'

'I know.'

Children are dancing together in front of the band. My grandma is standing among them, a little unsteady on her legs, which are covered in thick tights, wearing a flowery party dress and make-up. She is being supported by a strapping lad of about twelve, who might be a cousin of mine. 'That's my Grandma, my mother's mother. I wasn't expecting to see her here, she lives in an old people's home . . . more like sheltered accommodation next to the old people's home. Wait a moment, there's Paul.'

I grab Leon's hand, take him over to the buffet and tap Paul on the shoulder. He swings round, looks at Leon first with a frown and then turns to me. His face brightens. 'Ah. Little Margot, now I see. Well . . . *little* Margot . . .'

Paul has loosened his tie, and it is now hanging lopsided across his white shirt, which is stretched dangerously tight over his huge paunch. His hands grip my waist and give it a squeeze. 'Still plenty of you, I see. Keep it that way, dear. You look good enough to eat.'

'Happy anniversary,' I say, giving him three kisses. 'This is my boyfriend Leon.'

Paul's small brown eyes sparkle as they shake hands. 'Familiar face.'

'Leon's a photographer. An art photographer. He's been in the paper.'

'No, that's not where I know him from.' Paul turns to Leon. 'Do you ever go to Café de Sport? To play darts?'

'No,' says Leon. 'I don't think so.'

'Well you've got a familiar face all the same.' Paul sticks his index finger in the air. His movements are uncoordinated. 'But . . . I'll crack it before the evening's out. I've got a really good memory for faces.'

'Where's Agatha?' I ask.

Paul scans the room in annoyance. 'I really haven't a clue. Perhaps she's gone off with a strange man.' He winks at Leon. 'Women! You've got to keep an eye on them all the time, even when they're over sixty. Mark my words, lad. Have you two already had something to drink?'

'Not yet, I wanted to congratulate you first.' I put my arm on his shoulder in parting and take Leon over to my parents. They're sitting with Dick and Anne at one of the tables, close to the band, which is now playing 'Red Red Wine'.

'Take no notice of Paul,' I say. 'He always thinks he knows everyone from somewhere.'

'Give the running commentary a rest, will you. I can think for myself.'

I stop for a moment. I want to ask him to loosen up a little, but decide against it. It will sort itself out.

We've hardly reached the table when my father jumps up from his chair. He's wearing the light yellow shirt he's had for years and reserves exclusively for parties and celebrations, with a blue tie and smart grey trousers. 'We were just talking about you. I thought you weren't coming.'

'Of course I was,' I say, kissing him on both cheeks. 'Dad, this is Leon.'

'Hello, Leon,' says my father. Leon is at least six inches taller than my father, who almost has to crane his neck to look at him. 'Nice to meet you. We've heard a lot about you.'

'Not that much really,' my mother says. She smells strongly of perfume and there's a light coating of powder on her face. Before she says hello to me, she shakes hands with Leon. 'I'm Margot's mother.'

'No need to tell me. It shows,' says Leon. The corners of his mouth curl into a smile.

'It does, doesn't it?' My mother smiles shyly, cocks her head a little to one side and straightens the front of her glittery blouse.

Dick gives me a hug. 'Glad you could make it, sis. We were worried you were going to cancel.'

I feel slightly needled. 'Why does everyone always think that?'

Anne joins her husband and kisses me on both cheeks. 'We never see you these days. Recently it seems like you don't want to know us.'

'Don't be silly! This is Leon.'

'The reason,' says Dick, shaking his hand.

'Hello,' says Anne to Leon.

Now the introductions are out of the way, four pairs of eyes are staring at Leon like he's the evening's main attraction, and in a sense he is.

'Maybe you should put a jacket on,' says my father, plucking at my blouse, his face radiating disapproval. 'This is rather . . . chilly.'

I burst out laughing. 'This is how it's meant to be. I haven't got a jacket with me.'

'It's certainly different, isn't it?' my mother remarks. 'Not what we're used to from you.'

'I like it, Mum.'

'Don't let us cramp your style. And don't worry about what Dad says, he hasn't got a clue about fashion. By the way, have you two had anything to drink?'

I shake my head.

She waves at a waiter walking around with a tray. The young man turns on his heel and stops at our table.

'Red wine for you?' she asks.

'No, white.'

She takes a glass off the tray and looks at Leon. 'Beer?'

'No, the same.'

'There's beer as well, you know.'

'No thanks. Wine is fine.'

She takes a glass off the tray and hands it over to him. 'Well, that's nice. The whole family's complete. Gosh. Come over and sit with us, we want to know all about you, Theo.'

'Leon,' I correct her. 'Leon, Mum.'

'Those boots are really something,' I hear Anne say.

When I look up it turns out she's not talking about mine, but Leon's. They're black and grey, with long toes and a kind of reptile print.

'Thanks,' says Leon, moving one foot demonstratively back and forth. 'A friend of mine brought them back from Australia. Crocodile leather.'

'Poor crocodiles.'

'Personally I don't have much sympathy for the creatures.'

A little later my father calls the waiter over to the table again to give everyone a refill.

Leon puts his hand on his half-empty glass. 'No more for me. I've got to drive.'

'Are you going back to Amsterdam tonight?' asks my mother incredulously.

'No,' I say. 'We're spending the night in Helvoirt, Leon's got a bungalow there.'

'You know they've got hotel rooms here? Lots of people are staying the night.' She nods in Leon's direction. 'Then he can have a drink too.'

I look inquiringly at Leon. He shakes his head briefly, almost imperceptibly to the others.

'Leave it, Mum. Leon's working tomorrow.' *Why am I lying?*

'On a Sunday?'

'He doesn't have an ordinary job.'

'Well, tell us all about it,' says my mother, who has slid close to Leon and is watching him with interest. 'I've heard you're an artist. Can you make a living from that?'

'Things are going fine,' he says curtly.

'Leon often goes abroad on assignments,' I say, backing him up. 'He's just come back from Denmark.'

'Oh how nice. What were you doing there?'

'Taking photos for a multinational. More and more listed companies are brightening up their annual reports with art photos.'

She's doing her level best to feign interest. My mother is far from unworldly, but annual reports and art photography are beyond her ken.

'Since I had to retire on medical grounds I've been keeping rabbits,' says my father. 'Did Margot tell you?'

Leon shakes his head. 'Not that I can remember.'

My father straightens his shoulders. He's glowing with pride. 'Last year I bred the best lop-eared rabbit in the Southern Netherlands.'

'Impressive,' says Leon charitably. 'How do you do that?'

I could have warned him to ignore my father as far as possible on this point and not to give him the slightest encouragement to start talking about his animals, but it simply didn't occur to me. For the next ten minutes Leon is force-fed an impassioned monologue on blood lines, selection procedures and the effect of heat and special feed on the growth of rabbits. To my surprise Leon assumes the role of victim with good grace. My father needs little more than the occasional 'oh' and 'of course' to start him on the next rabbitological topic. Leon gives me a confidential wink. My father doesn't notice.

I feel two hands on my shoulders and look round. It's Uncle Paul.

'Come on, lovely girl, you're sitting here chattering the whole time, Agatha and I didn't hire an expensive band for nothing. Time to take to the floor.'

Before I can protest I'm pulled to my feet and Paul more or less drags me onto the dance floor. Not that I really mind. I've always liked dancing. That was one of the things John and I had in common. Many men just hang around the bar at parties, but John could always be found on the dance floor. I haven't seen him yet and I honestly hope it stays that way, since I don't feel like having to avoid him all evening.

Paul holds one of my hands high in the air and grasps my waist firmly. He twirls round like an expert dancer, but can't help losing the rhythm now and then. He really has had too much to drink. And he's not the only one. I feel a bit light-headed from the frequent pirouettes and the two glasses of wine. When the song is over, Paul holds me tight. 'One for the road.'

My feet and hips start moving automatically to the beat of the next song.

Through the dancing throng I see Leon sitting with my parents by the wall like a dark shadow. His arms are crossed and he's gazing over the top of all the heads into his very own horizon.

My father is still gesticulating wildly: he's really got his teeth into Leon. For a moment I feel sorry for him. I should have warned him.

In a flash I see John go by. Less than twenty feet away from us he is supporting Grandma on the dance floor. He's holding her firmly by the elbows, making sure she doesn't fall. Her movements are wooden, but her face is all smiles. It's wonderful to see Grandma enjoying herself, among all the people she cares about. I realise with a jolt that this might be her last party. Once she's sitting on the sidelines again, I'll go and talk to her. Sweet of John to take care of her. To his credit, he's always done that. Grannies, small children, teenage girls in glasses, they could all count on John. That was the glue that kept us together, at parties like this we were in our element.

John catches my eye. He smiles and winks. I smile back, slightly embarrassed, hoping that Leon hasn't seen. It's not a nice feeling, being unable to be completely myself at a party for my own family.

'Whoopsadaisy!' cries Paul again and I twirl round again under his solid, short arm.

Out of the corner of my eye I see my mother leaning over towards Leon. Leon takes a sip of his wine. His eyes wander and linger on John. I feel doubt setting in. Shall I go back the table? I decide to wait until this song's over. It's a long time since I danced and it feels too good.

Shortly afterwards I see that Dick has taken my chair. He and Anne are talking animatedly to Leon. I can't see his face from here.

The band moves on to the next song. Paul looks at me mischievously and keeps me on the dance floor. Perspiration is dripping from his forehead.

'I really am going to sit down after this one,' I shout in his ear.

'You must be joking!' he shouts, leading me to the other side of the dance floor.

I'm not entirely happy about leaving Leon alone, but as long as my family are keeping him occupied not much can go wrong. He's a grown man. I don't need to hold his hand all evening.

As soon as the music dies away, Paul is relieved as my partner by a man I don't recognise at first. Fine features, tanned skin and short grey hair. He must be reading my thoughts. 'Have you forgotten me already? Surely not?'

'Now I see it,' I cry excitedly. 'Cor from Switzerland.'

'Still me.' He puts his hands on my shoulders. 'My goodness, little Margot, how you've grown!'

'I've not grown any taller in the last five years,' I say.'

'But wider you have.'

Not until about six songs later – it could just as easily be seven – am I able to tear myself away from the dance floor and uncles and aunts and go back to the table.

Leon's chair is empty and he's nowhere to be seen.

'Where's Leon?' I ask my mother, who's been left holding the fort and is eating a pastry.

She looks up in confusion. 'I've no idea, darling. Perhaps he's dancing or he's gone to the toilet. He's certainly a handsome man. Nice clothes, and charming too. Are you happy with him?'

'Yes, very.' Gratefully I take a few gulps of the wine which has been left for me in my absence.

'That's good. He seems very nice. Dad likes him too, I think.'

Under the table I squeeze my mother's hand. 'I'm really glad about that.'

'We've missed you, all of us,' she says, serious now.

'I know. I'm sorry. I've just been really busy. And I'm not around here much anymore.'

'Are you really having a nice time in Amsterdam?'

'Yes,' I say truthfully. 'But I do miss you all.'

'Speak of the devil,' says my mother. She pushes her plate away and gets up. 'I'll leave you two in peace for a moment.'

As my mother heads for the dance floor, Leon makes straight for me. I can see right away that something isn't right. He's avoiding the dancers with agitated movements and he looks like he's spoiling for a fight.

He stops in front of me with his hands in his pockets.

'What's wrong?' I ask.

He looks demonstratively at his watch. 'We've been here for two hours and you've been on the dance floor for an hour and a half. Thanks a lot.'

I frown. 'Oh, come on, Leon, don't be so difficult.'

'Difficult? Me? I've been sitting here for an hour and a half listening to your father telling me about his rabbits and about how kind it is of John to help him build his new hutches, your brother waffles on at me for half an hour about leaky taps and your sister-in-law never tires of talking about her gifted children – while you're off having a ball. Not my idea of a good time.'

'Don't make such an issue of it. It's a party!'

His hand closes round my arm like a vice. 'That's fine by me, but we're going.'

'Behave,' I say, and try to pull free, but he keeps a tight hold of me and won't budge an inch.

'I said we're going. Now.'

It all erupts like a festering sore. The people around me may not be interesting artists or rich art collectors, but we understand each other, we share a common history. The talk with my mother and the conversations on the dance floor with my uncles and aunts confirmed my suspicion that without realising it I've turned my back on everyone since the break-up with John. And they really don't deserve that. After those dreadful lonely days in Amsterdam it's wonderful to let myself go to the music, and get closer to my family again. I feel good, welcome, and I'm reluctant to lose that feeling. This all crosses my mind as the band strikes up 'Let the Party Begin' and everyone around us starts leaping about and singing along.

'I'm not going. I haven't seen my family for ages. It's not even eleven o'clock yet!'

'I think you'd better,' he says, icily. 'Because otherwise you can walk to Helvoirt.'

My mouth almost drops open. 'Do you know what? Suit yourself. I've had it up to here with your ordering me about.'

Leon gives me a withering look. He lets go of my arm.

A group has gathered round us, they've picked up on the sudden tension and are watching us expectantly.

'Just sit down,' I hiss. 'Get a drink like everyone else. Then we can stay here overnight. You don't have work tomorrow. Stop being so difficult.'

The next moment John appears, a little unsteady on his feet. His hair is dishevelled and his eyes are beaming with pure pleasure. He puts one arm round me and the other round Leon, probably since he'd fall over otherwise. His weight presses us together a little.

'Hey, what's this I hear,' he says in a hoarse voice. 'Are you two going already? Don't be such party poopers, it's just warming up.'

With a fluid movement Leon grabs John by the collar and

swings him round with enormous power. John's face expresses nothing but surprise as his body is swept backwards by the force. He stumbles and lands sideways on the dessert buffet. The cake, the bottles, everything falls over in a diabolical game of dominos and clatters to the floor. John tries to stop himself but can't help sliding off and taking the tablecloth with him, together with everything left on it.

Around us people are clapping their hands to their mouths and holding on to each other.

Everyone is staring at Leon, who hasn't moved yet and hasn't taken his eyes off me for a second. He's barely noticed the havoc he has caused – or he doesn't care.

'Well?' he says.

The music stops.

'What do you mean, well?' My whole body is shaking and trembling.

'Get your bag.'

'Do what you have to do, but I'm staying here.'

He jerks round and leaves the room. All the guests shrink back from him. A gap seems to open up automatically for him to walk through, flanked by my tipsy family members, looking in turn at me and Leon, who goes into the hall and disappears from sight.

I run after him on impulse.

Leon is standing by the cloakroom. He's taking his coat from a bewildered young girl.

For a moment, a fraction of a section, our eyes meet. Then he turns on his heel without a word and walks up the stairs two steps at a time.

'Arrogant prick,' I call after him.

38

'Shall I try to sort out a room for you? Or do you want to stay over with us? Cor and Anita will be there too, but if you want, I can—'

'No, I'd rather go to my own place,' I interrupt my mother.

It's two in the morning. The band left over an hour ago and most of the guests trickled out of the room with them.

Apart from my parents, John and me, Cor and Anita are still in the foyer of the hotel.

My head is spinning with exhaustion and my ears are ringing.

'Shall I call you a taxi?' asks my father.

'No need,' says John. 'I'll take her home.'

My father looks at him probingly. 'Haven't you had too much to drink, son?'

'Not at all. Four or five beers spread over the whole evening.'

'I'm not so sure about that . . . You'll take care of my daughter, won't you? She's the only one I've got.'

John nods and looks at me. 'Are you coming?'

I follow him outside. The indicators on his Astra flash in the dark when he presses the key. John holds the door open for me. I slump into the car and put my belt on.

In the confined space the roaring in my ears gets worse. After Leon's departure the rest of the evening passed me by in a blur. My mother took me to the toilets, where I had a crying fit. She offered to get someone to take me home, but that was the last thing I wanted. So I freshened up, applied new make up to my swollen eyes and plunged back into the thick of the party. I spent virtually all evening on the dance floor. Dancing to forget, dancing to avoid thinking of anything else. I immersed myself in alcohol, the high of the music and finally exhaustion. There was a storm raging inside me, I was furious with Leon. He really went too far. I have a problem with aggression. Men who get into fights, that dreadful macho behaviour – I hate it.

I still haven't totally calmed down, although alcohol and tiredness are scattering an anaesthetising layer over most of my emotions.

John gets in beside me and pulls out of the complex in the direction of town. 'How shitty,' he says. 'I really had no idea—'

'There's no need to apologise. Leon was out of order.'

'He was jealous. I should have realised. I should have—'

'Please, shut up about it.'

A quarter of an hour later John stops the car outside my flat and lets the engine idle. Despite the cold and the late hour people are still out and about. Saturday night in the centre of a provincial capital. Groups of young people are roaming about along the narrow canal that flows past my flat. They are singing and slurring.

'I'll wait till you're inside, OK?'

'Yes, that would be nice.' I rummage in my bag, but can't find what I'm looking for. 'Shit,' I mutter.

'What?'

'My keys. I've got a feeling they're at Leon's, in my other coat.'

'You're joking.'

'No I'm not.' Against my better judgement I take everything out of my bag, every trivial little object, and open zips, feeling in every nook and cranny. 'I really don't have them on me.' I lay my head against the headrest and sigh deeply. The lamps along the canal seem to be swaying slowly to and fro in the night.

'What now?' says John.

I sigh again. 'Good question. Dick has a spare key.'

'He'll have gone to bed long ago. I saw him leave at about eleven with Anne and the kids.'

'I know.'

John coughs and rubs his face. 'It feels awkward, but . . . can I offer you a bed?'

'I'm afraid there's nothing else for it,' I hear myself say. The voice seems to come from someone else.

I've lost count of how many times we've driven this route, home from town in the evening. It feels unreal, as if I'm in a time warp, a year back in time. No, further back, when John was still the John I fell for. The sweet, handsome, considerate, strong John.

'Funny, isn't it,' John says next to me, as he takes the key out of the ignition and the dashboard light goes out. 'You and me. Here.'

I look at him in the semi-darkness, dumbstruck.

He runs his hand through my hair. 'Come on, let's go inside. You'll be falling asleep in a minute, and I won't be able to carry you.'

'Thanks a lot.'

'It wasn't a dig. You look terrific.'

'I ease myself out of the car and stagger over to the front door of a house that for seven years was my home. I've stood here, on this exact spot under the carport, thousands of times, summer and winter, with full shopping bags, looking for my key.

John opens the door and lets me in. I take off my coat and

hang it on the hatstand, in one flowing movement, without looking. I'm reeling.

'Are you coming?' says John.

I follow him into the living room. After weeks of living in Leon's loft, this room suddenly appears very small. It's not a small building by any means, but it feels almost like a doll's house.

'Nightcap?'

'I don't think that's a good idea. I don't want to make myself ill, if I haven't already.'

'Just water then?'

'Water's fine.'

While John is busy in the kitchen, I sit down on the sofa. The light-headedness persists, as does the annoying whistling in my ears, alternating with beeping.

John sits down next to me and gives me a glass of water.

I take a couple of sips. I look at John over the rim of my glass and read concern in his eyes – that and something else that I haven't seen in him for a long time. 'Don't get any ideas,' I say, softly. 'Really, John. It was a very strange evening, but we're not going to make it any weirder than it already is.'

He throws his hands up. 'Hey, this feels just as odd to me as it does to you, you know.' He coughs with his fist to his mouth, loosens his tie and kicks off his shoes.

We sit next to each other in silence for a moment. John finishes his bottle of beer, and I sip the water.

'Well,' he says. 'What now?'

'I want to go to bed.'

'Shall I take the sofa?'

'No need.'

He raises his eyebrows. 'Really?'

I shake my head and empty my glass. 'No.'

We follow each other upstairs to the bedroom in silence. He turns the light on.

'I haven't tidied up.'

'No, I can see.'

'If I'd known . . .'

'Doesn't bother me.' I get undressed, but keep my underwear on. When I see John running his eye over me I realise that the lingerie I'm wearing is not ordinary. I no longer care if he notices or what he thinks. It's like my arms and legs have suddenly become several pounds heavier. All I want is to sleep.

John turns off the main light and switches his bedside lamp on. It diffuses a soft, yellowy light through the bedroom, which is otherwise totally white.

I slide under the covers and lay my head on the pillow. Still that whistling in my ears. When I turn over I'm looking straight into John's eyes.

'I never realised what I was putting on the line,' he whispers. 'I know I shouldn't . . . mustn't be thinking about any of this, but I can't help it. You're a very beautiful woman, always have been. I took you too much for granted.' He reaches out.

I take his hand and kiss it softly. 'It was very sweet what you did this evening, with Grandma. I know how tiring that is.'

'I like doing it. Hopefully someone will do it for me later, when I'm old and decrepit.'

'You're a good person, John.'

His eyes are glistening. 'You only think that because you can't read my thoughts.'

'I think I can read your thoughts perfectly well.'

He closes his eyes for a moment. Then he rubs his thumb along my lips. 'I've fallen in love with you all over again,' he whispers.

I start crying silently and the tears roll down my face onto the pillow.

'Why are you crying?'

'I've no idea.' I really do have no idea.

John slides across the bed until he is lying against me and puts his arm round me. I smell his scent, that familiar scent, a mixture of aftershave and shower gel, and lay my head on his chest.

Then he works his way out from underneath me and lies on top of me. He buries his face in my neck, cautiously, feeling his way. 'My God, how I've missed this,' he moans.

I lie there in silence. I don't know what I think any more – or what I ought to think, and still don't feel like I'm clear-headed enough to know what I'm doing. The movements I make are not prompted by love or any other motive, they're routine, a reflex, made without thinking.

As he enters me, I immediately regret what's happened, regret coming here, regret that I'm now lying underneath him, swaying to his rhythm. I just feel dirty. What brought me here was a cry for love. I needed someone familiar, someone who would put his arms round me and tell me everything was going to be all right. But it won't be all right – it's just getting worse. I like John as a person, but I don't love him any more, and my body makes that brutally clear by switching off.

I read once that sex is all in the mind. It's true, I now know, it's simply true. Nothing is happening to my body, no tingling, no breathlessness, none of that. I lie underneath him like a rag doll and just want him to get a move on so that it's over quickly.

I close my eyes and think of Leon, the way he sat in that chair in London, his dark look as I spread my legs for him, the nervousness and excitement that shot through me. I think back to the first time he actually fucked me, the evening after I'd collected my things from John. Just the memory makes me feel my pelvis contracting and my body coming alive. Leon's eyes, Leon's hands, Leon's smell. When I open my eyes and stare at the chair in the corner of the bedroom, I can immediately picture him sitting there, watching, directing. Taking photos in his head. I can almost see the glowing tip of the cigarette he takes a drag on. By the curtain I see a dark shadow moving, a tall dark silhouette. That's it. I'm losing my mind completely, I've gone stark raving mad, I'm starting to hallucinate. Leon isn't here. Yet I feel his presence when I close my eyes again and concentrate.

I miss him. I miss him so badly it hurts.

John quickens his tempo, raises himself up and grunts incoherent words in my ear. But it's not John's words that echo in my mind, it's not his teeth biting my flesh, it's not his body that's taken over mine and not John who, to my own dismay, brings me to an orgasm that makes me cry out loud.

John rolls off me and brushes my hair out of my face. 'Wow,' he says, panting. 'Wow, Margot. Am I mistaken, or . . .? That's never happened before, has it? Not with—'

'I'm going home.' I push the duvet off me and start collecting my clothes.

Stupefied, John sits up in bed. 'You can't be serious.'

'This was wrong. I shouldn't have done it. Forget it.'

'*Forget it?*'

Stiffly, I put on my skirt and blouse. I realise too late that my thong is somewhere under the covers. Too bad. I just want to go.

'What on earth have I done wrong?' he sounds completely nonplussed.

'Nothing. You haven't done anything wrong. *I've* done something wrong. Terribly wrong.' I turn round on the threshold and shake my head. 'I don't love you.

I really don't.'

He jumps out of bed and hurriedly pulls on a bathrobe. 'I don't believe you.'

'Do me and yourself a favour: forget it.' Through a mist of tears I go downstairs and open the front door. The cold of the night hits me in the face when I go outside. The neighbours' security light comes on.

John is standing in the doorway in his bare feet. 'Margot, you can't go home. You haven't got a key.'

'I'm going to my mother's. I should have done that in the first place.'

'You can't go banging on their door at this hour,' he calls after me. 'It's four o'clock!'

'Bye, John.'

39

It's Monday and demolition work at Ce Truc is in full swing. I dropped by in the morning, just over an hour after the first workmen had set to work with gusto. It did me good to be able to establish that at least something in my life is going according to plan. But that's the only thing.

Joost is fluttering nervously around the workmen. He shows them what can go in the skip and what needs to be carefully loaded in to the small lorry to be transported to the storage facility.

My presence doesn't make much difference. The project has been prepared and discussed in detail, and everyone knows exactly what to do. The reason I'm here nevertheless is officially to give moral support to Joost, who's seeing his restaurant demolished before his eyes and is visibly upset by it – unofficially because I didn't want to sit at home with nothing but my gloomy, destructive thoughts for company.

As the space around me turns into a war zone with terrifying speed, the parallels with my own life are not lost on me. I've blown everything. Everything.

By letting Leon leave I've put myself in an impossible position. He'll never want to see me again. His ego's too big for that. He was the best thing that ever happened to me and I sent him away.

As a result, although I don't see it as the greatest loss by any means right now, there are far-reaching consequences for my business. Its tottering foundations rest entirely on Leon and his connections. Now that I've wilfully kicked that basis from under my feet, my business will collapse like a house of cards. In a little while, when I feel better again, I'll have to start actively looking for a new job. Not a pleasant prospect.

And yet, if I could turn the clock back, I wouldn't change a thing. Now I look back on it, the seed for Saturday night's outburst was already sown in the events of the previous week. Leon probably sees it differently. It's likely he thinks I've opted for my family, maybe even for John. But that's not it. I opted for something that I'd just regained and was in danger of losing all over again: my sense of self-worth. If I'd gone off with Leon on the evening of the party, I would have completely lost my identity. I *couldn't* do that, couldn't let it happen, if I wanted to stay true to the person I should love most of all: myself. However much Leon has come to mean to me, by doing that I'd have reduced myself to little more than his serf – a spineless slave to his whims, with no face of my own and no autonomy.

No, I don't regret that decision.

It's what happened afterwards that makes me cringe with shame.

'One, two . . .' the workmen roar in chorus. They are taking the panelling off the wall with crowbars. The wood creaks loudly and dust spirals into the room.

My mobile rings. I can't hear the sound but can feel the phone vibrating in my pocket. Against my better judgement my heart skips a beat.

Leon won't call. He'll never call me again.

Hurriedly I take it out of my pocket and look at the screen.

It's my mother.

'. . . a bit . . . again darling?'

'I can't hear you very well. Wait a moment, Mum.' I go into the corridor and put a hand over my ear. 'What did you say?'

'I asked if you were feeling a bit better again now.'

'Reasonably.'

'What's all that noise I can hear in the background? Are you at work?'

'Yes, they're demolishing an old interior around me.'

'Is this a good time?'

'Of course it is. What's wrong?'

'I'm calling because I'm worried we may have given you the wrong impression yesterday. We left you to your own devices not because we don't care. We didn't want to intrude.'

'I do understand that. Don't fret about it.'

'I wanted to tell you that your father and I were talking about it only yesterday evening. We'd both hate you to be unhappy.'

'If I am, there's nothing you can do about it. You did what you could and I hugely appreciate that.'

'Perhaps not entirely. Your father may see things a bit differently, he doesn't think about much more than his rabbit hutches, but I have my own opinion. I don't think Leon's reaction was that over the top at all. Your father used to be exactly the same kind of hothead, did you know that? I only had to look at another man and he'd fly into a rage . . . None of us gave it second thought at the time, but it must have been very hard for the lad. Everyone knew everyone else and he didn't know anyone – and you basically left him to fend for himself.'

'He should have been able to cope with that,' I say agitatedly. 'He's a grown man.'

She pretends she hasn't heard me. 'Jealousy is a sign of love, Margot. But even more of insecurity. That exceptional, handsome artist of yours isn't nearly as self-assured and arrogant as he'd have himself and us believe.'

I step aside for two workmen who are carrying sections of panelling outside. 'I don't believe that.'

'It's not a matter of believing it. Just take it from me that it's true. Aunt Anita is sitting here next to me and she says the same.'

I groan. Great, my mother discussing my love life with my aunt – if only that were all, but I know better.

'She agrees with me. That man really cares about you. You're important to him.'

'I thought you wanted me to get back together with John?'

'We want you to be happy. I saw the difference, darling. Even though we didn't see much of you, I've never seen you glowing like you have been recently. You look fantastic, your new work is doing you good . . . That Leon is good for you. I don't think it was a sensible move to send him packing.'

'I didn't send him packing.'

She says nothing. For a moment I think she's rung off, but the timer is still running on the screen. 'Mum?'

'I'm still here. Listen, I'm not going to interfere anymore, because of course I don't know if there's anything else involved. That's none of my business anyway. It's your life. I just wanted to say how we see things. Think about it.'

'There's no point any more.'

'I'm not so sure about that. Well, I won't interrupt your work any longer. Keep your head and don't do anything silly. And you know: if anything happens we're always here for you.'

'I know that, Mum. You're a darling.'

'Lunch break!' A deep male voice shouts.

I look at my watch. It's twelve o'clock. Joost is coming towards me. His eyes are darting back and forth behind the thin lenses of his glasses. 'I'm not cut out for this. What an unbelievable mess. Horrible.'

'It'll all be all right,' I say. 'The worst will be over by tonight.'

'You think so?' Joost turns round and we look into the room together. There's a pall of dust and the floor is strewn with pieces of wood and rubbish.

'Yes, really.'

'Shall we go and have lunch somewhere? There's not much I can do here.'

'I'm not very hungry.'

Joost bends over to me. 'Have you got a hangover?'

'No. I'm just not hungry.'

'Perhaps I shouldn't say it, but you look terrible. What did you get up to at the weekend?'

'Just stupid stuff.'

He smiles broadly. When I don't react, he gives me a searching look. 'Nothing too stupid, I hope?'

'Leave it,' I say dully. 'Where did you want to eat?'

My telephone rings again.

'You're popular today,' Joost remarks.

'It just looks that way,' I mutter, and glance fleetingly at the screen. An unknown number.

'Yes, hello.'

'Hello, this is Detective Charles Burghardt, North Brabant Police. Is that Margot Heijne?'

'That's right.' My heart misses a beat. Why would a detective be ringing me? 'What's wrong?'

'Are you at home?'

'No. I'm at work, in Amsterdam. What's it about?'

Silence.

'We'd rather tell you in person.'

I grip the telephone with both hands. 'Then I'll jump straight in the car.'

'Shall we say two o'clock at your place?' the man says.

'Two o'clock will be fine.'

40

It's ten past two when I drive into the street along the canal and I see a police car parked outside my door with two wheels on the pavement. The moment I park my car in the permit-holder's space, two people get out. A dark-haired, heavily-built man of about forty and a young woman with a narrow light-brown face and a brown ponytail. She's wearing a uniform, the man wears corduroy trousers and a thick red coat. They both have utterly serious expressions.

The whole long way home I wondered what could be wrong. It can't have anything to do with my parents or Dick and Anne. It flashed through my mind that it might be about Leon. Perhaps he got into trouble after he drove home on Saturday night. I soon abandoned that idea. What policeman would pay me a visit about something to do with Leon? Perhaps there's been a burglary, or I've committed some misdemeanour I'm unaware of. Although that idea is not pleasant either, at least it's easier to bear than the thought of something terrible happening to someone I care about.

'Burghardt,' says the man, shaking my hand.

The woman nods at me encouragingly. She has small, slim hands, but has a firm handshake. I don't catch her name.

'Come in,' I say.

In the hall there is a note stuck to my letterbox saying in block capitals PLEASE EMPTY!!! THIRD REQUEST!!!

'I haven't been home much,' I explain, with a vague gesture towards the letterbox. 'I live . . . er, lived with my boyfriend half the time.'

They nod and follow me upstairs.

I feel myself growing more nervous by the second. In the living room I point to the sofa. 'Have a seat. Coffee, tea?'

The heating hasn't been on for weeks. I turn the thermostat to twenty and go through into the kitchen.

'Don't go to any trouble, Ms Heijne. We don't need anything to drink. Have a seat.'

As there are no seats left, I fetch a chair from the kitchen and put it beside the coffee table, diagonally opposite the sofa. 'Sorry it's so cold in here.'

'We'll keep our coats on. You are the partner of John van Oss? That's what his mother told us.'

John. Something's happened to John.

'Ex-partner,' I say, almost breathlessly, and I look from one to the other.

'Did you live with Mr Van Oss for long?'

'Seven years. We split up about six months ago.'

'But you saw him this weekend?'

I cringe. 'Yes.'

The man looks in a small notebook that he takes from the inside pocket of his coat and reads aloud: 'A family celebration.'

'Yes, that's right. John is more or less one of the family. He's going to help my father with his rabbit hutches. My father's a rabbit-breeder, you see.' Why am I telling them all this? It's pure nervousness.

'Did you go home with him after the party?'

'I didn't intend to originally. But I'd left my house key behind in Amsterdam. It was too late to get a spare key from my brother Dick, so we drove to his house.' I'll leave it at that. I have no idea what they're after.

'Had your ex-partner been drinking?'

I have the feeling I need to watch my words. Perhaps John took the car out after I left and caused an accident and they're now collecting evidence against him. No, it can't be that. I would definitely have heard about that from my mother. Still I remain on my guard. 'I don't know,' I reply. 'Everyone had drunk quite a bit. So had I.'

'Did you spend the night with Mr Van Oss?'

I shake my head. 'No . . . Or not really. In the end I left and stayed the night at my parents' house. They don't live very far away.'

'What time was that?'

'I haven't a clue. Four o'clock? Four-thirty? It must have been something like that.'

'Did you see him or speak to him after that?'

'No.' I rub my face with my hand and look up. 'This is about John. What's wrong?'

The man coughs and exchanges a knowing look with his female colleague.

She looks at me with sympathy. 'This morning Mr van Oss did not show up at work. That was unusual for him, he was always there around eight. He didn't answer any of his phones and a colleague went over at about ten o'clock to check up on things.'

I stare from one to the other. 'Yes?'

'His house was locked, but the car was outside. No one answered the door, not even after his colleague had rung the doorbell repeatedly and banged on the door and windows. Then he called us and we gained entry to the house.'

My hands are clenched in my lap.

'Our officers found your ex-partner dead.'

'Dead?' I exclaim. 'That's impossible. There was nothing wrong with him. He can't be dead!' My eyes double in size. I look from one to the other again. 'No. It's impossible . . .'

'It would be a great help if you could tell us exactly what happened when you were at your ex-partner's house on Saturday night. Did you drink anything, was there an argument?'

I lower my eyes and put my face in my hands. 'We went to bed together. I shouldn't have done that. It was unbelievably stupid. I have a new boyfriend, who I had a fight with at the party, and . . . I shouldn't have done it, but it happened. I left immediately afterwards and stayed at my parents' house.'

'The boyfriend you had an argument with, who is that?'

I look up. 'Leon. Leon Wagner. He's an art photographer.'

The man makes a new note in his book. 'Did your ex-partner say anything to you before you left the house? Threaten to harm himself, for instance? Did he ever get depressed?'

I shake my head wildly. 'No. No. John is . . . was always really cheerful. He said he didn't believe me. And that I couldn't go to my parents' because it was too late. It was the middle of the night. He wanted me to stay.'

'What didn't he believe?'

'That I didn't love him. That it had been a mistake.' Again I look at the two people sitting on my sofa with their coats still on. 'What on earth has happened to John?'

XI

John regained his old place in the family brilliantly, or perhaps he'd never really relinquished his place. That was distressing, too upsetting. He was determined to do everything in his power to win her back. And it has to be said he made rapid headway.

I hadn't expected them to let it get to that point so quickly. I was deeply disappointed in her. Call me an incorrigible romantic, but I'd rated her higher than that. Much higher. It was shocking to have to watch as he made advances, slid closer and closer to her on the sofa in his living room and how easily she finally gave in to him. Then they quickly went upstairs. I climbed onto the flat roof of the kitchen and saw her getting undressed for him, the two of them winding up in bed and her finally – I'm not mistaken on this point, even though I'd like to banish it from my mind – starting to scream when he brought her to a climax. Yes, that really disappointed me – cut me to the quick.

It only confirmed the feeling I'd had for so long: John was a malignant tumour that must be cut out. She would never have allowed anyone to do that who hadn't previously been intimate with her. She gets too attached. Not only to things – to people too.

Maybe she really cared about the poor sucker, maybe not. I will never find out, simply because I have to allow for the fact that Margot's utterances after John's death will not necessarily be an accurate representation of the facts. They will not necessarily be a reflection of her real feelings for him while he was alive. I have to see them in context: the suicide of an ex-boyfriend shortly after she had sex with him. I'm not very familiar with these feelings myself, I'm too level-headed for that, but Margot is an emotional person. She will be consumed by guilt. She'll need support, she'll want to talk to someone who understands what she's going through. And guess who knows exactly what she's going through? You bet.

The fact that things went far too easily for him tonight, ran completely counter to my well-thought-out plan that – admittedly – only developed once I'd studied the contents of his fridge earlier this month. What I found there among the French cheese and bottles of Diet Coke would make it so terribly easy to kill him that it was almost an anticlimax. Fortunately there were still plenty more obstacles to overcome before we reached the grand finale. To start with, from that flat roof I was looking at an undisputed victor. A victor wouldn't do what I wanted to make him do.

But as I watched, paralysed, the tide turned, as if it was meant to be. There was an argument. I don't know why she took the decision, but she got dressed and left, on foot.

He stayed behind in the living room, flabbergasted, poured himself a glass of beer, pounded on the sofa with his fist and lay looking at the ceiling for ages.

No longer a victor.

Everything came together, a perfect fit. I had to do it now, wait no longer, hesitate no longer. Still I stood wavering for over a quarter of an hour before I rang the bell, since the intoxicated state I was in had too much of a hold over me for me to act immediately and lucidly.

A fortunate coincidence was that John opened the door at

once, without any suspicion. It probably didn't even occur to him that anyone else could be ringing the bell except for his beloved Margot, who had returned after her impulsive departure. So he looked surprised when saw me standing there. Not frightened, not shocked, just surprised.

I took out my pistol from under my coat and aimed it at his chest. 'Forgive the cliché,' I said softly. 'Personally I'm not a great fan of this bold approach, but unfortunately I haven't got much time. I want to talk to you for a moment.' I pushed the door further open, closed it behind us and forced John to get a notepad and a pen, after which I got him to close the blinds in the kitchen. He sat white-faced at the kitchen table. The scent of her still hung around him. I could smell it, together with the beer.

I sat down opposite him. First I let him talk. As long as he thought there was a way out, he could provide me with important information. And that's what he did. John was a good talker, without doubt. He could have talked the hind legs off a donkey. I saw him thinking, his eyes turning in all directions as he tried to think of a way out of the situation, tried to win me over, while I stared at him icily and asked him question after question. Keep on talking, he must have thought. As long I'm still talking I'm alive.

People are so predictable.

After half an hour I knew enough. Enough to get him to write a heart-rending, realistic letter to communicate to his next of kin. But first I had to get him to the point where he really wanted to write that letter, from the heart. That would make it more real, more plausible for the people who knew him – and hence also for the police.

'OK,' I said. 'We can do this two ways. It's your choice. The party's all yours. Are you going to do it yourself? Or do you want me to do it?

He looked at me uncomprehendingly.

'Forgive the cliché again,' I said, clarifying things. 'But I must, and I really hope you'll understand this, make use of the circumstances. You're not the type who's got the balls to jump from a block of flats. After our conversation I'm convinced you haven't got the aggression necessary to crash a car into a wall. And in this house I unfortunately haven't seen any beams that could take your not inconsiderable weight . . . But you're a diabetic, John. That creates possibilities. You possess potentially lethal quantities of insulin and you're used to injecting yourself. The most obvious plausible thing would be for you to take this route after Margot has left you for good. And of course, as you must realise, if you refuse I'll simply shoot you. Bang. Straight through the head.' I made an upward movement with my pistol and he shied away like a jumpy horse. 'That's no problem,' I went on. 'But imagine, John, it makes so much mess . . . All that blood, those bone splinters, bits of brain. Think of your next of kin, about your dear mother you were just telling me about. She'll want to say goodbye to you, embrace you one last time, as you lie peacefully in your coffin. That won't be possible if your face is damaged, then they won't let the family look at you. I know that from experience. And what's more . . .' I looked away for a moment, as if I was thinking it over, '. . . if you're difficult, I can assure you it'll be very quiet at your funeral, because you won't be the only one who dies tonight. I don't like to say this, but I know where your mother and the rest of your family live and I'll get them out of bed tonight one by one and gun them down. To get even with you, John, for making me mad. And because I simply enjoy it . . . I admit it. That's all the reason I need. As I just said: it's in your hands.'

It was an experiment, purely to see if he would take the bait. If not then I would have to switch to plan B, and the result of that was difficult to predict. I would have to tie him up without causing any injuries or bruising, and then administer a number of lethal injections. No easy task, risky, subject to many, many unforeseen factors. Too many. John wasn't a puny, unsightly little man, but a solidly built chap in the prime of life. I wasn't planning to get into a wrestling match with him. I could easily come off worst.

But John didn't realise any of that. He was so shaken he didn't even realise that I didn't want to use a gun anyway, because of the many drawbacks inextricably bound up with such a solution. Suicide – and of course that was what I was aiming for – would only be plausible if there were traces of gunpowder on the hand holding the gun, in exactly the right spot and exactly the right quantity. That meant that that he would have to pull the trigger himself, and the fact is that's a tall order. Then there was the question of noise. The neighbours were undoubtedly sound asleep, since it was four-thirty by now, but the sound of the shot might startle them awake. There was a good chance they'd simply go back to sleep afterwards – certainly if there was only a single shot. Still I couldn't just blindly assume that. For all I knew one of the neighbours might suffer from insomnia, or one might be a professional who would immediately recognise a pistol shot and leap into action. I had too little time to conduct a detailed investigation of the neighbourhood. It would mean having to make a getaway as fast as possible. And running away is not my style.

I like to look at my handiwork.

But John knew nothing of all this. John had enough problems of his own, that night at the kitchen table. He knew he was going to die, whatever happened, and he opted to do it himself. I could see from his whole attitude that he'd given up hope, but I remained alert.

He cried as he was writing the letter. Believe it or not, he snivelled like a child. He started talking incoherently about his mother, who would miss him so terribly. He told me how much he loved Margot, and that he'd only come to realise that recently, precisely when she had turned her back on him and things were going so well for her. Something had broken in him. His tears dripped onto the paper, causing the ink to run. He made mistakes, crossed words out and the end result looked muddled. That seemed to me to suit his frame of mind.

I handed him his own supply and put down the hypodermic needle, still pristine in its packaging. When he saw that he started to shiver, as if the situation was only now fully dawning on him.

'Intravenous injection gives a better result,' I said. 'Quicker too. It's a nice death, John. You'll fall into a coma quite quickly and won't feel anything. And I'll stay with you till you're dead. That must be a reassuring thought. You're not alone.'

His eyes clouded over and he shivered terribly, so violently I was frightened he wouldn't be able to find a vein.

'Make a tourniquet with your belt,' I advised him.

He did it. A fatalistic mood took hold of him, actually something very beautiful that you seldom see. Resignation at its best. He took plenty of time to tie the striped cotton belt round his upper arm. The he looked for minutes on end at the inside of his arm, as if his veins were moving, dancing before his eyes. They slowly swelled and stood out clearly in purple relief against his white skin.

I didn't want to hurry him along, because the trance he was in was to my advantage. But I was definitely in a hurry. It was already a quarter to five. The coma that follows the direct injection of an overdose of insulin into a blood vessel can last several hours, after which death normally ensues. However, in exceptional cases the patient may revive. Not without permanent brain damage, but he may survive. It all depends on physical resilience, the amount of insulin . . . There are so many factors to take into account. That was why I wanted to be on the safe side and get him to inject himself twice – I had to get away before sunrise.

I watched breathlessly as, still snivelling and babbling, he filled the hypodermic, put the needle in his lower arm, pressed the plunger down slowly but surely, emptying the liquid into his vein.

'And another one,' I said, the pistol still trained on his chest.

He looked at me in confusion.

'Yes, John. Go on. Another one.'

His movements became uncoordinated, but he managed to inject himself again. Then his eyes rolled back in their sockets and he started shaking violently. It was a strange experience to witness a biochemical short circuit. It had a dramatic effect on the functioning of his body. All the blood drained from his face. The shaking became more intense before subsiding. Then he collapsed onto the tiled floor and it became very quiet and peaceful. I knelt down beside him and looked at his face, a grimace of muscles and flesh.

With Edith it was so much more beautiful.

I took a bottle of water out of my pocket, unscrewed the top and took a couple of gulps. My throat had gone dry from the tension and all that talking. The minutes crawled by. Only when I had checked his vital signs for the tenth time two hours later and he was still not breathing, had no pulse and his pupils did not react to the bright light from my pocket torch, did I leave.

My job was done. I had created the circumstances.

The next step is up to Margot.

41

The detectives have gone. In a daze, I sit on the sofa staring into space, with my coat still on. I can't get my head round it, I just can't. John has committed suicide, with his own insulin. He addressed me personally in his suicide note.

I'm the reason he's dead.

How could he do such a thing? How *could* he? I can't even cry. I can't manage it. It's as if I've no feelings left, no emotions. As if I'm empty, used up.

All kinds of thoughts flash through my mind. If I'd stayed with him, slept off the alcohol in his bed instead of at my parents', would things have been different? If I hadn't simply gone off and left him distraught, but had explained to him very calmly over breakfast next morning that I really didn't love him any more, would he have made a different choice? If I hadn't gone to bed with him . . . If I hadn't left my keys in Amsterdam . . . If I hadn't had an argument with Leon . . . If we *had* taken a hotel room . . .

If, if, if.

I curl up and put my hands round my knees. Why? Why did he see no other way out? I can't understand it. The detective asked me if John ever had spells of depression, and however hard I think, the answer is and remains: no. John was the life and soul of the party, jovial, sociable, outgoing: a people person. Of course he was sometimes grouchy, silent, withdrawn, dismissive and angry, but no more than anyone else. I can't remember him ever talking about suicide. Ever. It's so unreal.

I try to resist the idea that he's not there any more. Perhaps it was a cruel joke to punish me. Has John got friends in the police who would do him this kind of favour? Were they fake police in a fake car? Am I dreaming all this?

I'm so nervous I start biting my nails. Perhaps I'll only be able to believe it when I see him, when I can touch him and see he's no longer breathing, feel his heart no longer beating. Or when I can talk to other people, who assure me that it's all really true. As long as I sit here alone on the sofa, it remains too abstract.

I grab the telephone and ring Dick's mobile. He answers immediately.

'Dick? Something terrible's happened.'

Dick gives a deep sigh. 'I know. Half the village is in uproar. How did you find out?'

No fake detectives.

Not a dream.

'From the police,' I say.

'The *police*? What were they doing at yours?'

'They came to ask some questions . . . Why didn't you tell me if you already knew? That's very unlike you.'

'Mum said you were working in Amsterdam and she didn't want to disturb you. It wouldn't have made a difference in any case . . . We were going to call in this evening when you were at home.'

'Have you talked to his mother yet?'

'No. I wouldn't know how to reach her. Hasn't she moved house?'

'She lives in Tilburg.'

'I didn't even know that.'

'Dick, where are you now?'

'At home, with Mum and Dad. Anne's here too, and the next door neighbour. There'll be some more people coming, I expect. Everyone's pretty upset. Me too. I heard from Mum that John took you home after the party.'

'I was with him that night.'

'You're joking!'

'Didn't Mum say anything then?'

'No. I can't get much out of her anyway.'

Suddenly I feel like my heart is going to burst. I fiddle with the zip of my coat and run through my mind in fits and starts what I've already told the police: that I didn't have the key to my flat and spent part of the night with John. I even tell Dick that I went to bed with John and immediately regretted it, and then at about four I went to our parents' house. 'In his suicide note he said I was the reason.'

'Suicide note? Christ, Margot. It gives me the shivers, you know? How awful . . . Are you alone at home?'

'Yes.'

'Stay where you are, I'm on my way.'

It becomes clear to me yet again how important my mother is to the village. My parents' house has been turned into a modest crisis centre. Mum is constantly making coffee, giving every visitor a bowl of homemade vegetable soup and hasn't sat still for a second. It's her way of dealing with it, I realise. As long as she can keep herself occupied and look after others, she's too busy to give in to her own grief. Her grief is as clear as day. We are all full of it. Plus rage. Blame. Pity. Guilt. Questions.

The telephone never stops ringing and the back door keeps opening and shutting. All people who are shocked and want to know more. Gradually I realise that perhaps it wasn't very wise of me to come here. I have a special role in this horror story. The village is already rife with gossip about John's suicide note, and someone has revealed that I have the starring role in it.

An hour, a bowl of soup, six cigarettes and three cups of coffee later I withdraw to my old room. Alone. The heating is on low and it's chilly. I sit down on the bed against the wall and close my eyes for a moment. Downstairs I can hear people talking, their voices muffled by the walls. I hear footsteps in the hall and the toilet being flushed.

In my first lucid moment of the day, the first moment in which, very briefly, I'm not paralysed with grief, I decide to call Joost. I was due to go and see him tomorrow.

He answers the telephone with his typical hoarse voice.

'It's Margot,' I said. 'Something awful's happened.' I explain to him that John, a good friend of mine, has committed suicide, that I'm completely shattered and can't work tomorrow.

'John? Not that ex of yours?'

'Yes, that John,' I say. In all the commotion I've forgotten that Joost has met him, albeit very briefly.

'Did he suffer from depression?'

'No, he . . .' I begin, but cut myself short. It's none of Joost's business. 'I'll be back on Wednesday,' I assure him. 'The plasterers and floor-layers know exactly what to do, so please don't get worked up about it, you don't need me around. Just make sure you're there at seven, they'll do the rest. I'll be back on Wednesday, and Thursday as well. It's just that I won't be able to come to the opening on Friday. I hope you don't mind. Friday is John's funeral.'

'Girlfriend, how can you worry about your work when you're going through something as awful as this? Take all the time you need. I'd just as soon keep Ce Truc shut for another week . . . I mean it, you know. If we can help with anything you must tell me, you hear?'

'It's really not necessary. But thanks anyway. I'll see you on Wednesday.'

He tells me to keep my chin up and rings off. Joost's reaction was heart-warming, but probably because no one in Amsterdam has brought him up to date yet on the rift with Leon. If he'd known about that he would have been a lot less accommodating and understanding.

It's almost ten o'clock when Dick drops me back at home. He hugs me and tells me to stay strong. 'You can sleep at ours if you don't want to be alone tonight. Anne can make you up a bed in no time.'

'No,' I say. 'I'm just going to bed. I'm shattered.'

Dick gives me a questioning look. 'Are you sure?

'Don't worry.'

'Did you have any appointments for tomorrow?'

'One, but I rang to cancel that this afternoon.'

'OK.' He hugs me again. 'Sleep tight. And try not to blame yourself.'

The living room has warmed up, but nevertheless I can't stop shivering. I sit down on the sofa and stare at the mirror, incapable of moving. I'm consumed with guilt and can't get my brain to stop looking for excuses, different choices that would have led to new, positive scenarios in which everything would have taken a different course. *If, if, if* . . .

With trembling fingers I take a squashed packet of cigarettes out of my coat pocket and prise one out. I press the lighter impatiently. There's no flame. I remember there's a lighter next to my PC. I walk unsteadily into the bedroom and am immediately confronted by the framed photo that Leon sent me.

It dominates the wall above my bed, to the right of my computer: the old man with the blue eyes that look at me reproachfully. Pain. My finger slides jerkily over Leon's signature in the right-hand corner of the photo. His handwriting becomes blurry because of the tears welling up in my eyes. And the realisation suddenly hits me like a sledgehammer. 'You've been through this too,' I whisper. 'And for you it was a thousand times worse than for me. You really *loved* her. She was everything to you. And you found her yourself. In your own home.'

I collapse onto the bed and pull my knees up, put my arms round them and lie still, listening to my own breathing and heartbeat.

The cigarette falls out of my hands.

42

The whole village has turned out. In the church all the pews are full. People have positioned themselves along the walls, at the back of the church by the candles, and next to the pews in the aisles. The 'Ave Maria' resounds through the high, vaulted space.

I sit in the second row, flanked by Dick and my mother, heads bowed, wrapped up in their own thoughts. I stare at the oak coffin in front of the altar. There is a sea of flowers on top and in front of it; the floral tributes cover it almost completely, like a multi-coloured veil. Roses, gypsophila, lilies, red and white. Children's drawings stick out of the wreaths. I can only read a few of them, there are so many. 'Words fail us – The Heijne Family'. 'Farewell, John – Bull's Eye Darts Club'. 'We'll never understand – The van Burens'. Goodbye, Mate – Your Colleagues at Lentico'.

I thought I wouldn't be able to cry any more, that I'd never be capable of producing tears, but they keep coming. The paper handkerchief my mother slipped me at the beginning of the service is sticking to my hand like a soggy ball.

I sniff and look at Dick. He gives me an encouraging nod and squeezes my arm for a moment. I look ahead again. John's mother, her sisters and their husbands and children are sitting in the first row.

John was her only child, and his father died years ago of a stroke. His mother has no one now. Her whole family has been snatched away from her. My heart goes out to her, to that thin woman in her black suit and her knot of dyed brown hair.

As the opening bars of 'You'll Never Walk Alone' ring out, the coffin is lifted by six silent men dressed in black. They are from the darts club, friends of John's, and I know them all. They walk slowly, carefully, with chins raised and faces taut with grief, down the aisle to the door of the church. Starting from the first pew, people stand up, following the coffin respectfully. We shuffle on behind. My father supports Grandma and helps her with her Zimmer frame on wheels.

A huge cortege of cars drives at a snail's pace past the snack bar and the supermarket to the cemetery on the outskirts of the village. Other motorists stop for us, people on bikes dismount to stand and watch. Somehow it heartens me that so many people have turned up. John was loved, a people person. He wouldn't have wanted it any other way.

At the cemetery John's coffin is placed on metal crossbeams over the grave. A circle forms around the hole in the ground. The priest says a few final words and sprinkles holy water over the coffin.

It's chilly and I shiver uncontrollably. There's been no sign of the sun yet. A thin layer of frost covers the closely mown grass and the withered brown beech hedge.

I scan the crowd and recognise most of the faces, but a few are strangers to me. They must be colleagues of John's. I get the feeling that every single person John ever met has come to his funeral.

Suddenly I see a face that doesn't belong in this context. For a moment I think I'm mistaken, but it really is her. She's standing diagonally behind the priest between John's coffin and my old neighbours. I can see only a portion of her face and pinned up hair. Our eyes meet and she nods to me, lowering her bright blue eyes.

Debby. She must have heard the news from Joost.

The pub was not designed to cope with the hordes of people wanting to get in. Waiters are walking to and fro with visible haste, and I hear them hissing to one another that more rolls and an extra coffee machine are needed. All the tables are occupied, and many people are standing at the sides, like in the church, but now with a roll in one hand and a cup of coffee in the other. It's warm – very warm after the freezing cold outside, and the windows are steamed up. The atmosphere has become a little more relaxed, but still charged.

I'm standing with my parents, Grandma and Anne and I bite into a soft ham roll. Dick is queuing for the toilets with his sons. I am looking for Debby. Maybe she's gone home, didn't want to intrude and it was enough for her that I knew she was there.

I want to talk to John's mother, who I know only as Tilly. That's what she always wants to be called. Not Mum or Mother, but just by her first name. There is a queue for her too, as there is for the book of condolences.

'It was a nice service,' says my father. His eyes are moist and red-rimmed. 'Worthy of the lad.'

Debby suddenly pops up next to me, almost startling me. Her blue eyes are surrounded by dark make-up and her hair is in a tight bun at the back of her head. She'wearing a long tailored coat with a dark fur collar. 'Hello, darling,' she says, taking my hand and kissing me on both cheeks. She smells of Opium and her skin is cold from being outside, as are her fingers. 'I'm so sorry. How awful. I heard from Joost and didn't want to leave you to face this on your own.' She looks around. 'But you're not exactly alone. It's like a state funeral. Marvellous.'

'Debby, these are my parents. And my sister-in-law Anne.' As they shake hands and Debby gives everyone her condolences, I add: 'Debby lives in Amsterdam.'

'Shame I didn't know John,' she says softly. 'He must have been very popular.'

'Yes, he was,' my mother replies. 'We still find it hard to believe he's not here any more. It's so unreal.'

'I know the feeling,' says Debby. She looks at me in sympathy and takes my hand. 'I want to give you Richard's condolences. And Leon's. He's in pieces.' She looks away for a moment, as if plucking up courage, and then rubs the back of my hand with her cold, thin fingers. 'Leon was very shocked. He told us about the fight he had with John that night. At the party. He blames himself.'

I clench my teeth. 'That's nonsense,' I say as softly as possible, in the hope that my whispering will be lost on the general hubbub. 'Leon has no part in this.'

'It's brought it all up again, the whole business with . . .' She stops in mid-sentence and forces her face into a joyless grin. 'Well, anyway. He hasn't left his loft for days.'

'Good of you to come,' I say, and realise at that moment that I would have preferred it if Leon had come himself. Again I clench my teeth, because at the same time I cannot escape the dark, unbearable thought that if Leon hadn't stormed off, I'd never have ended up going to bed with John. *If, if, if* . . .

'Well, I'll leave you alone now,' she says, with her soft, melodious voice. 'Take care.' Her cold lips tickle my cheek.

'Will you please give Leon all my love,' I say.

She raises one corner of her mouth into a half-smile in

response. With a nod of the head she bids farewell to my parents and disappears.

'Was that a friend of yours?' asks my mother.

'Yes.' I watch her leave until she disappears from sight. 'A good friend of Leon's too.'

'She looks like a model,' says my father, deeply impressed by Debby's appearance. 'Or a film star.'

'She's lovely, isn't she,' I say flatly.

When I look up I see Tilly standing by herself. I separate myself from the group and go over to her.

As soon as she spots me, she straightens her frail shoulders and lifts her chin. Her whole demeanour radiates pure hostility. John's mother was never an overly loving or accommodating person. There was a reason why John was always in and out of my parents' house and saw so little of his mother. He sometimes secretly called her Eucalypta, after the witch in a children's TV programme. The name was appropriate not just physically. Tilly exudes an obstinacy and strength that you wouldn't expect from her delicate figure.

I slow down a little. 'I'm so sorry,' I say. I don't dare take her hand.

Tilly looks me up and down. 'I want to have a word with you soon, but definitely not today,' she snaps, turning demonstratively on her heel.

I stand there helplessly and try to make eye contact with my parents, but they are busy talking to Uncle Paul and Aunt Agatha.

43

'They each need to be eight and a half feet wide,' I say. 'The height is seven feet and the arch begins at six feet on either side.'

Hopefully the measurements are being noted down correctly at the other end of the telephone line. All I can hear is some vague grunting.

'Have you got that?'

'Yes, we've got that. You wanted ten of them?'

'That's right, ten. Can you deliver them to an address in Amsterdam?'

'In that case there'll be an extra thirty euros delivery charge.'

'No problem.' I give the delivery address for the wooden panels – Debby's – and the address to which the wood yard can send the invoice: Night View. The orders for Night View are mounting up. It was an excellent idea of Richard's to have all invoices sent direct to the client. I could never have paid it up-front myself.

'When can I expect the panels?' I ask.

'In principle by the middle of next week. We'll make a start as soon as half the amount is transferred.'

I hang up and look at Taco. Loulou lies at his feet wagging her tail on the antique pink carpeting and the TV is switched to a commercial channel that's been broadcasting phone-in competitions all morning. The volume is turned up very loud.

'Could you transfer money to the wood supplier today?' I ask.

Taco gets up and stretches, revealing part of his slightly hairy, perma-tanned belly. 'Come with me a minute.'

Half dragging one leg behind him he leads me into his office. His foot is still in plaster. He has stretched a black sock over it.

In the office I try not to look at Edith's photo.

While Taco starts up the PC, my eyes are drawn to it nevertheless. She now looks less like me than when I first saw the photo. She appears younger and her hair is a different shade of red. Even her eyes aren't the same colour: they're green and brown. Her expression is different too, more provocative.

Perhaps I'm now more struck by the differences than by the similarities because I've got used to the idea.

'My ex-boyfriend committed suicide,' I say to Taco. 'Just like her . . . His funeral was a week ago today.'

He looks up from the screen in annoyance. 'Heavy,' he mutters and turns back to his computer. 'I'm sorry.'

'Thanks,' I say, clenching my teeth.

'Right, I'm in,' Taco growls. 'Have you got the bank details?'

I read out the account number and the name of the company while Taco, frowning as though he were long-sighted, peers at the screen and types in the information with two fingers. Then he pulls a drawer open and starts entering figures on a small device, and then types something else on his computer. He sniffs. 'I've transferred it.'

Outside I hear Taco's Rottweiler going berserk. 'Visitors,' concludes Taco, clicking his tongue. At the same time the doorbell rings, which is the sign for Loulou to shoot towards the front door yapping loudly.

'Lou! Quiet!' shouts Taco.

His deep, harsh voice makes me cringe, but the little white dog is not very impressed.

Taco pushes himself up from the desk and goes into the living room towards the front door.

I stand in the doorway of the office.

'And that goes for you too, you stupid animal!' he roars as he opens the door.

Only then do I see who is coming in, someone who, just like me, is rooted to the spot. My mouth goes dry.

For the past week I have been getting used to the idea that I'd probably never see him again. Last night I googled his name and put the few press photos of him that I could find in a separate file in my PC. Leon obviously doesn't like being photographed. In all the shots he was looking slightly away from the lens and his hair was covering part of his face. I read every report containing his name: Dutch, German and English press articles on exhibitions and essays on art photography where he was discussed as one of the most successful photographers in Europe. The rave reviews made him seem suddenly very far away – an inaccessible icon from a world I'm no longer part of.

It was deep in the night before I could get to sleep, with the help of half a bottle of white wine.

And now Leon is here. When I least expect him. My hair is in a scruffy ponytail, I have hardly any make-up on, and I'm walking around in an old work sweater and the jeans I know he'd like to see consigned to a bin liner. Almost all the beautiful feminine clothes I own are still hanging in Amsterdam, in Leon's wardrobe.

We stand facing each other in silence.

Taco looks from one to the other, scratches his neck and mutters: 'OK, I think I need to go and clean out the kennel for a bit. Make yourselves comfortable.' The door closes behind him with a faint click.

Silence.

We both stand there, with fifteen feet of antique pink carpet between us and a small dog scampering nervously from one to the other, its tail whizzing across its back like a white propeller.

Leon is the first to speak. 'I didn't see your car.'

'It's parked at the side, by the main entrance.'

He takes a step forward. 'My condolences,' he says softly.

I nod.

'And sorry,' he adds. 'I don't think I've behaved very well recently.'

My mother's words come back to me. 'I haven't behaved very well either,' I say, looking down at the floor then back up at Leon, who is sizing me up. 'It's a mess.' And that also sums up my state of mind in a nutshell.

'You could say that.'

I look up. 'I heard from Debby that you . . .' No, I mustn't bring that up, not now we're seeing each other again for the first time, not here, while Edith, with her shrouded, provocative gaze, is leering at us from Taco's office and blowing cigarette smoke in our direction.

'What did you hear from Debby?'

I shrug my shoulders. 'That you were feeling like shit.'

'She was right.'

Leon starts moving and comes towards me.

I stand there, too confused to move, feeling awkward.

Leon pulls me towards him and puts his hands on my back, as if he's afraid I'll run away from him if he doesn't stop me. Two warm, big, wonderful hands stroking me right through my thick sweater.

'I've missed you, princess.' His voice sounds hoarse.

I'd like to say something but the words stick in my throat. I inhale his scent, feel the warmth of his body and when I look into his eyes, I'm moved by the love and consolation they reveal. And I see so much more in them besides. I don't want to cry, not now, but my emotions are so close to the surface that it wouldn't take much for my heart to burst. 'Me too. I've missed you too.'

'Is there anything else you have to do here?'

'Not much.'

'Let's go then,' he says softly

'Where?'

'To the bungalow. There's wine in the fridge.' He grins, but his eyes are not smiling. 'Entre deux mers.'

It's no joyful reunion and the conversations we have are not relaxed and light-hearted. All our actions and words are inexorably overshadowed by an immense sense of grief and painful memories.

John's parasite is back and has assumed monstrous form, bigger and more powerful than ever. It ruthlessly smashes each glimmer of hope that surfaces only every so often. I must not laugh, is its compelling message. I must not make love or think about the future.

I must not be happy.

My parasite has found a kindred spirit in the dark man lying next to me on the bed with his arm around my shoulders. Leon knows what I'm going through, better than anyone. He's been through the same thing. There's no one who can understand so well the dark labyrinth I am trapped in. I know that. He knows that. Through bitter, devilish fate we are condemned to each other. That unspoken awareness colours our whole conversation.

In the few hours that we lie together and empty the bottle of wine, taking turns to put it to our lips, I discover a different

Leon. I talk and he just listens, without interrupting me, without judging and without expressing any form of jealousy. Yet that is what he must have felt overwhelmingly when I told him I'd been to bed with John. I spared him nothing. I wanted to clear things up, confess everything, because I knew that if there was any chance of a future for us, it could not be based on lies. It's too important to me. He just nodded, took a swig from the bottle and stared blindly at the bare wall opposite the bed.

Meanwhile dusk has fallen. The bedroom curtains are still open, but the thin nets are letting hardly any light through. Outside bare treetops wave gently in the wind.

'I just can't believe that John committed suicide,' I say. 'He wasn't the type.'

Leon turns his head away. 'That's precisely the idea that drove me nuts. Accept that that's how it is. Let it pass.'

He's not talking about John.

'Sorry,' I say. 'I realise that this . . . for you—'

He puts two fingers to his mouth. 'Ssh. Don't talk about it any more. Don't think about it any more. Let it rest. They're dead, Margot, both of them, just dead. That was their choice.'

'I find that difficult to believe.'

'I know.' He bends over me and kisses me gently on the mouth. 'It was just the same with me,' he whispers. 'I wish I could help you. All the thoughts you're having now, I had them too. Every one of them. And they nearly pulled me under.' He pulls me towards him, so tight I'm scared I won't be able to breathe. 'Accept that we're alive.' He nestles against me. His tongue glides over my lips, searching for a way in.

I taste the wine on his tongue and briefly, very briefly, something contracts in my abdomen and I want to go further, undress him, skin against skin, become one.

I must not be happy.

I pull my face away and grab his to slow him down, looking at him searchingly. 'I can't,' I whisper. 'Not now.'

His hand slips under my blouse.

I stop him abruptly and wriggle out from under him a little. 'I really can't.'

He sinks back into the pillows with a sigh.

'I can't get John out of my head. The point where I can process it like you've done with Edith is still a long way off.' I turn on my side and run my hand over the cotton duvet. 'Too much has happened just to shake it off. Recently I've been lying in bed thinking about it every night and I still can't make sense of it. Not yet.'

'Are we still just talking about John or am I missing something?'

I shake my head and wait till I've managed to structure my confused thoughts in such a way that I can formulate them rationally. 'It's all lumped together,' I say finally. 'Since I met you everything's been a whirlwind. I've neglected my family, which they didn't deserve. I've quit my job, burned all my bridges and by doing that I've made myself dependent on you and Richard. I've thought a lot about that. About that and . . . about the consequences of moving in with you. John and I . . . we had other things in common. With you . . . I don't want to rush into anything anymore.'

'Define rushing into something.'

'Getting into a relationship again based on . . . just a crush.'

Leon stares straight ahead. 'Don't beat about the bush. What's your problem?'

'You're abroad half the time. And I'm expected to wait in that factory of yours till you come home. I've seen where that can lead and it's not the kind of life I want.'

'What exactly are you getting at?'

'Richard's Marianne. She's one of the saddest people I've met. She doesn't want to live in that house in the polder, she feels terribly lonely there. And it's awful to see how Richard treats her.'

Leon says nothing, not even a grunt of agreement.

'Why aren't you saying anything?'

'Because I see things differently. It's shitty for Marianne that things have turned out like that over time, but you're not Marianne and I'd really appreciate it if you didn't compare me to Richard. Their situation is totally separate from ours.'

I shake my head slowly. 'Can't you see the similarities? Marianne's situation is more or less the same as the one I'd be putting myself in if I go back to Amsterdam with you. It boils down to the same thing. Everything revolves around you. Your trips abroad, your exhibitions, your acquaintances and friends.'

'No, I want to—'

'I don't even feel comfortable there when you're away,' I say, interrupting him. 'It's not a home. Debby stayed over with me one night because I felt uneasy there.'

He raises and eyebrow. 'You'll watch out with Debby, won't you?'

'Why?'

'Deb's a nice girl, but she's as bi as they come.'

'Bi? And you only tell me that now? That explains why she was walking around naked and wanted us to take a bath together.'

He stiffens. '*Wanted to* or *took*?'

'*Wanted to.* When she'd finished her bath she got into bed with me naked. I didn't know how to handle it, so I pretended to be asleep.'

'And what else?'

I shrug my shoulders. 'Nothing. Nothing happened.'

'No?'

'If it had, I'd tell you.'

'I found her with Edith once,' he says, so softly that I have to strain to hear him.

I turn my head to the left.

'In the bath. Lovely.' He grins mirthlessly. 'I was invited to join them. That was Edith. She could be like that. Very impulsive.'

'What did you do?'

He grabs the packet of cigarettes on the bedside table. The flame of the lighter bathes his face in an orange glow. He gives the burning cigarette to me and lights one for himself. 'What do you think?'

'I don't know. Debby's a beautiful woman.'

'I was furious. I dragged Debby out of the bath, threw her out bare-assed and chucked her clothes out of the window.'

'Yet the two of you are still friends.'

He shrugs his shoulders. 'We all have our faults, but I hadn't expected her to try on something like that again.'

'And what about Edith?'

'Edith . . .' He takes a drag on his cigarette. 'Listen. Why are we talking about dead people all evening? He pulls me towards him and kisses my forehead. 'Shall we give it a rest? And talk about things we *can* get our heads round instead? What do you think of the bungalow? Better than Amsterdam?'

'Yes, much better. But . . .'

'Can you imagine living here?'

'It makes no difference, Amsterdam or here,' I say flatly. 'It comes down to the same thing. I was just trying to—'

'Forget that for a moment. There are loads of other possibilities. I thought you liked this house. Close to the woods, not far from your family. That's true, isn't it?'

I remember cycling here as a child, on Sundays with Dick and my parents. 'I used to come this way sometimes,' I say. 'And it occurred to me then that people who lived in a house like this, on the edge of the woods, must be very happy.' I turn to face him. 'Odd, isn't it? That it all seemed so simple then? We're not so happy at all.'

Leon stubs his cigarette out and buries his face in my hair. 'Not yet. But this is a start: your fear about playing second fiddle, you need to stop worrying about it. I have very different ideas regarding that. You're not the only one who's lain awake in the past few weeks. I want to deal with a few things very differently.'

My phone rings. The ringtone jangles through the bedroom and startles me. I grope in my bag and find it.

'Tilly,' I hear a curt woman's voice say. 'Listen, can you come over tomorrow evening? I want to talk to you.'

'Of course,' I say. 'What time?'

'Eight o'clock.'

'I'll be there.'

She rings off straight away.

'Who was that?' asks Leon.

'Tilly. John's mother.'

'What did she want?'

'She wants to talk to me.'

After a long silence he says: 'Sorry. I'm going too fast. It's still too fresh. We'll talk about it later.'

I just nod.

We lie next to each other in silence until it's so dark I can no longer even make out any vague shadows. The darkness is total. Later, much later, I wake for a moment to find him laying the duvet over me and tucking me in.

44

Since her husband died Tilly has lived in a rented flat in Tilburg. Hers is one of a group of six-storey blocks positioned between a busy through road and a wide canal along the railway. Each building has its own large car park and plot of grass bordered with bare trees, a few rubbish skips and a glass recycling bin. I can count the number of times I've set foot in that flat on the fingers of two hands. Tilly is like a ride on the ghost train at the fair: her unexpected outbursts have made me wince more than once. John had definitely inherited his sociable, charming genes from his father's side. When he'd had a bit to drink John often ridiculed her but couldn't stand anyone else saying a word against her. 'With her you have to read between the lines,' he'd say to excuse her behaviour. 'At heart she's very sensitive and sweet.' I never discovered those qualities in her, though I did regularly feel intimidated and driven into a corner.

That feeling descends on me once again as I press the bell next to her blue-painted front door.

Tilly opens the door, and without a word steps aside to let me in. Her small flat is tastefully decorated with light-coloured, English-looking furniture. At the window there is a huge cage containing a bored parrot.

But the moment I enter her modest living room, I immediately see a letter lying on the dining table. Tilly has put it in a plastic cover, to prevent it from being damaged.

John's suicide note.

With my arms wrapped around me I go over to the table and start reading.

By the time you read this I'll be long gone
I hope that you'll understand that I was given
no other choice
    I cant see it any other way

Tilly, Mum I LOVE YOU
perhaps I'll meet you up there one day
I hope DAD is waiting for me I still miss him
every day.
Margot last night I loved you More than ever
I thought it was all right but I DONT
understand a damn thing anymore
    I AM AN ARSEHOLE.

SORRY SORRY SORRY I cant bother
you any longer
it is not your fault
I am doing this because I love
    You ALL!

No choice
this is shit

I LOVE YOU ALL

Jt

When I look up from the letter Tilly is standing there watching me in silence. Like me she has her arms folded. 'Read it yet?' she says sharply.

I nod. I wish I could cry, but I can't any more. I just feel dazed. 'Well?'

'I think it's awful. I still can't understand what—'

'What did you do to my son?'

I look up in confusion. 'Do?'

She starts to nod violently. The loose skin along her cheeks and in her neck reacts in slow motion to the rapid movements. 'Yes, do. You were with him that night. Something happened. I want to know what.'

'I went home with him after the party,' I say as calmly as possible.

'And then?'

I look up, straight into her eyes. Small, dark eyes in which I find traces of humanity for the first time in years. She's been crying. And not just once. Her eyelids are swollen, the whites bloodshot. My heart goes out to her again, to this strong, very difficult woman who has no one left. She's not warm or eager to please, but she's definitely a mother. And John was her only son. Her only child.

'I'm waiting,' she says, her voice filled with pent-up fury.

I hesitate and lower my eyes. I've told the police that I went to bed with John. My mother. Dick, and even Leon. But now I'm standing face to face with John's mother I can't bring myself to say it. I suddenly feel very dirty.

She takes a couple of steps forward and angrily grabs the letter off the table. She holds it next to her, pointing to it. 'This, Margot, this: *I loved you more last night than ever. I thought it was all right—*'

'I've read it,' I interrupt.

'*I was given no choice*,' she suddenly shouts. '*I'm doing this because I love you all.* What kind of nonsense is that? A suicide note? My son killing himself because he *loves* everyone? Absurd. This isn't John. This is *not . . .*' she spits the word out 'John. I want to know what happened to my son.' She lifts her head and looks straight at me, as if she's braving a storm. 'What the hell happened to him and what did you do to him?'

She has a right to know. There's no getting round this. He was her son. 'I slept with him,' I say softly, without looking at her. 'John had had too much to drink and so had I and I'd had an argument with my new boyfriend. It just happened.'

'And then?'

'Then I regretted it and left.'

'What did you say to him?'

'That I was sorry I'd let things go that far.' I take a deep breath. This is infinitely more difficult than I could imagine. I stop speaking for a moment to summon up my courage. 'That I didn't love him. I went to my mother's house.'

'How did he react? What did he say?'

I shrug my shoulders helplessly. 'Not much.'

'I'm asking *what*.'

I press my lips together. 'He said he didn't believe me.'

'And what else?'

'That it was ridiculous to get my parents out of bed in the middle of the night.'

'And that was it?'

I raise my hands. 'Yes, that was it.'

'I don't believe you. I know my son. And I knew his father before him. They were cast in the same mould. Suicide?' She pauses for a moment and her eyes sparkle slyly. 'No, I can't believe that and I think you know more than you're letting on.'

My eyes grow wider. 'Why's that?'

She looks at me with a contorted expression. The tension causes her facial muscles to twitch irregularly. 'What do you think? You were the last one with him.'

'Have you told the police this?' I ask.

'Are you afraid of that then?'

'No!' I shout. 'Why should I be? I think it's awful. How can you think that I have something to do with it? I haven't slept through a single night since John died.'

'Guilt?'

'Yes, guilt,' I say, loudly. 'Because I left. Because I left him alone. If I'd thought for a second that he would commit suicide, I would have sat up with him all night and held his hand. But he didn't give that impression, Tilly. Not for a moment. He was upset, he'd had too much to drink, he was dumbfounded, you name it, but he wasn't depressed, he didn't threaten to harm himself, he wasn't eerily quiet, nothing like that.'

'So you agree with me that something's not right?' is all she says. She seems to have calmed down all of a sudden.

I rub my fingers over my closed eyes. 'I try to reconcile myself to the fact that he really did it, but I can't manage that either.'

'Then tell that detective. He doesn't believe me.'

I look up. 'But if John . . .' I say. I can't express the rest, it's too frightening.

She nods violently. Again the soft, thin skin along her cheekbones follows in slow motion. 'Exactly, Margot. Exactly. If he didn't, who did?'

I can't remember how I got home. The idea that John might have been murdered – *has* been, according to Tilly – gnaws away at me. I can't imagine anyone who could or would want to do such a thing. Does John have debts I don't know about? But if so, how? John isn't the impulsive type, addictions like gambling or drugs are completely out of character for him. He was a social drinker and he didn't even smoke. Suddenly I'm reminded of Tom. He was furious when he found out that John was having an affair with Mieke. It spelled the end of their marriage and a close friendship going back years. Tom went through the same thing as me, he was betrayed by two people he trusted. Could that have made him . . .? I shake my head. Not Tom. Impossible.

Not many people knew John was a diabetic. He didn't make a big thing of it. If he had to inject himself, he withdrew discreetly, he didn't want to be seen as a special case. Only family and friends knew. One time John injected himself when Tom and Mieke were there. That was on holiday in Italy. He wanted to take blood from us all to show us that it didn't hurt and to measure our blood sugar levels – just for fun. Mieke and I offered our fingertips, but Tom stuck his hands under his armpits and shouted 'no way!' He found it really gruesome. Later he looked away when John injected himself. Try as I might, I can't see Tom as someone who would kill his old friend, and definitely not with insulin.

I don't know what to make of that suicide note either. If John was murdered he must have written it with the murderer there. It doesn't make sense. Why would John do that? What could make him decide to pull the wool over all our eyes? Why didn't he fight back? Why didn't he just refuse to write the letter – if he knew he was going to die anyway? Was the threat so great that he . . .

I change position on the sofa. My contorted posture has made my feet start to tingle. I reach towards the coffee table and light a cigarette.

What am I doing? I must stop this, at once. It's bad enough that John's taken his own life; I can't even get my head round that. But John murdered? No, too weird for words. That's going much too far. I must be losing my mind.

Threat.

I'm doing this because I love you all. No choice.

Was John threatened? Could someone have forced him into this, because otherwise something would happen to a member of his family? Me? Tilly?

I get up and go over to the bookcase, where a business card that one of the two police officers left here is sticking out from between two heavy books. There's a mobile number on it. The detective was very friendly and said I could ring him anytime if something occurred to me that might be important, evenings as well.

I grab the phone off the table and key in the number. The telephone rings on the other end of the line and there's a series of clicks, as if my call is being transferred.

'Detective Sam Tienen.'

'Er,' I stutter. 'Not Burghardt?'

'Charles Burghardt is tied up with a case. He's having his calls redirected to me. Can I help you with anything?'

'I don't know. I'm the ex-girlfriend of John van Oss.'

'John van Oss . . . I've heard about that, but not the details. Suicide.'

'I suspect there's more to it,' I say. My voice is trembling. Just like when I visit the doctor, I feel slightly nervous, and have the idea that I'm wasting someone's time and so must make sure I summarise my thoughts as concisely as possible. 'I just want to ask your colleague what that's based on. Suicide, I mean. You see, John's mother and I don't believe that—'

'Before you go on,' he interrupts. 'I'm afraid I know too little about this case to go into this. If it can wait till tomorrow or the day after, I'll make sure that Charles Burghardt calls you back himself. Is that OK?'

'Yes . . . that's all right. Shall I give you the number?'

'I've already noted it down.' He reads back my landline number.

To be on the safe side I give him my mobile number too. 'He really will call me back?'

'You can take my word for it. It's just that he's busy with a case right now and I can't disturb him.'

'I understand,' I say.

'Is there anything else I can do for you?' the voice is toneless, without any real involvement. It's a routine question.

'No thank you.'

45

The traditional Japanese restaurant is less than a third of a mile from my flat, tucked away in an ancient quarter with historic alleys and narrow, shallow canals that flow past and underneath the buildings. I'd heard about this restaurant a number of times, but had never been there before. It is in a loft and has room for only a limited number of diners.

Our hostess is wearing a kimono and seems to me to be of Japanese origin. She is not the only Oriental face in this pink and black room: the tables are occupied exclusively by people with the same features as our hostess and I can't understand a word of their conversations.

Leon has just ordered a seven-course menu. We are drinking lukewarm sake and dry white wine.

'At that party I promised your father I'd take some photos of his rabbits,' says Leon in a subdued tone.

I groan. 'You're joking.'

He smiles and takes a sip of wine. 'According to him there's a huge demand for rabbit photographers. I could always retrain.'

I burst out laughing and cover my mouth with my hand. 'Oh, how awful! What am I doing to you? You know, I had to do that a lot as a child, hold his rabbits still on one of those wobbly camping tables so he could take photos of them. Keep pushing those ears down, and hold the animals down on the table so that they didn't jump off. It took us hours to finish a roll of film. With any luck there'd be one photo that was any good. My father's a walking disaster area with cameras. And I'm not the greatest assistant, I'm afraid.'

Leon puts his glass down. 'I'll drop by in the next few weeks. If I'm still welcome, at least. It strikes me as fun, rabbits. A bit of a change from smug bank directors and naked women.'

The Japanese hostess appears at the table and serves us small hors d'oeuvres. In staccato Dutch she explains what it is. Raw mackerel, seaweed, mushrooms. 'Good taste,' she says, concluding her explanation. She nods as she speaks as if there are batteries hidden in her neck.

Leon and I smile at her and turn our attention to the artistically arranged bowls. I've eaten with chopsticks before and thought I was pretty good at it, but Leon takes the biscuit. With consummate ease, as if he knew nothing else, he empties the small bowls in no time.

'She's right too. Good place, this,' he says. Then he suddenly looks straight at me. 'Do you feel a bit better?'

'The mist has cleared at least. For weeks I felt as if I was walking round with a pair of tights over my head.'

He nods and drinks a slug of sake. 'I hate it.'

'What do you hate?'

'Margot . . . I want that body of yours next to me at night, I want you to be there when I get home. I want to have something to come home for.'

I can't answer immediately as I'm chewing a piece of raw fish. It's cool, soft and slightly salty and slips down my gullet as if by itself. 'I've heard you say "I want" three times now. What's in it for me, except—'

'Except for amazing sex?' He raises an eyebrow teasingly.

At the table opposite a few people look up. They may not speak Dutch, but they certainly understand it.

'That has nothing to do with it. That's not what I mean.'

'Then say what you do mean.'

As I take another mouthful, I think back to the day I'd painted the bedroom apple-green. Again I see John's disapproving response. It was those reactions that made me creep further and further into my shell and start trusting my own feelings less and less. Leon is a completely different man from John, but he too has his compelling list of demands. 'I don't want to be your pet,' I say finally.

'What?!'

'You say you want me to be there when you get home. You probably mean it in a sweet way, but I've told you before that I have a problem with the idea of playing second fiddle.'

'I wanted to talk about that this evening,' he says.

The bowls are cleared away by the hostess. She asks if everything is all right. We nod at her in silence. She disappears behind a thick curtain.

'I want to give it up.' He searches for my hand across the table.

'Give what up?'

'The assignments. I've been sick of them for a while. Or perhaps sick is an understatement. I really am sick to the back teeth of them. Those guys want me because I'm the best, famous in a small world,' – he says it sarcastically – 'but when it comes down to it, you're simply bought and paid for. In which case you have to do what they want.'

I watch as he stiffens and stroke the back of his hand.

He calms down a little. 'There are some great people among them, but all in all I'm simply fed up with it.'

'Since when?'

'For some time.'

The next course appears. In halting Dutch we are given an explanation of exactly what the beautifully cut pieces of fish and vegetables are.

'I wanted to stop last year,' Leon goes on, as soon as the hostess has withdrawn. 'But when Edith died I fell into a black hole: I lost all desire to try anything new, so I went on doing what I was used to.' He snorts. 'Back to square one, actually.'

'What else would you have done? If Edith were still alive?'

'The plan was to go to China and do a photo reportage on the conditions Chinese labourers work and live in. Edith was going to go with me. Then we were going to travel on to America, or back to Europe, we hadn't decided. The idea was to make the same kind of series in the West, but of the people who use the Chinese products. A pair of designer trousers will have cost all in all less than three euros by the time it leaves the factory, but the end user pays two hundred and fifty. I wanted to reveal that discrepancy.'

'You can still do that, can't you?'

He takes a bite of some dark stuff that according to the commentary is supposed to be seaweed. 'It's less topical now than it was last year,' he says as he chews. 'Oh, I don't know.'

'But you do know you're fed up taking photographs on commission.'

'Yes. It's great having two homes and a good car. It's nice staying in expensive hotels and eating in these kinds of restaurants. But it doesn't mean a thing. Earning money, spending money . . . I was happier when I was travelling around the polders, looking for shots, in peace and quiet. I had a part-time job in a camera shop then and much more time for my own stuff.'

'I remember you telling me that.'

'Photography is my thing, it's what I'm good at. But I notice I'm beginning to hate it more and more. I haven't even had time to do any more work on my new project. In the past it never even occurred to me to leave the house without a camera. Now when I see the bag, what I'd most like to do is give it a good kick. That's not good and it's because of all those assignments. I've got to get back to my personal work, for a few years at any rate. That'll have financial consequences, but I don't think I'll lose any sleep over that.' He looks up. 'So, princess . . .'

I move the chopsticks aside and study his face. Leon obviously has the same attitude towards his work now that I had towards All Inclusive when I met him in London. No wonder he understood so well what was going through my mind.

I have the strong feeling that now it's my turn to support him. Edith would have gone to China with him, but I'm not Edith. I'm still nowhere near finished with Night View and I've got so many other ideas. No, if I'm honest: I really don't want to leave. 'How do I fit into this picture?' I ask. 'For the time being I'm going to be busy with designing and furnishing. Suppose you get it into your head to take off to Africa or God knows where for three months? What then? For me it comes down to the same thing.'

He shrugs his shoulders. 'You need to go on doing what you're doing now. I can help you, if you want, take some work off your hands or something. And do my series and exhibitions in between . . . there are so many possibilities. I just don't want it to take over my life any more. Perhaps you can plan your work so that you can take a month off now and then and come with me – if it comes to that. But those are all just details. The question is whether you like the sound of that. I'll be home a lot, pestering you a lot.' He grins.

I smile. 'I like being pestered by you.'

'Good job. Will you think about it?'

'Does this all depend on me?'

'No. I'm stopping anyway. I was planning to talk to Richard tomorrow morning. I've been thinking about this for long enough already. Denmark was the last straw. But it would be great to know that it will be "we" in the future.' He looks into my eyes, takes my hand and kisses it. His eyes are half hidden by his hair. 'It'll be really great,' he says. 'Believe me.'

I've managed to talk about the future for the whole evening. For the first time since John's death I feel my appetite for life returning, I dare to believe that nice things are set to happen. Leon makes me feel like I'm the only woman in the world and encourages me to make the most of myself. Since I met him my self-image has turned 180-degrees and I've been happy with who I am and what I'm capable of. Motivated by Leon, under his care and with his support, I had the courage to quit my job. The career change feels so really good, so natural in fact, that now it only seems strange that I didn't dare do it much earlier. I'm no longer frightened of failing. I have every confidence that I'm standing on the threshold of something that will grow much bigger and better.

I can't see that future apart from Leon. I love him and he intrigues me. Leon has so many different facets that it seems like I'll never be able to fathom him completely. Every time I've peeled off another layer there is undiscovered territory beneath, and it's all equally exciting and inspiring. Leon has the aura of a street fighter and the heart of a creative intellectual. Apart from that the sex is unusually good, refreshing, even breathtaking. He brings things out in me that I didn't even know were there.

And I enjoy every second. It's no trouble for me to imagine myself leaving everything behind and following this man, who's now lying next to me asleep and breathing peacefully, all over the world from one creative impulse to the next. I start forming a vague picture of it.

The warm pastel shades of pleasant prospects in which I wallow on the border of waking and sleep, are cruelly and suddenly daubed with red and black paint.

I must not be happy.

I can no longer get to sleep. Just like yesterday and all the nights before it, back to the first sleepless night after the news of John's death, I'm lying in the dark staring into space again, wide awake.

How can I act as if nothing's wrong, while that indefinable feeling keeps gnawing away at me that there's something that doesn't add up about John's suicide?

46

This morning Leon left early for a gallery in Antwerp, an appointment he couldn't get out of. After he left I had a shower and drove to see the carpet supplier. There was a problem with the colour of the carpeting. Fortunately it turned out to be less serious that it sounded on the telephone. The carpet man is obviously more critical than I am or ever will be. I only saw the difference when we put the samples next to each other in day-light – and Night View has no windows. I was able to negotiate a ten per cent discount for Taco.

Now I'm on my way to see Marianne. She wants to explain to me what I could do to avoid paying unnecessary tax and at the same time make the work easier for her. To put it mildly, I'm not really looking forward to it. To be honest, I even regret getting involved with her without thinking it over first. She lives too far away from where I live – if there are no tailbacks it's over an hour's drive, though that can easily double in bad weather or at the wrong time of day. But that's not really the main reason. There's a negative aura around that spotless house, despite the cat and despite the child.

When I get as far as Utrecht the telephone rings. The radio is on so loud I don't hear it at first. I turn the volume down and answer it.

'Charles Burghardt, Noord-Brabant Police. Is this a bad time?'

I automatically make for the right-hand lane and tuck in behind a lorry. 'No, I'm in the car.'

'Alone?'

'Yes.'

'I heard from a colleague that you'd called. Sorry I'm only getting back to you today. May I ask why you got in touch?'

'This week I went to see John's mother, in Tilburg.' I pause for a moment. Thinking something is very different from actually saying it. Especially to a detective. Maybe he'll certify me crazy. I clear my throat. 'She's . . . convinced that John didn't commit suicide and felt like she was the only one who thought that. She asked me to tell you that I find it difficult to believe as well.'

'You do?'

'To be honest honest, yes I do.'

'And what are you basing that on?'

'Suicide is so . . . so terribly unlike John. You didn't know him, but I lived with him for seven years. He wasn't depressed, not even impulsive. On the contrary, John was someone with a sense of humour and a great ability to put things into perspective. Of course he had his quirks, and he was certainly no saint, but suicide . . . Maybe I'm just imagining things, but . . . there are passages in the letter that both Tilly, his mother, and I find odd.'

'You mean the sentences: *I'm doing this because I love you all and I was given no choice?*'

'Yes,' I say, almost breathlessly. My eyes light up. I'm not imagining things. The police have noticed too. 'Yes, those.'

Burghardt coughs. 'In principle we've not found any indications to suggest anything but suicide. The windows and doors were shut. No signs that force was used on the body. In this specific case the cause of death seems obvious. And there was a suicide note in his own handwriting. All in all it's a clear-cut case.'

'But . . .?' I ask, because I have the idea that this was only a preamble.

'Ms Heijne, I hope you'll understand that I'm not deaf and blind to the opinions and feelings of people who knew the victim well. But at the same time I have to keep it in the back of my mind that denial is a normal reaction under such circumstances. The situation was confusing for your ex-partner. Excessive drinking, exhaustion because of the late hour, a rejection that may have been hard to take . . . It's certainly not inconceivable that the whole thing became too much for him and he acted on impulse. We see examples every day of people seemingly acting out of character. Unfortunately, I should say.'

'But?' I ask again.

'What I'm trying to say is that a suicide like your ex-partner's is not unique, but it *is* rare. In the course of our investigation among family, friends and work colleagues no one indicated that they had picked up any signal that he might have been suicidal. His GP confirmed that. That doesn't often happen. Usually there are signals in advance. So, to cut a long story short, I did dig a little further.'

'And? Did you find anything?'

There is a moment's silence on the other end of the line. 'Do you understand the consequences if we no longer treat this as a suicide?'

'How do you mean?'

'Then we'll start considering this as a murder.' The detective pauses for a moment. 'I'd like it if you could find time to drop by the station today or tomorrow, and answer a few questions about your current partner, Leon Wagner.'

Burghardt could just as well have slapped me in the face or punched me in the stomach. I'm so startled I involuntarily jerk the wheel. A driver starts honking his horn alongside me.

'Ms Heijne? Are you still there?'

'Yes, I'm here . . . This is a huge shock.'

'Is there a reason for that?'

'Leon . . .' I say. 'I . . . I don't know what to think.'

'Don't think anything for the moment. Let it sink in gradually, then we'll talk about it later at the station. When could you drop in?'

'Early evening,' I say hurriedly. 'I'm on my way to my accountant right now. After that I can come straight back to the station.'

'Fine, so I'll see you later. One thing, which you possibly know already: I'd like to ask you emphatically not to mention a word of this to third parties, and especially not to your partner. It could have unfortunate consequences for our investigation.'

'Of course, yes,' I say hesitantly. 'I understand.'

'Take care and I'll see you this evening.'

'See you this evening.'

I'm still behind the lorry, but I'm unable to carry on driving calmly. It's as if I find myself in a featureless landscape; no trees, no grass, no cars, but bubbles and strange angular floating objects I've never seen before in my life and can't put a name to. Jerkily I steer the car towards the crash barrier and come to a halt on the hard shoulder. I have just enough presence of mind to put my hazard warning lights on.

From pure stress I start biting my nails. Leon left the party before me. What time was that? I can't remember. Did he drive straight home? I've no idea, we didn't talk about it. Did Leon know where John lived? That's never come up, but he talked to various people at the party and someone may have told him. Maybe even my own father.

I close my eyes and in my mind's eye I can see how Leon grabbed John and threw him off, the fierceness in that movement, the sudden aggressive outburst that revealed a completely different side of Leon. A violent, explosive side.

At the same time images flash past of Leon in Amsterdam. His reaction to my visit to John earlier that day was fuelled by pure jealousy. Leon must have heard hours before I got home that I'd been to see John. Still, he didn't start arguing or shouting at me. No sulky silence or blame. None of that. He stayed calmly on the sofa and didn't even look at me. He ordered me to get half undressed and the words he spoke next couldn't have been more out of sync with his actions.

Leon had everything under control, including his own reaction. He'd considered every step; Leon the director.

Jealousy.

I bend my head and see my knees are trembling. I grab them in an attempt to keep them still, but my hands are trembling just as badly. My whole body is shaking.

Leon once found Debby and Edith together in the bath. When I asked him what he'd done with Edith, he changed the subject abruptly.

The seed of a dreadful idea has been sown. It takes root with unprecedented speed and grows and grows, invading me and making me tremble with horror.

'Please let it not be true,' I whisper, but my voice sounds hoarse and broken.

47

My first impulse after Burghardt's telephone call is to turn round at once and drive to the police station. I can't think about anything else anyway; the sooner that conversation is over the better. I drive on past the junction all the same, I don't know why. Perhaps it's easier to switch my mind off and work through the day's schedule as if nothing's wrong.

Throughout the long journey to Marianne's house I try to think as lucidly as possible, but the seed that Burghardt has planted is thriving and has developed a diabolical symbiosis with John's parasite.

Miraculously, by the time I sit down in Marianne's conservatory-cum-office and put my box of documents on her glass desk and unpack it for her, I have calmed down a little. My heart is no longer pounding like crazy and I manage to make a relatively calm, perhaps even normal impression. Except that almost everything Marianne says passes me by. It's about mileage allowances, but the point of her detailed explanation doesn't stick.

Lola has been parked in a playpen for the occasion, which she clearly disapproves of. She screams regularly, her high-pitched voice is piercing in the bare room.

Outside a pale sun has broken through the thin cloud cover. Further into the polder it is raining heavily. The leaden, vertical column is approaching slowly.

'Did you understand everything I just said?' she says, sitting down opposite me and pouring me another coffee.

'I think so.'

'You really must do it, you know. Many of the miles you drive are for business. You're robbing yourself if you don't declare them. I can't simply guess the totals afterwards or fill them in for you, so you've really got to do it for yourself. If you keep proper records, they can add up nicely in your favour every year. Besides which, you're entitled to it.'

I nod and am about to pack my things again when the phone rings.

'Yes,' I hear Marianne say, in between Lola's screams. 'Just a moment, Richard. What was that?'

Silence. I see her face cloud over.

'You can't be serious! Why's that?'

She bends her head and notes down figures with spindly strokes on a notepad.

'Ridiculous . . . I'm really amazed . . . Yes, you're right. I agree . . . I'll look it up. Have you got a minute?'

I put my hands in my lap and watch as Marianne leafs assiduously through a diary and makes notes.

'Rich?' she goes on. 'Listen. This month there are only two, but there are eight assignments planned for the first quarter of next year, including that . . . Yes . . . I understand . . . OK . . . I've . . . Of course. I won't do anything yet.' She rings off. When she looks at me she makes a rather nervous impression.

'Problems?' I ask.

'That was Richard. He's in Amsterdam at Leon's. It's all kicking off, I'm afraid.'

'I thought that Leon had to go to Antwerp?'

Frowning, she glances at her diary, as if she's overlooked something. 'That was this morning.'

'But what's wrong?'

'Leon said he wants to stop doing photo assignments with immediate effect.' She leafs absently through the diary. 'That's out of the question of course. He can't do that.'

'How many assignments has he got coming up?'

'At least ten. She twists a loose lock of hair round her finger. Her doll's face is taut. Then she looks up. 'Do you know what's behind this?'

I feel awkward. Finally I say: 'He did tell me, yes.'

'And you didn't try to stop him?'

I shrug my shoulders. 'Why should I? It's his life, his decision.'

Her eyes suddenly harden. 'You do understand, of course, that this will have consequences.'

Marianne is the second person today to draw my attention to consequences. Her unexpectedly fierce reaction suddenly gives me a very different picture of her. Not a pathetic little wife stowed away in the country by her egotistical husband, but a lioness standing right behind her man.

'Consequences for what?' I ask.

She passes her hand over my files and documents. 'For this, for example. I'm doing this because you're Leon's girlfriend.' Then she sniffs and brushes a couple of rebellious curls from her forehead. They spring straight back. 'But come on. We haven't got to that point yet. Let's not get ahead of ourselves.'

For some reason I get the feeling this will be the last time I see Marianne. The very last time I'll be welcomed into this house, this cold, impersonal house. If there's anything else I want to know, I need to ask now. Without further ado I ask her outright: 'Do you know if Edith had an affair?'

She looks up in alarm and narrows her eyes. 'What?'

'I was wondering. Leon blurted out something to that effect. He didn't go into it any further.'

Marianne quickly recovers. 'That depends what you mean by affair.'

'What are you trying to say?'

'Edith was . . . Well. There were rumours.' She looks me straight in the eye. 'That Edith was more relaxed than most of us in that respect. And she often walked about naked, regardless of whether anyone was there.'

'Rumours you say?'

'You can never be sure about that kind of thing,'

'Did Richard ever talk to you about it? I mean . . . he and Leon are pretty close, so he should know how—'

Marianne gets up abruptly. She slides the cardboard box towards her and starts demonstratively packing my records. When she's finished, she shoves the box into my hands. 'I think you'd better go now.'

48

I think I'm losing my mind. Or maybe I already have, and went stark staring mad long ago, completely gaga. I'm no longer capable of thinking clearly. Generally speaking, I can find the way to the police station in town in my sleep, having driven past it so often. But now I pass the cul-de-sac three times before I recognise the large modern building for what it is and leave my car in the car park in front.

I enter a large, virtually empty hall and go over to a counter where two uniformed policewomen are talking. One of them looks up.

'I have an appointment with Detective Burghardt,' I manage to say.

The policewoman makes a telephone call and gestures towards a bench.

I sit down nervously. My heart is pounding in my ribcage. The seconds pass so slowly it feels like I'm in a vacuum.

'Margot Heijne?'

I look up.

It's the young woman with the light-brown skin, who I immediately recognise as Burghardt's colleague. This woman has sat on my sofa, in my living room. She is wearing her hair down now and flashes me a most friendly smile. 'Would you come with me?'

I get up and follow her to a closed door. She swipes a card and leads me into a long, bright corridor. Nothing remains of the relative quiet of the hall in here. The odd door is ajar, and I see people walking around with files, talking into mobile phones and lost in thought at their computers. Some in uniform, others not. There is a smell of coffee and a vague odour of detergent.

'Here it is,' she says, opening a door for me. 'Charles?'

Burghardt gets up from behind his desk and walks towards me. His light shirt is slightly crumpled and dark circles are visible beneath his brown eyes.

The door is closed behind me. The policewoman does not stay for the interview.

'Hello, Ms Heijne. Nice that you could come today. Can I offer you some coffee?' He shakes my hand. A warm handshake, slightly too firm.

'No, thank you. I've had too much coffee today already.' My voice sounds more high-pitched than usual.

'Tea or water?'

'Yes, tea please, thank you.'

He disappears into the corridor and returns a moment later with two plastic cups dangling between his thumbs and fingertips. He puts one down for me. 'Sugar?'

'Yes, please.'

Burghardt rummages in his drawer and puts two crumpled sachets of sugar and a plastic spoon on the top of the desk. 'There you are.'

Only then does he look at me and really make contact. He folds his hands in front of him on the desk. 'So . . . here we are then. How are you?'

'Not great,' I say truthfully. My voice trembles slightly. I look down at my shoes. They're in urgent need of a polish. 'I just don't know what to think any more.'

'That's understandable. I'm going to record this interview so that I can listen to it again later. Are you OK with that?'

I nod and see Burghardt start a recorder.

'The point is this,' he begins. 'If, and I stress if, your ex-partner did not commit suicide, the logical conclusion is that he was murdered.' He gives me a penetrating look. 'A murder committed in a very cunning manner. It implies that the murderer didn't act in a fit of anger, but that each step was premeditated. It would have to be someone who knew precisely what they were doing, and it must have been someone who knew the victim.'

I'm startled. 'Why do you think that?'

'The absence of any signs of a break-in, for one thing. Your ex-partner – if there is any question of murder, I hope you'll keep that at the back of your mind – would have let his murderer in during the early hours of the morning. As I told you on the telephone this afternoon, no signs of violence were found on his body. From this we can conclude that there was no struggle. But the main reason is the motive. A murder like this is not committed at random. There must be a reason. We have ascertained that John van Oss had no debts, and as far as we could establish did not keep dubious company. No addictions, no criminal record. That brings us as a matter of course to the sphere of personal relations, the only area where your ex-partner could have made enemies. And I'm inclined to think: did make enemies.' He pauses to take a sip of his coffee. 'Your ex-partner had an affair with Mrs Mieke Dingemans, who at the time of the relationship was married to Tom van Dijk. Of course we have interviewed them both. They're back together again, as you may know.'

'No, I didn't know. I haven't spoken to them for ages.'

'In any case, on the night in question they weren't even in Holland, but were touring Egypt. They only returned home last week.'

'That's why they weren't at the funeral,' I think aloud.

Burghardt ignores my remark. 'In view of that we're left as far as we can see with only two people who may have had a motive and the opportunity. Some members of your family stated that on the evening of his death your ex-partner had a violent clash with your current boyfriend. I'd like to know more about that. I'd like to hear your side of the story.'

I scratch my eyebrow and look at my shoes again. My heart is racing and there's a lump in my throat that seems to be getting bigger. I clear my throat, and then again.

'You drove together to the party from your present boyfriend's home?'

I nod. 'Yes, in his car. Leon didn't want to go out that evening. He'd just come back from Denmark and he was tired. He didn't know anyone at the party. He just didn't feel like it.'

'What was your partner doing in Denmark?'

'He was there on an assignment.'

Burghardt nods. 'OK. Go on.'

'In the end he came with me after all. There were lots of relatives there I hadn't seen for ages. I may have drunk too much and I started dancing. Actually I kind of neglected Leon all evening.'

I look up again. The detective is looking at me impassively. 'When I caught up with him again, he was angry and wanted to go home.'

'Not an unusual reaction in itself,' says the detective. 'And then?'

I shrug my shoulders. 'I didn't want to go. It was also the way he said it. It wasn't a question: it was more of an order. Leon can be very pushy sometimes.'

Burghardt has shifted in his seat and is looking at me with increased interest.

'I don't mean that in a bad way,' I hasten to add. 'He's also very sweet, really, I—'

'Don't worry about what I might be thinking. I'm just trying to get a better picture of the evening, your boyfriend and your relationship. Please continue. We have plenty of time. How exactly did Leon Wagner ask . . . order you to go home with him?'

I swallow and cough again. My throat is parched. 'He grabbed my arm and said I could walk to Helvoirt if I didn't go with him. I was still living with him then.'

'You don't any longer?'

I shake my head.

'What is the reason for that?'

'It seemed best if I just stayed at home, for the time being. I wanted to get everything straightened out in my mind first.'

'Have you seen Leon Wagner again since that evening?'

'Yes. He wants us to get back together again.'

'Do you want to?'

I bite my lower lip. 'Yes,' I whisper. Why am I starting to cry now?

'OK, let's go back to the party. Your partner wanted you to go home, but you wanted to stay.'

I rub underneath my eyes with my forefingers to wipe away the tears. 'We were actually having an argument when John came up to us and put his arms round me and Leon. He said he'd heard we wanted to go home and that we shouldn't be such killjoys. I can't remember exactly, but it was something like that. I don't think John realised how tense the atmosphere was.'

'Or perhaps he did,' remarks Burghardt. 'Had your current boyfriend already had contact with John van Oss? Did they know each other?'

I shake my head. 'No.'

'You said that you were dancing all evening and catching up with your family. Is it possible that Leon Wagner and your ex-boyfriend spoke to each other earlier in the evening, that there was an altercation?'

I shrug my shoulders in confusion. 'That's possible . . . but I don't know.'

'What was Leon Wagner's reaction to the hug?'

I close my eyes. Tears flow down my cheeks. 'He grabbed hold of John and threw him against the buffet table.'

'And after that?'

'He said I had to go home with him. He didn't even look at John. It was a mess. I didn't want to go. So he left. Alone.'

'Can you remember approximately what time it was?'

'About eleven, I think. But I'm not sure.'

'You stated that after the party you went home with John van Oss and were intimate with him. You left more or less immediately afterwards. Can you add anything to that?'

I look up. 'What could I add?'

'Did you talk together, and if so what about? Did your ex-partner threaten to harm himself when you left? Something to that effect?'

'No. Honestly. A number of people have asked me that. He was just . . . bewildered. He said I couldn't just leave like that and couldn't get my parents out of bed in the middle of the night.'

'But you went anyway?'

'Yes.'

'And he didn't come after you? He didn't try to stop you?'

I shake my head. 'He stood in the doorway. He wasn't even dressed.'

'What exactly did he have on?'

'His dressing gown.'

Burghardt nods and makes a note. Then he looks up again. 'What exactly did you say to your ex-partner when you left?'

'That I didn't love him any more. That I was sorry, something like that. And that he shouldn't contact me again.'

'Had you both had a lot to drink?'

'Yes.'

'When did you re-establish contact with your present boyfriend?'

'After the funeral . . . Exactly a week after John's funeral. Friday of last week.'

'Did he contact you himself?'

'No, I was with a friend of his, who has a . . .' I look at the detective. If I say that a friend of Leon's has a night club, will that make him look more suspicious? 'A kind of nightclub, which I am refurbishing. I was working there when Leon dropped by. It was more of a coincidence, really. He was also surprised to see me there.'

'Coincidence . . .' says Burghardt, giving me a piercing look. 'Could Leon Wagner have known that you were there?'

From Burghardt's remark, I realise that Leon's visit to Taco may not have been such a coincidence at all. He may be on to something. Leon and Taco have been friends for years and my appointment had been made a while back. 'It's possible,' I say softly.

'And then?'

'What do you mean?'

'What did you do after you bumped in to Leon Wagner at that friend's place?'

'I went with him to his bungalow.'

'In Amsterdam?'

'No, he has two homes. The bungalow is in Helvoirt.'

'And did you stay there?'

'We did that night.'

'What did you talk about there?'

'John. Only about John.'

'How did he react to that?'

'He was very understanding. He told me I had to let it rest. That the idea that John might have been murdered would drive me crazy. It happened to him. His girlfriend committed suicide a year ago. He's been through the same thing.'

Burghardt starts leafing through a file. Then he looks up. 'Edith Benschop.'

I nod.

As he continues leafing through the file he says without looking up: 'Ms Benschop took an overdose of sleeping pills and tranquillisers, as a result of which she lost consciousness and finally drowned in the bath.'

'His bath,' I say softly. 'He found her there. She'd been dead for two days.'

Burghardt goes on leafing through and reading. Then he looks at me. 'Would you describe your boyfriend, Leon, as a jealous sort?'

A jolt goes through me. I'm speechless and sit looking at the detective as if frozen to the spot.

'You don't have to reply. We're not in court here.'

'Yes,' I say finally. 'But he—'

Burghardt interrupts me and goes on bombarding me with

questions. He wants to know how Leon expresses his jealousy. Whether he has ever inflicted pain on me or abused me – no, of course not.

I try to answer as well as I can and with every word I say I feel I'm making Leon more suspicious than he probably already is in Burghardt's eyes. I'm fully aware that I'm sitting here discussing the most intimate details of my love life with a total stranger. Things that are between myself and Leon and don't concern any-one else.

Then Burghardt raises doubts about Edith's suicide. I reply to his pointed questions, tell him everything I've found out about her in dribs and drabs, things that Leon told me only after much insistence and in confidence. Burghardt keeps pursuing the relationship between Edith and Leon.

I tell him about my suspicion that Edith had an affair with Debby. I tell him about Leon finding them in the bath together and his reaction. I tell him how Marianne reacted to my ques-tions when I visited her this morning. The words just keep on coming and they are registered inexorably by the recorder between us on the desk.

It feels like a betrayal.

I'm betraying Leon.

I must restore the balance. 'Leon is very good to me,' I say, realising how feeble those words must sound now. 'More lov-ing than John ever was. I . . .' I look up and try to make eye contact with Burghardt, who is sitting looking at me with his fingertips together and an unfathomable expression. 'I love that man. I don't want him to have had anything to do with it.'

'No one's being charged with anything. Can you wait a moment?'

Burghardt gets up from his desk and turns the recorder off. Then he disappears into the corridor, closing the door behind him.

I pick up my cup of tea and empty it in a few gulps. The liquid is now lukewarm.

The detective doesn't return until about ten minutes later. 'Ms Heijne,' he says, 'I want to thank you for being so forthcoming. You can go home, or do whatever you planned to do today. It would be nice if you could stay in the area. You've already got my card, haven't you?'

I nod.

'If anything else should occur to you, you can always call me. Were you going to talk to or see your boyfriend today?'

'He's coming over to my flat this evening. We were going out to eat.'

Burghardt puts his fist to his mouth and coughs. 'I've just phoned a colleague in Amsterdam. If we can find him quickly and he cooperates, Leon will be brought to this station by my Amsterdam colleagues for questioning.'

My eyes widen. 'Will he be arrested?'

'No. We just have a few questions for him. Please don't worry. It *is* important, though, that you don't ring him or let him know what's happening in any way.' He manoeuvres me towards the door and holds it open for me. As far as he's concerned the interview is over.

Suddenly I realise there's something he hasn't told me. Something very important. I turn round in the corridor. 'You said just now that there were two people left,' I say. 'Two people who might have had a motive and had the opportunity.'

He nods and scratches the top of his arm.

'So who is the other person?' I ask.

'You, Ms Heijne.'

I didn't go straight home, but left my car in my permit-holders bay by the canal and walked into town. I can't remember how long I wandered around aimlessly in the busy town centre where the first Christmas decorations had already been put up and carols were ringing out from the shops. Jollity that was out of step with the inner storm that was driving me along. I kept walking. The pale winter sun sank behind the tall buildings and gradually gave way to a crescent moon which only appeared every now and then through a thick blanket of cloud. I walked past the shops, through narrow alleys and across squares, reached a drawbridge at the edge of the town centre, crossed it and found myself in an old residential area, with small houses crammed together. Through the windows I saw people with plates on their laps watching TV and lying stretched out on sofas. There wasn't a living soul in the street. The cold was biting. I turned round and started walking in the direction of my flat.

All I could think of was Leon, who was probably now being questioned by Burghardt in that impersonal police station. Leon, who under glaring fluorescent lights with a plastic cup of coffee or tea in front of him would have to talk about Edith all over again, and whose freshly healed wounds would be torn open by Burghardt's pointed, targeted questions. With good reason? Was I so blinded by love that I simply couldn't or didn't want to see all the signs indicating that Leon killed both his girlfriend and John?

It is dark when I open the main door to the block of flats. I try the light switch without success. There must be a problem with the electricity; it's not the first time the lights have failed. The hall is pitch black. I grope my way towards the smooth banister and climb the stairs a step at a time. I hear faint noise coming from the other flats. A television is on somewhere and someone is practising on the piano, the same tune over and over. When I reach the top I look for my front door key. My fingers are still trembling as I put the key into the lock and enter.

The next moment something starts to move in front of me. No more than a rustle, a displacement of air, caused by a man-sized, ink-black shadow.

XII

As I drove here this afternoon I recognised the rage I was feeling all too well. That was why on quiet stretches I drove a little over the speed limit. I forced myself to concentrate on the job in hand. It worked. I managed to manoeuvre the car through the busy traffic in a controlled way.

Once in her flat I began to wonder if it was sensible to let myself go like this. I'm not terribly well prepared and that might mean having to improvise. But, I reminded myself, I'd done the same with that awful John, an improvisation that I really enjoyed, albeit in the strictly technical sense. Because emotionally that murder palls beside Edith's. It didn't give me anywhere near the same degree of satisfaction. And that's ultimately what drove me here. Even more than the rage, the resentment, the serving of the common good . . . Hunger.

While I waited for her to get home it struck me that I couldn't have chosen a better moment. Margot is vulnerable; she's prey to violent emotions that could make her decide upon an irreversible, destructive act. Tomorrow everything may change. If I wait, it may be months before such a chance presents itself again. And I mustn't be blind to the possibility that a second chance will never come.

That would be a pity.

From the first moment I saw Margot and her unusually coloured eyes, she has never left my mind. That slightly worried smile around her mouth and that body of hers . . . She looks so much like Edith. I'm sure it will be just as wonderful with her, no: even better. Edith and John's murders were bloodless. This time blood will flow. Lots of blood.

What a wonderful prospect.

For hours I walked round her flat and killed time by searching through her living areas and her personal things. Yet I couldn't allow myself to get too carried away by the excitement racing through my whole body. It was a premature stage, and I was dealing with unknowns. For instance, she might arrive home with a friend or relative. Funnily enough, that possibility aroused only pleasant tingling sensations. I had planned my exit strategies. I trusted my ability. There were countless ways of keeping myself out of the picture and then waiting for a good moment to slip away – or else to strike.

But she came home. And she was alone.

I heard her footsteps on the stairs. One person. I heard the key being inserted into the lock. I crept to the door and waited.

Just as I expect, she's so disorientated by the shock that she doesn't react at first. Paralysed with fear, a short circuit in her motor system. What a marvellous gift from Mother Nature, and so useful at the same time. Quick as a flash I unroll the clingfilm further, winding it round her neck, shoulders and arms, and push her to the ground. She lands on her back and kicks into the void, like a she-tiger in her death throes. She has no idea what she's fighting against, or perhaps it's only a convulsion. She can't breathe. It must be an extremely unpleasant experience for her. She yanks with her head and tries to scream, but no sound comes out.

I let her thrash for a few seconds and watch as she tries to pull her arms loose. Her fingertips claw at the clingfilm. She can't reach it properly and because she bites her nails, she just brushes the surface a little.

'Lie still or I'll have to hurt you,' I say. That's a bit mean of me. I'm going to hurt her anyway, but she doesn't know that. I want to avoid a struggle.

She doesn't listen. She keeps on kicking and now she hits the coffee table, which shifts a little from its position. Her mouth forms a scream, which is muffled by the clingfilm that she's partly sucking in in an attempt to breathe.

Good. For a moment I gave in to the desire to see her struggle. And a wonderful sight it is too. Now I must act, to prevent something from falling over, or stop her getting the idea of stamping on the floor to alert the downstairs neighbours.

I leap onto her and sit astride her thighs. 'You're not going anywhere anymore,' I pant. Shit, she's strong. Much stronger than I expected. She should be without oxygen by now, but she keeps tossing and turning and twisting her body. I have nothing but respect for such resistance. It makes it so much more beautiful.

I push down on her forehead with my hand to keep her pressed to the floor, holding the knife in my other hand. A splendid Italian cutthroat razor that I first saw about a year ago. Or more precisely, first saw the potential of. I hold it close to her face. 'Do you want to breathe?'

Suddenly she stiffens. I think she understands me. Or perhaps the lack of oxygen is finally getting to her.

'This will be easier if you stay still.' Very carefully I prick the clingfilm under her nose with the tip of the razor. A slit, very small, you can hardly see it. I'm not giving her any more. Her first priority must be to breathe; then she'll have no time for funny business.

It works. She lies still and concentrates on her task. She

breathes in. She breathes out. The clingfilm makes a whistling sound around her nose.

'I hope you'll understand that you must cooperate, because otherwise I'll be obliged to seal off your air supply. Nod if you understand.'

She nods. She understands. She doesn't move as I get off her, retrieve the roll of clingfilm from under the sofa and wind it around her legs. She submits to all this meekly. It's called swaddling. as people do with very young babies. It evidently produces a pleasant sensation to be wrapped so tightly, as in a warm, protective womb.

I don't think Margot sees it like that.

Her hands, the only part of her body that have not been wrapped, are sticking out of the clingfilm at crotch level. They're no longer groping around. They're just lying there, with those gnawed nails. Resignation. I've seen it before and it remains a magnificent sight.

I sit astride her again and put my hands either side of her face. The tip of her nose stands out like a white cap against the taut clingfilm. Around her mouth the material is full of condensation. There is a dazed look in her eyes. She can't see me in focus. But she can see me. For the first time, I suspect. And she stiffens. Her facial expression is heavily distorted by the clingfilm, but I recognise the surprise. Her eyes widen, although her eyelids are being forced partly shut by the clingfilm and obscured by strands of hair tangled in the wrapping. No, on second thoughts: not a pretty sight.

'I could say I was sorry, but I'd be lying,' I say. 'To tell you the truth, I'm just starting to enjoy it.'

She twists her head from left to right and again tries to scream, but it makes scarcely any sound. A few layers of clingfilm are very effective.

'It makes it easier for everyone if you cooperate.'

I take hold of her feet and drag her across the wooden floor towards the bathroom. It's less than twenty feet, but it leaves me out of breath. She really does weigh a ton. In the bathroom I turn her onto her stomach.

Then I put the plug in the bath and turn the hot tap on. That's vital. Without hot water it will take hours, and may not work at all.

Margot has a small old-fashioned hip bath in a shade of beige. It looks a bit grubby, though I expect it's from age rather than because Margot neglects her household chores.

She is still having difficulty in breathing. The lack of oxygen is making her calm. Very calm.

I grab her head and move it to the side. There is no muscular tension in her neck. She is definitely breathing. I can feel the faint flow of air around her nose. She's unconscious.

With a huge effort I manage to manoeuvre her into the bath. She looks odd: a fat woman wrapped in clingfilm who barely fits into her own bath. Her buttocks are virtually trapped in the deep section, the bundle her legs are wrapped in rests on the seat section. That way she can't drown.

'Should you be able to hear me, you may like to know that this razor belongs to your beloved boyfriend. It's got Leon's fingerprints on it. In a minute we're going to put yours on it too. It has to look as natural as possible. Of course I'm wearing gloves. But you'll understand that.'

She doesn't respond.

'I'm going to free one arm,' I say, cutting the clingfilm and wriggling her arm out of the transparent cocoon enclosing her. Her hand is now resting in the water, which is quickly rising. Another five minutes or so and the tap can be turned off. Perhaps sooner. It's a small bath and her body fills it almost completely.

'OK, here we go.' I notice how the tension has taken hold of my voice. I can't remember how often I've done this in my mind, picturing every detail until I reached a state of ecstasy.

I dig the tip of the razor into her wrist. Her skin is tough and doesn't yield easily. It may also be due to the razor itself. It looks super sharp, but it's become rather blunt. Leon probably hasn't used it for quite a while. I had to hunt for it in his bathroom this afternoon. If he'd thrown it away, that would have been a bad omen. I might well have called everything off. This razor was part of the plan, part of the fantasy I've been carrying around since Edith's murder: bath, razor. I finally found it in a toilet bag at the bottom of a cupboard.

I push the razor into her hand and press her thumb onto the handle, then do the same with her fingers. I make smudges, then push it into her other hand.

'Nice, isn't it?' I say softly. 'Your fingerprints and Leon's. So romantic.'

Margot is completely unconscious. She doesn't even come round when I make the first incision. The blood gushes out immediately and produces red clouds in the water. It looks like a lot but that's an optical illusion. I make a second incision. Deeper now, rather carelessly. Clumsily even. I do that deliberately. Of course I know how to cut wrists in such a way that it's over quickly. But I don't want any doubts to be cast on her suicide. I've got to put myself in her position. She's confused, she wants to end her life, but then again she doesn't really want to. So it's a cry for attention and she makes a mess of it. She nicks her flesh, is alarmed by the pain, the blood. Recovers, cuts again. Makes an incision. And another. Now deeper. In zigzags, shaky.

It's the details that make all the difference.

It's now time for her right wrist. The same method, but much more carelessly – her cutting hand is already wounded and painful and apart from that she's right-handed.

Now the blood is flowing freely out of her body, billowing through the water.

I bend over her and place my hand round one of her breasts. Squashed by the clingfilm, but big, full, feminine. I caress the other and feel a tingle coming over me. Should I . . .?

No.

Later. When I'm home. Don't leave any traces, don't deviate from the plan. My memory is many times sharper than the razor I'm cutting with. I can recover the feeling and the images time after time and do what I like with them, in a safe place at a safe time.

Not here. Not now.

Now all I can do is wait, wait and watch.

That clingfilm has to go; it's restricting my view and ruining the picture. I cut it loose around her throat and pull it over her head. That's better. Her face is free now. Just like she's sleeping. Just like Edith.

I turn the tap off and sit on the edge of the bath to watch the most beautiful spectacle I've ever seen. This is art. True art.

Still I feel the rage welling up. 'You took Leon away from me,' I whisper to that bloody still life. 'Do you know his assignments make up eighty per cent of my income? You understand I can't let something like that happen? First you drive him crazy with that ex of yours, making him uncontrollable. I solved that efficiently, and now you deem it necessary to tear him away from me, just like your predecessor. But that's all over now, Margot. Everything will go back to how it was. Leon is not a lone wolf. He seeks people out. Not crowds, like me, but just one. And he focuses on that one, on that one special person he feels a strong bond with and will do anything for. I know him through and through, dear. When he's thrown upon his own resources, he comes automatically to me. Like a moth to the flame. Then he'll do exactly what I tell him to. He said this afternoon that you had nothing to do with his decision, but you and I know better, don't we? I know him better than he knows himself. All those so-called pieces of wisdom of his . . . Let's be honest: they come from me. I taught him all he knows. He's my project, the best so far. I made him. You should have seen him this afternoon when they came for him. He was at a loss. Suspicion of murder . . .' I chuckle. 'He'll probably be released by this evening, or else tomorrow. Poor guy, he's done nothing wrong. But you, dear Margot, can't know that. It's all got too much for you. For you it all ended here and now. You don't want to go on in the knowledge that your beloved boyfriend is a murderer . . . That's why I'm here. Call it fate. That sounds nice.'

She doesn't move. She's lying there quietly bleeding to death. Slowly, very steadily. The bath is turning red. No longer pink. It's really red now. A wonderful, glorious bloodbath.

I could watch her for hours, but sadly I have to go now. Perhaps she's arranged to meet someone, and her brother or a girlfriend will be outside at any moment. I can't stay any longer, the risk of discovery is becoming too great. She'll be dead within the next half hour anyway. And should she come round, she'll be so badly weakened that she won't be able to make it to the living room. At any rate she'll no longer be capable of alerting anyone.

Reluctantly I get up and start cutting the rest of the clingfilm free. I stuff everything into a plastic bag and toss in my gloves. I check very carefully to ensure that no red droplets find their way out of the bath. I put on a new pair of plastic gloves, take a new plastic bag out of my overalls and repeat the procedure. No blood must stick to my gloves, or to the outside of the bag. I take off my plastic overshoes and my protective clothing. They also disappear into the bag.

I drop the razor into the water.

I look around once more. Not a splash. Terrific. I grin at myself in the mirror.

I always get what I want. I never fail. Never.

49

It's as if I'm being sucked downwards from a weightless position, becoming heavier and heavier and descending faster and faster, until I land on my back with a thud and everything obeys the law of gravity once again. And starts hurting. Pain in my arms, my lungs.

I can feel a mattress under me, warm and gel-like. Tiny, mechanical beeps. A sucking sound, rhythmical, slow, coming from somewhere behind me. Footsteps on linoleum, muffled voices, further away.

Someone's touching me. I can hear rustling above my head. I smell chlorine and detergent.

Where am I? I can't remember how . . . I can't remember anything. Yes, I can. *Oh no . . . No!*

In a reflex I open my mouth and suck in air. My lungs fill with oxygen. And again, like a swimmer coming to the surface after a deep dive. Again. I can breathe. My face is free, no longer covered. No more of that wet clingfilm. Wet . . . Water. I have a vague memory of water.

I move my arm. Free. The other arm is fixed.

'Keep that arm still, dear,' a woman's voice says. 'Don't tug at it. That's where the drip is. You've lost almost four pints of blood.'

And then a familiar voice, but it sounds far away, like someone's talking through a hollow pipe, echoing slightly. 'Margot? Open your eyes. Say something.'

Something strokes my skin, something thin and hard. Pressure on my upper arm. A hand on my head. Someone brushes my hair out of my face.

'Say something.'

I blink. Everything is white. A blinding white light and moving shadows, closer.

Shadows.

I close my eyes again.

'Please say something.'

I don't want to. I want to go back to weightlessness, back to the dark, where I no longer need to hear, feel or see anything. The dark where there is nothing, no fear or pain or confusion. Simply nothing.

A hand against my cheek. 'Answer me. Say something. Margot, say something.'

I open my eyes and immediately shut them again. 'Pain,' I say softly, pulling my face into a grimace.

A woman's voice says: 'You'll get some painkillers in a minute. First you have to wake up.'

I slip away again. Suddenly, without warning, everything is dark. There's nothing.

'Margot!'

I open my eyes wide. Why don't they leave me in peace? 'Leave me,' I whisper.

Rustling next to me, or above me. Footsteps.

A man's voice, from far away. 'Has she come round?'

Next to my head a patient woman's voice answers. 'Just now.'

'Functions?'

'Normal.'

'Can I get Burghardt?'

'Wait a bit.'

Come round?

When I open my eyes a fraction and try to focus a woman's face is hanging over me. She is dark-skinned and has big, green eyes that are looking at me with interest. She's wearing a white coat with a name badge on it that I can't read. The letters are so small and blurry.

A face appears next to her. Leon. 'Darling, I got the fright of my life. Why did you—'

The nurse puts a firm hand on his arm and exchanges a knowing look. Later, her look seems to say. Later.

That's good, later is good. Now I want to sleep.

'Your parents are on their way,' I hear Leon say. 'They'll be here any moment.'

'C . . . cold,' I start shivering.

Someone lifts my right eyelid and shines a light inside. 'You had a narrow escape, madam. If your friend hadn't found you, you'd no longer be with us. It was a very close shave.'

Found? Suddenly it all comes back. I came home, from that long, cold, lonely walk. I opened the door and was pulled inside. Something was wound over my face so that I couldn't breathe. I finished up on the floor. I fought hard, very hard. But it was pointless. He was stronger. Him! It was . . . it was . . . 'Richard,' I whisper. 'It was Richard.'

'What do you mean, darling? Calm down,' says Leon. Then, more softly: 'Could she be delirious?'

No answer.

'Mr Burghardt,' the nurse raises her voice. 'I don't think—'

Heavy footsteps approach. 'Who is Richard?'

'My manager,' Leon answers.

I open my eyes again. Burghardt. Leon. The nurse. All three of them are standing round the bed looking at me expectantly.

Their faces are revolving around each other like a kaleido-scope.

'You didn't do this yourself?' asks Burghardt.

'What?' I ask. 'What . . . have I done?'

'You were found in the bath with slashed wrists. Did you not do that yourself?'

Suddenly I feel sick. My stomach contracts and a wave of bile comes up. Someone supports me. Something metallic is pushed under my chin. The cold, sharp edge presses against my collar-bone. 'Come on,' the nurse sounds sympathetic. 'That's it.'

I shudder at this nasty taste in my mouth. Another wave comes up, splashing beneath me in the bowl. The nurse wipes my face with a moist tissue.

'Richard,' I say. My voice sounds so weak that I can scarcely imagine anyone can understand me.

'*Richard*? What do you . . .?' Leon's voice.

'I want you to stay in the corridor for a moment,' Burghardt says. 'My colleague will accompany you.'

I hear footsteps leaving the bed.

Burghardt bends over me. 'Are you a hundred per cent sure, Margot?'

I nod. 'Yes.'

'There's no need to be frightened. You can tell me what happened. Are you sure you're not mistaken?'

'He pulled something over my face. I couldn't breathe.' I cough violently. Something dribbles from my nose. Someone wipes it away. 'I finished up on the floor. From that point on I can't remember anything. It was Richard.'

Burghardt stands up and turns to someone standing by the door. A tall, dark shadow. 'Would you come with me for a moment?'

The nurse is still sitting by my bed. I try to make eye contact.

'Can I sleep? It hurts . . .' Only then does it dawn on me what the detective just said. *Wrists.*

I press my chin onto my chest. My wrists are bandaged.

'I didn't do that,' I whisper, 'really I didn't.'

'I believe you,' says the nurse.

Then everything goes black.

XIII

I've failed. The blow has hit me much, much harder than I could ever have imagined. I was careless, let myself get carried away.

While I was sitting in the café opposite her flat, and Leon's Audi came screeching round the corner, I realised that I should have finished things off. I'd used the wrong method. Or perhaps the location wasn't right and I should have taken her somewhere where she would have been found less quickly. I should have thought about it for longer and made more and better preparations.

But I didn't do any of that. I let hunger prevail over reason.

Leon most likely came straight from the police station, and that's less than a quarter of an hour's drive from Margot's place. I had expected the police to hold him for longer. Something else I didn't take into account is that he wouldn't slink off quietly after the questioning, but would want to confront her with it. Because that's Leon: straightforward, loyal and direct. I know for certain that he regarded me as his best friend, even though he doesn't really know me. He sees only what I let him see, hears only what I let him hear. Others might say I'm manipulative. I call it common sense. And that common sense means that my personal share of unpleasantness has always been reasonably limited.

So far, that is. Because as I sat in that café, I knew that I might just lose this battle.

I just had to wait and see. Perhaps Leon was too late and there was nothing he could do. I just stared at the entrance to the flat, and waited. Minutes passed and nothing happened. For a moment I toyed with the idea of going across and ringing the bell. Why not? I was in the neighbourhood anyway . . . Perhaps I could have helped? Perhaps I could have talked Leon into making some phone calls, going for help, while I looked after her.

And also stopped her breathing.

Those kind of idiotic, desperate thoughts went through my mind, while the clock went on ticking and the door stayed shut.

An ambulance would be there any moment. I had to know what was being carried out on the stretcher. A body bag? Or a dying woman with hastily rigged drips?

From this position the ambulance would obscure my view of the stretcher, so I went outside and stationed myself at the corner of the street. As I got there I heard the first siren. The second quickly followed.

I withdrew into a doorway. Five or six minutes later the whole crowd came out. No one paid any attention to me, they were all too caught up in their work. But I saw what I needed to know.

She was alive.

For long enough to say what she had seen? This time I decided not to wait and see. Time was a luxury I couldn't afford.

I had to act. Immediately.

I would rather have gone to South Africa in style, but now it was out of necessity.

50

My parents and Dick have gone home now. The nurse urged Leon to follow their example, but he refused to leave me alone. After various fruitless attempts to get him to change his mind, her attitude softened. She offered him a cup of tea and then an extra bed was wheeled into the room. 'Would you go to bed?' she said, before leaving the door ajar behind her. The light was demonstratively turned out.

Leon pushed a stool next to me and put his elbows on the mattress. In the dark I listened to his side of the story. He spoke softly, almost whispering.

Richard had been there when the police arrested him in his loft in Amsterdam. Leon and Richard had talked over Leon's 'resignation' as well as they could and Leon had just ordered a takeaway when the police rang the doorbell. Despite his amazement he decided to cooperate – he'd done nothing wrong after all. Richard's reaction had been a lot less laconic. He immediately offered to call in a lawyer and noisily questioned the reason why Leon was being taken to the station. Leon turned down his offer and said he would call him as soon as it was over.

At the station Burghardt had tightened the screws, confronted him with painful extracts from the extensive police report on Edith's 'suicide', which had been faxed through to him by his Amsterdam colleagues. He'd shouted terrible things about me and John, and used information that he could only have found out from me. As a result Leon knew that Burghardt had talked to me, and he put two and two together. The detective brought up the supposed affair between Edith and Debby, and rubbed in the fact that I'd slept with John on the evening of the party. Burghardt was convinced that at that point Leon had blown a fuse, just as he had with Edith. Because the similarities were striking: infidelity as the trigger, jealousy as the motive, with a staged suicide as a result. Burghardt picked at all Leon's recently healed wounds, not missing a single one, and poured acid into them. Then he turned the screws even tighter: he asked Leon if he had witnesses who could confirm that he had driven home after the family celebration. Of course he had none.

When they finally let him go, Leon had reached boiling point. He intended to strangle me or hurl me out of the window – his exact words. Because he assumed I wouldn't let him in, he used the key. He found me literally bathing in my own blood, with a scarcely perceptible heartbeat. He almost collapsed on the spot. He pulled me out of the bath, used his shirt to stem the blood and rang the emergency services.

I shift my position and let my eyes wander over Leon. A warm feeling engulfs me and for a moment, a fraction of a second, I forget everything. Perhaps this is fate, it flashes through my mind. My mother always says there's no such thing as coincidence. People meet for a reason. Each new encounter is part of a learning process.

Perhaps I had to enter Leon's life to give him a second chance. His life more or less ground to halt after he found Edith dead. He kept blaming himself, so much so he could only find consolation in a self-imposed punishment: continuing doggedly down the dead-end street that left him increasingly jaded and no longer brought him any joy. Leon in turn crossed my path at a